A ROYAL REQUEST

INSPIRATIONAL ROMANTIC SUSPENSE

BOOKS & AUDIOBOOKS
BY PAIGE EDWARDS

PRESSLEY-COOMBES SERIES

CATHERINE'S INTRIGUE #1

DEADLY BY DESIGN #2

DANGER ON THE LOCH #3

SKYE FALL #4

ROXBURY HEIRS / ROXBURGH SCIONS SERIES

FACING THE ENEMY #1

FLAT DECEPTION #2

TRAITOR IN THE SCOTTISH ISLES #3

DEADLY DEPTHS #4 ~ COMING FALL 2026

SOLDIER'S LEAP SERIES

A ROYAL REQUEST #1

STAND ALONES

HEIRS OF FALCON POINT - CREATOR

SINISTER SECRETS- ANTHOLOGY

A ROYAL REQUEST

INSPIRATIONAL ROMANTIC SUSPENSE

PAIGE EDWARDS

Cover Design: Cynthia Edwards

Published by Balquhidder Books, LLC

ISBN: 978-1-966494-04-1

Praise for Paige

"A modern-day spy thriller set amongst the windswept and remote Scottish Isles of Uist. *Traitor in the Scottish Isles* is a fast-paced, riveting story that takes readers into worlds they can only imagine. Paige Edwards has created two wonderfully unique and completely different characters in Cairstie and Sheridon. The contrast between the pampered girl and the hard-bitten, slightly cynical, dangerous MI6 operative couldn't be more apparent. A fun, exciting story. I highly recommend this read." – Reader's Favorite 5-star Review.

"The action is non-stop in Paige Edwards' romantic adventure novel. Her plot is uniquely complex, informing an astute audience that there is more than one moral at the end of this story. *Skye Fall* is an exciting novel in a class of its own." – Readers' Favorite Five-Star Review.

"Paige Edwards has woven a gripping and riveting multilayered story that grabs one's attention in the first few pages of the book and just doesn't let go!" – InD'Tale Magazine Crowned Heart Review

"*Danger on the Loch* grips your attention with its mix of romance and mystery to which any reader regardless of age can relate in terms of identity, family, and relationships. Castle Rannock is a brilliant setting that breathes with a life of its own. With its stone walls, secret passages, and staircases, it exudes an air of mystery and foreboding that you want to unravel. Paige Edwards has created a mystery case worthy of someone like Sherlock Holmes to crack." Readers' Favorite Five-Star Review

"Paige Edwards' romantic suspense novels never disappoint. I know when I pick up one of her books, I'll be drawn into high adventure with characters who come to life off the page."– Kathi Oram Peterson, author of Danger Unknown and Treacherous Legacy

"The estate is a character in itself made only more haunting by the diverse characters within it. As part of the Pressley-Coombes Series, this meets reader expectations and terms of offering high-tension suspense and feel-good romance."— Readers' Favorite Five-Star Review

"Filled with vivid description, unique characters, and page-turning tension, Paige Edwards is the perfect blend of suspense and romance."— Sian Ann Bessey, USA Today best-selling author

"Edwards knows precisely how to blend suspense, romance, and depth of feeling in such a thrilling manner it will leave readers anxious for more." – Esther Hatch, award-winning & best-selling author.

"I can't wait to read more from Paige Edwards." — Sarah M. Eden, USA Today Best-selling author

"Paige Edwards has created an exciting world of high society, complete with dark secrets, budding romance, and heart-breaking decisions that will keep every reader turning the pages." – Traci Hunter Abramson, award-winning & best-selling author.

"Fabulous characters, great heart, and a determined villain all combine to make *Skye Fall* a novel fans of romantic suspense won't want to miss!" – A. L. Sowards, author of Codes of Courage

For Anabelle

Acknowledgments

Many moons ago, a friend of mine went into labor and asked if I would watch her children while she and her husband went to the hospital. A few hours later, a beautiful daughter joined their growing family. Her parents named her Anabelle, for which the main character in *A Royal Request* is called. This story is for her.

In this business of writing, beta readers are worth their weight in gold, but Mandy Biesinger, A. L. Sowards, and Robbin Peterson were absolute platinum for mine. Mandy, a dear friend that I met at my first book signing, pointed out issues that led to a major rewrite, which improved the story considerably.

Also, thank you to my critique group for early eyes on the manuscript: Ellie Whitney, J. C. Wade, Kyla Beecroft, and Cindy Ray Hale. To my launch team: I couldn't have done this without you. You are amazing humans and friends who share a love for clean and inspirational fiction. I can't thank you enough for all you.

Every author has secret weapons in their arsenal. Mine are my editors. To Ellie Whitney, who puts up with my perpetual comma splices (sometimes I add them just to see if she'll catch them . . . She does;), and Bev Rosenbaum, who found things in this story that no one else saw, you ladies improve my books 100%.

Special thanks to my husband, Ladd, who counseled me to take this manuscript in another direction, which allowed the story to blossom in a fresh new way.

Readers, you are the reason I write. Thank you for your generosity and support. I hope this book provides you with an escape from life's challenges and demands.

Lastly, thank you to my Lord and Savior, Jesus Christ, whose redeeming love provides grace, comfort, and joy to all those who seek Him.

Chapter 1

I SLAM my door behind me as I enter the flat and flop onto the sofa to wolf down my Chinese takeaway. Picking up the controller, I click on the telly, and a beautiful face flashes across the screen. Long, shiny, dark hair. Big blue eyes. Her slender throat and creamy skin make me salivate, and a longing fills me—one I haven't experienced in ages.

She's just the way I like my women.

I crank up the volume.

"Tell me, Anabelle," the television presenter says, "May I call you that?"

"By all means."

Anabelle's long lashes sweep her cheeks, and my heart leaps at the sheer charm of it. She's lovely. Just like Stella . . .

"Did you urge your father to hire Genesis, your employer, to renovate the family's estate?" the presenter asks.

"I'd love to say he signed those contracts for pure, unadulterated nepotism," she says cheekily, flashing perfect, white teeth. "But it's a bit more boring than that. Dad chose Genesis because they provided him with the most comprehensive renovation package for Soldier's Leap."

I straighten, and my breath catches in my throat. *Soldier's Leap?*

"When you say, father, you're referring to Viscount Huddleton?" the presenter asks Anabelle.

She flushes, her cheeks blooming with color. "Yes." Anabelle glances away as though embarrassed.

I edge forward on the sofa, my breath rasping loud in my ears. I can scarcely believe my good fortune.

"How challenging are renovations on a Grade II listed property?" The presenter natters on with that false persona of his, but I'm only half listening now as I jump to my feet.

"Lots of hoops to jump through, I'm afraid." Anabelle tilts her head, her long, dark hair shimmering. "But everyone on the team is an expert in their field, which makes a massive difference on a project of this scope."

I tug at my collar and pace to the window with its view of overflowing bins. Then, I grab a pen off the coffee table and jot down the name of the company handling the renovation.

My gaze lifts and lingers on the woman's creamy neck and blue eyes, my fingers itching to touch her. I drop the pen beside the cold remnants of my meal.

Pivoting, I pace the room, my exhaustion forgotten as a plan takes root. Soldier's Leap should be mine by right, passed down from my great-grandfather.

Glancing at the telly once more, my gaze lands on the lovely woman and the ancient hunting lodge situated behind her.

One day, Soldier's Leap and Anabelle will both be mine.

Chapter 2

Buckingham Palace Gardens, London, England – six months later

Anabelle Dewhurst sighed as rain peppered the sea of open umbrellas around her. If boredom were an Olympic sport, she would be taking home the gold. A sudden gust ballooned her dress, flipping her hemline to her thighs. She grabbed the chiffon and hastily shoved the tea-length gown back into place, then leaned toward her brother, Wills, and pushed up the sleeve of his morning coat to peek at his watch.

His eyes twinkled, and he adjusted his wrist for her convenience. "Seven hours," he mouthed. "Then you fly back to that Scot of yours."

Anabelle bit her bottom lip. Several weeks ago, all had seemed well between her and her boyfriend, Brodie. But after returning from corporate meetings in London, he'd semi-withdrawn into work, raising the question foremost in her mind, had Genesis objected to him dating a fellow employee? Or was he losing interest?

She sucked in the corners of her mouth, then bit her lip again for good measure. She and Brodie weren't coworkers, not exactly—it was much worse than that.

Brodie was her boss, and Soldier's Leap, Genesis's latest renovation project, belonged to none other than her father. To make matters worse, Dad appointed her the family's representative. Talk about complicated. The entire situation placed her and Brodie on a precarious teeter-totter.

Anabelle sighed again, this time drawing a sharp look from her mother. Seven more hours might as well be a thousand until her flight left for Edinburgh. All she had to do was survive the Queen's Garden Party first. Not the King's. His Majesty did not sponsor this activity, though he often supported his wife by attending when his schedule permitted.

Wills edged closer. "Dial it down a notch."

Anabelle pasted on a smile. Wills was right. Mother deserved every accolade for her decades of service. If only it didn't require such a grand event for her to receive it.

Shifting, she glanced at her father, who leaned on his brass-tipped cane and hadn't said much since their arrival. Dad's normally ruddy complexion resembled that of a jaundiced baby. Was he ill? Or was that hue cast on him by the umbrella he held?

"Is something going on with Dad?" Anabelle whispered.

"No. Why?" Her brother raised a single brow, a talent he'd achieved during childhood.

"He looks yellow," Anabelle stated as her heel sank into the soggy lawn.

Balancing on one heel, she tugged her foot free from the grass her shoe seemed intent on aerating. When she wiped off the mud, the metal buckle sliced into her finger. Anabelle hissed.

One glance at her red, dripping hand, and the umbrella Wills held over them did a fast spin. Her lungs compressed, and she clutched her brother's arm, gasping for air like a floundering fish.

"What's going on?" Mother asked.

"Anabelle cut herself," Wills said.

Warm blood trickled down her fingers, and dark spots obscured her sight, blackness closing in. *Not here.*

Wills pressed his umbrella into Mother's hand and yanked the bright satin handkerchief from his morning coat and covered Anabelle's injury.

"I think I'm going to disappear," Anabelle whispered.

"Nonsense," Mother said, bracingly.

Dad moved to Anabelle's side and withdrew a handkerchief from his trouser pocket, not the statin one in his breast pocket, but a cotton one, soft from years of washing, and pressed the fabric around her fingers. "This will staunch the flow. Eliza, hand me your gloves; they'll hide the blood."

Wills slid his free arm around Anabelle while Dad and Mother moved in tandem to cover the blood stains. In no time at all, her sight cleared, and her swimming vision solidified.

"Close shave, that." Dad patted Anabelle's cheek, his eyes assessing. "Are you feeling more the thing?"

"Yes. Thank you." Anabelle exhaled and gave him a weak smile. "Disaster avoided."

When she was two, a stray dog bit her leg, requiring twenty stitches and a ridiculous number of shots, and she had fainted at the sight of blood ever since. While Anabelle could not recall the incident, the trauma remained. Blood and sharp objects did her in every time.

She lifted her chin and encountered a number of curious faces bent in her direction. She raised her brows, daring them to comment. But their manners and reason for their admittance soon got the better of them and everyone slowly returned to the business at hand.

Not for the first time today, Anabelle semi-envied her sister, Cressida, who was still too weak from chemo to attend this event. Generally, Anabelle and Wills avoided them, too, but when Her Majesty intended to honor Mother's service on behalf of the crown, they'd made the exception.

Now that her lungs were once more fully operational, Anabelle took in the scene. Men and women, adorned in fancy hats, morning suits, and dresses, stood on Buckingham Palace's private lawn, awaiting Her Majesty's arrival. Earlier, the Queen's equerries, her appointed military attendants, had arranged all six thousand guests into "human lanes."

Mist blew sideways under Wills's umbrella, raising goose pimples on Anabelle's flesh, just as the palace's garden door opened. The band struck up, and the royal family appeared on the steps, then descended onto the lawn on the final note. How they greeted so many people each quarter astounded Anabelle. Never good with idle chit-chat, she was grateful not to have been born an HRH. Being titled "Her Royal Highness" meant a life of public service, with every move and word speculated on by the press—horrors. The Windsor's held her deepest sympathies.

Anabelle's mobile dinged inside her father's suit pocket with an incoming text. He'd kept it for her as she hadn't brought her clutch bag.

"Dad, can I check it?" she asked.

He passed her the device while Mother chatted with the woman next to her. Shifting to shield herself from prying eyes, Anabelle opened her mobile, then bit back a gasp. She refused to call more attention to herself on the palace lawn, surrounded by thousands of people dressed in posh attire.

"Jecca's engaged! Look." Anabelle shifted the screen toward Wills and her father. In the picture, her bestie held up her hand, displaying a diamond solitaire and a toothy grin.

Wills scowled and turned away, his jaw bunching. What was up with that? Shifting the screen toward her father, she stifled the urge to give Jecca a bell this very instant.

"Have they set the date?" Dad's gaze slid to Wills, who stared into the distance, his expression blank.

Jecca, along with Anabelle's sister, Cressida, were her closest friends. Though Wills had mates of his own, the three of them still enjoyed a close bond. Doubtless, Jecca's nuptials would prevent them from spending time together as her bestie's fiancé had little in common with their group. The old saying, opposites attract, certainly held true in Jecca and Geoffrey's case.

Jecca's news sparked a niggle of worry inside Anabelle because Georffrey seemed rather demanding and self-absorbed, but her bestie clearly cared for the fellow. Returning the mobile to her father, she glanced at Wills, who remained silent. At one point, she had suspected he fancied her friend, but Wills never acted on it, so she must have gotten it wrong. Anabelle, like most people, misinterpreted situations on occasion.

The rain struck the ground like minuscule torpedoes and increased in volume, the earth growing soggier by the minute. Anabelle shifted onto the balls of her feet to keep her heels from sinking further into the lawn.

"Stop fidgeting," Mother whispered beside her. "The Queen is coming our way."

"Bother," Anabelle muttered. Of course, Her Majesty, and not one of the lesser royals, chose their "lane." And Anabelle knew why. She narrowed her eyes at the woman behind the queen consort. Grandmama Poole. No doubt, she had orchestrated this on her daughter's behalf.

Anabelle side-eyed her brother, then grimaced.

Grandmama, the Lady Barbara Poole, the seventy-two-year-old Dowager Countess of Seybourne, was one of the Queen's six companions and steamrolled everyone in sight, including Anabelle, who, despite working in Scotland, had agreed to stand three hours in torrential rain in the hope that Mother might receive a royal handshake.

"It will be over soon, then you'll be jetting back to Scotland." Dad patted Anabelle's arm.

He had hired Genesis, her employer, to renovate the family's Scottish medieval hunting lodge—though that might be a humble descriptor for the hodge-podge monstrosity Dad inherited upon his mother's death.

Last year, he finally gained access to Soldier's Leap when the renters' decades-long lease expired. The lessees had agreed to maintain the property when they signed the contract but had, instead, left the place in a shambles, and with no forwarding address.

"Doubtless, you're pining for home every bit as much as I am for Brodie." Anabelle slipped her arm through her father's. He disliked court events and used the running of High Ridge Hall, his estate in the Cotswolds, as an excuse to avoid them.

"You'd be right." Dad flashed one of his rare smiles, his color much improved.

Had she imagined the whole thing? He appeared perfectly fine now.

A hush fell upon those around them, and everyone stood a little straighter as the Queen progressed up their "lane" with Grandmama at her heels. Anabelle and her family followed suit, squaring their shoulders, and standing at attention. Dad might be a prosperous businessman with a title of his own, but Mother's family had served the crown for centuries.

Her Majesty, wearing a pale-cream dress and a chic, matching, wide-brimmed hat trimmed in black, stopped to chat with a nearby fellow. Mother pasted on a bright smile as she waited her turn, and Dad placed a hand on the middle of her back, lending his unspoken support.

A sudden spasm of nerves in the pit of Anabelle's stomach made her nauseated; nonetheless, she soldiered on, strapping her party manners about her like an ancient buckler and shield. Turning, she caught Wills's dour expression, one that perfectly echoed her emotions.

The Queen inched forward and spoke with the lady next to Mother, a retiring crusader for a mental health charity that Anabelle supported. Then, Her Majesty shifted toward Mother, who immediately dipped into a curtsy.

"Lady Eliza. How lovely to see you again. Thank you for your service," the Queen said.

"It was a pleasure, Your Majesty." Mother appeared ever gracious as she smiled and gripped her hat to keep it from flying off in a sudden gust.

"And how are you, Lord Huddleton?" the Queen asked while Grandmama fought with her umbrella, which appeared intent on flipping inside out.

"Can't complain, ma'am." Dad bowed. "Though I strongly wish the weather were more cooperative for your event." His quiet charm sparkled through his words.

Her Majesty leaned forward and dropped her voice. "That makes two of us."

She turned to Mother. "I haven't seen Peter lately. Where's he been keeping himself?"

The Queen referred to Mother's second cousin, the Duke of Devon.

"I believe his arthritis objects to the rain," Mother said.

"Peter always did enjoy his creature comforts." The Queen nodded. "Good for him. It's a foul sort of day for a Garden Party, don't you think?"

"Indeed." Dad bowed, his lips curving.

With her umbrella now behaving, Grandmama swung in Anabelle and Wills's direction. "Ma'am, you remember my grandchildren, William and Anabelle Dewhurst?"

Wills bobbed his head, and Anabelle dipped into a curtsy, her knees knocking. She caught Her Majesty's humorous expression and was charmed, despite herself, and a genuine smile stretched Anabelle's lips.

"I do indeed." Her Majesty nodded. "How good to see you again." She shook Wills's hand, then Anabelle's. "Lovely girl." The Queen addressed Grandmama as though Anabelle wasn't standing before her. "Quite beautiful, Barbara."

Feeling rather like a specimen under a microscope, Anabelle forced herself not to squirm. Grandmama had foisted one young man after another on her, in the last year, hoping she'd break things off with Brodie, a heathen Scot, and marry a fellow of her choosing.

The Queen tilted her head, and Anabelle's stomach cramped. *Bother.* Her Majesty hadn't finished with her yet.

"You must visit London more often, Miss Dewhurst. Barbara tells me you are to be married. May I offer my congratulations? I should very much wish to attend."

Anabelle's tongue knotted and all but choked her. She opened her mouth to speak, but no sound came out, so she curtseyed, relying on years of ballet lessons to save the situation while her mind scrambled.

The Queen, along with her entourage of attendants and bodyguards, moved off.

Mother squeezed her arm. "Oh, dear," she whispered, for Anabelle's ears alone. "Mama's done it now."

Anabelle looked at her mother in dismay and swallowed, her stomach dropping to her knees. Grandmama was at it again. Only this time, she had accepted Brodie, something Anabelle never dreamed possible—not with the way Grandmama opposed his Scottish pedigree. Perhaps her concern about Anabelle becoming an "old maid" had won her over at last.

But Grandmama's approval hardly mattered.

Anabelle had a much bigger problem. She was not engaged.

Chapter 3

Killicrankie, Scotland

Brodie Maxwell scanned the work order, shifted in his seat, then read it a second time. *Och.* This was a mistake. He lifted his gaze and ran it over the group of team leads until it landed on Tara Tanner, the head designer on the Soldier's Leap renovation who sat on the far side of the conference table from him.

"According to these work orders, Anabelle selected the wrong fabric for the corporate suites. How long will that set us back?" Brodie asked.

"At least two weeks, and that's only if Corsco can manufacture a special run. They're trying to squeeze us in between other projects and promised to ring me back. I haven't reached out to the draper yet but hope they're available once the fabric arrives." Tara tapped a varnished fingernail on the tabletop and shook her head, her red hair swinging about her chin.

"How many weeks are we talking if they can't?" Brodie kept his eyes on the work order.

"Six."

His heart skipped a beat. *Six weeks?* "Have Anabelle find another use for that botched material."

"There's more." Tara's mouth puckered, like she'd sucked a lemon.

"Yes?" Brodie's temple pounded.

"It appears Anabelle changed the agreed-upon colors in the stencil motif. I didn't catch it until I returned from my purchasing trip to Istanbul. Mick's crew has almost completed half of the east corridor."

Brodie inhaled sharply through his teeth. Why had Anabelle altered the work orders without speaking to him or Tara first?

"I don't understand. It's so unlike her." Tara's puzzled expression mirrored his own internal confusion.

As the Dewhurst family's on-site representative, Anabelle had the power to veto his decisions as project manager if she deemed them unacceptable. Still, she always met with him and Tara before doing so. These work orders went against their agreement and were so unlike Anabelle's professional ethics that he intended to give her the chance to defend herself before he acted.

He eyed the Gantt chart on the table's surface. "Those modifications occurred long before your buying trip, Tara." He reeled himself in, bottling the Scottish brogue he slipped into when moved by strong emotion. "You are the lead designer, which means the ultimate responsibility for those errors are yours."

Tara leaned forward, her eyes hard as obsidian. "I may be the lead designer, but as the Dewhurst family rep, Anabelle has obviously gone over my head."

However much he disliked disrupting deliverables, Anabelle's concerns over Tara's decisions on two prior occasions had proved valid. Did Tara carry a professional grudge for being shown up? The woman was a bit of a diva, but an incredibly talented one, and they were lucky to have her on the team.

"The bottom line lies with you." Brodie moved to the next item on his agenda. "Randy?"

"Ahh." Randy Watson, the general contractor, scratched his neck, the nervous tic always a precursor of bad news. "The geothermal system isn't working. One of the lines collapsed. Repairmen arrive next week to fix it."

Brodie kept a lid on his frustration. "Are we still under the manufacturer's warranty?" "Yes." Randy bobbed his head, his dark hair moving in sync to the motion.

"Any hidden costs?" Brodie asked.

"Everything's covered."

"Brilliant." Thank goodness for that. "We can set out space heaters until that line is repaired."

"On it." Randy typed into his mobile, then picked up his coffee mug.

"Anything else?" Brodie asked as Randy had a habit of pausing between issues.

"One of the glamping pods suffered damage from the last batch of holidaymakers."

"Are the Mellencamps aware?" Brodie referred to the married duo Lord Huddleton had hired to manage the place.

"Yes." Randy fiddled with his coffee mug. "Mellencamp notified me about the issue. I've a crew working on it as we speak. Mrs. Mellencamp's retained the deposit and will bill the family if the repairs exceed the amount."

"How extensive is the damage?"

"It's nothing we can't handle ourselves, but my guys are working overtime to repair it before the next group arrives."

"Very good. Thank you." Brodie made a few notations in the margins of his chart, then turned to Mick Aiken, a fair-headed man in his late twenties with a perfectionist's eye for detail. He ran a crew of skilled craftsmen who came highly recommended by Genesis to handle the stenciling and filigree work throughout the mansion.

"Mick?" Brodie raised both brows, eager to end the meeting so he could leave for the airport to surprise Anabelle.

Since Anabelle represented her family, they walked a professional tightrope relationship. He might be the project manager, but she had final say, something that kept them both on proverbial eggshells to ensure they avoided issues such as those that had arisen in today's meeting.

But Anabelle rarely questioned his decisions, except when they veered from the Dewhurst family's best interests. And since he not only watched the bottom line, but held the family's happiness as a top priority, they rubbed along smoothly enough. Only once had the two of them locked horns, and it took days to regain their equilibrium as a couple. After the dust settled, Brodie thoroughly agreed that Lord Huddleton, Anabelle's father, could not have chosen a more devoted family advocate.

Brodie flipped through several pages on his Gantt chart, then glanced at Mick expectantly.

Mick cleared his throat. "My crew finished the gold leafing in the entrance hall yesterday and will start on the restaurant today."

The entrance hall adjoined the former grand drawing room, a space now occupied by an upscale restaurant featuring elaborate plasterwork and Corinthian columns. Bookings were already several months out.

"Excellent." Brodie nodded. "How long will it take to redo the stencil?"

Mick calculated the numbers on his mobile and glanced up. "One week to eradicate what's been done, and another two or three to reapply the corridor."

"Did it ever occur to you with the rooms flowing one into the next, that those hues would clash?"

"Not for me to say. I was just following the chart."

"Can you paint over the stencil to tone down the colors and speed things along?" Brodie asked.

"Not in the least." Mick shook his head.

"Anabelle could help with the removal if Tara frees her up." Randy earned a glare from Tara for that remark.

"Get her on it when she returns." Anabelle was not only the family rep but a junior designer at Genesis who worked every bit as hard as he did. When corporate caught wind of this catastrophe though, they'd insist he sack her . . . Unless he spiked their guns by circumventing that action with something less severe.

"If I hire British gilders and put my crew back on the stenciling . . ." Mick's voice faded as he worked out the timing.

Brodie rubbed the stubble on his jaw as he weighed these latest disasters. All that stood between them reaching their contract deadline were the few weeks he'd padded into their schedule.

"How many spare hands do you need?" Brodie asked.

"Four at best, plus anyone on the team with extra time."

Brodie flipped through the Soldier's Leap catering profits. He could use their slush to cover the extra labor. "Hire them."

Checking the time, he groaned internally. This latest kerfuffle had tacked on forty-odd minutes. Anabelle's plane had landed, and his intent to surprise her at the terminal fizzled. But if he hurried, he might catch her before she boarded the train.

"That's it for now. Our catering staff has prepared a tasting table downstairs. Please let them know which dishes are your favorites. They're finalizing their summer menu and would appreciate your input."

Mick and Randy pushed out of their chairs and took off for the kitchen without further prodding. Tara lagged behind them, mincing around on those spiked heels while he shut down his computer and stored it away.

Using the office sector's external door to access the long drive up to the mansion, Brodie jogged to his car, ringing Anabelle on the way. *Please don't catch the train.* He jumped in his BMW and backed out, then, passing the newly seeded lawns and sculptured shrubbery, he headed for the gate.

Anabelle's voice came through the speaker. "This is Anabelle. Leave me a message."

"Lass, I hope ye get this. I meant to surprise ye, but our meetings ran late. Could ye hang tight? I've booked us supper at Luigi's," he said, naming their favorite Italian restaurant in Stirling.

Taking the last broad sweep of the drive, he reached the electronic gate and braked, waiting for it to open. Across the road, the eastern end of Loch Tummel drew his eye and held his gaze. White horses capped the waves as wind buffeted the deep blue water, lined with heavy forest and steep drops. Low clouds scudded, sailing across the azure sky. *Breathtaking.* Work demanded so much of his time that he rarely took time to soak in the spectacular views.

He swung onto the carriageway and accelerated. Anabelle's lack of response worried him. He'd worked long hours so they could spend evenings together upon her return, to make up for his neglect. He took full responsibility for the rocky patch they'd been going through.

Corporate wasn't thrilled to discover they were dating and had asked him to end the relationship–right after he'd asked Anabelle's father for her hand. Securing an agreement with Genesis had taken serious footwork on his part, which had delayed his proposal. To complicate matters, the engagement ring he'd designed and specially ordered from South Africa was delayed, stalling his proposal even further. But during that interim, he'd come up with an alternative plan to Genesis's mandate that employees could not date coworkers by creating a new company of his own, one where he and Anabelle worked together without corporate interference.

So, he'd agreed to keep things professional at work, but after hours? What he and Anabelle did on their own time was no one's business but theirs.

Dealing with Genesis and the jeweler had slowed his and Anabelle's relationship trajectory, making him unable to propose. Yet, as the weeks multiplied, Lord Huddleton, doubtless, questioned his trifling with Anabelle's affections. If the situation were reversed, Brodie would not be so accommodating.

His mind looped back to those signed work orders. Corporate would demand Anabelle's release. But had she truly gone over his head? The idea niggled away at him.

He sent her a voice text.

Brodie: Approaching airport. Did you get my message, lass?

Anabelle: I'm so sorry. My mobile battery died, and I didn't receive your message until I plugged it in on the train.

Brodie tugged his tie, loosening the knot as disappointment choked him. Making a U-turn, he zipped out of the airport, then rang the restaurant to cancel their reservation.

No quiet dinner. No time alone. This blasted renovation couldn't end soon enough. Taking the roundabout, he reentered the highway and started for Soldier's Leap.

Chapter 4

The Uber rolled to a stop outside the Soldier's Leap family wing. With a happy sigh, Anabelle stepped onto the drive, lifting her gaze to the hunting lodge's Baronial architecture. A sense of homecoming enveloped her as the driver retrieved her bag from the boot.

"Here you are, miss." The driver set her luggage on the ground beside her.

"Thank you."

The driver jerked his chin by way of acknowledgment, then hopped behind the wheel and headed down the drive, pea gravel crunching beneath the tires.

Gripping her suitcase handle, Anabelle dragged it to the door and punched in the code, then entered, nudging the door shut with her knee. The original staircase rose before her on this side of the wall, dividing this section of the house from the formal entrance and newly erected staircase in the formal entrance for paying, corporate guests.

Anabelle touched the baluster and took in the filigreed, Art Nouveau railings. Though opulent by today's standards, welcome wrapped her in its warm embrace.

Rather than lug her case up the steps, she headed for the music room, her heels echoing on the gray-veined marble. Crossing the semi-circular alcove where the grand piano stood, she ran her fingers over the ivories where Granny had taken her first lessons. Roots. The family connection burrowed deeper the longer she lived on the estate, and a strong desire to learn all she could about her Grandmother's Scottish forebears took hold.

The Sawyers, who had leased the property for the last eighty-plus years, had accidentally flooded the basement, obliterating all the family's documents and history—a heartbreaking discovery, indeed. But as the reno continued, Anabelle had high hopes that somehow other family artifacts would surface. Thus far, nothing had. But she continued to search. If records existed, she intended to find them.

Clasping her suitcase handle once more, she left the music room and strolled the full length of the adjoining library to the lift outside the small drawing room and rode the elevator to the next floor.

When she first moved into the family wing, Brodie had voiced concern about her living alone in such a vast space, instead of staying on the public side of the mansion with the other team leads. But Anabelle couldn't explain in a satisfactory manner how she never felt alone inside Soldier's Leap. Besides, someone needed to keep an eye out for any issues that might arise during the reno. The last thing they needed was another flood.

The door at the end of the corridor, which led to the attic, stood slightly ajar. Odd that. She always kept it closed. Perhaps Randy, their general contractor, had visited during her absence. Leaving her case beside her bedroom door, she marched down the hall and shut it, ensuring the latch held.

She paused as her mind grappled on how to inform Brodie that the Queen of the United Kingdom had invited herself to their nonexistent wedding. Perhaps he'd find the situation humorous, and they'd have a good laugh, or, horror of horrors, would he think she was hinting for a proposal? The last thing she intended was to prod her stubborn Scot of a boyfriend into marriage.

The entire last year had produced one construction disaster after another, not to mention Genesis's policy on not dating co-workers. After Brodie dealt with that kink, all but signing a contract with corporate for the two of them to keep things professional on the jobsite, Genesis backed off. But that fiasco had soured their relationship with corporate.

That's when Brodie had broached the topic of starting their own company when this reno concluded.

Even with an exit plan in the works, Brodie did not take his responsibilities lightly and gave this project his complete focus. But as the winter days gave way to spring, then early summer, his responsibilities had quadrupled.

Sighing, she grabbed her suitcase from where she'd left it beside the master suite's double, pedimented doors and entered what had once been Julia and William Lindsay's set of rooms. Stepping across the plush carpet, she set her case on the bench at the foot of the ornately carved, four-poster bed.

On her pillow lay a small bouquet of pink tulips. Butterflies erupted inside her chest and fluttered against the walls of her heart. Rounding a bedpost, she lifted the nosegay. Tucked within the leaves lay a typed card.

"You were missed."

She closed her eyes and savored the gesture. Brodie had missed her. For a man of few romantic notions, these flowers went a long way to pacifying her bruised heart. Sadly, she hadn't checked her messages before boarding the train and missed a surprise supper with him at their favorite restaurant.

Inside the bathroom, she found a glass and gave the flowers a drink from the tap. Still smiling, she set the tulips on her dressing table, then toed off her heels and padded barefoot to the French doors and stepped onto the balcony. She filled her lungs with the clean, sweet air and gazed at the beds below where peonies, allium, and gentians abutted roses in every color under the sun. Lovely. Her heart swelled, then warred with mixed emotions: happiness and an ache, soft and undefined. In six months, Soldier's Leap would no longer be her home, and though she could return whenever she chose, she would never be a permanent resident again.

High Ridge Hall, her father's estate in the Cotswolds, though beautiful, went to her brother Wills, along with her father's title, when he passed. While growing up, Anabelle rarely spent more than her school holidays there, along with fleeting trips home after university, thanks to Grandmama Poole's insistence that Mother, Anabelle, and her siblings reside in London to attend society gatherings. Only Dad had the effrontery to defy her, staying at High Ridge despite Grandmama's edicts.

Poor Mother, ever the peacemaker, was torn between pleasing her widowed mother and spending time with Dad in the country. Thank goodness Anabelle had only been born an "Honorable." Titles did not mean much in today's world, but Grandmama chose to ignore that particular memo. The royal orbit in which she traveled stuck to the old traditions. To her way of thinking, titles were everything.

That had led to Grandmama's vociferous opposition to her dating Brodie. "He'll only ever be a laird, and that's only when his father dies. You can do much better than marry a wild Scot and live in the back of beyond."

Thankfully, Granny Dewhurst, her father's mother, had been nothing like Grandmama Poole. Anabelle had enjoyed a close relationship with her until her passing two years ago.

Stepping back into her suite, Anabelle changed into a fresh blouse and trousers, then pulled her hair over her shoulder, combed out the tangles, and touched up her makeup. Still with time on her hands, she entered the dressing room and unpacked, then dumped her dirty clothes down the laundry chute. When she turned to leave, small grooves on the plaster, just inside the door, made her halt. Why hadn't Randy's team repaired the walls before they painted them?

She ran a fingertip over the indentations. Were those words? Tingles crept up her torso, and she dashed to her desk for a sheet of tracing paper and a pencil, then trotted back. Holding her breath, she pressed the paper to the wall and lightly rubbed lead over the ridges.

A word took shape before her eyes.

Belinda.

Granny's sister, along with her brothers Robbie and Wills, had died as a children. Anabelle's fingers trembled, and she dropped the pencil. Retrieving it from the floor, she applied the graphite several centimeters above Belinda's name, where a dual set of ridges appeared in the plaster.

Robert.

William.

Her throat tightened, and her eyes stung. The lessees had not erased their names when they'd remodeled Soldier's Leap in that horrid Victorian revival style.

Hardly daring to hope, Anabelle ran her hands down the wall where barely noticeable grooves, far below the others, scratched the surface. Kneeling, she placed the paper over the lines and repeated the process.

Belle.

Granny! A lump clogged Anabelle's throat, and tears scored her cheeks.

Belinda, Robert, William, and Belle. Granny and her siblings. Who had written their names on the wall?

Rubbing her hands over the surface with wider sweeps, Anabelle encountered no more indentations. She sat back on her bare feet. Had someone marked the children's height here, much like her own parents had tracked her and her siblings' growth? Perhaps their mother, Julia, had done so. She had died from consumption during World War II while her husband, William, served in Egypt with the British Army.

Shortly after Julia's passing, William arranged for the children's passage to Canada on the *SS City of Benares* to protect them from enemy bombings, but Belle contracted measles before their departure and remained behind.

During the Atlantic crossing, a German submarine sank the passenger liner carrying Granny's siblings and seventy other British children. The following year, Belle's father, William, contracted typhoid when it swept through his military camp, leaving Belle an orphan.

Up until this time, Belle had stayed with her nanny, but after her father's death, her trustees sent her to live with an elderly cousin when the war department commandeered Soldier's Leap as a military hospital. After the war, Granny's trustees leased the estate to a school for the blind. By the time Granny married Grandpa Simon and moved to High Ridge, Grandpa's estate in the Cotswolds, she had reached her majority, only to find that her trustees had signed a long-term lease with the Sawyer family.

Her grandparents had fired the trustees, but the eighty-five-year lease proved binding.

As for Granny's family, Anabelle knew nothing save for the snippets her grandmother shared—snippets that filled Anabelle with a raging desire to find more information about Granny's people.

Idly, Anabelle ran her fingers over the indentations, her thoughts on Julia, who had likely tracked her children's progress, unconcerned about marring the plaster walls, unknowing of what lay ahead. The bottled emotions Anabelle held inside erupted into a physical ache, and she rubbed her breastbone to soothe the pain. Julia, her great-grandmother, had died when Granny was only five.

Sometime after the Sawyers took possession of Soldier's Leap, they moved all her family's records to the basement, where the later flooding obliterated their history.

Questions continued to circle as she slipped on her shoes and went downstairs to wait for Brodie. She unbolted the door that connected the family wing to the main entrance, with its soaring ceiling and inlaid insignia of a medieval soldier. Then she headed to the team's offices, where she had a clear vantage point of the drive from a large window.

Ever since Genesis's scolding about dating a fellow employee, Anabelle, a self-professed rule follower, had struggled with her and Brodie's relationship. Guilt. It left her feeling like a sneak. And Brodie's responsibilities in recent weeks had tripled, adding to the chaos swirling inside.

If the five love language theory spoke truth, hers, words of affirmation, and Brodie's, that of physical touch—both were rather thin on the ground.

To top things off Grandmama had thrown a spanner in the works, fibbing to the Queen about her upcoming nuptials. Anabelle fidgeted with the window latch.

Grandmama's lie forced Brodie down on one knee or ended their relationship.

Anabelle twisted a curl around her finger, while shame flamed her cheeks. She'd rather die than broach this debacle to Brodie.

But broach it she must.

Chapter 5

The private gate swung open, and Brodie nosed his BMW up the drive to Soldier's Leap. Only staff and the family used the single-lane track, while the main entrance led to the guest car park, which provided for corporate events and restaurant patrons.

Taking the tight, hairpin turn, Brodie crested the hill, with the hunting lodge's white limestone walls and slate-capped conical towers playing hide and seek through hedgerows of rhododendrons and hawthorns. Despite the manor's higgledy-piggledy additions, the structure's fairy-tale appearance hearkened back to its days as a royal hunting lodge.

He eased up on the petrol and let the car tick over, idling the engine while he soaked in the view. A feeling of well-being swarmed his senses. Och. He tapped the steering wheel and admitted an attachment to the once ungainly place.

Over the last year, he had been so caught up in the project that he hadn't absorbed the new elevation's effect–until now. Though its occupants had suffered misfortune during the Second World War, Anabelle's people, the Lindsay's, had left a cheerful imprint on the estate.

Following the lane, he parked in front of the estate office entrance, firmly shelving the work order issues until he and Anabelle were on the clock. Doubtless, Anabelle had a logical reason for what had occurred. Why darken their evening with business differences? They had so few private moments.

A curtain twitched into place at one of the windows, then the office door opened, and Anabelle stepped outside. His heart lifted at the sight of her slender form. Anabelle's bone-deep beauty would last long after others' good looks faded, something his architectural eye had noted from their first introduction.

Compared to her taller siblings, Anabelle's average stature did not bear comment, but she didn't need height. Her natural grace and that undefinable *something* drew the eye and held it. For months, he'd struggled to label the uncanny phenomenon.

In a nutshell, Anabelle had presence—an inner elegance, and she had it in spades. That presence had captured his attention when she was a first-year university student while he moved toward pursuing an advanced degree. They'd enjoyed a flirtatious friendship, but nothing had come of it. So, when he ran into her last year, he did not hesitate to act.

Snatching the mixed bouquet of tulips and hyacinths off the passenger seat, he hopped out of the car. Anabelle closed the distance between them, and he tugged her into his arms, burying his face in her neck, scents of blossoms and sunshine encircling him.

He closed his eyes as his world righted itself. "Och, lass, 'tis happy I am to see ye."

She shifted in his arms and lifted those impossibly blue eyes of hers, fringed by dark lashes. Never one to deny such an open invitation, he dipped his head and savored the softness of her lips, careless if any of the team could see them through the windows. They weren't on the clock. Genesis could eat their edict.

"I must have just missed you." He held out the bundle of pink tulips and white hyacinths.

"They're lovely. Thank you." She accepted the bouquet and breathed in the hyacinth's sweet scent. "You're spoiling me with all the flowers."

She appeared so completely bowled over by the tulips, that he vowed to bring her tulips more often.

"You deserve spoiling. We've been working far too many hours, so I planned to surprise you at the airport."

"I'm sorry about that. Why don't we order something from the kitchen and eat in the family wing? I'm sure Joanna has leftovers from today's menu."

"Sounds perfect."

"Mr. Maxwell, on that, we are in perfect harmony."

He took her free hand, and they crossed the drive to the family's external entrance. Anabelle punched in the code, then relaced their fingers as they entered the Lindsay wing.

Pausing at the base of the stairwell, he examined the gold leafing.

"No, you don't." Anabelle tugged his arm. "No work allowed."

Grinning like a loon, he let her tow him through the ballroom, where natural light poured through the clerestory windows, sparkling off the crystal chandeliers, to the dining room beyond, a shortcut she used to bypass the lengthy corridors.

While Anabelle rang the kitchen, he soaked in the tooled leather wall coverings and carved paneling Gerard's team of skilled artisans had repaired. The walnut table, polished to a dull shine, seated twenty and smelled of beeswax.

"Brodie, which do you prefer?" Anabelle placed a hand over the mouthpiece. "Joanna has smoked salmon with asparagus spears and shallot potatoes or vegetarian consommé?"

"The salmon."

He turned back to examine the dining room that cleverly concealed a sleek galley kitchen that their wood specialist had created behind custom, hinged panels, along with a matching island that divided the space, yet kept the open concept. The sheen of pale silk draperies brightened the overall design. Doubtless, Anabelle's family would enjoy many happy meals here.

"Two salmon, please. We're in the family dining room." Anabelle paused. "If it isn't too much bother, could you bring up a vase? Thank you so much. Cheers."

Re-pocketing her mobile, Anabelle drew him to a window seat. "I found something just before you arrived. I can't wait to show you." Excitement pulsed through her words.

"What is it?" He sat on the cushion beside her, sinking into the tufted upholstery, and played with a lock of her hair.

"When I unpacked, I found grooves on my dressing room wall . . ."

As Anabelle shared her discovery, his heart melted. How difficult it must be to not know anything about half of your family. He'd grown up in Kirkton Glen, a small valley in the Scottish Highlands, where his ancestors had been baptized, married, and buried for nigh on four hundred years.

The same could not be said of Anabelle's ancestors.

Her mother's people, the Poole's, were titled aristocrats, and every last one of them had served the crown. But Anabelle had always been closer to her father and his mother, Belle, who lived with them during her waning years.

"Discovering all four children's names etched into the wall is almost miraculous." She rubbed her chest as though it ached. "How did their names survive all these years?"

"If I remember correctly, the original plaster in the dressing room was covered with paneling, the wood in such poor condition that Gerard couldn't save it. The names must have been on the wall beneath."

"You would think the painters would have prepped the walls before they sprayed them." She held up her hand. "Don't get me wrong; I'm delighted they didn't, as those names are the only things to survive the Sawyers' occupancy." Her blue eyes clouded with worry as she looked at the etchings. "Seeing them made me realize how little I actually know about Granny's people, and that unsettles me."

"If you're keen to trace your ancestry, why don't you hire a genealogist?" He ran his thumb over the back of her hand.

"The records were lost, Brodie."

"Have you tried the *kirk*?" he asked.

"The church is a ruin. If any records existed, they're long gone," Anabelle huffed, her bottom lip sticking out like a toddler in a full-on pout.

"Perhaps the minister moved them to Pitlochry, Calendar, or the cathedral in Dunblane. Come on, Anabelle. I've never known you to give up. Where's your fighting spirit? Your people were a big deal in these parts. Just because the private collection is gone doesn't mean all their information is lost."

"You're right." Anabelle perked up.

"What about your great-grandfather's war records? Didn't he serve in Egypt? That might be a good place to start."

"I already ordered his records. Other than regimental notes and

William's physical description, which I found vastly interesting, nothing shed any light on his family."

"Perhaps the region's historical society has something on the Lindsays."

A rap sounded on the door, putting an end to their conversation.

"Come in," Anabelle called.

Joanna Seward, a robust woman who ran the catering staff, entered, pushing a cart.

Brodie inhaled, and his mouth watered. "That smells delicious."

"I think you'll be pleased, Mr. Maxwell." Mrs. Seward's blue eyes sparkled beneath her gray hair as she spread a linen tablecloth, set the table with their meal, and placed a basket of rolls with pats of stamped butter, shaped like a soldier, between the crockery.

"Thank you, Mrs. Seward." Anabelle rose, tugging him to his feet.

Together, they approached the table. He pulled out Anabelle's chair, and she sat and spread a napkin across her lap.

"We have strawberries and cream, coffee, tea, and tiramisu for dessert." Mrs. Seward rattled off the after-dinner options.

Brodie sat across from Anabelle, his stomach growling.

"I'll have an herbal tea with the strawberries." Anabelle dimpled up at the woman, her white teeth flashing.

"Tea for me as well." Brodie nodded.

"Aye." Mrs. Seward inclined her head, then wheeled the empty trolley into the corridor.

For the first few minutes, the faint clink of cutlery sounded as they tucked into their meal. Brodie glanced at Anabelle across the table and vacillated on sharing what had occurred today at work. But having no desire to ruin their evening, he shoved the issue aside. It could wait.

Anabelle remained unusually silent during his musings.

He set down his cutlery. "What's troubling you?"

Anabelle looked up, her utensil raised halfway to her lips, then set it back on her plate. "We're in a terrible fix, Brodie. I'm horribly embarrassed and don't know how to tell you . . ." Her voice trailed off.

His gut tightened. This night was not to be without issues, after all. "If you tell me what it is, we can deal with it."

"Oh, Brodie, I'd love nothing more than to pack Grandmama off to the

Outer Hebrides." Anabelle dabbed her lips with her napkin. "I'm not sure you're aware, but she's one of The Queen's attendants."

Anabelle's grandmother, a force to be reckoned with among the royal courtiers, was the only person who turned his fiery Anabelle into a wide-eyed rabbit.

It was his mother, and not Anabelle, who had updated him on Lady Barbara's appointment. Anabelle never mentioned it—until now.

"What's Lady Barbara done?" He tore off a piece of roll, buttered it, then popped it into his mouth.

A dark flush crept up Anabelle's neck. "She's invited the Queen to our wedding."

He choked on the bread. Keeping his gaze on Anabelle, he reached for his water goblet and knocked it over. Liquid splashed across the white tablecloth. Anabelle bolted around the table to his side.

"Drink this." She pressed the crystal to his lips.

It was either swallow or drown. He gulped and sputtered as the water pressed painfully against the obstruction before the roll dissolved and opened his passageway. He inhaled a lungful of air, then pushed out of his chair, snatched up his napkin, and dabbed at the tabletop. "I hope this doesn't leave water stains."

"What's a water stain compared to the alternative?" Anabelle glanced at the door, then lowered her voice conspiratorially. "The staff waxes this furniture so often, I doubt it left a mark."

He chuckled but immediately sobered as her words sank in. "Why is the Queen coming to our wedding?"

Unbeknownst to Anabelle, he had designed a ring with a South African jeweler, but the blasted shipment had been delayed for months.

"It's Grandmama's way of forcing an engagement. I'm dreadfully sorry, Brodie."

"And I suppose it was impolite to correct the Queen?" The corner of his mouth twitched.

"Rather." She caught his expression. "You find this humorous?"

"I do." He dropped the sopping napkin onto his plate. "How many marriages are forced by royal decree these days?"

"None within the last century or more."

"What a story to tell our children."

“There you go with those imaginary children.” Anabelle rolled her eyes.

“Would you prefer I get on bended knee here and now?” He had not intended to propose without a ring, but he’d do it to salve Anabelle’s worries. Silently, he cursed Genesis’s employee rigamarole and the jeweler’s tardy shipment. Had the ring arrived on time, they’d already be engaged–assuming Anabelle said yes.

“I’d prefer a proposal without coercion, thank you very much.” She stuck that adorable nose of hers into the air and sniffed.

“Aye. On that, we agree.” He tugged at his shirt collar. No matter what he did now, Anabelle would think he’d proposed because of the Queen . . .

“This is such a muddle. What are we to do?” She looked up at him, her eyes imploring.

“We’ll figure something out. Her Majesty can’t march us up the aisle until we’re ready.”

Anabelle’s pupils darkened. “She wouldn’t dare. Would she?”

“I doubt it.” But he wouldn’t put it past Lady Barbara to plan another coup.

Chapter 6

Early morning sunlight filtered through the upper windows as Anabelle stepped through the family wing's connecting door into the main entrance hall, eager to view the progress made during her absence. She paused on the inlaid marble floor beside the Lindsay family crest of a mounted soldier and craned her neck to take in the gold leafing Mick's crew had completed on the vaulted ceiling.

Lovely. Not even the most demanding nitpicker could fault the craftsmanship.

The hall converged upon a row of Corinthian columns interspersed with a lush embankment of greenery separating the hall from The Soldier restaurant. No one would ever believe the space once served as the grand drawing room. She entered the restaurant, her footsteps muffled by the tarps strewn across the floor. Scaffolding stood against the back wall, blocking the terrace doors.

She pushed aside the plastic sheeting that covered the windows and peeked outside at the newly filled swimming pool sparkling in the morning sunlight. Her gaze wandered to the pickleball and tennis courts that abutted the family's private walled garden.

"You're back." Hugo, Mick Aiken's gangly assistant, said.

Anabelle jerked and spun about. "Oh." She pressed a hand to her chest to still her racing heart. "I didn't hear you."

Hugo, a man of few words, and Mick, the lead stencilor, both clad in off-white, paint-spattered overalls, leaned against opposite sides of a ladder three meters away.

"Sorry." Mick gave her an infectious grin. "You jumped a mile."

"I thought I was alone."

Gerald, the New England wood preservationist, waved. "Glad you're back, Anabelle." Without stopping to chat, he hurried on his way.

"Are you inspecting our work?" Mick swept an arm toward the newly gilded plaster.

"Yes. You and your team have done a fabulous job."

"Thanks. They're a talented bunch. I've some questions about the corridor stencil, though. Care to have a look?"

She accompanied Mick back onto the marble tiles and headed toward the corridor in question, Hugo hurrying ahead of them.

"Mind your step. The floor is somewhat slick." Mick placed his hand on her elbow to assist her. "After you." The plastic sheeting crackled as he parted it for her to enter the corridor closest to the front of the house.

"Thank you." Anabelle stepped through the partition onto more tarps.

She waited while Mick tucked the barrier back into place, then turned, almost bumping into Hugo. She flung out her arms to regain her balance and hit him in the chest.

"I'm terribly sorry."

Hugo grunted, stared at her for a moment, then moved out of the way.

Lifting her gaze to the stenciling, Anabelle's jaw dropped. *No. No. No.* Instead of the soft neutral colors used elsewhere, the stencil pattern had been switched to a garish magenta that clashed not only with the wood paneling but also with the upper walls and soon-to-be-laid carpet.

Anabelle blinked several times, her mind a mass of confusion. The stencil ran the entire length of one side of the corridor, just below the moldings. Why had Mick switched the colors? This was an utter disaster.

Covering the lower half of her face to conceal her expression, she fought for words. Why hadn't Tara monitored the stenciling during her absence? It fell under her realm of responsibilities. Anabelle always checked job sites at the close of each day to encourage the workers and identify issues before they became a concern.

"Your crew executed the motif exceptionally well. I'm confused, though. Did someone change the color palette?" Her heart thumped in distress, but she refused to cause a stink until she got to the bottom of this disaster.

"You didn't change the colors?" Mick waved at the magenta hues, a look of confusion in his eyes.

"No. I did not. They're hideous."

"On that, we both agree." Mick scratched his shoulder, opened his mouth, then closed it again. "I thought . . . Nevermind."

Anabelle swallowed her frustration. "Obviously, there's been a miscommunication. Why don't we leave off on this until Brodie weighs in on the changes?"

Mick saluted. "My guys will be thrilled, eh, Hugo?"

"Ugliest assignment we've ever had." Hugo itched his armpit.

Anabelle drew out her mobile and took several pictures, determined to address this at the morning's design meeting.

Leaving Mick and Hugo, she rode the lift to the basement to check on Seward and the new chef who had arrived earlier in the day.

Raised voices reached her on exiting the elevator.

"This is my kitchen. You and these *frauleins* are in my way," a male, German-accented voice shouted.

Before Anabelle left for London, Mr. and Mrs. Mellencamp had hired a Viennese chef from a Michelin-starred restaurant. When Anabelle expressed concern about territorial issues that might arise in the shared kitchen between the chef and Joanna Seward, the head of Soldier's Leap Catering, Brodie assured her that the Mellencamps had it covered. But from the sounds of this argument, they most definitely did not, which meant, she had to deal with the issue as the family rep.

She hurried down the corridor and pushed wide the two-way swinging door.

Mrs. Seward jerked, pivoting toward her, face flushed—an unusual phenomenon for the unflappable head of catering.

The chef, a blonde man with gray eyes rimmed with the lightest lashes Anabelle had ever encountered, snapped his head in her direction and glared.

"Is something wrong?" Anabelle moved deeper into the room.

The chef lifted a pale eyebrow and looked down his hooked nose at her. "And who might you be?"

"Anabelle Dewhurst, I'm a representative of the family who owns this property."

The chef's cheeks darkened, but he did not apologize. "Konstantin Wagner." He dipped his head slightly. "If I am in charge of the restaurant, I cannot do so with people under my feet."

"Mr. Wagner, it's good to meet you. Welcome to Soldier's Leap. We're delighted to have you on site. Have you toured the restaurant space yet?" Anabelle asked, hoping to diffuse the argument.

"Not yet, no. I wanted to start my rubs first."

"I understand. This is Joanna Seward."

"I run the catering service from this kitchen." Mrs. Seward straightened to her rather impressive height, her chest expanding. "I have a right to be here," she added with a sniff.

Bother. Anabelle swallowed. Who would have imagined that a junior designer would have to settle squabbles among the employees? She certainly hadn't seen that in the job description. But if she didn't end this, a third world war would likely erupt on the premises.

With the restaurant booked months in advance of its grand opening, Soldier's Leap could not afford to lose its chef or the income from its thriving catering service.

"The two of you need to work out a schedule. I understand that was shared when the Mellencamps interviewed you for the job. As Mrs. Seward leaves in thirty minutes, you and your staff will have the kitchen all to yourselves." Anabelle kept a firm lid on her rising impatience with the diminutive chef.

"I must start my rubs." Wagner's pale lashes shielded his narrowed eyes.

Anabelle lifted her chin. "Then may I suggest you use one corner of the kitchen for your prep until Mrs. Seward leaves at half two? In the future, your shift begins at half two as outlined in your contract."

Mr. Wagner untied his apron and tossed it onto the stainless counter, then marched across the room, muttering, "Fine. I will return in thirty minutes . . ." And he stomped off accompanied by a string of expletives.

Temperamental chefs weren't uncommon, but Anabelle had not anticipated such foul behavior on Wagner's first shift.

"Miss Dewhurst–" Joanna Seward began.

Anabelle held up a hand. "I'm dreadfully sorry, Joanna. Let him settle in, and tell me if there are any further issues."

She scanned the generous commercial space, taking in the gleaming surfaces. Mrs. Seward ran a tidy kitchen, and her catering service provided considerable revenue. The woman had not stormed off like the new chef, but her frustration did not bode well if this situation continued. With the restaurant booked months in advance of its grand opening, Soldier's Leap could not afford to lose its chef or the income from its thriving catering service.

If these two couldn't learn to play nice, both cooks would quit, and she'd be stuck finding an alternative plan.

CHAPTER 7

SHE'S BACK.

My heart jumps. Does she like my tulips?

Of course, she liked the tulips, I tell myself. All women like flowers.

Last night, I sneaked into the family wing, intending to display the flowers in the dining room, but curiosity drove me upstairs. I wandered about until I found her suite and left them on her bed.

I couldn't help myself and looked through her things, even her unmentionables in the top bureau drawer. But I didn't take anything. I can control myself.

Unfortunately, I took too long and had to dart up to the attic and down the opposite side of the house when I heard someone enter the lift. That was too close.

Today, a day later, my breath races when I think about my gift. Did Anabelle find my card? Did she read it?

Footsteps. I whip my head in their direction, and my hand trembles when Anabelle walks past. I fill my lungs with her scent—something floral with a punch—a heady combination.

My mouth waters when she looks at me, and it's all I can do not to follow her. To listen to her soft, cultured voice. To touch her shiny, dark hair.

Sighing, I turn away. I promised myself that if Genesis hired me, I would focus on claiming Soldier's Leap. I lied.

I've found a way that Anabelle and I can both be happy. This way, we both get Soldier's Leap, and I get Anabelle. She'll learn to love me.

I know it.

Chapter 8

Brodie entered his office and placed his jacket on a hook, turning when Tara barged in without knocking. Though Randy, the general contractor, had recently hung the new doors, the coded locks and handles had not yet arrived.

"I made a mess of things. Corporate knows about Anabelle's amended work orders."

Brodie stiffened.

"Let's start at the beginning." He motioned for her to join him at the small table he used for less formal meetings, rather than traipse down the corridor to the large conference room. "How did Genesis find out?"

"I might have let it slip." Tara winced, avoiding his eyes. "Paul rang right after our meeting last night." Tara tossed her bob, the sleek fall of red hair returning almost immediately to rest on her shoulders. "He could tell something was wrong, and it all poured out. Now he's pushing for disciplinary action." Tara rapped the table with her knuckles. "What if he lets Anabelle go? I can't meet our deadlines without her. She's incredible. It would take three designers to replace her."

Brodie rubbed the bridge of his nose but didn't interject. As project manager, he'd found that if he didn't fill the silence, people often divulged information they didn't intend to share.

"I don't have nearly enough material to complete those en-suites." Tara wrung her hands, now in full panic mode. "I've called my normal contacts, and no one has openings."

The beginnings of a headache throbbed in Brodie's left temple. He couldn't deal with Tara's panic just now. He had to fix this. Pronto. Maybe if he reworked their schedule, he could shorten the delay.

He tugged at the knot on his tie, then slid out his mobile and texted Anabelle.

Brodie: Steer clear of the offices today.

Thanks to Tara, he needed to sort this with corporate if he hoped to keep Anabelle on the payroll. Unfortunately, her signature appeared at the bottom of both work orders, irrefutable evidence he couldn't deny. But something in the back of his mind niggled. There must be more to this situation.

Footsteps reached him from the corridor.

"Hello?" Anabelle called. A second later, she rapped on the partially open door and peeked around the doorframe.

His temples drummed, the headache spreading to his left eye. *Blast.* He'd hoped to solve this before she arrived.

"I saw the lights." Anabelle beamed, her blue eyes shining. "How long have you been here?"

"A while. Did you receive my text?" he asked.

"No."

Tara cleared her throat, drawing Anabelle's attention.

"I'm sorry. Am I interrupting?" Anabelle's mobile dinged. "That's probably your text." She checked her mobile and nodded.

"Are you going to tell her?" Tara demanded.

Tara caused this problem for Anabelle with corporate, and now the woman wanted *him* to spill the bad news?

"Tell me what?" Anabelle's gaze darted between him and Tara.

Brodie pressed two fingers to his throbbing temples.

"Have you seen that stencil in the corridor? Mick said someone changed the work order to that hideous magenta." Anabelle's forehead creased. "It clashes with everything, even the woodwork."

"Why don't you join us?" Brodie motioned toward a chair at the table.

He did not want to hold this conversation, not until he had time to speak to corporate. Unfortunately, Tara had eliminated that option.

"Why do I suddenly feel like I've entered the headmaster's office?" Anabelle situated herself across the table from Tara, her eyes full of questions.

His stomach churned as he placed a color-coded folder on the table's surface, then sat halfway between Anabelle and Tara.

If Anabelle mentioned the stencil disaster on her first morning back, certainly that proved her innocence. And why hadn't Tara brought it to his attention over the last few days? That infuriated him almost as much as the error. She must have slacked on her site checks.

Running his thumb over the edge of the folder, he glanced at Anabelle, who gazed at him expectantly. Unable to remain seated, he crossed to his desk, opened the top drawer, and riffled blindly for something to do–anything rather than broach the topic at hand.

The documents for his and Anabelle's startup company caught his eye. He hadn't left them in such disarray but had clipped them together. Had someone gone through his desk? In his rush to the airport, he had left them inside the top drawer, unlocked documents that listed Anabelle as the design lead.

His ears rang with high-pitched static. Had Tara found those, too? The woman's insatiable curiosity kept her in the know, which she manipulated to her favor. But her inability to stay out of everyone's business caused most of the team to keep her at arm's length.

Brodie covered one eye, the socket now on fire. If he didn't get this headache under control, it would become a full-on migraine. As a long-standing habit, he compartmentalized his life into segments, just as he took care to keep things between himself and Anabelle professional during business hours, ensuring none of the team complained about his granting Anabelle special favors. In fact, most of the team had no idea they were an item.

Unable to stall any longer, he returned to the table and opened the folder. "Anabelle, you're a valuable asset to our team. When you took on the role of family representative, you agreed to discuss any design adjustments before implementation to ensure cost analysis and the meeting of mandatory deadlines."

"That's right." Anabelle scooted forward in her chair. "Am I correct in guessing that whatever this is..." She pointed to his folder. "Has something to do with the stencil?"

She'd always been a quick study, and an intuitive one at that.

"Among other things." His throat muscles constricted.

She glanced across the table at Tara, who snatched the folder from Brodie and pulled out two pieces of paper, her gaze clouded with worry.

Anabelle's stubborn little chin shot into the air. *Brilliant.*

"I hope one of the errors includes the corridor's motif. That magenta stencil must go. I intended to speak to both of you about it this morning."

"Did you make these changes?" Tara placed one of the work orders in front of Anabelle.

"Why would I do that?" Anabelle turned confused eyes on him. "They're hideous."

"It appears two work orders were placed, altering agreed-upon designs, without conferring with Tara or me." Brodie pressed on with a heavy heart. "Until now, our renovation has met each deadline, but both of these changes have wreaked havoc on our deliverables."

Anabelle's expression darkened. "And you think I had something to do with it? We had an agreement. I would never do something like that without confirming with you first." She folded her arms, and her body went ramrod straight in the chair.

Nausea roiled in Brodie's gut.

"Did this occur while I was in London?" Anabelle's gaze shot darts his way.

Bullseye. He should have mentioned this last night. Big mistake. "Two work orders were changed, one switching the colors in the stencil's motif."

"To that nasty magenta? I most certainly did not fill that out," Anabelle said through clenched teeth, her lips barely moving.

"You deny changing the colors?" Tara pushed the second paper across the table. "What about the drapery material?"

"What are you talking about? What drapery material?" Anabelle reached for the paper, her eyes dropping to the work order.

"The special-ordered material for the en-suites." Tara blinked, her reaction one of bafflement by Anabelle's denial.

"The custom weave fabric?" Anabelle perused the work order, shaking her head. "I don't understand this. I spent days finding that William Morris design, which ties perfectly to the décor. I would never have ordered it in Dupioni silk for south-facing rooms, though. And even if I did, we don't have nearly enough yardage."

"So, you deny filling these out?" Brodie asked.

"I do." Anabelle stared him down, her gaze sparking.

Brodie rubbed his face with both hands. What a disaster.

"That is your signature at the bottom." Tara rose halfway from her chair and tapped the signature lines on both forms.

Anabelle stared at the paper and swallowed. "That certainly looks like my signature, but I didn't sign these. Why would I order silk for south-facing rooms? It will fade and rot in the sunlight. Besides, we need five times the yardage listed in these mods for the en-suites."

Brodie kept his gaze on Anabelle's signature.

Anabelle's moniker was on the bottom of both forms. The facts were against her.

"If it were just the material, I would let this drop." Brodie rubbed his temples where his head throbbed so hard he could barely hear himself think. "The stencil in the corridor is halfway completed. Mick's crew will need a solid week to remove what's been done before they reapply the correct palette. That will halt their progress on the gold leafing and plasterwork." The labor alone would kill their budget.

Anabelle's hands trembled, along with the papers she lifted from the table.

"All our reputations are on the line." Every single member of the team, to be exact. Not to mention Genesis's. His name as project manager would hinder his "rising star" status if he didn't deliver on time—and that would hurt their startup.

The trouble was, if Anabelle did not sign those documents, someone else had deliberately done so to get her sacked. Or were they trying to sabotage the renovation?

Unfortunately, he had nothing except the way he felt about her to stand in her defense. He needed proof to settle his doubts. Because those signatures were dead ringers for hers.

"Why would I do that when we agreed on the motif's colors for the entire ground floor?" Anabelle dropped the forms on the table's surface.

"It's your signature, Anabelle. If we had proof, I could fight corporate, but as things stand, my hands are tied," he said quietly.

"I did not sign them. Why would I choose a magenta palette for the stencil, or silk for sun-drenched walls? Give me some credit for better taste than that."

The computer hummed in the background while his eyes bored into her soul for the answers he sought.

"Are you going to sack me?" Anabelle asked at last.

He must act, or corporate would handle Anabelle much more severely. Sweat plastered his shirt to his back. Tara had placed him in a bind. The kindest option he could offer Anabelle was probation. Sacking her would destroy her career and, most likely, their relationship.

Sometimes, he really hated this job.

Refusing to look either woman in the eye, he pushed out of his chair. "You ladies work out how to utilize that wasted fabric. As for the other, both of you will lend Mick's crew a hand to speed up the process of replacing that stencil."

"Me?" Tara's voice rose for the first time.

"You are partially accountable for this fiasco. If you had checked the job sites regularly, things would never have progressed to this point."

Tara lowered her head, bright spots of color in both cheeks. "I know. I should have checked sooner. It's just that Anabelle is usually so reliable, I've never needed to follow up before."

"What did the workroom have to say? I assume you contacted them?" Brodie asked.

"I did," Tara flipped her red bob once more. "They've agreed to adjust their schedule once the fabric arrives from the weavers. Unfortunately, the weavers aren't available for another month, which tacks six weeks onto our schedule."

Six weeks? Brodie coughed to clear his throat's obstructed passageway. "Now that we have a new timeline, let's put this behind us and move forward."

Tara nodded and left the room, her over-confident attitude, for once, missing.

With Tara now out of hearting range, Brodie placed both hands on the table. "Tara mentioned the work orders to Paul. I believe you, but until I can prove otherwise, I have no other option but to place you on formal probation, Anabelle. It's the most lenient disciplinary action I can offer under the circumstances."

"Very well." Hurt and anger warred deep within Anabelle's eyes.

The expression impaled his heart as she left his office with her head held high, closing the door behind her with the softest of clicks.

A slam would have been better.

Chapter 9

Anabelle leaned against the terrace balustrade, taking in the estate's lush gardens and outdoor pool. Down the hillside near the loch, newly built glamping pods peeked through thickets of ancient Caledonian pine, larch, and beech. She sighed and rubbed the back of her arms as the sun dipped behind Ben Morven, a mountain the Scots called a Munro. The light muted, leaching the sky's fiery hues to lavender gray.

Brodie was avoiding her. Part of her did not blame him. Unfortunately, the other bit did—the bit that expected loyalty from the man she loved. Unfortunately, her gift to see both sides of a situation did her no favors in this instance.

Her Majesty's demand for an invitation to a nonexistent wedding, and now her probation, both issues out of her control, had left her flummoxed. With so much inner angst humming through her body, if she didn't do something physical, she'd go mad. Stepping off the terrace, she marched across the manicured lawn toward the gardener's barn, where a boxing bag hung. It was closer than the basement gym and more private. No one from the team would find her there.

On reaching the structure, she noted the bolted door.

"Bother," she huffed, then plopped onto the stoop and planted her chin on her fists, her emotions at war with the peaceful setting.

Minutes passed. An occasional nightingale sang from the trees, and the lavender sky deepened to purple, then grayed to black. One by one, stars emerged, diamonds sparkling against black velvet.

Three young deer, barely more than fawns, exited a thicket and bent to graze, their ears forward, their bodies poised for flight. Anabelle tracked the small herd as they nibbled the grass. The frustration she had battled since this morning's disaster rose and choked her, and she lowered her face into her hands. She yearned for Granny's comforting arms.

Whenever life overwhelmed her, Granny would say, "Set your emotions aside and examine your issues from every angle. Can you do anything to improve your situation? If so, do it. If not, leave it with God."

Anabelle straightened her shoulders. Feeling sorry for herself accomplished nothing. Granny might be beyond reach since her passing, but her teachings lived on inside Anabelle.

Filling her lungs, she expelled a shaky breath. Someone had forged her name on those addenda. If she challenged the signatures as counterfeit, would Genesis believe in her enough to hire an expert to prove her innocence?

Doubtful. Her shoulders slumped. Experts took time and money. Working on such a slim profit margin, Genesis had neither. But either way, her reputation as a designer suffered. Proving her innocence would give her the chance to eventually recover and take command of her career.

Whoever had forged her name must be a member of the team. No one else understood the significance of altering work orders so late in a project. But why would they do such a thing? Everyone on the team stood to lose a large bonus along with their professional reputations if the renovation exceeded the deadline.

She mulled that over for a while.

The better question was, who wanted her gone?

Tara mentioned the work orders to Paul. But sacking Anabelle only slowed the reno, and spinning up a replacement took time, time the team could ill afford. As much as she'd like to point the finger in Tara's direction, she couldn't. Tara had big plans for her bonus.

Randy? He had a contracting business to uphold and was seriously dating a woman he met over the holidays. The fellow even mentioned settling down. For that, he needed a sparkling reputation to provide for a family. She shrugged it aside.

Gerald? Goodness, no. The cranky Bostonian hadn't the least interest in ruining his reputation.

Mick? The fellow worked like a well-oiled machine and could usually be found atop a ladder with a double-ended brush in one hand and a pot of paint in the other. He, like the other team leads, had laser focus and a stellar clientele. But Hugo, his assistant with the protuberant eyes, followed her every move. She shuddered. The fellow made her flesh crawl.

The deer lifted their heads, froze for two beats, then bounded across the lawn and disappeared around the far side of the manor. Through the gloom, a shadow separated from the forest, and a man stepped onto the lawn, head down, shoulders hunched. His movements triggered the terrace lights, casting a long, distorted shadow behind him.

Brodie? Anabelle caught her breath and pushed to her feet. Brodie's perennially erect carriage and purposeful stride broadcasted confidence. Not tonight. Never had she witnessed such dejected body language in Brodie.

What was he doing out so late?

He ambled up the terrace steps and entered the house, not once glancing in her direction. Was he on his way to speak with her? She tugged her mobile out of her pocket in anticipation, but as the minutes lengthened, neither call nor text lit up her screen.

She wrapped her arms around her middle. Since they started dating, a day never passed without a goodnight kiss, no matter how busy their jobs kept them.

Did he suspect her of guilt?

A mosquito bit her arm. She slapped it absently, still mulling over his behavior.

As a child, she fibbed a time or two, but her conscience bothered her so badly that by the time she hit double digits, she had stopped altogether. How could Brodie, who knew her better than anyone, believe that she had altered those work orders?

Coals of temper burst to life, sparking red hot. *It's your signature, Anabelle.* But why would she sabotage the renovation? That made no sense at all. Surely, Brodie had reasoned through that. Besides, if she and Brodie intended to open their own firm after the reno's completion, those forged addenda delayed their departure.

Her mobile lit up, her heart right along with it.

Brodie: Night, lass.

Probation. I didn't see that coming.

I'd been sure they'd sack Anabelle after I signed those work orders—so sure, that I found us a small derelict cottage where the two of us can be together, without interruptions, a place where we can bond away from the outside world.

I sigh, my foot tapping the floor. I've never worked this hard to get a woman's attention, but Anabelle is worth the delay. Once we're together, Soldier's Leap will be mine. Who else would her father leave the place to but her? When he does, illegitimacy will not keep me from my inheritance, not like it did Gran.

Once Anabelle understands how things will be, she'll fall in with my plans. She's nothing like the others. She's loyal.

She won't reject me.

Chapter 10

In the attic, where the team stored the newly purchased artwork, furnishings, and fixtures until rooms below were ready to receive them, Anabelle set the bolt of material she carried onto the floor and removed the sheeting from yet another set of overstuffed chairs. Retrieving the dupioni silk, she draped it over a bookcase and let the lamp's natural light setting give an accurate read on the colors.

Intent on finding a way to put the fraudulently ordered fabric to good use, she stepped back and frowned, her shoulders dropping. The material's cool hues clashed with the orange undertone of the wood.

All morning, she'd searched without the slightest glimmer of luck. If she intended to salvage her career, she needed to find a solution for this material's use, or Tara might push for her release. This mix-up reflected badly on her, too. And Tara resented it.

As for Brodie, he had holed up inside his office to rejuggle their deliverable schedules. If anyone could find a way to meet their deadline, Brodie would, but his preoccupation had dealt her a crushing blow. Two months ago, if someone asked where she saw herself in five, ten, or thirty years, she would have said, "At Brodie's side in both private and professional sectors."

Even though Brodie had placed her on probation to protect her from corporate's push to have her dismissed, had those forged signatures raised doubts in him about her innocence? Brodie, a master chess player when it came to life, often proved hard to read.

Gathering up the silk, she lowered the plastic sheeting, then grasped the floor lamp and moved to the next grouping of furniture, the extension cord trailing behind her. She wiped a grimy hand across her brow and repeated the process—again without success.

Her spirits plunged. Being falsely accused had wounded her in ways she never dreamed possible. Someone she knew had done this to her, of that she had no doubt, and that betrayal stung.

Squaring her shoulders, she moved to the next grouping and read the label taped to the plastic sheeting: Business Center. Tara had designed the corporate workspace. Altering her selections might raise conflict.

But as Anabelle reached the section beyond, inspiration struck, and she returned to inspect the center's furnishings. A half dozen computer desks, several overstuffed lounge chairs, French Provincial rolling chairs for the workstations, side tables, and Art Nouveau accessories stood shoulder to shoulder, lined up like soldiers in formation.

Tara's mix of styles created a luxurious yet functional space. Even the Business Center's rug proved unique, but in hues that did not blend well with the rest of the reno's design.

Anabelle eyed the office furniture and tapped her index finger on her chin. One glance at the bolt of dupioni silk, and a smile tugged at her mouth. The large-scale pattern did not repeat often but appeared wide enough for what she had in mind.

Using her hand to approximate the size of the large flowers, she then counted the windows on her printed layout. Her smile broadened, and she whipped out her mobile and rang the design workshop in Stirling.

"Hiya, Margaret, it's Anabelle Dewhurst from Genesis."

"Hello, Ms. Dewhurst," Margaret responded in her formal manner.

"I'm terribly sorry to ask, but we might have a last-minute change. Has your workshop started on the blinds for the Soldier's Leap Business Center?"

"Let me check." Computer keys clicked in the background. "Ah. No. We have not."

"We'll still need the blinds we ordered, but I wondered if your workshop could create toppers using the Abyssaly Vintage print by William Morris in Dupioni silk." She had enough yardage in the misordered print to cover toppers in the deeply shaded business center.

"Very boho." Margaret's voice warmed. "That would look exceptionally well together. Unfortunately, doing so will throw off our delivery schedule if we add toppers to the order."

"I do understand. Thank you, Margaret. Cheers."

Anabelle stared off into the distance. Drat. Margaret ran the largest design workshop in the region. No one else would have an opening for such a fast turnaround. Anabelle drummed her fingernails on her mobile case as an idea took hold, and she rang her mother.

"Darling, what a pleasant surprise to hear from you," Mother answered.

Anabelle stifled a giggle. It had only been two days since she last saw her, but Mother was always delighted to hear from her children.

"Hold on," Mother said.

Muffled voices came through the line. She must have covered the mouthpiece with her hand. She had never mastered the art of putting someone on hold, but she could text and video chat like a pro. Mother's endearing quirks warmed Anabelle's heart, and a sense of homesickness swept through her.

"I'm back. The chemist was filling a prescription and needed me to sign for it," Mother said, coming back on the line.

"Chemist? Are you sick?" Concern filled her. Mother was rarely ill.

"No, dear. Your father's under the weather."

"What's wrong with Dad?" Why hadn't he mentioned it when she was in London?

"Nothing. He's just a mite tired, but I'm sure you didn't ring to chat about that." Mother's volume increased like it always did when she was excited. "Has Brodie proposed?"

Anabelle snorted. If Mother only knew. "Things are rather hectic at present."

"That's too bad. Grandmama was asking just last evening if you had selected a wedding date. The Queen's schedule is filling quickly."

I'll just bet it is. Anabelle pressed her lips together. If she told Mother about her probation, Grandmama would hear about it and ring Brodie's mother, and ruffled feelings would ensue. Anabelle expelled a lungful of air. Though she longed to confide in her mother, Dad always proved the safer bet when she needed a familial shoulder.

"Mother, could you overnight me Granny's sewing machine?"

"Whatever for?"

"It's a long story, but I'm in desperate need of a machine and have zero time to locate one with all the attachments I need."

"I'll be happy to see that you get it, darling."

Dad spoke in the background, but Anabelle couldn't make out his words.

"Just a moment, Anabelle. What is that, dear?" Mother asked Dad.

Anabelle paced to the closest window, a full-length sheet of glass that overlooked the terrace and newly filled pool beyond. A lone swimmer executed a flip turn at the far end and started back in her direction.

She wiped the grime from the pane to see better. Who was in the pool? Had the water even had time to heat after its recent filling?

Placing a hand on the glass, she squinted against the glare. The swimmer reached the shallow end and hoisted himself out. Water sloshed onto the deck at his feet. Wow. That fellow was ripped. Really ripped. When he tugged off his goggles, Anabelle caught her breath. *Brodie* glanced up at the window where she stood in plain sight, gaping at him like a teenager.

She spun away, but not before the corners of Brodie's mouth lifted, and his white teeth flashed. Her cheeks burned, and she chided herself for ogling him. Well, not for ogling him exactly—more like—for getting *caught* ogling him.

Tempted beyond contrition, she peered out as Brodie ran a towel over his hair, then started for the basement stairs, doubtless to access the gym showers in the house's lowest regions. Brodie had not looked *that* fit at university. Anabelle placed her hands on her cheeks.

Here at Soldier's Leap, Brodie worked long hours in his button-down, fitted shirts. Even when she rose early and went for a morning hike or jog, he beat her to the office. They'd shared private moments–stolen good-night kisses, late-night texts, and an occasional dinner–but she had never seen him without his shirt.

And nothing had prepared her for that physique.

The pool's completion during their chilly spring had not tempted anyone to use it until this morning. Brodie, doubtless, swam laps to assure the heater was up and running before he deemed it acceptable.

"Anabelle, darling? Are you still there?" Mother's voice interrupted her musings.

"Yes," Anabelle croaked, then coughed to clear her throat.

"I'm terribly sorry that took so long. I'll overnight Mother Dewhurst's machine to you within the hour. You'll have it by tomorrow. I must say, I'm glad you want it. The machine's been sitting idle since she passed. I almost donated it to the local charity shop, but your father wouldn't hear of it."

Anabelle's heart tripped. "I'm glad I asked for it, then." The idea of donating Granny's belongings unsettled her. "Mummy, you won't give Granny's things away without speaking to Dad or me first, will you?"

"You sound just like your father. We all loved Mother Dewhurst, but she's been gone two years, Anabelle. It's time we cleared her rooms. We can't keep them as a shrine to her memory."

Anabelle closed her eyes. Mother had a point. Granny's things couldn't stay there forever. But whenever she visited High Ridge, she made a point to sit in Granny's rooms. Having her things just as she'd left them felt as though Granny had just stepped outside, not left them altogether.

"Wait until I'm home, and I'll help you sort it out." Anabelle stalled, needing one last chance to say goodbye.

"That's very thoughtful. I'll look forward to having you all to myself." Mother blew a kiss through the receiver. "I must dash. Love you, darling."

"Ta." Anabelle slumped onto one of the chairs, the plastic crinkling beneath her.

Grandmama would hound Mother for a wedding date in the very near future. What could she tell them? That she and Brodie were going through a rough patch due to his placing her on probation? That he had all but barricaded himself in his office? That right now, their chances of marrying were as probable as her flying alone to Mars. Disquiet's sharp edges snagged her heart as her precarious situation with Genesis struck home with greater force.

She clicked off the lamp and carried it downstairs, balancing the bolt of material under her opposite arm. Returning to her workstation, she distracted herself by sketching a window topper that showcased the silk print. Satisfied with her drawing, she placed an online order for notions and batting to be delivered the next day, then texted Randy.

Anabelle: Do you have time to cut eight pieces of lumber for window treatments?

With the design workshop booked solid, she intended to tackle the upholstery job after hours—even if she cut the wood herself. Whoever had forged her signature wouldn't get rid of her so easily.

A few minutes later, her phone chimed.

Randy: Send me the dimensions, and you'll have them today.

Armed with resolve, Anabelle opened her AutoCAD program, intent on using every inch of that William Morris silk print. Excitement fizzed inside her. She could do this. Tara said she didn't care what Anabelle did with the material. Well, she'd use it to improve the business center's design and tie the room in with the rest of the house.

Tara walked past on a cloud of Chanel, dressed in a black and white ensemble much better suited for a Parisian runway than a reno project. "Ah, there you are, Anabelle. Mick needs an extra hand in the corridor. One of his crew has taken ill."

"Me?" Anabelle didn't know the first thing about professional stenciling.

"Yes. If we are to make up time for your blunder, you need to help repair the damage you caused. Mick assured me that he could teach you what you need to learn."

Seething internally, Anabelle bit her tongue to repress a scathing reply, rose from her desk, and shut down her computer with quick jerky movements. If she remembered correctly, Brodie requested both of them to help with the stenciling. But dressed like that, Tara had created the perfect excuse to bow out.

Anabelle sighed. Brodie wouldn't be the only one putting in long hours, not if she intended to complete those toppers off the clock.

Taking the corridor, she passed the newly installed staircase, which mirrored the original inside the family wing, then crossed the entrance hall, and turned the knob hidden in the paneling to enter the family wing. She needed to change into something more conducive to paint splatter.

Anger swirled with every step, and she narrowed her eyes. If Brodie thought she'd tolerate his preoccupation, he'd soon learn that she was not the woman to sit quietly in a corner. She had things to say.

And say them she would.

Chapter 11

I RUN my hand up the banister, my gaze rising to the second floor, examining the newly repaired wainscoting. No one could differentiate where the old paneling ended, and the restoration began. My chest swells with pleasure at the magnificent repairs.

When Anabelle and I are together, we will live at Soldier's Leap, the home where I should have grown up.

I rub my jaw. Prior to this renovation, the property didn't have a residual income. Doubtless, that was why Lord Huddleton's family had leased the place for decades.

I shrug. Anabelle and I will figure out a way to make this work. Living here, together, where I belong, is what matters.

First, I must win Anabelle's heart. I drum my fingers on my thigh. To do that, I need to study everything about her.

In private.

CHAPTER 12

BRODIE WHISTLED as he donned his trousers and button-up after showering in the gym bathroom. Catching Anabelle's stunned expression earlier when he climbed out of the pool had alleviated much of his earlier frustration about the reno's sabotaged deadline.

While he wrangled with their deliverable schedules over the last few days, Anabelle's probation kept him tossing at night. He believed her. He'd never known her to lie.

Unfortunately, the facts proved otherwise—unless he upended them, which is why he'd overnighted a specialist that packet, one he needed to check on.

Returning to the office, he pressed a number he'd added to his mobile.

"Crouch Forensics," a woman answered.

"I'd like to speak to George Crouch. The name's Maxwell."

"One moment, Mr. Maxwell."

Brodie paced the office as the second hand ticked away the minutes.

"Crouch," a preoccupied-sounding male answered.

"Mr. Crouch, this is Brodie Maxwell."

"I received your packet."

"Did you have a chance to look it over?" Brodie cut straight to the chase.

"I am backlogged, Mr. Maxwell, but I will take a preliminary look at it later in the week or the first of next."

"I appreciate that." Brodie rubbed his neck. That was not the answer he'd hoped for.

"I'll patch you back to Helen to set up your billing," Crouch said.

Brodie gave his information to Helen and rang off. Crouch had a reputation as a bulldog in his field. If Anabelle said she didn't sign those documents, then Crouch's findings would back her up.

With that accomplished, his focus shifted to the reno's deadline. The penalty for exceeding it destroyed Genesis's profitability margins, not to mention its professional reputation. And Brodie fully intended to ensure both were a success.

Returning to his desk, he rang a carpet sculptor.

"Hiya, Ralph. Brodie Maxwell."

"Brodie. Good to hear from you." Ralph Chalmers had attended primary school with him, taking over his father's sculptured carpet business, a niche market, upon his father's retirement. "What can I do for you?"

"We've had a small opening in our schedule, and I was wondering if you could move up your arrival at Soldier's Leap by two weeks?" Brodie had sent business Ralph's way on more than one occasion. Crossing his proverbial fingers, he hoped to collect on it now.

"Hang on. Let me check with Nancy."

Nancy, Ralph's wife, set his schedule and ran the office. With so few custom carpet designers, clients were at Ralph's mercy.

"Nancy's switching things around. When do you need me?" Ralph asked.

Tension eased from Brodie's shoulders. One hurdle down. "Does the first week of August work?"

"It does."

"Thanks. I owe you."

"You don't owe me a thing. See you in August."

"Cheers." Brodie's mobile screen darkened. He rotated his neck, easing the pressure. If he shifted a few more projects around, they just might make that deadline.

Knock. Knock. Tara rapped her knuckles on the doorframe and pushed it wide, her over-strong perfume itching his nose. He fought back a sneeze.

"May I help you?" Brodie frowned at the interruption.

Tara sat on one of the leather chairs opposite him. "Genesis just offered me the lead designer position on the Slovakia Project when we wrap here."

"Congratulations." The Slovakia Project, a woolen mill conversion into upscale flats, was corporate's next endeavor. "When's your start date?"

"I haven't decided if I'll accept."

What kind of eejit turned down a deal like that? Brodie cocked his head, suspicions rising. Where was Tara going with this?

"I heard that you're starting your own company. Are you in the market for a designer?" she asked.

Ah. That explained the fancy outfit and strong perfume. Since he never once mentioned starting his own firm, Tara must have snooped through his office. "Where did you hear that?" Brodie leaned back in his chair and folded his arms behind his head.

"Someone mentioned it," Tara sputtered.

"I think not." If Tara lied about overhearing his plans, had she lied about Anabelle's work orders, too?

He rejected that train of thought. The signatures on those documents were so similar to Anabelle's that only a professional could detect discrepancies.

"You've been digging through my files. If there is one thing I value in an employee, it's integrity. If, and that's a mighty big if, I do start a firm, Tara, I will choose a lead designer who mirrors my ethics."

White spots speckled Tara's red-stained cheeks as she rose from her chair.

The sudden knots inside his neck released. He and Anabelle never spoke about their future plans at the office. If Tara ever found out, the woman would have no compunction about tossing Anabelle aside to promote her own career.

Did Tara feel threatened by Anabelle's talent? If so, she had good reason. Though a junior designer, Anabelle's executions were nothing short of brilliant.

"I think we're done here." He shut down his computer and raised a brow when Tara delayed her exit.

She stomped out like a spoiled child. The woman's diva behavior swung like a pendulum, from one extreme to another. Brodie cocked his head to the side. Was Tara desperate enough to hire someone to forge those work orders and discredit Anabelle?

He found that hard to accept.

When Crouch analyzed those signatures, he would have answers. And if a member of his team was involved, he intended to turn them over to the authorities.

Clad in a T-shirt and dungarees, Anabelle beelined it for Brodie's office, but his closed door made her hesitate. She hovered, waffling with her hand only inches from the wooden panel. Mick found her a few moments later, her fist still raised to knock.

"Ready?" Mick asked her.

"As ready as I'll ever be." Reluctantly, she followed him to the corridor, more than ready to obliterate that magenta stencil.

Mick knelt and opened his work bag, then fished out two pairs of rubber gloves located next to paint pot samples, a spool of wire, stencil brushes, and rollers. On rising, he climbed the ladder, disconnected the paint well from the top rung, and placed it on the ground between them.

Anabelle put on gloves while Mick took the spare roller and loaded it with paint. After he evened the amount, he handed it over. "This base should block the color. I've already given the upper wall a good sanding."

"Thanks." Anabelle accepted the tool, then ascended the second ladder.

She stretched as far as she could reach and covered the hideous magenta motif in one swipe. "That's an excellent primer. Who's the manufacturer?"

"Shearer. One coat does the trick, and it has low VOCs." Mick mounted the metal rungs.

A few minutes later, Anabelle ran out of paint, moved her ladder two meters, reloaded the roller, and climbed back up, careful not to press the applicator too hard. The last thing they needed was to sand and repaint the lower wall from new drips below the moldings.

"Randy mentioned your grandmother yesterday. He said she was a famous composer."

Anabelle paused to look at him. "She was. In fact, Granny took her first music lessons right here at Soldier's Leap."

"Did she teach you to play?" He reached to cover a spot he'd missed.

"She did."

"Was she an easy taskmaster?"

Laughter bubbled from her core. "Hardly. Granny always expected me to give my best."

Mick reloaded his roller with the same care he had hers. The fellow's exacting manner doubtless placed him in high demand. The ladder creaked under his weight as he climbed back up.

They painted for a while in silence.

"The lower paneling covers some awkward angles in this corridor. How old is this place anyway?"

"Over four hundred years. Probably much older than that. Soldier's Leap started as a tower house, then was added to by successive generations."

"Hence the awkward angles Brodie's softened?"

"Yes. But I like the awkward bits." Anabelle lifted her chin in defense of her home.

"How did your family get this place anyway?" Mick asked, openly curious. "It's always interesting to find out how these places wind up in families."

"Granny inherited it when her father passed."

"So, she was an only child?"

"Her three older siblings died during the last World War."

"The Blitz?" Mick's gaze sharpened on her.

"My great-grandfather booked passage for the family to Canada so they could avoid the bombings, but Granny contracted measles and remained behind, intending to join them when she recovered." Anabelle squeezed the handle and pressed heavily on the roller. "Their ship was torpedoed."

"War is an ugly business." Mick's mouth flat-lined.

Anabelle dabbed guiltily at the run she created from too much pressure. "I'm dreadfully sorry about that." She indicated the dripping paint.

"I've got it." Mick descended from his ladder and switched with her, repairing the issue with two swipes of his roller. "There." He flashed a charming smile. "Good as new."

"I'm afraid I'll never make a good stenciler. It requires too precise a hand."

"We all have our talents."

They worked on, with Anabelle determined not to cause any more drips.

"Why is the place in such a sad state?" Mick climbed off his ladder and moved it further down the wall.

"The house was commandeered as a hospital until the end of the war, then became a school for the blind. Granny's trustees encouraged her to sign a long-term lease, much like Spencer House in London, as her finances could not cover the upkeep.

"Unfortunately, the family in possession did not hold up their end of the bargain, and Granny, who barely remembered the place, didn't insist on it. When she passed, Soldier's Leap came to my father."

"That's incredible." Mick reloaded his roller and ascended his ladder. "What happened to her before she became a famous composer?"

"She lived with her great-aunt. Then, when she was old enough, she attended boarding school."

"The posh and their boarding schools." Mick grumbled as he ran the roller along another stretch of wall. "So, how did you get saddled as the family's representative? Isn't that kind of a conflict of interest?"

She had no desire to rehash the convoluted tale, or they'd be here until midnight. "Since I work on-site, it was the logical choice."

"Is that why your father hired Genesis?"

Anabelle's skin suffused with heat.

Mick, apparently unaware of her embarrassment, craned his neck, his focus on her application. Satisfied with her work, he switched on the fans to speed the drying process, then moved to the far end of the corridor and primed the surface in preparation for the stencil.

"It's fairly early in your career to achieve team status on something of this magnitude." Mick rolled the paint.

"Nepotism, you mean?" Anabelle asked, her voice tight.

"I thought so at first—but only at first. Your talent dispelled any doubts I originally carried." Mick shrugged.

Slightly flustered by his left-handed compliment, she remained quiet. After a time, Anabelle's thoughts meandered to Brodie and their complex situation. She blew a loose strand of hair out of her eyes in frustration. Two weeks ago, she had blithely gone about her duties, enjoying quiet evenings with Brodie and watching Soldier's Leap come back from the brink of dilapidation.

"Do you mind if I turn on some music?" Mick called, startling her from her reverie.

"Not at all." Tunes might distract her from the worries pressing on her heart.

"I like oldies," Mick said. "Is that all right with you?"

"Yes."

A few seconds later, Paul McCartney's voice filled the air. "Hey, Jude . . ."

"I love the Beatles." Mick's eyes sparkled as he joined the song.

Who would have guessed Mick had such a fair voice? He certainly didn't shy from using it either. Tossing her worries aside, Anabelle chimed in. Randy caught them belting out "Yellow Submarine" at the top of their lungs thirty minutes later.

"You're having a sing-off and didn't invite me? I'm offended." Randy entered the corridor and gazed up at their work.

"Good thing you didn't. I've heard you sing." Anabelle waved her roller in his direction.

"Ouch. I'm mortally wounded." Randy slapped his chest and staggered.

"We still love you," Anabelle assured him, fighting a smile at his antics.

"Speaking of which, where do you want me to stack the wood you asked me to cut?" Randy halted beside the base of her ladder and rested a hand on the fourth rung.

"Would it be an inconvenience if you set it inside the family wing?" Anabelle climbed down and set her roller in the pan.

Randy's brows rose ever so slightly. "Not at all."

"Brilliant." Anabelle pivoted and called to Mick, "I'll be right back."

"Need any help?" Mick asked.

"I've got it." Randy lifted the plastic sheeting at the end of the corridor and held it wide for her to pass.

"Where is this pile of wood you cut?" Anabelle ducked through the opening.

"On the front steps." Randy's steel-toed construction boots thudded against the marble floor as they crossed to the entry hall and accessed the front porch.

Anabelle punched in the Lindsay wing code and held the door wide as Randy hoisted the one-by-fours and followed her inside.

"Where should I put these?" Randy looked at her over the lumber in his arms.

"Here is good." She indicated a spot on the floor just inside the door. Until she set up Granny's sewing machine, she didn't see the point in Randy lugging that lot about. She grabbed one end of the pile and helped Randy as he lowered it to the floor.

"You planed these." She ran her hands over the smooth wood and glanced up.

Randy shrugged. "It's more finished—easier to work with."

"That was kind of you, but I feel guilty for pulling you off task."

"It's no big deal, Anabelle. The machines were just sitting there. I did it during break."

"I truly appreciate it."

Randy glanced around. "It's been a while since I was over here. You okay living on this side of the Great Wall?" He referred to the enormous lath and plaster divide that separated the family wing from the rest of the mansion.

"You sound like Brodie. Trust me, it's lovely staying here."

"If you say so. Good luck on that project." He turned to leave.

"Thanks again," she called after him as he went out the door.

She gazed at the pile of milled lumber, eager to get started. When she finished those toppers, no one would accuse her of sabotaging the reno. Not Genesis. Not Brodie. And most assuredly, not Tara.

But the fact remained, someone had forged her signature, and until she found out who did it and why, she worried that they would strike again.

Chapter 13

Anabelle sat on her heels, her knees stiff after spending most of the night cutting out window toppers. Still keyed up about her probation, she pushed to her feet and headed to the music room, passing the ancient grandfather clock as it chimed half two in the morning.

She needed to start sewing, but Granny's machine had not arrived. Doubtless, something had interfered with the shipping.

Deep shadows distorted objects in the dimly lit corridors, and Anabelle's satin-lined robe, a trifle too long, trailed behind her like a damsel in a gothic novel. She snorted at the fanciful imagery. No ghost stories clung to the house's history, odd indeed, considering its age. She adored Soldier's Leap and dreaded leaving when the project ended.

The proceeds from High Ridge, Dad's estate in the Cotswolds, could not support both properties. Hence, the construction of those hideous holiday glamping pods down near the loch, the restaurant, catering service, and corporate events retreat center.

Like most owners of British country houses, Dad had retained one wing of Soldier's Leap for the family. Brodie's designs and Randy's careful execution had converted Soldier's Leap, a former rabbit warren of small choppy rooms, into a medieval fairytale castle, complete with slate-capped turrets.

Indeed, the elevation and interior were so cleverly altered, that if Anabelle had not witnessed the structural changes, she would never believe them unoriginal to the house.

Pausing just outside the music room, she examined the repaired woodwork. Gerald had matched the patina perfectly, proving once again that Brodie had chosen master craftsmen. Soldier's Leap, with the original hunting lodge at its core, now flowed cohesively from one room to the next.

The reno had gone according to plan until this week. Whoever forged those work orders had wreaked havoc on Genesis's deadlines. Brodie would drive himself into an early grave reorganizing their schedules as the accrued fees for extending the deadline were a corporate loss Genesis could ill afford.

Could someone on the team have altered those work orders? Though illogical, that seemed the most likely scenario, one she had grown to accept as an outsider could not have done it.

But this situation placed every team member in a bad light if corporate exceeded its target date. In a nutshell—the extended world of design and its associates all had long memories. To make matters worse, Genesis had entered their reno in global architectural magazines, trade show videos, podcast interviews, and even several television shows featuring Grade II properties.

This project would make or break their reputations. Even if, by some miracle, they met the deadline, her own standing, due to those falsified work orders, was all but lost. A shaky breath escaped her lips, and her spirits plunged.

She entered the music room and drew her robe more tightly around her against the cool marble floor, then sat on the piano bench and softly pressed the newly tuned ivories—the same keys Granny had taken her first lessons on as a child.

Her throat constricted, and she ached for her grandmother's presence. Even after over two years, she missed her—missed her with a pain that time had not eased. Often in the days and months following her loss, questions arose that Anabelle longed to ask, questions only Granny could answer—answers she had taken with her to the grave.

Pressing the damper pedal, Anabelle started into *Dido's Lament*, a musical score Granny often played when she missed Granddad Simon, but her faith that they would reunite after this life upheld her until her death, almost half a century later.

Granny's buoyant attitude and practical life application skills often raised questions about Anabelle's ancestors. Had Granny inherited her nature from her parents? William's war records provided some indication of his stalwart nature. Still, Julia, his wife, remained an enigma, dying when Granny, the youngest of the Lindsay children, was barely five during the ill-fated sinking of the *City of Benares*.

The longer Anabelle remained at Soldier's Leap, the more she yearned to know her family's history, especially Julia, the great-grandmother she knew so little about.

Granny never spoke of the years shortly after losing her family.

"It does no one any good to remember those times," Granny told her once when Anabelle had pressed for answers.

Anabelle longed for her grandmother's wisdom and loving arms, and the opportunity to unburden herself about the forgeries and her subsequent probation. Doubtless, Granny would have found Grandmama Poole's inveigling Her Majesty to attend Anabelle's nonexistent wedding highly amusing.

She hit a sour note and replayed the stanza. *Almost* . . . she could feel Granny beside her. A persistent tear spilled over and splashed on the keys.

In the old days. Granny would hand her a tissue and tell her to blow her nose.

Anabelle wiped her face, recalling Granny's timeless counsel, "Fix it if you can, or give it to God."

Anabelle had fixed the fabric issue, but she had no control over the Queen's request. Or did she?

A rush of indignation surged, and her brows snapped together. She and Brodie might not be engaged, but they were either dating, or they were not. She refused to live another day in limbo. At half two in the morning, Brodie did not have a meeting or phone call to use as an excuse to evade her. She intended to speak to him whether he liked it or not.

Gathering her courage like armor, Anabelle exited the family wing, heading straight to the estate offices. Texting Brodie was not an option. She did not intend to warn him of her impending arrival; that gave him time to prepare. Blind-siding him was the only way.

Brodie worked late and pulled all-nighters when pressed. The man rarely slept. He might be part vampire—like one of those Cullens she'd read about during her romantasy phase.

By the time she reached Brodie's office, she had armed herself for battle. But no light glowed under the door. Odd, that. She pushed it wide just to make sure.

Empty. Now what? She couldn't march up to Brodie's room and rouse him from sleep. What if someone saw her? Call her old-fashioned, but she had standards about such things. Besides, she didn't believe he had gone to bed, not after a day like yesterday. When Brodie worried, he worked. He made things happen. Or . . . he relieved stress with physical activity.

Spinning around, she traversed yet another corridor to reach the former orangery. Randy had replaced the rotted beams with steel beams and glass cladding, then installed an indoor pool in their place. As for the basement, which had suffered extensive damage from flooding, new drains, geothermal heating, and a state-of-the-art gym filled the space.

She entered the women's locker room to glance at the pool, but the lights were off, and the water lay calm. *Hmmm.* That left only one option.

Regaining the corridor, she eyed the lift. Its ding would warn Brodie that someone was about. So, she gathered her robe to keep from tripping and took the stairs to the basement, pausing outside the gym.

Metal clanged inside as someone racked a set of weights. Anabelle peeked around the door frame. Brodie, clad in shorts, a pair of trainers, and a sleeveless T-shirt that clung to his glistening body, met her eyes in the wall mirror. He froze for a nanosecond, then straightened and grabbed a hand towel.

"Couldn't sleep?" Brodie lifted a dark brow and ran the towel over his face and arms.

Trying not to gawk, she stepped into the room and shut the door.

"I think it's time we had a chat, don't you?" Anabelle folded her arms and lifted her chin. "Do you, or do you not, believe that I signed those work documents?"

Brodie sat on the weight bench and draped the towel around his neck. "For what it's worth, I never believed you did—not entirely," he amended.

"Then why are you so offish?"

"Anabelle, lass." He sighed her name. "Do ye know how much I hated placing ye on probation? It's fair ripped me up inside, even if it was the lightest disciplinary action, I could give ye."

"But if you believe I'm innocent . . ." She let it hang.

"The proof is stacked against ye. Trust me. I'm doing what I can to clear your name."

"What does that mean?" She squished her forehead. The whole thing sounded like he was blowing hot and cold.

"I'm not at liberty to say at this point."

Stubborn Scot. She paused for two beats, hoping the pressure would make him give way, but Brodie showed no sign of capitulating.

Anabelle swallowed her nerves and dove headfirst into the deep end of her innermost fears. "And where do you and I stand in our personal lives?"

"I'm all in, Anabelle." Brodie half rose, took her hand, and gave it a gentle squeeze.

"Then why have you kept me at a distance?"

"You're on probation. If any member of the team sees us together, they might ring corporate and say I went too light because we're dating."

"Can you really see Randy, Mick, or Gerald or even Tara doing that?"

"No. But someone on our team likely amended those documents. What I can't work out is why. No one benefits from such an act. The only thing I can figure is that one of the workers has a personal vendetta against you as the Dewhurst's family rep." His mouth flattened. "Until I have facts, it's best that we keep a cordial distance. It's the only way I can protect your reputation and career."

Anabelle huffed. Brodie had such outdated ideas. How like a man to think he held all the cards in the decision-making process.

"It would have been nice if you told me what was going on, don't you think? I'm not a mind reader." She moved closer, her temper rising.

"I thought if your feelings were hurt, your reactions would be more authentic." He lifted his shoulders.

Her temper flared, and she stabbed her finger into his sweaty chest. "That's heartless. How would you feel if I put you on probation and kept you at a distance?"

"I probably would have reasoned it through."

Anabelle threw both hands in the air. "Quit making all the decisions in our relationship without conferring with me first. In case you haven't noticed, you are not my boss when it comes to what's between us." She folded her arms. "Why not ring me about your magnanimous plan during one of your nocturnal work-out sessions?"

She edged closer, the toe of her slipper ramming into the bench's metal leg. *Ow.* The pain intensified her frustration. Narrowing her eyes, she bent until her face was on Brodie's level. "Your plan is chauvinistic. From now on, include me in the process before you make random decisions. And ring me after hours. I can't live like this, Brodie."

"Och. I'm sorry, lass. I'm a right clod for treating you thus. I'm not always the best communicator, but in the future, I promise to include you in decisions that affect us both."

"And the detachment between us? It stops now. Not spending time together is killing me."

"Just time?" His mouth twitched.

"A kiss or two wouldn't hurt, but if you insist on this separation, I'll lose it at work and say things we'll both regret."

"Like what?" His eyes lit with anticipation. "I love that sassy mouth of yours."

She glared at him, but it did no good. He continued to smile in that knuckleheaded way that turned her heart to mush. "I insist on seeing you. I miss us."

"Why do you think I'm down here lifting weights in the middle of the night?" Brodie rubbed the towel over his head, then tossed it aside, no longer sweating.

"Because you don't sleep like a normal human?"

"Wrong. I missed you." He pulled her onto the bench beside him.

"So, you work out?" Why didn't he just give her a bell if he missed her? Sometimes, men made absolutely no sense.

"I hoped I could sleep for a few hours if I got tired enough. The last two days have been rough, and I'm not referring to rearranging our deliverables schedule." He pushed her hair aside, then kissed her neck just below the ear and hauled her onto his lap.

Her brain short-circuited. Trust Brodie to use her weakness to get his way.

"You're not so . . ." She sputtered breathlessly.

Not giving her a chance to finish, Brodie planted his mouth on hers in a searing kiss.

She pushed on his chest and turned her face away. "You wretch."

"Tell me you didn't like it." His eyes danced, matching green devils in his handsome face. "Or this." He cupped her face and lowered his mouth, connecting their souls by the tenderness of his lips.

Her bones melted—right along with what was left of her brain cells. It had been two days since they'd kissed. Wrapping her arms around his neck, she returned the favor, her pulse racing so fast that she sank against his chest, the only sturdy thing holding her up. The room faded to nothingness, and wild shivers erupted all over her body as his insistent mouth branded hers.

Brodie groaned and set her away from him, shoulders heaving as he rested his elbows on his bare knees to catch his breath.

"That's exactly why I can't talk to you until this forgery is settled," he gasped.

With every ounce of willpower, Anabelle stayed put, her fingers gripping the edge of the bench. "You talk to me after hours, or I'll kiss you in front of the team."

A tantalizing smirk curved his lips.

"I mean it." She threatened, moving out of grabbing range. If Brodie kissed her again, she'd cave. And he knew it.

"All right, lass, a compromise it is."

With that agreement, she started for the door.

"No goodnight kiss?"

Stopping on the threshold, she pivoted. "I think you've had enough kisses for one night." With a final wave, she left the gym with a silly smile on her face.

She made it all the way upstairs to the family wing before her mobile buzzed with Brodie's picture and a short reel.

"Sweet dreams, lass. I'll be thinking of you." She touched his face on the screen and, smiling, floated the rest of the way to her room. Stepping out of her slippers, she draped her robe over the bench at the end of the bed, then climbed onto the mattress and pulled the duvet up to her chin. Warmth suffused her, and she drowsed almost immediately.

Her mobile vibrated. Groaning, she lifted the electronic device off the bedside table and read the words.

I love you.

I love you, too.

She texted back, then placed the mobile under her pillow and drifted toward sleep.

Then it hit her, and her eyes popped open.

The text had not come from Brodie, but from an unknown number.

Chapter 14

She loves me.

I hum under my breath as I feed the electrical wire through the basement wall.

My plan is working perfectly. Now that I know she cares, I don't feel so bad about what I'm doing. It's taken me days to run this line, but I'll be able to watch her, even when the internet goes down.

I need to know her habits. Her likes. Her dislikes. Everything.

For a second, I pause and worry that she's becoming an obsession. But she loves me, I remind myself as I wire the electronic device and check the viewer.

Her bed shows up on the feed. Success!

Anabelle sighs in her sleep, her dark hair framing her face. She's beautiful. Perfect for me in every way.

The urge to visit her room burns inside me, and my fingers itch to touch her creamy skin.

CHAPTER 15

BRODIE PASSED copies of the updated Gantt chart around the conference table to the team leads first thing the next morning. "I've rearranged the deliverable schedules. It will drastically change all of our plans to make this work. But it will allow us to hit our deadline."

Barring further disasters, the team wrapped a month short of the holiday season. Though the delayed container carrying Turkish marble prevented them from making their first bonus, the new schedule allowed them to reach their main financial incentive.

Randy scanned the printout and whistled. "That was some juggling act. We even reach the November deadline."

Tara studied the chart in silence, as did Mick, while Gerald Smith, the wood preservationist, grunted his approval. Lance Billings, the head groundskeeper, along with Konstantin, the restaurant's main chef, and Joanna, the tearoom and catering manager, nodded in tandem. Thanks to Anabelle's timely tweaking of kitchen shifts, Konstantin no longer overlapped with Joanna's crew.

Only the Mellencamps had not attended the all-hands-on-deck meeting, as they were knee deep in handling the holiday lets changeover down at the glamping pods.

"Barring any unforeseen disasters, we finish mid-November, save for the ensuite bathrooms' shipping container of Turkish marble. Locals will handle those installs when it arrives."

After only six hours of sleep in three days, countless conversations with suppliers, and calling in favors with manufacturers, Brodie's very bones ached. "You'll receive overtime and a bonus incentive for meeting the alterations. Any questions?"

"I don't know about the rest of you, but I'd better get cracking. We don't have a lot of wiggle-room." Mick rose from his chair.

The rest of the group filed out in silence. Randy, the last to leave, slapped Brodie on the shoulder as he walked past, then shut the door smartly behind him. Brodie could always count on Randy. Last year, shortly after his arrival on the construction site, the two had struck up a friendship.

Brodie gathered the spare copies off the conference table and returned them to the file cabinet. One last action needed doing before he pressed the pause button on his day. Booting up his computer, he emailed the team, attaching the updated Gantt chart before hitting send. That should thwart any miscommunication if the person who faked those work orders attempted to sabotage anything else.

He leaned back in his chair and closed his eyes. His entire body hurt from lack of sleep. A wee wink or two . . . For just a moment . . .

Buzzing. More Buzzing. Brodie jerked in his chair. How long had he been out? Blearily, he glanced at his watch. Twenty minutes!

His mobile vibrated on the desk, startling him fully awake. He blinked several times, ran a hand over his face, and then read the message.

White Glove had attempted a delivery.

Brodie shot out of his chair and bolted down the short corridor to the office's external exit. He reached the drive just as a lorry backed away from the front entrance. Waving both arms, Brodie stepped in front of the vehicle as it turned around. The driver slammed the brakes and rolled down his window.

"Sorry about that." Brodie came abreast of the driver's side.

"Are you Brodie Maxwell?" The fellow pushed his flat cap off his head, then slapped it back on again.

"I am."

"Identification, please."

Brodie dug his wallet from his trouser pocket and handed over his license.

The driver checked the identification and returned it to him. "Sign here, sir."

Brodie scribbled his name on the electronic pad, and the driver handed him a box. When he read the South African address, his heart raced.

"Thank you."

The driver nodded, and Brodie stepped away from the vehicle, clutching the box. *Finally.* He stood there until the lorry disappeared down the main drive.

Two of the ground crew manned electric trimmers on the nearby hedges. Needing privacy, Brodie crossed the drive, pea gravel crunching under his loafers, and rounded the side of the house. A worker, wearing waders, stood in the pond cleaning the filter.

Continuing along the path, he passed the Greek marbles under a pergola smothered in pink climbers. Once again, he encountered Lance's team of gardeners deadheading spent blooms.

Where could a fellow find privacy on such a vast estate? Brodie eyed the family's private walled garden. The locked gate beckoned him, much like the one from *The Secret Garden.* With only a slight hesitation, he let himself inside, the metal latch clanging shut behind him.

The place was blessedly free of workers. He exhaled.

Peeling off the tape securing the package, he found an ornate box stamped in gold from Shimansky Jewelers. His hands shook as he lifted the lid and stared at the engagement ring he had created for Anabelle.

The round, three-karat diamond flashed fire in the sunlight, much like Anabelle herself when her ire was up. He examined the platinum band where blue-diamond baguettes graduated in size toward the center stone. He had selected the rare gems to match Anabelle's eyes. The piece was stunning.

Months ago, he flew to London on a trumped-up excuse to ask Lord Huddleton for Anabelle's hand. Then disaster struck. First with the jeweler's delay, then the Queen's request. And now those forged work orders.

He replaced the ring in its velvet container, returned it to the cardboard box, and folded the flaps shut. How could he propose to Anabelle without her believing he'd been forced?

Until Crouch conducted forgery tests, he could not clear Anabelle's name. Which meant his hands were tied. If he put a ring on her finger, the team was sure to comment. He didn't mind in the least, but if the forger rang corporate and accused him, Genesis might reprimand him for going too light on Anabelle.

Brodie wandered the garden, absently admiring the Japanese pond and waterfall, its arched bridge, and the trellis swing covered in star jasmine and columbine. Espaliered fruit trees hugged the encircling stone walls. Crossing the carpet of newly laid sod, he paused beside a stand of birch and rang the forensic specialist.

"Forgery," Crouch's receptionist answered.

"Hiya. It's Brodie Maxwell. Is Mr. Crouch available?"

"Transferring you now."

A few clicks on the line and George Crouch's voice boomed through the receiver. "Mr. Maxwell, you are a most persistent fellow."

"I'm afraid so." Brodie bypassed the usual chit chat and cut to the topic uppermost on his mind. "Do you have any updates?"

"Just preliminaries, mind you, but after an early examination, both signatures appear to be forgeries. Good ones, I'm afraid."

"That's excellent news. What does that mean for Anabelle Dewhurst?" Brodie asked.

"It means that Miss Dewhurst did not sign those documents. Unfortunately, I have no idea who did." Mr. Crouch sounded puzzled.

"Could it be a member of my team?" Brodie hoped not.

"Not unless they hired a pro. This forger is an incredible mimic. Their only mistake was the amount of pressure they applied on the pen and an incremental deviation on the w."

"May I update corporate with your findings?" If so, he could remove Anabelle from probation.

"I'm sorry. Until I've completed the entire analysis, I cannot make a legal statement."

Brodie snapped a leaf off one of the birch trees. "When will you have one?"

"A month. Perhaps two."

Brodie rubbed the back of his neck. Anabelle would be forced to stay on probation when this fellow could prove her innocence now. It hardly seemed fair. He'd call corporate and speak to Paul Symonds, the VP over

Genesis's UK division. If Paul didn't allow him to retract Anabelle's probation, Brodie had no other option but to delay his proposal.

Again.

He yanked at his tie. After seeing the ring, it made the wait impossible.

"Thank you, Mr. Crouch. Did you notify the police?" Brodie asked out of curiosity.

"Not yet, but you can be sure they will receive my professional analysis. This is a new forger, a dangerous one for private collectors, auction houses, and museums."

And Soldier's Leap, Brodie added silently before ringing off.

He strode across the lawn, let himself out of the secluded garden, and patched a call to Paul.

Mr. Crouch didn't believe the forger to be a team member, but Brodie wasn't so sure. Creatives were ultra-talented, capable of mimicking styles they admired. It wasn't uncommon. Look at how many popular authors who had stolen ideas from their up-and-coming mentees.

Brodie rubbed his elbow and stared off into the distance. Did a criminal live among them, one who acted like everyone else, but harbored a very great secret?

Chapter 16

Anabelle hung her turquoise dress inside the rosewood armoire and stepped into paint-spattered dungarees. While tying her hair into a messy bun, movement in the garden below drew her to the window. She twitched the material aside just as Brodie exited through the family's garden gate.

Of late, he was here, there, and everywhere, performing installation checks before the Quality Control Inspector signed them off. How like him to ensure that the newly laid sod met superior standards. With that crease denting the flesh between his eyes, he must have disliked something he'd found.

Gnawing her lip, Anabelle slid on a pair of Crocs and left her suite to help Mick.

Because some forger had attacked her professionally, last night's text still gave her a twinge. Could the two possibly be connected? No, it was just a wrong number. No need to bother Brodie; that would only add to his worries. That had been intended for someone else, surely. Anabelle pushed the text to the back of her mind.

When she reached the foyer, team members bustled about with an air of purpose, not stopping to chat per usual. Brodie's updated Gantt chart had put everyone in hyperdrive. Her heart lifted at his finding a solution, despite the forger's near success in sabotaging everything they had worked to achieve.

Anabelle reached the corridor, and soon she and Tara were rolling a topcoat over yesterday's primer. Since she had zero training as a stenciler and projects of her own to complete, Mick's new crew needed to handle matters after today.

Two hours later, she speed-walked down the corridor and called the lift. After a three-minute wait, she spun, intending to take the stairs and slammed into Brodie's chest instead.

"Ooomph. Sorry," she said.

"I'm not." Brodie gripped her elbows to steady her. "I have news that can't wait."

"You caught the person who forged my signature?" Hope stirred within her.

"No, but I think you'll like this almost as much." He dropped her arms and stepped away.

"Doubtful."

"Randy's team found a leak in one of the bedrooms and traced it to the attic." Brodie paused dramatically.

"And?" she prompted.

His mouth quirked. "So impatient." Brodie punched the lift button.

"Can't you give me a hint?" she asked.

"It will spoil the surprise."

"I hate surprises." Anabelle folded her arms and scowled.

The elevator doors dinged and slid wide to admit them.

"I know," he winked, the corner of his mouth lifting.

They rode to the third floor in silence.

"This way." Brodie indicated with an outstretched arm.

They traversed the corridor to the attic stairwell, and Brodie opened the door.

"What's the surprise?" she asked.

"You never give up, do you?" Brodie waited until she preceded him up the stairs. "It's one of the things I love about you."

"Did I ever mention that stubbornness is one of your least favorites of mine?" She tossed the comment over her shoulder.

"Diamond cuts diamond, lass." They reached the top step, and Brodie waved her forward with a flourish.

Passing multiple groupings of furnishings, they reached the far corner of the attic, where Randy and two men dumped a pile of lathe and plaster into several wheelie bins. Anabelle coughed at the content-filled air.

"What's all this?" Anabelle directed her question to Randy and the rubble.

"We traced a leak. The roofers left loose flashing around a chimney, and the moisture saturated this wall before it spread downstairs."

Anabelle narrowed her eyes. "A two-year-old roof should not leak." Her family had covered that expense when the Sawyers complained about water damage. She recalled her father's grumblings about the unexpected bill, which the Sawyers should have paid under the lease's stipulations. By the time Dad's legal team added the expenditure to the list the Sawyers owed, they had swanned off to Europe without a forwarding address.

"I agree," Randy said. "We have roofers scheduled to fix the issue."

Brodie stepped past the rubble and paused, his eyes on the plank floor. He rubbed away the plaster's powdery residue and tapped the mismatched planks. "Odd. That bit is newer than the rest." He glanced at Anabelle over his shoulder. "Do you know what room is below?"

Anabelle gave it some thought. "I'm fairly certain the master dressing room is below this section. Why?"

"The wood here is much newer than the original planking. Any idea why?"

She wrinkled her nose. Brodie brought her up here to look at a patched floor?

Randy tapped the planks. "I never noticed it. I was too busy trying to chase down that leak."

"Anabelle, when Randy tore down the wall, he found something." Brodie indicated a battered steamer trunk. "That was inside a walled-up room, along with a bedstead and desk."

She glanced at the trunk's flat lid and rusted lock. "What's inside?" she asked, her voice sounding as though she had jogged up four flights of stairs.

"Why don't you take a look?" Brodie nudged her gently.

With a drumming pulse, she edged forward, bending to undo the rusty latches, then held her breath as she heaved open the lid. Layers of brittle tissue rustled like dry leaves.

Her questing fingers pulled back the paper and revealed a folded garment, sadly yellowed with age. Anabelle didn't dare touch the delicate satin and lace overlay with her bare hands.

"Someone preserved this with great care. I need to wash up and locate some gloves. I won't take but a moment." Anabelle straightened.

"Hold on." Brodie passed her a thin packet of wet wipes.

"Thank you." Excitement filled her as she scrubbed the excess oils from her hands.

"Are you surprised?" Brodie thrust his chin toward the trunk.

"I'm more than surprised. I'm delighted. That steamer trunk likely predates the Sawyers' occupation."

"Aye." Brodie agreed.

"How do you figure that?" Randy rested his hands on his tool belt.

"I spent a year studying furniture and accessories in design school. Judging by the style, that trunk dates somewhere between 1800 and the turn of the last century. Which means, it must have belonged to Granny's family."

Brodie withdrew a pair of gloves from a trouser pocket, and a sly grin curved one side of his mouth.

"You came prepared." She slipped the white fabric onto her hands.

"I know how you operate. You would never risk damaging anything so delicate."

"What do you think it is?" Randy returned to the trunk, his eyes filled with curiosity.

"At a guess, I'd say clothing. By the way it's been packed away, it must have been important, but it's hard to tell with the yellowing that's occurred." Anabelle knelt and reached inside, gently lifting the material.

The fabric unrolled, revealing a lace and satin floor-length gown with a train.

Anabelle gasped. "It's a wedding dress. Just look at that lace. It's exquisite. Just look at that train!" Despite the stains, the dress stole her breath.

"It's not exactly white." Brodie eyed the dress doubtfully.

"A little water, vinegar, and sunshine should brighten it up." Anabelle stood, holding the dress away from her by the shoulders. "I wonder who it belonged to?"

"Whoever wore it was just about your height." Randy pointed out.

"A gown like this was designed by a master." She inspected the dress. "I'd love to have it analyzed."

Brodie fished around inside the tissue paper. "There's more."

"There is?" She draped the gown over Brodie's shoulder. "Don't touch the material."

"That thing smells like nasty gym clothes." Randy waved in front of his nose as if he could dispel the odor.

Anabelle ignored him.

"You're right." Excitement coursed through her as she peeled back the crumpled paper. Inside lay a long, beaded veil. When she raised it, seed pearls pattered onto the floor like raindrops and rolled across the planks.

"Oh, no," she cried.

"A shame, that," Brodie murmured.

"I've never seen its like." Anabelle examined the veil's fine stitching.

"That's bobbin lace." Randy, who'd gone back to stand beside Brodie, pointed to the gown on Brodie's shoulder. "My Gran made it, like her mother before her."

"Bobbin lace? Is it popular in this region?" Anabelle asked.

"I wouldn't know." Randy shrugged. "But the women in my family have always made it."

Anabelle laid the veil over the gown on Brodie's shoulder.

"I am happy to be your lady's maid." Brodie bowed slightly, careful not to dump his stained cargo.

"You're hired." Anabelle fished about one last time, but the only item left was a small prayer book. She opened the cover and squinted at the faint, spidery writing.

"Randy, can you make this out?" she asked.

He took the prayer book in his calloused hands and squinted at the words. "On the advent of your marriage. Grandmother Morrison."

Morrison. She'd never heard that name before. Maybe the dress belonged to the Sawyers after all. "Is there a date?" Anabelle asked.

"No."

"Surely, a publication date will give us an idea." She glanced over Randy's shoulder and groaned. "It's in Latin."

"Bring it here." Brodie, still balancing the gown and veil, held out his hand.

Randy passed it to him.

"1907." Brodie whistled.

Zips of excitement bubbled inside her, like a fizzy drink swallowed too fast. "Do you think *Grandmother Morrison* is Julia's grandmother?"

"It's a possibility." Brodie lifted the yellowed gown and ruined veil.

"Don't touch them! I'm going to have them professionally cleaned."

"Anabelle, it's unlikely that you can save this gown." Brodie's voice gentled. "The veil's a lost cause."

"None of us knows a thing about Granny's people. World War II and the basement flood destroyed all her family's records. I'd like to preserve this if it belongs to our Lindsays."

"Why go to the expense?" Brodie eyed the dress with distaste.

"Because it might be a piece of family history." Anabelle removed the gown and veil from Brodie.

"All I'm saying is that I'd save the expense until you know if it belongs to your family."

"The Maxwells display ancient weapons in their ballroom. Maybe I want to display this gown in the same way."

Randy laughed. "She has you there, Brodie."

"You don't have proof that this is your great-grandmother's wedding dress," Brodie insisted as she folded away the gown and veil.

"Then I'll find it."

Chapter 17

"Where are we going?" Anabelle tugged at the blindfold wrapped around her eyes.

"No cheating." Brodie slid his arm around her and covered the bottom of her scarf, then steadied her when she stumbled on the uneven cobbles as they crossed a hilly street.

"Can't you give me a hint?" she asked.

"Nope."

"You didn't even stop to consider my request," she protested.

"That's because it's a surprise. If I gave you a clue, you'd figure it out."

"Hmmm."

"Besides, we're almost there."

A door squeaked, and Brodie guided her inside a quiet building smelling of damp. She wrinkled her nose. An old structure.

Brodie untied the knot at the back of her head, and the blindfold fell from her eyes. They stood in the aisle of an old stone kirk with a hammer-beam ceiling.

"What are we doing here?"

"I thought you intended to meet with the minister, so . . ."

Her heart turned to mush. To help her, Brodie had brought her to meet the local minister, sacrificing his time from the reno's never-ending demands. If she didn't already love him to pieces, that would have sealed the deal.

She kissed his cheek. "Brodie Maxwell, I love you."

His eyes warmed, and he stepped close, cupping her jaw, his intent clear.

Footsteps echoed on the stone floor. Anabelle cleared her throat and stepped away to greet the local minister.

"Minister," Brodie addressed the diminutive fellow with spectacles. "Brodie Maxwell. We spoke earlier."

"Mr. Sheffield will do. We don't stand on ceremony here in the countryside." Sheffield blinked his rather myopic eyes and studied them in turn. "Come to my office. It's more comfortable there."

For such a short man, Anabelle half trotted to keep up with the minister as he moved through the congregational pews. Mr. Sheffield opened a side door and ushered them into a small, yet thoroughly modern office.

"Please be seated." He rounded his desk and plopped into his chair.

Brodie pulled out a seat for her, then took his own, facing the minister across the desk.

"Mr. Maxwell, your call intrigued me, so I did some digging." Mr. Sheffield's glasses glinted, further distorting his magnified eyes.

Anabelle gripped Brodie's hand.

"Unfortunately, the church was relieved of any valuables during the bombings. But I did call the cathedral in Dunblane, along with the national archives. No one has discovered their whereabouts."

Anabelle's hopes plummeted, and she bent her head to mask her disappointment. Brodie rubbed the back of her hand with his thumb. Doubtless, those records, if they'd survived the war, were moldering away in someone's damp basement.

"I'm sorry to hear that," Brodie said. "We hoped that the Lindsay records were moved to this kirk."

"Do you have any suggestions on where I should go next?" Anabelle straightened her spine. She'd not give up. Someone must know where the records were kept.

"You might try meeting with the more aged members of this congregation. Perhaps one of them knows something useful."

"That would make the members nearly one hundred." Anabelle couldn't imagine anyone living to that ripe old age.

"Families talk, and many have lived here for generations." Mr. Sheffield splayed his hands. "I'll mention this at our Sunday services. If someone remembers anything, I'll ring you."

"Thank you, Mr. Sheffield. You have been most kind to meet with us." Anabelle rose and shook his hand, doing her best to hide the disappointment that bogged her down.

"The Historical Society in Edinburgh has digitized records from this region. They're a rather haphazard collection, I'm afraid. But they might be worth a visit."

"That's a marvelous idea." Anabelle gave Minister Sheffield a full-on smile. "I'll do that."

The minister stood unmoving, blinking his nearsighted eyes as she and Brodie left his office. The door closed behind them with a decisive snap. Brodie chuckled under his breath as they started through the choir section, their footsteps echoing on the stone floor.

"What's so funny?" Anabelle paused to read a tombstone beneath her feet. The writing, faint from years of wear, made her half bend to decipher the words.

"I believe you just gave that minister unholy thoughts."

"Nonsense." Sometimes Brodie had the silliest notions. "Look. I think it says Lindsay."

Going down on one knee, Brodie joined her.

"Can you make it out?" Excitement coursed through her. *Could it be?*

"I think you're right." Brodie ran his fingers over the faint divots in the slab. "The date's in Latin. Seventeen something. I can't make the rest out."

"Too early." Anabelle huffed and sat back on her heels. But if one Lindsay had attended this kirk, perhaps Julia's grandparents, the Elliotts, had as well. Rising, she wandered to a series of elaborately carved tombstones mounted on the interior wall.

"Can you spare a few more minutes?" With Brodie's time at a premium, Anabelle disliked asking, but these stones were in Latin, and she needed his expertise.

"I've time."

"Brilliant." But after deciphering each tombstone, she admitted defeat. No other Lindsays appeared among them.

Sitting inside the basement cupboard, I check my feed. Everything is in working order. For a minute there, I thought last night's power outage had scrambled my equipment. Missing one night of Anabelle sleeping has me antsy, so I press the button and replay the previous night's recording where she lies on her bed, her dark hair spread across the pillow, one arm extended.

A ferocious longing fills me, an insatiable hunger that drives me to pace the small, enclosed space. Need rises in me, and my gaze returns to the feed. My hands shake, and I thrust them into my pockets.

Hunger, stronger than anything I've ever experienced, claws at me. I can't lose control. Not now. Not after all my careful planning. It took months to join this team so I could be near her and walk these halls.

I bang my head against the wall, fighting the urge to claim everything that should be mine.

Chapter 18

Seated at her workstation, Anabelle tallied the number of actuals against their corresponding orders. "Brass rings—one thousand, three hundred, and twenty-two," she muttered, bolding the final tally on the printout.

"Anabelle, you have visitors." Mick stood in the doorway to her and Tara's office, his feet covered in white booties, so he didn't track paint on the refinished floors.

She continued counting.

"Earth calling, Anabelle." Mick clapped to catch her attention.

She lifted her head, startled. "I'm terribly sorry. I was so focused. Could you repeat that?"

"You have visitors in the entrance hall." Mick offered her a pair of booties.

"Did they give you a name?" Rising from her desk, she accepted the shoe coverings and slipped them on.

"I'll leave that to them." Mick's smile flashed, oozing with charm.

Their friendship had deepened during her probation, when most of the team steered clear of her, save for Randy. Even the chef and catering staff held her at arm's length.

"How is the stencil coming along?" Avoiding the blocked corridor, she and Mick traversed through the Business Center to the back hall. Newly erected scaffolding on two walls of The Soldier restaurant abutted the main entrance, where Mick's crew were busily gold leafing the faded pillars.

"We're making good progress. Hugo'd like me to hire a few of the temps for a more permanent basis."

"Are you and Hugo partners?" Mick was such a nice fellow; she couldn't imagine him in business with the creepy Hugo.

"No. Hugo was my first hire."

"I see."

On gaining the vast entrance hall, Anabelle spied a couple near the front door, a set of luggage piled at their feet.

"Mother. Dad. What are you doing here?" Anabelle rushed forward with outstretched arms and enveloped both parents.

"Surprise!" Mother returned the hug with interest.

Dad kissed her cheek, his coloring the hue of putty.

Concern swarmed up her spine, but the entrance hall, where anyone could overhear, was not the place to express her concern. "What do you think of your ancestral home, Dad?"

"It's a lot to take in." High Ridge, the elegant Georgian pile he owned in the Cotswolds, did not compare to the reno's earlier Baronial style.

"We can have a look later. I'm sure you've had a long trip. Did you drive?"

"We did," Mother said.

Dad avoided flying whenever possible and rarely left High Ridge and its immediate surroundings. What had brought them?

"Right this way." Anabelle clasped two suitcase handles and rolled them across the entrance hall to the hidden door in the paneling. She punched in the code, then led her parents to the salon on the far side of the family wing.

"Why don't I order us some tea, and then the Mellencamps will get you settled." Anabelle buzzed the kitchen. "Joanna, my parents are here for a visit. Could someone bring us some tea?"

"Aye, and I've scones and a baklava cooling on the racks," Joanna said.

"Sounds lovely. My parents will be pleased with those options."

"Very good." Joanna rang off.

Anabelle texted Mrs. Mellencamp next.

Anabelle: My parents arrived just now. Could someone prepare a room?

Mrs. Mellencamp: "I'll send one of the staff over."

Anabelle: "Brilliant. Thanks."

Turning back to her parents, Anabelle found her mother wandering the room, while her father, looking a mite better, relaxed on the sofa.

Anabelle plunked onto the cushion beside him. "Tea is on the way."

"I can't get over the changes. The house is beautiful, Anabelle."

Busy with High Ridge, Dad had visited only once since Soldier's Leap had come to him just before his 60th birthday last year.

By comparison, High Ridge passed to Dad when he was in his twenties. But Anabelle favored Soldier's Leap, with its smoothed-out quirks and homely vibe, and she couldn't help thinking that her sister would feel the same.

"After tea, would you like a grand tour?" Anabelle asked. With the renovations and major changes, she was anxious for his approval.

Mother glanced at Dad. "I wouldn't mind a bit of a lie down first. If you don't mind, we'll wait on the tour."

"What time do you get off work tonight?" Dad asked.

How did she tell them that unless she slept, she worked?

"I see Brodie hasn't popped the question yet." Mother indicated her bare ring finger with a small nod. Her parents exchanged a meaningful glance.

Anabelle tensed. Grandmama and the Queen were bad enough without her parents joining their ranks.

Joanna Seward bustled into the room, pushing a tea cart, followed by Drina, a member of the housekeeping staff.

Anabelle exhaled, relieved to sidestep an unwanted conversation.

"Drina, Mrs. Seward, I'd like you to meet my parents, Lord and Lady Huddleton."

The young maid's eyes bulged, and she dipped into an awkward curtsy. "Pleased to meet you."

"Thank you for your help." Mother smiled in an obvious attempt to put Drina at ease.

Still looking somewhat bewildered at meeting actual toffs, Drina addressed Anabelle. "Mr. Mellencamp will be taking up the luggage and asked if you have a room preference for your parents."

"The yellow suite." Anabelle nodded, thinking it would best suit her parent's needs.

"That's a lovely one." Still wearing that goggle-eyed expression, Drina backed out of the room.

"Oh, dear. I so dislike it when your father's title bowls people over." Mother returned to the sofa.

Joanna pushed the cart to Father's side.

"Is that baklava?" Dad eyed the multi-layered, honey-coated pastry.

"Yes." Joanna nodded. "Baked today."

"It looks delicious. I'd like one of those, and a cup of tea, please. Two sugars. No cream." Dad seemed under the impression that Joanna was part of the Soldier's Leap staff.

"I'll serve, Joanna. You don't need to wait on us." Anabelle disliked special treatment, especially when that was not part of Joanna's job description. "I'll send the cart downstairs on the dumb waiter."

"Very good." Joanna checked the tea cart one last time, then departed.

"You have very attentive staff." Mother gave her stamp of approval.

"We don't have personal staff. Joanna is an employee, just like me, and manages our tearoom and catering team." Anabelle added two sugars to her father's cup, then plated the baklava he so admired. "What would you like, Mother?"

"Just tea for me, darling."

Anabelle poured the hot water over her mother's favorite Oolong to steep before she passed her the porcelain cup and saucer.

"Thank you." Mother set the pretty China on the end table beside her.

"Mummy, did you bring Granny's sewing machine?" Anabelle selected a small plate and added a few slices of banana and strawberry to it, then sat between her parents.

"We did. When I told your father you needed it, we decided to bring it ourselves. So here we are." Mother waved airily.

"I'm so happy you're here." Anabelle beamed at them.

Dad finished his last bite of baklava and wiped his mouth with a napkin. "That was the best pastry I've had in ages."

"Soldier's Leap Catering is immensely popular." Anabelle popped a strawberry in her mouth and chewed, the sweet flavor bursting on her tongue.

"I can see why." Dad leaned back against the sofa cushion, taking in the ornate plasterwork ceiling. "Has all this been redone?"

"No, only cleaned and repainted. But the plasterwork and Corinthian columns in the restaurant are being gilded as we speak."

"It's a very peaceful setting." Dad closed his eyes and appeared to doze.

"Mother, what's going on with Dad? He doesn't look well," Anabelle pitched her voice low, so as not to disturb her father.

"He's been exhausted of late, but the doctor did a full set of labs on him, and he checked out fine." Mother paused, appeared to search for words, then at length spoke, "I must say, we expected Brodie to receive us alongside you. Have you had a falling out?"

"We keep things professional at work." Anabelle shifted, disliking her mother's change of topic.

"Very sensible of you both."

Mother glanced at her bare finger again, making Anabelle long to sit on her hands.

She had best warn Brodie that her parents were here and asking embarrassing questions.

"You seem quite settled." Mother picked up her teacup and saucer.

"I love Soldier's Leap. From the first moment I arrived, it has felt like home."

"You've certainly worked wonders on the place. Doubtless, it'll be a wrench for you to leave." Mother slipped her arm around Anabelle and kissed her cheek. "You were always so restless in London, much like your father. The two of you flourish away from the city. If Grandmama didn't insist on it, I'd spend more time in the country myself."

Anabelle eyed her mother curiously. "If you could choose where you lived without hurting anyone's feelings, which would you pick?"

"High Ridge." Mother's eyes brightened. "I'm happy wherever your father is. City. Country. It doesn't matter to me." Mother glanced at Dad with misted eyes, a faint smile hovering on her lips. "But he loves High Ridge, so that would be my choice, too."

"Even though you're always so busy in the city?" Anabelle asked.

"That's to keep me from missing your father." Mother laughed.

"If you miss Dad so much, why do you stay with Grandmama Poole so often?" Anabelle shifted, unable to grasp the situation.

"Grandmama's alone, darling, and I'm the only child who can tolerate her for lengthy increments."

Speechless, Anabelle could only stare. All this time, she had assumed Mother preferred London's social whirl, but compassion for her cantankerous mother kept her in London.

Drina rapped on the doorframe, gaining Anabelle's attention. "The yellow suite's ready, Anabelle, and Mr. Mellencamp's sent up the luggage."

"Thank you, Drina."

Drina nodded and left as silently as she'd arrived.

Mother rose with fluid grace, her gaze on Dad's sleeping form. "Anabelle, could you send supper up to our room tonight? I think we'll turn in early. Your father's exhausted, and I must confess to being a trifle wilted myself."

"Of course. Let me know if you need anything."

"Pierce. Wake up, darling." Mother gave Dad's shoulder a gentle shake.

He opened his eyes. "Did I drift off? I'm sorry."

"It's no bother, Dad. Our entire team lives in a chronic state of exhaustion to reach that deadline."

"And we've popped in at the worst possible time." Mother exchanged another of those undecipherable glances with Dad.

"I'll visit during breaks." Anabelle led her parents to the lift at the end of the corridor.

"I must say, I am astonished at what you've done. Who would have thought this higgledy-piggledy pile of stone could feel so welcoming?" Dad pushed off the sofa and followed her and Mother upstairs to the first floor.

On reaching their suite, Anabelle opened the double doors with a flourish.

"This is lovely." Mother stepped into the room, turning slowly to take in the large four-poster in gold silk bedding, the muraled ceiling, white woodwork, French Provincial furniture, and the pale-yellow walls.

She walked into the adjoining sitting room with its bayed window and festooned draperies. "It's absolutely sumptuous."

Dad eyed the bed.

"The mattress is very comfortable. I'm sure you'll sleep quite well," Anabelle said. "I tried them all out before we made the purchases."

Guilt assailed her for taking the master suite when, by rights, Dad should have claimed its use. If she had known of her parents' impending arrival, she would have moved out but consoled herself that all ten family suites were large and inviting.

Anabelle left her parents to settle in; their impromptu visit, so out of character, left her uneasy. Didn't they trust her to represent the family to Genesis? Or were they here for something else altogether?

Chapter 19

THE WHIRRING of crickets serenaded Brodie as he crossed the estate's U-shaped drive, the crisp evening air welcome after a stressful day. The porch-light burned above the family wing door. He jogged up the steps and rapped. Stepping back a pace, he took in the darkened windows and frowned. Anabelle must have gone to bed.

Just as he turned away, she opened the door.

"I wasn't sure you'd still be awake." Brodie pivoted, drew her into his arms and kissed her.

"I'll be up for hours yet." She tugged him inside, then closed the door. Lacing her fingers with his, she cut through the ballroom to the family dining room, rather than taking three separate corridors to reach her destination.

"Have you eaten?" she asked.

"No." He and Randy spent all afternoon overseeing the repairs on the geothermal line a landscaper had severed with a backhoe.

"I saved you a plate."

"You're marvelous. I was going to scrounge through the office break-room and see if anyone left something in the fridge."

"Are you our fridge thief? Mick mentioned the other day that someone had eaten his schnitzel. That wasn't you, was it?"

"Maybe?" Brodie raised one shoulder.

"You know what? Don't tell me. That way, if someone inquires, I won't betray you."

He chuckled. Anabelle couldn't lie to save her soul; her face betrayed every emotion.

A sleek galley kitchen, hidden behind wood panels, provided every bell and whistle Anabelle's family could possibly need. When in use, the table seated twenty-five. Right now, a sewing machine rested at one end beside a stack of pattern pieces.

"What are you doing?" Puzzled, he moved to the table while Anabelle warmed his food. "Is this the notorious fabric that has caused such a fuss?" He squinted at the pattern.

"It is." The microwave dinged. Anabelle retrieved his plate and set it on the table with cutlery rolled in a napkin. "Don't spill on it. I have big plans for that material."

"I can see that." Brodie pulled out a chair, bowed his head, and blessed his food. When he finished, he stabbed a fork into a delicious-smelling meat dish covered in a sauce of some sort. "What is this?"

"Something French that I can't pronounce. Konstantin's been experimenting." Anabelle retook her seat behind the sewing machine.

Brodie popped the bit into his mouth and chewed. After swallowing, he said, "It's excellent." He speared another bite.

Anabelle placed two pieces of material together and ran a seam down one side, pulling out pins before she ran them over with the needle.

"I didn't know you could sew," he said between swallows.

"Granny taught me. This is her machine. I asked Mother to overnight it, but she and Dad brought it with them instead."

"Your parents are here?" His stomach flipped.

"They showed up this afternoon unannounced." Anabelle snipped the thread and met his eyes.

He set down his cutlery and tugged at his collar, guilt curdling his supper. *Brilliant.* He'd asked Lord Huddleton for Anabelle's hand in marriage over two months ago. Doubtless, Huddleton had arrived to discover why he delayed his proposal. Since he was her father, Brodie could not fault him, and if their roles were reversed, he'd do the same.

"I don't know how I'll entertain them. We have so much to do."

Anabelle selected another piece of fabric, pinned it to the lining material, then lowered the flat thing holding the needle.

Anabelle deserved the most romantic proposal he could deliver. With her parents' arrival, whatever he slapped together now would be rushed at best.

Rising, he came up behind Anabelle and placed both hands on her shoulders. She meant more to him than any job or professional accolade—infinitely more than this blasted renovation—a renovation guaranteed to launch him into the architectural stratosphere if he delivered on time.

Anabelle reached the end of yet another seam and cut the thread.

"I love you, lass." His throat squeezed. "I wish we could get married this instant."

"What's brought this on?" She twisted in her chair to look up at him, her eyes concerned.

"I'm juggling too many balls, and you're being pushed onto a back burner. I don't like it. You're worth more to me than any fame this renovation brings. Ye know it, don't ye?" he asked, slipping into Scots with the deep emotion of the moment.

"If I didn't, I do now." She patted his arm like a mother comforting a bairn.

He knelt beside her and laid his head in her lap, exhaustion tugging at his seams. She stroked his hair, and tingles rippled across his scalp.

"Mmmm. That feels good."

"It can't possibly be comfortable kneeling in that position. Go to bed, Brodie. You're dead on your feet."

He lifted his head and sighed. "The second I move, I wake up, and when I doze off, I dream of Gantt charts."

"That sounds rather horrid." She smoothed his hair off his forehead.

He chuckled. "Remind me never to take on another project like this."

Anabelle snorted. "I'd be wasting my breath, and you know it."

"Aye. You're right." Rising to his feet, he tugged her out of her chair and held her close, resting his head on hers.

"You'd never be happy with a mediocre project," she murmured into his chest.

"Perhaps not, but I wouldn't mind a long stretch between them."

During their next break, he intended to marry her if she agreed to his proposal. "Och, lass, but I love ye." He bent to kiss her.

"You have a fine way of showing it." Lady Huddleton spoke from the doorway, one hand on her hip.

Startled, Brodie lifted his head.

"Mother, we didn't see you there." Anabelle's grip on him tightened, then she dropped her arms and stepped away.

"I came down for a glass of water."

Sure, she did, and he was an astronaut. Brodie reined in his thoughts.

"Isn't there a pitcher and glasses in your room?" Anabelle sounded puzzled.

Bless her, she didn't question her mother's motives, whilst he had no difficulty reading Lady Huddleton's thoughts.

"I must have overlooked it." Lady Huddleton advanced into the room, her slender frame as willowy as Anabelle's. "It's good to see you, Brodie."

"It's good to see you again, Lady Huddleton." Brodie inclined his neck in a half-bow.

"You have impeccable manners, Brodie, even when you're upset that I've interrupted you." Lady Huddleton's eyes gleamed with amusement.

He rather admired Anabelle's mother, or Lady H., as he had dubbed her, for calling a spade a spade in this instance.

"What's all this?" Lady Huddleton indicated the fabric strewn across the table.

"I'm working on a project for the Business Center. It's the reason I need Granny's sewing machine. Brodie popped by after overseeing a repair." Anabelle joined her mother at the table.

Lady H. studied the pattern. "Do you need help with this?"

"I do rather. Would you mind terribly?" Anabelle visibly brightened.

"I'd love to be of service. What else will I do while you're working?"

"Dozens of things. Go for a swim. Play tennis or pickleball. Take a boat out on the loch. Visit Stirling." Anabelle counted off the topmost activities. "Turn your visit into a holiday."

"We'll be sure to tour the area while we're here, but I can also lend a hand." Lady H. took Anabelle's fingers in her own. "It will be a pleasure to sew again. I haven't made anything in ages."

Anabelle's father worked alongside his employees, but Lady H.'s prestigious upbringing did not seem conducive to menial labor. Where had someone like her learned how to sew?

"I've flummoxed your boyfriend, Anabelle." Lady H. laughed, a girlish peal filled with genuine mirth. "Don't stand there gawking, Brodie. Of course, I can sew. Mother Dewhurst insisted I learn. I find it rather therapeutic."

"Mother makes beautiful quilts for hospice." Anabelle directed her remark to Brodie.

Lady H. patted Anabelle's shoulder, then glanced at her bare finger, and a frown marred her expression. "Still holding back, Brodie?"

"Mother!" Anabelle's face flushed.

Lady H.'s barb landed plumb center. She had every right to be out of sorts with him. She and her husband had waited months for their engagement news.

Since the ring's arrival earlier in the day, the diamond had all but burned a hole in his pocket, and he cursed Anabelle's probation for delaying the proposal.

"I'll bid you both goodnight," he said stiffly and nodded to Lady H.

Lady Huddleton closed her eyes for a moment. "I'm dreadfully sorry. I was horribly rude. Please forgive my deplorable lack of manners."

"No worries, Lady H. I understand." He blew Anabelle a kiss and quit the room.

He refused to ask Anabelle in a rushed manner. She deserved a well-planned proposal, one that showed how much he loved her, and not because her parents pestered him into it.

Och. Her parents.

Lord and Lady Huddleton would likely retract their blessings when they found out that he'd placed Anabelle on probation.

Chapter 20

The app on Anabelle's watch dinged, reminding her of her meeting. She saved her file, then turned off the workstation computer. Glancing at the office's other occupant, she hesitated, then squared her shoulders.

"Tara, I'm taking lunch. My parents are visiting, and I'm going to give them a tour of the estate."

"Don't exceed your break." Tara didn't lift her eyes from her computer screen.

"I won't."

Anabelle snatched her jacket off the back of her chair and hurried down the corridor to the back of the house, her heels sinking into the newly installed wool runners. When she reached the entrance hall, she found Mick atop a ladder gilding a Corinthian column just outside The Soldier restaurant and Hugo loading his paint brush.

Despite the creepy vibe Hugo gave off, he deserved to be treated decently, so she paused to exchange pleasantries. "You've made progress."

Hugo grunted, then proceeded to ogle her legs.

Anabelle shuddered and glanced up at Mick who rested a forearm on the top of the ladder.

"We have. For fear of sounding stuffy, I won't mention how pleased I am with the new additions to my team."

"I'm glad they've worked out." She waved and continued across the foyer to access the family wing. Her parents stood waiting inside the small foyer.

"Oh, good. You're ready. I need to watch the clock. My team lead expects me back on time." She eyed her mother's lightweight blouse. "You might need a jacket. The wind's chilly."

"It's just you and me today, Anabelle." Dad slapped a flat cap onto his head.

"Aren't you coming, Mother?" Anabelle asked. "I thought you wanted to see the estate?"

Her parents shared another of those glances where an unspoken conversation appeared to pass between them.

"Not this time. I'm neck deep in that sewing project."

"All right, then." Rather disappointed that she couldn't show both parents the changes, she pasted on a smile. "You're in for a treat, Dad."

"Then, let's go." Dad pecked Mother on the cheek and opened the exterior door.

Anabelle moved onto the graveled drive and fell in step beside her father, taking the path through a stand of firs and birches to an ornamental pond with a fountain at its center.

Dad beelined it to one of the benches at the water's edge and patted the spot beside him. Anabelle joined him and leaned into her father's side.

"Your mother said she could tell from your tone that something was wrong, so we decided to visit."

Anabelle had always been a Daddy's girl, and because of their close bond, her father had always seen through every one of her smoke screens.

"My career's in tatters. Brodie was forced to place me on probation because someone forged my signature on two work orders, documents that have wreaked havoc on our delivery date." Anabelle blew a strand of hair out of her eyes.

"Who forged your name?" Dad asked through narrowed eyes.

Anabelle could practically see his hackles stand on end, ready to leap into the fray to protect his little girl.

"I have no idea, but they did a fabulous job. If I didn't know for certain that I hadn't signed those documents, I'd believe it myself."

"Test analysis will prove your innocence." Dad sat forward, his elbows on his knees.

"That's pricey. Genesis is running on a slim profit margin."

Her father rose and paced to the pond's edge, his eyes on the fountain. "I had no idea you were dealing with so much. I suppose that's why things have cooled somewhat between you and Brodie?"

She joined him and slipped her arm around his waist. "Possibly. You and I are too much alike, Dad. Neither of us are good at hiding things from the other."

"You'd almost think we were related," he agreed. "In a few months, this will be nothing but a blip in the rearview window."

Anabelle forced a smile that went no further than her lips. "If you say so."

They stood thus for a time until Dad broke the silence. "Why don't you show me the rest of the garden plantings?"

Taking his arm, Anabelle led him to the cottage garden, where the vegetation increased in height and color. Dad rotated, slowly taking it all in.

"I don't think I've ever seen such a wide variety of vegetation. It feels . . ." Dad trailed off. "My mother was born here but spent all her adult life in England. She longed to return, but the lease prohibited that. Even so, her memories of Soldier's Leap, though vague, were happy ones."

Dad lifted his gaze to the newly altered facade. "This is only my second visit to the place since the Sawyers vacated, yet I have the most incredible sense of belonging."

Anabelle squeezed his arm. "I like to think that our ancestors' goodness permeates the estate. I wish we knew more about them, but the flood destroyed the records."

"I'm glad I came. After so many years at High Ridge, I never gave much thought to Mother's people."

"I've been doing some digging. Just the other day, an attic wall collapsed, and we discovered a trunk containing a wedding dress and veil. A small prayer book was inside and said, 'Grandmother Morrison.' Does that surname ring any bells?" Anabelle bent to smell a blue rose, a rare find in both perfume and color.

"I've never heard of any Morrisons. I don't want to dash your hopes, but that trunk probably belonged to the Sawyers," Dad said.

Anabelle slumped. “I was positive it was your grandmother’s dress, even though Brodie warned me that we didn’t have enough information to make an informed decision.”

“He’s right. So many people lived here over the years, not just the Sawyers. It could have belonged to someone from the school for the blind or a hospital patient during the war when the government commandeered the place.”

“There’s a historical society in Edinburgh I intend to visit and see if they have information on Julia’s family.”

“With all your spare time?” Dad’s eyes twinkled.

“I’ll speak to Brodie.” As long as she clocked her hours and handled the installs, he’d likely allow it, especially while her parents were in residence.

She and her father roamed the rest of the gardens, pausing before a trio of scantily clad Grecian goddesses.

“Do you know why the attic floor is patched in one place? It almost looks like something was boarded up.”

“Could have been a burst pipe that needed repairing,” Dad suggested.

“That’s the most logical reason for it, but I’m curious. The patch is near where we found the trunk with the wedding dress. I’d like to get our contractor to pry up a few of those planks to see if anything’s underneath.”

“Sounds like we might have a mystery on our hands.” Dad gave her a conspiratorial wink.

“So, you’re okay with that?”

Dad nodded his assent.

“Then, I’ll speak to Randy and see when we can start.” Anticipation thrummed. What if Soldier’s Leap held secrets?

Chapter 21

Anabelle rubbed her gritty eyes. With full days on the computer, followed by hours of sewing on trim in dim lighting, she'd need specs if this kept up much longer.

Rising from the dining table, she stacked the pattern pieces, which lay strewn across its surface, into some semblance of order.

Her parents had gone to bed ages ago. Moving to the doorway, she glanced into the corridor to assure herself that Mother wasn't wandering about before she rang her sister, Cressida.

"Anabelle." Cressida, twelve months her junior, was the proverbial night owl.

"Hiya. Are you up for a sibling video chat?" Anabelle asked.

"Always."

"Righto. I'll send an invite after I ring Wills."

Wills joined them a few minutes later, hair tousled and bleary-eyed after being woken from sleep. "Cressy, what's on your face?"

Cressida, whose skin was covered in a green mask, stuck out her tongue. "It's a pore minimizer."

"You don't have big pores." Wills ran his hands through his disheveled hair, making it stand on end.

Cressida pointed to her face. "This is the reason why I don't."

"Okay, you two. It's good to see you both. It's been a while," Anabelle interjected.

"What's this about, Anabelle?" Wills asked. "It's late."

"Dad's exhausted and his color is off. I've never seen him like this." Anabelle drew her jumper more tightly around her.

Silence ensued as Wills and Cressida stared at one another.

"Dad hasn't bounced back after his last round of Covid," Cressida stated. "And Wills has taken on more and more of the estate management in the last few months."

"I didn't know. Why didn't you guys say anything?" Anabelle wiped her forehead with her sleeve.

"Nothing to say. Dad's getting old, and old people get tired. You know what an exhausting schedule he keeps."

"It's more than that," Anabelle insisted. "I've heard that Covid triggers all sorts of autoimmune diseases. He needs to be checked."

"Give him time to recover," Cressida insisted, itching her nose and dislodging a small bit of mask.

"Have you considered that it could be his kidneys? It runs in the family, you know." Anabelle pushed to see if her siblings knew more about Dad's health than they let on.

"He'd tell us, if he did," Wills said. "Was that the reason for this call?"

Anabelle bobbed her head.

"Well then, if we've covered everything, I'm heading back to bed. I need my zeds." Wills saluted, and his screen went dark.

Wills's quick departure left Anabelle and Cressida staring at each other, wide-eyed.

"He's been grumpy for a while now." Cressy shrugged, then patted her face where the mask had dried. "And he does get up before dawn and needs his sleep."

Truer words were never spoken. Wills was never at his best this late. "Sorry to interrupt your bedtime ritual, Cressy. I just assumed you guys would know about anything going on with Dad."

"Stop worrying. He'll bounce back."

"I suppose you're right. Thanks for talking." Anabelle blew her sister a kiss.

"Night."

She pocketed her mobile and faced the toppers Mother had sewn today while she was at work.

Returning to the far end of the table, she turned the window treatment inside out. Mother had finished the seams with her serger. If Anabelle hadn't known better, she'd insist the toppers had been professionally done.

She unplugged Granny's machine and stepped to the sash windows, closing the heavy draperies against the darkness and switching off the massive chandelier.

Dad's health weighed on her heart, disturbing her like a repetitive eye twitch. The Dewhurst men died from freak accidents or illness; none reaching sixty in the last century.

She longed to share her worries with Brodie, but he disappeared early that afternoon without a word to anyone. When she rang him after work, he did not pick up.

Moving down the corridor, she passed the grand drawing room with its adjoining lounge and telly. Dad had left a lamp burning after watching Sky News. She stepped to the end table and switched it off. Through the windows, flickering lights caught her eye. She cupped her hands and peered out, but everything went black. A second later, her mobile buzzed with an incoming text.

Brodie: Can you meet me in the garden?

Anabelle: Now?

Brodie: Aye.

Anabelle: Which one?

Brodie: The walled garden.

What was Brodie doing out in the family's private garden at this time of night? Puzzled, Anabelle slipped outside, then paused on the terrace while her eyes adjusted to the darkness.

"Hiya." Brodie's deep voice reached her before his form separated from the shadows.

"What are you doing out here? I tried calling you earlier."

"I had some errands and didn't finish until just now."

"Oh." She played with the hem of her blouse.

He joined her on the steps, took her hand, and ran his thumb over the back of her fingers.

"What's bothering you?"

She shrugged, her shoulders moving up to her ears and back. "I'm worried about Dad. He's exhausted. When I spoke to Wills and Cressida about it, they said he'd had a recent bout with Covid and hadn't bounced back. But I can't help thinking it's something else. His father died from kidney disease."

"And you've been worrying."

"Yes. I'm just being silly, but after losing Granny, the thought of something happening to Dad frightens me."

Brodie drew her close. "I'm sorry, lass."

The comfort of his arms surrounded her, and she snuggled close, leaning on his strength. "Why were you out here in the dark?"

"I had something up my sleeve, but perhaps it should wait." His Adam's apple bobbed.

"Is it something fun? I could use a distraction."

"Trust me, Anabelle, this seems in poor taste with—"

"Let me be the judge of that." She traced her fingers down the dark stubble on his jaw that had grown since his morning shave.

"All right, lass." His chest expanded, and his shoulders tensed with suppressed energy.

He clicked something in his hand, and Japanese lanterns sprang to life, hanging from the trees above the small bridge arching over the pond in the distance, the water reflecting their glow.

Taking her hand, Brodie led her across the newly laid sod. When they rounded a shrubbery, her breath froze in her chest, and her hands went clammy.

The bridge's wooden slats were covered in rose petals under the flickering lights.

The lanterns' soft illumination lit Brodie's smile, and everything inside her went still.

Water trickled, the only sound save for her heartbeat thumping inside her ears. She fought the huge lump forming inside her throat.

"Is this what you were doing when you disappeared today?" Her voice sounded unnaturally high as she indicated the lanterns and pastel-colored petals.

"Aye."

Anabelle covered her mouth, and shivers of anticipation raced up her torso. She clung to his arm to stay upright when her knees threatened to buckle.

Like a wooden pull toy, he towed her onto the bridge, then took both her hands when they reached its apex. "I spoke to your father today–again."

"Again?"

"I asked him for your hand months ago."

"You did?" She sounded like a parrot but couldn't seem to help herself. For the last few months, Brodie had been so preoccupied, that she had halfway expected him to call things off between them.

He drew her down beside him on the bridge and leaned against a post while she dangled her legs above the water.

"We had so many demands on our schedules, there never seemed an appropriate time. Then those forged work orders and . . ."

She appreciated his excluding the Queen's ridiculous request and her probation.

"But?" Ever since their second date, she had dreamed of this day, and now that it had arrived, impatience swarmed her heart. Why didn't he hurry this along? Anabelle scooted closer, until only centimeters separated them.

She indicated the romantic setting and batted her eyelashes.

"Ye aren't letting me ease into this tonight, are ye?" Brodie raised one of his dark brows.

"Not on your life, Mr. Maxwell. I want the whole package, and I want it now. No more dithering." The words slipped out of her mouth without thought. "There will always be something to hold us back from the perfect moment. Carpe diem, Brodie. Tonight is ours."

Even in the dim light, she could tell that her response moved him. His eyes softened, and he touched her hair, then slid his fingers down the side of her face, his hand sparking electric currents in its wake.

"I love ye, lass. Ye own my heart. Without ye, life is dull and colorless, a continuous round of work and duty. But since we met, you've changed my world. Knocked it clean off its foundation. You're my favorite part of every day. I want to see you when you wake, hold you while you sleep, and build a future with you at its center. If you feel even the least bit the same, would ye be my wife?"

"Yes! Yes!! Yes!!!" She launched herself into his arms before he could utter anything else. Her heart smacked against her ribs with such force she was sure Brodie and everyone inside the house could hear its thumps.

He crushed her to him, and his lips latched onto hers with a searing kiss that scattered her senses, and all but fried her brain cells. He took his time celebrating by exploring every inch of her mouth, face, and neck.

"We're engaged." She smiled against his mouth when she could speak, her voice hoarse.

"Och. I forgot." Brodie leaned back, putting space between them as he struggled with something inside his trouser pocket. An impatient yank, and a glittering diamond arced through the air and plopped in the pond beneath them.

Brodie said something in Gaelic that she did not understand, nor did she need a translation, as she had a good idea what it meant. Without hesitating, she toed off her shoes and slid from the bridge into the water.

She gasped. "I never dreamed the pond would be so cold."

"What are you doing?" Brodie leaned over her, hanging onto the railing.

"Getting my ring," she tossed at him over her shoulder.

"We'll fish it out in the morning when we can see what we're looking for."

"No, we aren't. I've waited long enough. I want my ring."

With rolled up trousers and bare feet, Brodie switched on his mobile torch and joined her a minute later, shining its light into the murky water.

Anabelle clamped her teeth to keep them from chattering, cringing as her feet touched the moss covered stones. The ring had landed close to where she stood. Peering about, she moved forward, then slipped on a slimy rock. Brodie grabbed her arm to keep her upright and lost his footing.

Windmilling his arms, he fell backward and crashed down like a felled tree. A huge splash shot up from the displaced water and doused Anabelle, soaking her to the skin. Brodie disappeared under the water, completely submerged, save for the arm holding his mobile above the surface like a coveted trophy.

Anabelle snorted, then bent double, the tips of her hair touching the pond, and laughed until her sides ached.

Brodie surfaced and flipped water from his eyes just as someone opened a bedroom window at the back of the house.

"What's going on out there?" Gerald Smith, their wood preservationist, hollered.

Anabelle cupped her mouth with both hands. "We're looking for a rock."

"Do it quieter. People are trying to sleep." Gerald slammed the window sash down.

"Rock collecting?" Brodie chuckled.

"It's the truth. Diamonds are the very king of rocks," she insisted.

"No diamond is worth a case of pneumonia. I suggest we return at first light when we can see what we're doing."

Trust Brodie to be the practical one. Well, she had no intention of being practical. She wanted her ring.

"Oh, ye of little faith." She switched on her mobile torch and ignored him, squinting at the moss beneath her feet. A glint among the gunk, then was gone.

"I saw something," she squealed.

"Are you sure?" Brodie slogged in her direction, rippling the water around them.

Anabelle held up her hand. "Can you shine your torch there?" She pointed.

"Aye." Brodie's mobile lit up the area near her feet.

Another glint, and she crouched, fishing about her toes—toes that had lost all feeling. "Gotcha." She lifted her ring, covered in a blob of moss.

"It's a wonder you saw it at all." Brodie took the ring from her and rinsed it off.

Then, standing in the middle of her family's pond, the two of them shivering uncontrollably, Brodie slipped the engagement ring onto her finger.

"I need another kiss." Anabelle lifted her face for a swift peck, but Brodie wrapped his arms around her and tugged her close, his warmth holding the chill at bay.

Above them, the rising moon sailed, spinning a silver trail of beams across the pond's surface. Anabelle snuggled against him and sighed, soothed by the choir of crickets and the lovely, magical night under an inky sky sprinkled with stardust.

He kissed her again, his lips caressing hers until she groaned with need.

Brodie, ever the gentleman, stepped away and dropped his arms. "Anabelle, we had best go inside; I can't feel my feet."

Chapter 22

Anabelle stood at the circulation desk beside her father as Hannah Robertson, the director of The National Archives of Scotland, approached, a slight frown on her face.

"This doesn't look good, Dad," Anabelle whispered.

"I think you're right," he agreed.

Ms. Robertson halted on the opposite side of the counter. "I'm sorry, Miss Dewhurst, but there aren't any Lindsays in our digital archives. The time frame for the records you requested is a point of embarrassment, as many of them were lost due to a prolonged period of thefts."

"I remember hearing about those record thefts on the BBC. I thought those records were found?" Dad chimed in.

"Most of our documents were located at Trent University, but unfortunately, those from your region were never recovered."

Anabelle bit her lip and glanced with dismay at her father. Ms. Robertson, a professional researcher, made no errors.

"Do you have any recommendations on where we should search next?" Anabelle flipped her hair over her shoulder as disappointment consumed her.

"Have you tried the Church of Scotland?" Ms. Robertson asked.

"Yes." The local kirk Ms. Robertson referred to had fallen into disrepair, which is why Anabelle had broadened her hunt.

"I'm sorry to hear that. I have your address on hand and will keep a lookout in case something comes to light. We receive new records all the time." Ms. Robertson's forthright gaze assured Anabelle that the woman meant what she proposed.

"Thank you." With a heavy heart, Anabelle tucked her arm through her father's and exited the building. Outside, she paused on the pavement at a complete loss on what route to pursue next.

"I'll ring the minister to see if anyone responded to his inquiry." Dad squeezed her arm.

She rubbed her temples where a headache throbbed. "Randy has time to pry up the attic floorboards tomorrow and see what's hiding beneath them. Maybe we'll get lucky and find family documents."

"Don't get your hopes up. The Sawyers probably patched the floor due to wood rot or a beetle infestation."

Anabelle gave him a sour look. "You're such a landowner."

"Probably because I am one." Dad chuckled.

They cut through a close, one of Edinburgh's small pedestrian alleyways, and entered the Royal Mile, with Anabelle picking her way across the cobbles, careful not to turn her ankle. Outside the Bank of Scotland, a piper played a haunting tune, the music carrying down the street.

"Delightful," Dad said when the song concluded.

Anabelle nodded, but she was still preoccupied with their recent visit to the historical society. "I was positive they would have information on the Lindsay family."

"Think of this as a treasure hunt. We've discovered two places where the records aren't. We cross them off and keep looking."

"You sound like her sometimes, you know," Anabelle said softly.

"Who?" Dad glanced down at her.

"Granny. She turned everything into a game."

"That's what this is, an adventure. Enjoy the hunt." Dad checked his watch. "We'd best go meet your mother."

"I don't know why she insists that I try on wedding gowns. Brodie and I haven't even set the date." Anabelle winced at her cranky words. Weeks and weeks of sleep deprivation were no excuse for her behavior. "I'm sorry. I didn't mean to sound petty."

"Humor her, love. That's all I ask. You're our first to marry, and Eliza wants to be part of this."

Anabelle didn't mind looking at dresses, but the Poole family expected pomp and circumstance due to their years at court, while Brodie's family, though their social equals, had simpler tastes. Until she and Brodie determined the venue, shopping seemed rather pointless, even with the Queen in attendance.

Cutting through the square past St. Giles, they reached Mother's location at Seton's Bridal.

A bell chimed when Dad opened the door to a modern boutique with a ceiling that soared two stories and contained a stained-glass skylight at its zenith, distilling diffused reds, golds, and blues on the room below.

Near the front of the shop, Dad located a comfortable sofa and sat down to read. "You ladies enjoy yourselves. I'll be right here if you need me."

"There you are, darlings." Mother rushed toward them, her face wreathed in a smile. Behind her, a short, stoutish woman in her sixties followed. "This is Mrs. Gordon. Her family has designed bridal gowns for generations."

"A pleasure, ma'am." Anabelle greeted the gray-haired woman dressed in smart business attire.

The corners of Mrs. Gordon's thin lips curved as she sized Anabelle up. Taking charge, Mrs. Gordon escorted Anabelle and her mother to a massive Alderwood table. "Would either of you care for something to drink?"

"Water would be perfect." Anabelle's throat had gone dry after her walk.

"Nothing for me," Mother said. "But I'm sure my husband would care for a glass."

Mrs. Gordon retreated to the back of the shop and retrieved a carafe of water, two goblets, and several leather-bound bridal books.

Mother leaned close and lowered her voice. "The dresses here are fairy-tale gorgeous."

When Mrs. Gordon returned, she placed several design books on the table, then poured water from the pitcher into a goblet, making quite a production of the presentation.

"Thank you." Anabelle sipped the liquid gratefully, the water soothing her parched throat.

"I'll leave you to it. Call me if you have any questions." Mrs. Gordon bustled off in Dad's direction.

Mother flipped open the first book, turned a few pages, then nudged it across the table in her direction. "I adore the ones with trains. They look so nice from the back." Mother tapped at a design with a long, tapered finger.

"They do, but I was thinking something less elaborate."

"Something a bit grand will be expected with Her Majesty in attendance, don't you think?" Mother cocked her head to the side.

"I'm not sure that I'm comfortable with such an enormous gown." The massive skirt did not appeal to her in any way.

When Mother buried her nose in the book once more, Anabelle snapped a picture of the gown and texted it to her best friend, Jecca.

Anabelle: What do you think about this? I could recycle it for a parachute after the wedding.

Jecca:

Then she sent Anabelle a picture of a dress covered in ruffles. The thing resembled a giant snowball more than a wedding gown.

Anabelle giggled. Wedding dress hunting was not for the faint-hearted. Good thing she and Jecca could make light of the situation.

Jecca shot her another picture, this time of a sheer gown in desperate need of lining.

Anabelle: Are you sure that isn't lingerie?

Mother lifted her head, and her gaze narrowed on Anabelle's mobile. "Would you please put that away? We need to focus."

"I'm sorry, Mother. Jecca and I were sharing wedding dress ideas."

"What do you think of this one?" Mother pointed to a hoop-skirted dress that looked more like a ball gown than Anabelle's idea of a wedding dress.

Mrs. Gordon returned with more binders.

"I'd prefer something without hoops." Anabelle cast a pleading glance in Mrs. Gordon's direction, behind Mother's back.

"We have some here." Mrs. Gordon rummaged through the books, selected one, then flipped through the pages. "Are any of these to your liking?"

Anabelle browsed the sketches, her eyes returning to those with lace. "These are beautiful."

"Not all brides can wear lace. Before you get your hopes up, let me drape a few swatches around your shoulders to see how your complexion responds." Mrs. Gordon hurried from the room and returned a few minutes later with a ringed group of lace panels.

"Come this way." Mrs. Gordon motioned for Anabelle to join her in front of a full-length mirror. "Watch your face and see how your skin responds." Stepping behind Anabelle, Mrs. Gordon placed the lace around her shoulders and tucked it up to her chin.

Almost immediately, a creamy glow softened Anabelle's skin tone.

Mrs. Gordon made a put-putting sound of approval. "It is most becoming on you, Miss Dewhurst."

"Thank you," Anabelle said.

"These are a mite plain, Anabelle." Mother turned the page where a gown with a long train took pride of place. "You need something more elaborate."

"I love this one." Anabelle returned to the sketch on the previous page, its train modest compared to the fifteen-foot one Mother preferred.

"You have exquisite taste." Mrs. Gordon nodded approvingly at the drawing Anabelle had selected. "That is handmade bobbin lace."

Good taste. *Another word for expensive*. "I've seen bobbin lace recently on a vintage gown."

"You have?" Mother pivoted in her seat, her eyes rounding in surprise.

"I found it in the attic. The dress is horribly yellowed, which is a terrible shame because the gown is lovely."

Mrs. Gordon's eyes brightened perceptibly. "There is a way to remove stains from lace. I would recommend having it professionally cleaned if I were you. Bobbin lace is rare and expensive. Very few make it these days.

"You know," Mrs. Gordon said breathlessly, her face animated, underscoring her passion for her industry. "Years ago, my grandmother and her cousin, Louise Morrison, made bobbin lace for this shop."

Anabelle stopped, mid-breath, her heart transitioning into a polka. *Morrison.*

"Louise's work was much admired." Mrs. Gordon smiled, her glasses winking. "Several royals and aristocrats commissioned Louise to design their gowns. Unfortunately, Louise's hands stiffened from arthritis, and she retired. We still have samples of her work. I have never seen such exquisite bobbin lace before or since."

"Do you have pictures of those gowns?" Mother asked.

"We do. They are just along here." Mrs. Gordon led them to an alcove outside the fitting rooms where a grouping of photos in gilded frames along one wall.

"That dress belonged to the Duchess of Atholl. Our shop created it for her marriage." Mrs. Gordon pointed to one of the gowns photographed on dressmaker dummies. "And this is Princess Mary's ball gown." She indicated another of the pictures.

"It's exquisite." Mother stepped forward, eyebrows high, looking impressed.

"This one belonged to Jenny Jerome. She married Winston Churchill's father."

"I heard her story on the BBC." Mother nodded. "Do you remember, Anabelle? Jenny was an American socialite who married into the aristocracy."

"I do." Anabelle eyed the delicate lace worn by Jenny Jerome.

"And this is the last one done by Louise, and it is my personal favorite." Mrs. Gordon pointed to the framed picture on the bottom right. "Louise made this for her granddaughter. It took her two years, because the pain from her arthritis was so great."

"It's stunning." Anabelle gazed at the familiar-looking gown, positive she had seen it before. She stepped close to examine the high, Victorian neckline and corseted bodice. The dress, complemented by the chapel-worthy train, was timeless and reminiscent of the one she had found in the attic. . .

An odd humming consumed her. Surely, no two gowns could be so similar?

"She's quite taken with that one." Mother patted Anabelle's arm.

"I would love to wear something like this. It's not over the top but dignified enough for the Queen to attend the chapel service." Anabelle kept her eyes on the picture, afraid that if she looked away, the dress would disappear, and she would wake up to find this only a dream. "The gown's timeless."

"Louise came from nothing, but she was talented. Her granddaughter married into a prestigious family. It's a shame the granddaughter, Julia, died so young." Mrs. Gordon shook her head as if saddened. "She and her husband were admired for championing good causes."

Julia.

Mrs. Gordon's voice faded as Anabelle read the name beneath the picture, and the hair on her arms rose.

Julia Elliott. Anabelle went still, hardly daring to breathe, while her eyes stung and her throat constricted.

"Julia married William Lindsay, the eventual heir of Soldier's Leap, an estate near Loch Tummel," Mrs. Gordon said.

Mother's eyes widened, and she opened her mouth as if to speak, but Anabelle squeezed her arm in warning. Mrs. Gordon would likely stop sharing if Mother said anything, and Anabelle needed that information.

"I've heard of Soldier's Leap." Anabelle's heart thundered so fast that she placed her hand against the wall steady herself.

"Aye. It's undergoing a renovation." Mrs. Gordon lowered her voice, even though they were the only customers inside the shop.

"Can you tell me more about Louise Morrison, the lace maker? Was she from around here?" Anabelle's gaze strayed to the gown her great-great-great-grandmother created.

"The Morrisons were shopkeepers here in Edinburgh," Mrs. Gordon informed her.

The fact that the woman shared her family's information so freely stunned Anabelle. Scots, for all their curiosity and friendliness, rarely disclosed personal facts with strangers. Perhaps pride in Mrs. Gordon's prestigious clients had loosened her tongue.

Now that Mother had caught on to her objective, Anabelle dropped her arm.

"You mentioned that this Louise Morrison was a cousin to your grandmother. What happened to your grandmother?" Anabelle asked to be polite, though she burned to learn more about her great-grandmother's people.

"She lived to the ripe age of ninety-three, and her mind was fully intact until she passed."

"She must have shared many stories with you," Anabelle said.

"Aye, and she taught me how to make bobbin lace."

Mother gave Anabelle a speaking glance, one filled with disapproval that she had pumped Mrs. Gordon for information without revealing her identity.

Anabelle cleared her throat. "Mrs. Gordon, I have a confession to make about why I'm so interested in your family history. I'm a direct descendant of Julia Elliott. We recently found a wedding dress at Soldier's Leap identical to the one in this picture." Anabelle touched the framed image of Julia's gown. "A prayer book bearing the Morrison name was tucked beside it."

The corners of Mrs. Gordon's mouth curved ever so slightly. "I have a confession to make as well. I recognized you when you entered the shop. I never forget a face."

"Surely, we've never met?" Anabelle wrinkled her brow in confusion.

"No, but you were on Skye News when they did a story on Soldier's Leap and mentioned your relationship to the Lindsay family."

Evidently, she and Mrs. Gordon had similar Machiavellian tendencies when it came to information gathering.

"It looks like I've been royally played." Anabelle's shoulders shook as she burst into laughter. Mrs. Gordon joined her, cackling merrily.

"I must fetch your father. He needs to meet Mrs. Gordon." Mother left them standing in front of the pictures.

"It is a grand day when relatives come to call." Mrs. Gordon's words warmed Anabelle.

Mother returned just then with Dad at her side, and Anabelle performed the introductions.

"Mrs. Gordon, this is my father, Lord Huddleton."

"Call me, Pierce." Dad shook Mrs. Gordon's hand. "I understand that our grandmothers were cousins."

"Och. Aye." Mrs. Gordon bobbed her head. "And I am Erica, Erica Seton Gordon. You must visit my husband sometime so we can look at photos. I have pictures of your grandparents." Erica glanced at Anabelle. "Miss Dewhurst—"

"Anabelle." No need for formality among family.

"A good name." Erica beamed, giving Anabelle's name her stamp of approval.

"I was named for my grandmother, Belle Lindsay Dewhurst."

"The composer?" Erica asked.

"Yes." Anabelle grinned, delighted that Granny was still remembered for her work.

Erica appeared somewhat gobsmacked, not from associating with an aristocrat, but by meeting descendants of a famous composer. Erica, a hard-working woman herself by the look of things, valued accomplishments over titles. Anabelle liked her already.

"Is there more family in the area?" Dad asked.

"Unfortunately, I am the only child of an only child. My husband and I never had children. We rescue dogs." A look of eagerness flickered across Erica's features when her gaze rested on Dad. "Would you like to meet sometime?"

"That would be delightful." Mother exchanged contact information with Erica, then they said their goodbyes and stepped outside the shop.

Dad and Mother started down the pavement. Anabelle gazed after them for a moment, then nipped back inside Seton's Bridal.

"Erica, if I bring Julia's dress to you, would you be able to tell if the stains are removable?" Anabelle stopped, unwilling to take it further. She'd loved the wedding gown from the moment she lifted it from the trunk. If Erica could clean it, Grandmama needn't know the dress's actual age.

"I would enjoy the challenge and adore seeing Louise's final work firsthand."

"Thank you." Excitement bubbled, and she embraced Erica.

Erica's eyes gleamed, and she patted Anabelle's upper arm. "Come back soon, lass."

Still grinning, Anabelle left the shop, her feet floating over the uneven cobbles. God had led her to Erica when all other avenues to locate her family had come to nothing.

Gracious. Anabelle's eyes widened. Erica's information took their family back two more generations. A blessing, indeed.

Catching up to her parents, Anabelle ordered a ride on her app. Less than five minutes later, the driver let them off at Waverly Station, and they boarded shortly thereafter.

"Anabelle, I can tell by that expression on your face that you are plotting something," Dad remarked after they settled inside their compartment.

"I asked Erica to clean Julia's dress. If she removes the yellow stains, I intend to wear it." If anyone had a vested interest in that wedding gown, it would be Erica . . .

"A second-hand gown?" Mother's hand flew to her chest.

"A vintage gown," Anabelle corrected. "You saw how lovely it was. The dress is a classic and would mean so much to me if I could wear it. Ever since I started the reno at Soldier's Leap, I've felt an affinity for Granny's family. The dress ties us to them."

Anabelle glanced at her father for backup. "Your Grandmama Poole will have something to say about that," he said.

"All Grandmama needs to know is that a bridal shop with a royal warrant created the gown."

"What about Brodie? Won't he care that you're wearing an old dress from the attic?" Mother raised both of her finely tweezed brows.

"Brodie wouldn't care if she married him in a matching tuxedo." Dad said, his tone amused. "Let her wear what she wants, Eliza."

Though Dad was on her side, Mother remained unconvinced. But Anabelle knew better than to argue the point; now was not the time with Dad looking so peaked.

"Erica probably won't be able to remove those stains. They're quite pronounced." A mischievous smile curved Anabelle's mouth. "But you're wrong about Brodie, Dad. He won't be in a tuxedo. We'll both be wearing skirts."

No Scottish Highlander would marry in anything but a kilt.

Chapter 23

Anabelle is engaged! I snap the mechanical pencil I hold, then grip the paper weight on my desk and hurl it into the wall. It dents the newly plastered surface.

Why did she do that?

She loves *me*! She told me so herself. I have the text to prove it.

I glare at the vase on the counter before me, a leaded crystal one that I spent a small fortune to purchase. The flowers beside await my arrangement.

I march to the kitchen drawer and retrieve the micro listening device I purchased off the dark web. I need the name of the person she's vowed to marry.

And this will give it to me.

Chapter 24

Brodie stood beside the microwave in the break room, warming his soup for lunch. The bell dinged, and he retrieved his soup and stirred it, grinning to himself as he considered the absurd gift he'd purchased to commemorate his and Anabelle's one-week anniversary–a desk fountain filled with green algae, guaranteed to make those blue eyes of hers sparkle.

"Mail." Mrs. Mellencamp poked her head around the doorframe, her hands loaded with a bouquet of roses and several parcels.

"Anything for me?" Brodie eyed the deliveries.

Mrs. Mellencamp stepped inside, set the flowers on the counter, and sorted through the envelopes. "Ah. Here it is." She handed him a thick manila envelope.

"Anything else?" he asked.

"The rest of these are for Anabelle."

Brodie's gaze landed on the flowers. Lord and Lady Huddleton had not held his delayed proposal against him once they understood what had occurred.

The microwave dinged. Instead of withdrawing his soup, he followed Mrs. Mellencamp down the corridor to the conference room and stopped in the doorway. Inside, Tara, Anabelle, and Gerald bent over the table discussing the pros and cons of wood stains and their eco-friendly varnishes.

"These are for you, Anabelle. Where would you like me to set them?" Mrs. Mellencamp, bless her, had no compunction about interrupting her coworkers when she had a job to perform.

Anabelle glanced up from the samples, and her gaze landed on the bouquet. "Does it say who they're from?" she asked.

"I'm sure I don't know. I don't make a habit of snooping through people's things," Mrs. Mellencamp said in her abrupt way. The long hours were wearing everyone down.

Mrs. Mellencamp set the bouquet on the conference table with a thump, then bustled out.

Anabelle's gaze snagged his, and her face lit with that secret glow she spared only for him. She tilted her head toward the flowers and raised her brows as if to ask if he'd sent them.

He shook his head and shrugged, curious to find out the identity of the sender. Had her parents sent them? For Anabelle's sake, he sincerely hoped so. Resting his arm against the doorframe, he found it difficult to tear his gaze away from his future wife.

Gerald muttered something, and Anabelle dropped her gaze back to her clipboard. "My notes have mocha latte down for the red room."

"I'm not sure I approve of that combo." Tara tucked her red hair behind her ear, her focus on the paint chip beside the flooring sample. "It's too dark and will shrink the room."

"I agree," Anabelle said. "But I thought we decided that stain would create an intimate vibe, one that you were aiming for." Anabelle skirted the conference table and dug through the flowers. "No card?" Her face hardened, and she lifted them in her arms, swung about, water sloshing from the vase, then dumped the bouquet in the bin. Crystal tinkled as the vase shattered inside the metal receptacle.

Brodie jerked upright as shock rippled through him at Anabelle's cavalier treatment of such an expensive arrangement.

"Did you just toss those gorgeous blooms in the bin?" Tara dashed to the waste container and lifted the flowers from the trash, picking glass shards from the leaves.

"I did," Anabelle affirmed without the slightest look of repentance. "I don't accept flowers from people who don't identify themselves."

"If you don't want them, I do. These roses are stunning." Tara sniffed the blossoms.

"Be my guest."

Brodie frowned. Anabelle was acting oddly.

"What's this?" Tara removed a small, dark object from the center of a rose and eyed it with a frown. "Is this something the florist uses to refresh flowers?"

Anabelle took the wee bit of plastic from Tara and examined it closely. "It probably fell off another package inside the delivery truck."

"No way to find the owner now," Tara said.

Anabelle lobbed the object into the bin, where it pinged against the inside of the metal container and plopped into the water at the bottom.

"Nice shot." Brodie applauded from the doorway, and all three glanced in his direction.

"Brodie." Gerald nodded, acknowledging his presence, but the American was not the man to be distracted. "What's the decision, ladies?" He turned back to the table, his brash, Bostonian accent grating on the ears.

"Keep the stain as is. It's too much bother to change." Tara adjusted several roses.

"I've wasted the last forty minutes for nothing?" Gerald snatched up his samples and strode from the room, his color high.

Not the least perturbed by Gerald's frustration, Tara eyed the adjacent parcels on the conference table. "Anabelle, you've some mail."

"I'll read it during lunch." Anabelle remained at the table, checking paint swatches against her clipboard.

Since being placed on probation, Anabelle never strayed from her tasks, doubtless to ensure no one accused her of bungling her job. But even Brodie found her behavior today odd.

"You're sure about the flowers?" Tara all but buried her face in the petals.

"Positive."

Brodie almost felt sorry for whoever sent the bouquet—but the other part of him aimed to find out who was cheeky enough to send roses to an engaged woman. Her parents would have tagged the flowers. So would her friends and sibs.

"I'm going to put them in a vase." Tara headed toward him. "Brodie, I thought you'd gone. You wouldn't know anything about that sparkler on Anabelle's hand, would you?" Tara smiled, her eyes watchful.

Most everyone knew he and Anabelle were seeing each other.

"And if I did?" he challenged. His and Anabelle's engagement wasn't a secret. They maintained a professional relationship while on the clock.

"That's a big ring. Are you sure you gave it to the right girl?" Tara tossed her bob, then continued to her office.

What a tiresome woman. If she weren't so good at her job, he would insist that Genesis place her on another project.

He edged into the room and joined Anabelle at the conference table. "Hiya."

Anabelle set her clipboard aside.

He shifted and scanned the information. "Those are detailed notes."

"I'm documenting everything. No one will forge my name again—not if I can help it."

"Forearmed is forewarned?" he asked.

"Exactly."

"That was nice of you to give Tara your flowers."

Anabelle turned a lovely shade of pink. "Better her than me."

"What does that mean?"

"This is the second time in two days that someone has sent me a bouquet." Anabelle huffed.

Weird. "Any idea who?" Brodie leaned against the table, trying to play it cool even though his blood simmered.

"They weren't from you or my parents."

"How do you know?"

"You always send me tulips and write sweet notes. You also sign your name. So do Mother and Dad."

He played with her hand, turning the engagement ring to catch the light. "It's clean."

"I wasn't overfond of green algae blobs."

He chuckled, but his mind remained on her revelation. "If it's bothering you, I'd be happy to find out who sent them."

"Do you know how many florists there are between here and Stirling?" Anabelle shook her head, her dark hair shimmering under the lights. "Mrs.

Mellencamp found both bouquets on the front steps with my name on a card."

Something vague shifted inside him.

"The night we made up, I went to bed and was just drifting off to sleep when I received a text. I thought it was from you. But I was wrong." She rubbed the backs of her arms as though suddenly chilled.

"You're sure?"

"Of course, I'm sure. The text came from an unknown sender."

"What did it say?" He squinted at the clipboard, but his entire focus remained on their conversation.

"I love you." She cringed, her shoulders rising to her ears.

"Why didn't you tell me sooner?" His unease erupted into downright worry. What kind of person texts "I love you" to a woman they weren't dating? A creeper, that's who.

"We've been working eighteen-hour days for weeks. I honestly forgot about it until the bouquets started arriving."

"Was that text the first time this person contacted you?" If he could establish a timeline of the events, perhaps they could determine who sent it.

"Yes." She paused, trailing her finger over the table's surface, then glanced up, a frown flitting across her features.

"Did you remember something else?" he asked, intent on her answer.

"The day I flew home, I found tulips on my bed. The note beside them said, '*You were missed.*' I thought they were from you, but you usually hand-write your notes; this one was typed. When you showed up on my doorstep with more tulips, I thought it rather odd, but sweet that you'd bought two bouquets. I thanked you for *all* the flowers. Remember?"

You were missed? "I'd love to say they were both from me, but I didn't put any on your bed." Bouquets, notes, and unsigned texts. Years ago, he'd streamed a series on stalkers–obsessive characters who escalated to physical violence.

Someone had targeted Anabelle. His stomach nosedived. "You should probably report this to the authorities."

"Why did I know you were going to suggest that?" Anabelle's shoulders slumped, and she exhaled loudly. "I'm not going to lie; this creeps me out."

"Would you like me to ring the police?" Anabelle could be in real danger.

"Bother." She sighed. "I'll do it."

"If you need a private place to meet with them, feel free to use my office."

"Thank you. I will. I'd rather not alarm my parents. They have enough to deal with without worrying about their daughter having a secret admirer."

Admirer? Not hardly. The person who sent the flowers and text had issues. Though Brodie maintained a calm exterior, anxiety scoured him, like carpet nails against flesh.

How had someone accessed Anabelle's room? Did they slip inside the family wing behind a worker? Or were they a member of his team with a code?

Brodie yanked at his tie, his soup long forgotten.

Anabelle had a stalker.

CHAPTER 25

ANABELLE FIDGETED on the hard wooden chair as the two policemen inside Brodie's office plied her with questions. They arrived an hour after her call, and if her deductive skills proved accurate, Detective Inspector Finlay Maxwell, a tall, handsome man with a commanding presence, appeared the senior officer. In contrast, Detective Sergeant Marcus Ogilvie, a shorter man with a thick neck and close-set eyes, seemed nervous and likely the junior partner.

"Ms. Dewhurst, from what you've shared, let me assure you that we take situations such as yours very seriously. Stalker behavior often escalates into dangerous territory if not caught early," DI Maxwell said.

Lovely. Anabelle suppressed a shudder.

"Has anyone displayed an abnormal interest in you recently?" Ogilvie crossed one leg over his knee.

"No."

"I find that hard to believe. Certainly, a beautiful woman like yourself is accustomed to admirers." Ogilvie gave her a blatant, unblinking stare.

Anabelle ground her teeth and leaned forward in her chair. "Are you suggesting that I asked for this? I'll have you know that I'm engaged to be married, and I don't make a habit of leading people on. *Sir.*" She emphasized the last word with narrowed eyes.

"I am most sorry, Ms. Dewhurst. We do not mean to offend." DI Maxwell shot his partner a silent warning.

Anabelle bit her tongue and forced herself to calm down. "Perhaps someone else from your department should take this case."

"I meant no harm. Perhaps we got off on the wrong foot," DS Ogilvie said.

"Perhaps you did." Anabelle inclined her head, imitating Grandmama Poole at her best.

"You mentioned an unknown person leaving messages and flowers. Is there anything else you can tell us?" Maxwell studied her, his expression intent.

Anabelle shifted in her chair.

The door opened, and Brodie slipped inside the office. Both detectives glanced his way. Detective Maxwell's expression broke into a grin. "Brodie."

"Finn." Brodie took the vacant seat beside Anabelle and linked their hands. "Good to see you."

Anabelle snapped her head in Brodie's direction. "You two know each other?"

Brodie snorted. "More than I'd like to admit. I should have known you'd be on the clock, Finn."

DI Maxwell's eyes shimmered with suppressed merriment. "Is this the lass you've hitched your star to, Brodie?"

"Aye. And I'm right worried about her," Brodie responded. "Anabelle, meet my cousin, Finn."

"Cousin?" Anabelle rolled her eyes. "Brilliant. I should have known. You're Finn?"

"Aye." Finn nodded.

"It's highly unusual during questioning for someone, other than a legal advisor, to attend," DS Ogilvie said, slightly narrowing his eyes at Brodie.

"Consider me her legal advisor, then." Brodie's cheerful tone was at odds with his hard expression. "I'm here to ensure that you lot take her statement seriously."

"You seem overly friendly for a legal advisor." DS Ogilvie's gaze shifted to her and Brodie's linked hands.

"Your investigative instincts are showing. We are engaged." Anabelle lifted her hand, the engagement ring flashing under the overhead lights.

"This is a complete waste of our time," Ogilvie growled.

"Pipe down," Finn snapped. "We're getting to the questions." He cleared his throat, then sobered, his expression now all business. "Stalkers often begin with little things. Sometimes, unnoticeable to the recipient. When did you first realize that something odd occurred?"

"When a bouquet of tulips appeared on my pillow." Why did they keep asking her this? Were they hoping she'd remember something else?

"Did the flowers contain a note?" Finn asked.

"Yes."

"What did it say?" Finn pressed.

"You were missed." Anabelle used air quotes.

"That doesn't sound so odd," Ogilvie looked up from jotting down notes. "Perhaps it was someone you dated who isn't aware of your engagement."

"The only person I've dated recently is Brodie. Initially, I thought the tulips were from him. Later, I learned that wasn't the case, which alarmed me considerably."

"Why is that?" Finn asked.

"Because it meant someone entered the family wing at Soldier's Leap, which is a private residence, and wandered about until they located my bedroom."

"Are work crews ever inside your wing?" Finn drummed his fingertips against the chair's arm.

"Very rarely," Anabelle stated. "And only with advance permission."

"Would any of the workers know which room is yours?" Finn glanced up from his notes.

"No." Anabelle shook her head. "Some team leads sleep on the opposite side of the house, but others, along with the crews, commute to the job site."

Finn nodded to Ogilvie, who jotted that down as well. "You spoke of a second issue. When did that occur?" Finn inquired.

"A few weeks ago, I received a text from an unknown number." Just thinking about it dug a pit in the place her stomach used to be. She tightened her grip on Brodie's hand. "It said, 'I love you.'" She raised her chin, her fighting spirit at odds with the hollowed-out emotions coursing through her.

Brodie slid an arm around her shoulders, reading her need.

"That's a big jump," Finn stated.

"Aye," Ogilvie agreed. "The perp has likely got himself a burner."

Okay, she didn't need to hear that. Cross that, didn't want to hear that her stalker's text had moved beyond notes and flowers.

"Anything else?" Finn asked.

He met her eyes, and she read sympathy in their depths.

"For the last two days, expensive bouquets in ornate vases have arrived on the front porch addressed to me. And a card showed up in today's post." Anabelle passed the envelope to Finn.

He opened the flap and removed the typed message, skimming the words, then reading them aloud.

Anabelle,

You belong with me. Return the diamond ring you're wearing. You don't love him. We belong together. You know we do.

I love you.

"Why didn't you tell me about this?" Two furrows dented the skin between Brodie's brows.

"It came with the post. I only just read it."

"I hate to say this, Ms. Dewhurst." Finn tapped the letter. "But your stalker is escalating. I suggest that you remove your engagement ring until things settle down. If you cooperate, perhaps that will slow his advancement into the next phase and give us time to find the culprit."

"Why should I give in to this person? Who's to say what they will demand next?"

"Finn is suggesting this for your safety, lass." Brodie rubbed his jaw with his free hand.

"I'm dreadfully sorry, Finn. I'm not trying to be difficult, but I don't want to give way to his demands."

"That's understandable. I'd like you to consider cooperating before making your final decision. There's one more thing we need to do before we leave."

"What's that?" she asked.

"May we inspect the family wing?" Finn stood, giving her little choice but to comply. "I'd like to get the lay of the land and check your room."

"Of course. Could we exit the way you arrived? I'd prefer not to raise my coworker's curiosity." She'd already been enough food for gossip.

"By all means," Ogilvie agreed.

Anabelle led them to the office wing's exit onto the drive, then crossed the gravel in awkward silence until they reached the family's private entrance. She punched in the code and held the door wide. Once inside, she showed them to the lift, passing the small drawing room where Dad spoke into his mobile.

He waved, pointing at the phone, and mouthed, "Chilton."

Dad's estate manager was likely reporting his daily update.

"That was my father, Lord Huddleton," Anabelle explained to the detectives. "His mother was born here at Soldier's Leap."

The four of them rode the elevator to the first floor with Finn and Brodie catching up on each other's recent activities.

Ogilvie gawked at the meticulously restored rooms with wide eyes. "Never thought I'd see the inside of this place."

Anabelle refrained from commenting. She was more worried about the sick expression on Brodie's face, the one that hadn't fully dissipated since Finn read the contents of the stalker's note.

"Here we are." Anabelle opened the double doors to the master suite. The cream-colored paneling and gilded woodwork drew the eye to the four-poster bed that put a king-sized mattress to shame. The suite's proportions complemented the massive and rather ornate furniture.

Ogilvie closed his gaping jaw and got to work, assisting Finn in a systematic search.

Anabelle took Brodie's hand and moved through the doorway into the suite's sitting room, then sank beside him onto the down-filled sofa. An urge to comfort Brodie consumed her, and she slipped her arms around him. "It's going to be fine."

He sighed. "I'm glad Finn is taking this seriously. I wasn't sure he would when he saw I was involved."

"What's the story between the two of you?"

"What do you mean?" Brodie hedged, making her roll her eyes.

"You two are more than just cousins. You have history. What kind of trouble did you get up to together?"

"Other than sneaking out at night to go fishing on the loch when we were lads, and cutting up in primary school, the local minister caught us breaking into the sacramental wine when we were twelve. A few years later, he busted us again when we rang the kirk bell in the middle of the Christmas service."

"You didn't," Anabelle gasped, almost choking with surprise.

"Aye. Minister Liddell gave us a lecture neither of us forgot. For all his preachiness, though, he understands high-spirited lads."

"Was he the reason you both became upstanding citizens?"

"Verra likely." Brodie nodded. "That and the tanning my father and Uncle Jamie delivered when they found out. Neither of us could sit for days without wincing."

Finn appeared in the doorway. "Ms. Dewhurst, we've found something."

Bracing herself, Anabelle reentered her bedroom, her heels sinking into the plush tartan carpet. Brodie followed her to the foot of the bed.

"See that dark object?" Finn pointed to a small dark spot, no bigger than the tip of her pinky finger. "We believe it's a camera lens."

Anabelle gulped, her eyes on the object. This was so much worse than she imagined. Her knees wobbled, and she sat on the edge of her bed. The idea of someone watching her as she moved about her room. *While she slept?* Her hands shook, a weakness brought on by fear.

Brodie's color heightened, and he looked as though he'd punch a wall. He reeled in his emotion, though, and knelt on the floor before her. "Are you all right? Can I get you some tea?"

"I'll be okay. Just give me a minute."

"Ms. Dewhurst, what's above this room?" Finn pointed to the vaulted ceiling.

"The attic."

"We'd like to go up and have a look around, see if we can spot other cameras, then we'd like to check out the rest of the family wing." Ogilvie had sobered considerably from his initial crack about her admirers.

"How may we help?" Brodie stood as if poised for action.

"When you hear us above you, could you bang on the ceiling?"

"Aye. The attic stairs are at the near end of the corridor, behind the door. There's a light switch just inside," Brodie informed both detectives.

"We'll be some time, as this could be a lengthy process." A grim line surrounded Finn's mouth.

The detectives trod down the hall, their footsteps muffled by the newly laid runner.

Anabelle remained sitting, her legs as unstable as jelly while Brodie entered the corridor and retrieved an extension dusting pole from the broom closet and returned. Being the project manager on the reno, he knew the house better than she did at this point.

Anabelle glared up at the camera. "I hate the idea of being watched. It makes my flesh crawl." She tucked her trembling hands underneath her equally useless legs.

Brodie set the pole against the wall, then drew her into the sitting room, well away from the camera. Stopping by the window, he ran his fingertips over her jawline and followed it with a kiss.

"Do you really want me to remove my engagement ring?" she asked, her voice the merest whisper.

"If it protects you from this peeping tom, then, aye, I do, but only until they catch him. Then that sparkler's going right back on, lass."

"I'm giving it to you for safekeeping." Her throat squeezed as she dragged the ring from her finger. "Don't give this to someone else. I'm terribly fond of it."

"Yer the only one for me, lass. I love yer fire and that sassy mouth of yers." He paused. "I was ready to give Ogilvie a Glasgow kiss for the way he kept gawping at your legs."

"He didn't gawp at my legs."

"Not when you were looking," Brodie growled.

"Did you glare at him?"

"More than that, I gave him the Witcher's eye," Brodie said with a sharp nod. "You'll not be receiving any more ogles from that quarter."

"My hero." Brodie's behavior would have amused her if they didn't have a creeper on the loose.

She shuddered as her thoughts returned to the purpose of the detectives' visit. Brodie swept his arms around her, and she leaned against his chest. For long moments, they stood thus.

"We'll get to the bottom of this." Brodie stroked her hair, and his words, spoken with confidence, soothed her.

Footsteps stomped overhead.

"Are ye okay?" Brodie asked.

"I'm good."

He dropped his arms, marched into her bedroom, retrieved the pole, and tapped it against the ceiling to lead the detectives to the correct location.

Still somewhat shattered by Finn's revelations, she tottered into the bedroom, disliking being alone and definitely not as brave as she pretended.

"Has anyone asked you out recently?" Brodie asked.

"No. The team knows we're seeing each other after hours. Tara even commented on my engagement ring."

"She did to me as well." He winked, then asked, "Has any member of the crew frightened you? Or behaved like you rebuffed them? Stalkers don't always comprehend that their victims dislike their overtures."

"No one." Curiosity drove her to ask, "How do you know so much about stalkers?"

"I watched a documentary on it a while back. It raised my curiosity, so I researched it a bit more. I'm glad the police are taking this seriously." His eyes riveted to hers.

She moved to his side and laced their fingers together.

"Good thing Ogilvie came to his senses. Doubtless, he saw you as a silly woman, jumping at shadows."

"A time waster, you mean?" She captured her bottom lip, her teeth sinking into the flesh as she mulled that over.

The cops moved above them. Brodie thumped the ceiling three times with the pole.

"Careful, or you'll need painters to repair any marks you create," she warned.

"I'll gladly pay out of pocket to keep that nutter away from you."

An answering knock sounded above them, and the camera disappeared. "Got it," one of the detectives yelled.

Brodie returned the dusting rod to the closet, then ducked his head back inside the door. "I'm going up there to see what they found."

Chapter 26

Brodie charged up the attic staircase and ground his molars to contain his fury. That monster had wired a camera over Anabelle's bed. As the lead manager of multiple projects, he'd learned to repress strong emotion, but enough was enough. If he found the culprit before the police, they'd have to arrest him for assault.

Panting, he reached the attic. Finn lifted his chin in greeting, then returned to tracking a wire with Ogilvie across the vast expanse of floorboards.

"Any idea where this goes?" Finn knelt to examine where the wire disappeared into the exterior wall.

Brodie rubbed his jaw, reeling in his anger to consider the question. Randy's team had insulated the walls and erected fire barriers between each floor. Drilling a wire from the attic to another floor would take some doing.

On a hunch, Brodie opened the casement window and hung over the sill. A wire ran straight down the side of the house, obscured from external view by a massive stand of firs.

"I'm fairly certain we'll find something in the basement." Brodie headed for the stairs, with the police just steps behind.

Sure enough, when they reached the basement, they located the wire where it entered the house inside the laundry. Anabelle's stalker had run the line along the skirting board behind a row of washers and drilled through the adjoining wall into a storage closet.

Finn whistled. "Whoever it is, they're organized. And savvy."

Brodie's stomach knotted. They were right. This fellow was a canny one.

"Why not use wireless?" Ogilvie puzzled. "It's loads easier and less invasive."

"Wi-Fi is traceable. We also lose internet on occasion," Brodie managed through gritted teeth as fear engulfed him. Anabelle's stalker had a brilliant plan, one that made his identity untraceable.

Finn, poking around the storage room, swore. "Get in here."

Brodie and Ogilvie joined him in the tight space.

"Look at this. The perp set up a viewing station to ensure they could watch uninterrupted." Finn indicated a monitor underneath one of the shelves.

"Old school, but effective." Finn whistled, then rang their chief. "We need a fingerprinting kit. The call-in on that stalker is accurate." He rang off. "They're sending a team. Brodie, could you remain here to ensure nothing is touched during our absence? Ogilvie and I need to search this side of the house for more cameras."

Brodie did not relish Anabelle being alone while in a vulnerable state. "Aye. I'll ring Anabelle's parents to sit with her until we have more information."

"Sounds good," Finn agreed, then he and Ogilvie headed for the stairs to complete their search.

Brodie pulled up her father's number, then hesitated. Anabelle didn't appreciate his taking charge without her input. These were her parents; he should run this by her first.

Though it went against his instincts, he rang Anabelle and filled her in on what had occurred. "Your parents won't thank us for shielding them from this situation."

She sighed a bit shakily. "You're right."

"Would you like me to call your father? I'm happy to do so."

"Yes." She hesitated. "Brodie?"

"Aye?"

"Thank you for including me."

"I don't mean to always take charge. I am trainable," he added, attempting to lighten the fear that still pulsed through her voice. "I love you, lass. I'll be with you soon."

He rang off, then called her father, raking a hand through his hair as he waited for Huddleton to answer.

"Hello," Lord H. answered.

"Lord Huddleton, could you and your wife sit with Anabelle? We have a situation I need to update you on . . ." When he finished filling in Anabelle's father, Lord Huddleton was already on his way, huffing through the speaker as he hiked up the stairs, obviously evading the lift to keep the connection.

"Soldier's Leap has a top-of-the-line alarm system, but I'd like to beef that up after the policemen perform their security check."

"By all means, do your utmost to protect our daughter," Huddleton said.

"Thank you, sir." Brodie exhaled. Implementing new locks and deadbolts, out-of-reach sensor lights, along with beefed-up firewalls and rotating passwords might do the trick.

"I'm going to take this one step farther," Huddleton said. "I'm going to get her a dog."

"A dog?"

"Aye."

"A puppy will take forever to train," Brodie shot back.

"I wasn't referring to a puppy. I'm talking about a guard dog or a retired police canine. That camera in Anabelle's bedroom is beyond disturbing. Her stalker means business. No one is messing with my daughter. I'm outside Annabelle's room." Huddleton lowered his voice.

"Excellent." Brodie prayed Huddleton didn't purchase a vicious beast, because Anabelle, in all likelihood, would grow attached to the thing and beg to keep it after the danger passed.

Meaning, the dog would be his as well.

"What on earth possessed you to buy me a dog?" Anabelle gazed at her father, then back at the Belgian Malinois Shepherd sitting on the drawing room floor beside his chair. "You've seen my schedule. I don't have time to care for a pet. What if it chews up Granny Belle's Steinway or urinates on the hardwood floors while I'm at work?"

Her father merely shrugged. "The dog needed a home, and your mother and I would rest easier if you had a watchdog, especially at night when you're alone in this wing."

"Your father and I will take her for walks while we're here." Mother spoke around a mouthful of pins as she attached cording to the window toppers she was sewing. "That way, you can focus on your job."

"That's kind of you, but I thought you were leaving?"

"Change of plans," Dad said.

With a stalker on the loose, having her parents extend their visit brought on a massive sense of relief. "I'm glad." Anabelle eyed the Belgian, who promptly returned her stare. "What's his name?"

"*Her* name is Daisy." Dad patted Daisy's head. She looked up at him, and Anabelle could almost see the dog smile.

"Seriously? Daisy?" Anabelle rolled her eyes. "What kind of a guard dog goes by Daisy?" Anabelle let the canine sniff her hand. Unable to stop herself, she stroked the animal's short, fawn-colored fur. Daisy nuzzled her, and everything inside Anabelle melted.

She knelt and kissed the dog's furry head. "You're a sweetheart." She scratched under Daisy's ears, and the dog leaned into her hand. "Her black mask and ears make her look like a small German Shepherd, don't they?"

"I think so. She's also very intelligent and needs lots of exercise," Mother said, jabbing another pin into the cording.

Brilliant. Anabelle stole a glance at Daisy. The dog returned the favor with soulful eyes, then lowered her head onto Anabelle's thigh, crumbling her defenses.

She'd always been a sucker for animals, and Dad knew it.

My feed isn't working. I start down the basement stairs to find out why, but voices stop me before I reach the bottom step. I look around the corner.

Coppers are in the storage closet talking about my setup. They've found it. That's what those coppers are doing here. Good thing I came down to check.

Quickly, I ease back around the corner before they catch me and hurry upstairs, my chest heaving. Do they suspect me?

I go outside behind the gardening shed. Shouting, I kick the wall—five. Six. Seven times.

All that work wasted.

I can't ever go back down there in case they've got that closet staked out.

My chest heaves, and I shake with fury. Anabelle won't get rid of me so easily. I won't let her. We belong together.

I glare at the house, thinking . . .

There are other ways to watch her and to make her mine.

Wood screeched as Brodie leaned on the crowbar and pried up a plank from the attic floor. Sweating profusely, he fixed the tool under the next one and applied pressure, but the stubborn thing refused to budge. He thrust all his weight on it. A slight rending noise, then the floorboard gave way, knocking him off balance. He landed on his rear.

"Oomph." Brodie staggered to his feet.

"Are you okay?" Anabelle rushed to his side.

"All I hurt was my dignity." Tonight, at Anabelle's insistence, he and Randy had come up here to satisfy her curiosity.

"Is that what you landed on?" Randy snickered. "Looked like it was your ar—"

Brodie glared at him. For the last twenty-four hours, he and Randy had installed deadbolts and safety features throughout the Lindsay wing before she requested they pry up the attic floor.

Randy was not Anabelle's stalker. He'd bet his life on it. The only thing Randy obsessed over was the woman he'd met during the holidays on a skiing trip in the Alps. The two were practically engaged.

Anabelle, who stood closest to the hole he'd created in the floor, shone her torch into the gaping abyss. "You aren't going to believe this."

"What?" Brodie crowded beside her, with Randy setting down his tools to join them.

"It looks like a shaft for a small lift or circular staircase," she said.

"Why would the master suite access the attic? Those rooms lie closest to the end of the corridor where the regular stairs are located."

Anabelle lay prone and pushed aside the debris blocking her view. "I'm fairly certain that's a stairwell. Maybe it's a secret passage." She lifted her head, her blue eyes shimmering with excitement.

Randy sat back on his steel-toed boots and stroked his close, cropped beard. "When we removed the paneling inside the master dressing room, it looked as though a section of the wall had been plastered over."

"Do you think that's where this goes?" Anabelle asked.

"Possibly." Randy nodded, moving close to have a look.

Brodie eyed the rafters above them. "Randy, when you tore down that wall up here, was anything else inside that room?"

"Just a few pieces of old furniture." Randy rubbed his neck. "It looked like a storage room as it didn't have any windows."

"Why would someone put a staircase inside the master suite that led to a windowless attic room?" Anabelle's brows knit, appearing every bit as puzzled as he was himself.

"How old is the house?" Randy asked.

"Perhaps four hundred years or more. I can be more specific once I examine the foundation. Why?" Brodie faced the contractor.

"This could have been an escape route during the Jacobite uprisings, then used later for storage." Randy kept his gaze on the floor, but his thoughts appeared far away.

"That makes sense." Anabelle scanned the area with new interest. A goodly number of Scots remained Catholic after the reformation and supported the Stewart cause. "Is it possible that my family hid Jacobites up here?"

"Probably." Randy bobbed his head. "You're in the heart of the Highlands."

Leaving them to their speculation, Brodie removed the splintered planks from the rest of the hole, then clicked on his torch to study the walls and the ironwork steps below, his mind performing mental arithmetic. "Off the cuff, I'd say this was added after the house was built." Following a hunch, Brodie lowered his upper torso into the hole and examined the underside of the remaining planks. "Unbelievable."

"What?" Anabelle and Randy asked in unison.

Brodie pushed himself out of the hole and wiped dust from his eyes, then jerked his chin toward the attic floor. "That was a hinged door before someone nailed it shut."

"Does that prove Randy's theory?" Anabelle asked. "I'll visit the National Archives and see what I can discover about Jacobites hiding in this area after the uprisings."

"In all your spare time?" Brodie teased.

Anabelle wrinkled her nose at him in that sassy way of hers, making him long to tickle her until she squealed.

He glanced away, his eyes dropping to the former trap door. Had the room been used to protect political refugees? Or had Anabelle's family locked away a mad relative like other aristocrats in bygone eras?

Chapter 27

After church the following Sunday, Anabelle, Brodie, and her parents pulled up in front of Erica Gordon's house, its pristine gardens walled with granite stone.

Leading the way up the walk, Brodie rapped on the bright red door, while Anabelle kept Daisy's lead gripped in one hand. Mother and Dad stood directly behind her on the stoop. When Anabelle mentioned that she had a dog, Erica insisted that she bring Daisy to play with her rescues while they visited.

The red door swung wide, and a short, jolly fellow stood on the threshold, his face wreathed in a smile. "You must be Anabelle. I'm Hank, Erica's husband."

"Nice to meet you, Hank. These are my parents, Lord and Lady Huddleton, and Brodie Maxwell, my fiancé."

Once the introductions concluded, Anabelle glanced at Daisy, then back at Hank. "Is it all right if I bring Daisy inside?"

"Aye. This way." Hank Gordon led them into the kitchen and opened the back door, revealing three mixed-breed dogs.

Daisy's ears pricked forward, and she whined. Instead of darting outside, she looked up at Anabelle with her soft brown eyes as if to say, "May I go play?"

Anabelle unclipped her lead. "Go on, girl."

Daisy needed no further encouragement and dashed onto the small terrace to greet Erica's pets. After a sniffing frenzy with the other dogs, Daisy romped about the fenced garden, frolicking, and yipping like a young puppy.

"We can sit here and watch the dogs from the window." Erica carried a stack of old photo albums to the kitchen table. "Pierce and Anabelle, you must sit on either side of me. I have pictures that will be of interest to you."

Smirking at Erica's bossy tone, Anabelle did as she was told, gathering around the well-scrubbed table, the surface soft from generations of wear.

"These are my parents." Erica opened a leather-bound album and pointed to a black-and-white picture. Despite the old-fashioned photo, the bride and groom were a handsome pair.

"And this is Grandmother with her cousin Julia, and Julia's beau, William Lindsay." Erica tapped a picture on the opposite page.

Anabelle scooted forward and squinted at the small image. Julia appeared in her late teens, with her hair piled high on her head. William's erect posture and striking light eyes bore testament to the genetics he had passed to his descendants.

"They were so young," Brodie commented.

A hard knot obstructed Anabelle's throat and prevented her from speaking. Brodie, who had taken the end chair, scooted close and slid his arm around her shoulders, while she leaned into his side and wiped her eyes.

Erica pointed to another picture where Julia stood, wearing the beautiful gown her grandmother Louise had created, with William at her side.

"My mother." Dad cleared his throat several times. "She's the image of Julia."

"It's uncanny." Mother reached across the table and patted Dad's hand.

Erica bustled from the room and returned with a box of tissues.

"Thank you." Taking one, Anabelle mopped her cheeks.

"Pierce has his maternal grandfather's jawline and nose, don't you think, Anabelle?" Mother's question helped pull her together.

"And eyes," Anabelle added, tapping the picture. "Don't they look just like Dad's?"

"You've got them too, Anabelle," Brodie add after apparent consideration. "But you inherited Julia's build."

"Trust an architect to notice structure." Dad winked.

Anabelle elbowed Brodie, who only laughed and kissed her cheek, not the least shy about their relationship in front of her parents.

"Erica, can I get a copy of this?" Dad touched William and Julia's wedding picture.

"Absolutely. But I have more in here of your grandparents." Erica flipped through several pages and stopped. "You must know that Julia took some persuading to marry William. His parents were not keen on the match and even disowned him for a time."

"Why?" Anabelle asked.

"Julia's grandmother, Louise Morrison, worked in a dressmaker's shop, a very prestigious one." Erica's mouth thinned.

Snobbery. Anabelle detested it in all its forms.

Erica tapped Julia and William's wedding picture. In an era when solemn facial expressions prevailed, the pair glowed with joy. "They were a love match." Erica turned a few more pages. "That wasn't always the case with society weddings. But William was of age and stood firm against his parents."

"You said they cut him off. What happened?" Anabelle burned with curiosity.

"William married Julia, and true to their word, his parents cut him off and made his second cousin, Irving Campbell, Laird Lindsay's heir. He was a wild young lad. So, for the first seven years of William and Julie's marriage, they lived in Edinburgh."

"I thought they always lived at Soldier's Leap," Anabelle burst out, unable to contain her surprise.

"No. But those were happy years, despite their frugal lifestyle. Things might have continued that way, but Irving booked passage on *The Titanic* and was lost at sea."

"Is that when William's parents changed their mind?"

"Aye, no other male heirs existed. Irving Campbell had lived a riotous life, even getting one of the maids in the family way. The laird was most relieved to reinstate his son by the time Irving passed."

Dad, who'd been quiet through Erica's revelations, closed the last of the albums. Meeting Erica, a connection to his grandparents, appeared to light a fire inside him, and he peppered her with questions. And Erica, bless her, did her best to fill the gaps in their history.

Meanwhile, delicious scents wafted through the kitchen from the slow cooker beside the sink, and Anabelle's stomach growled so loudly that everyone looked at her. Heat flooded her neck and cheeks.

"I'm glad you're hungry." Hank checked his watch. "And the food is ready." As he rose from the table where he'd sat watching Erica and Dad with a half-smile, a timer buzzed.

Hank crossed the room. "Are you at a good stopping place, Erica?" He opened the oven and removed a casserole dish, then turned off the crockpot.

"Aye. I think I've given Pierce much to think about." Erica removed several photos from their sleeves. "I'll make copies of these for you. I must say, it's lovely to discover family after so many years."

Anabelle and Brodie set the table, and Hank blessed the food. While they ate, Anabelle asked, "Do you know about the secret room at Soldier's Leap?"

Erica looked down, then set her food aside. "Aye. They built it to hold mass after the Reformation, then hid several family members inside who fought during the Jacobite uprisings."

"Did they escape?"

"All the way to the American colonies." Erica nodded. "Those were difficult times for Scotland."

"So, our family was Catholic?" Anabelle asked. For some reason, she always assumed they switched to Protestantism during the Reformation.

"For a time, they held out, until it became too difficult for them to worship."

"Is that why they fought to place a Stewart king back on the throne, rather than keep a German one?"

"Aye. It's what we've been taught anyway. You forget that clan chiefs wielded much power back then. If he supported the Stewarts, the clan did as well."

Anabelle sighed with relief. "My imagination sometimes runs away with me. For a hot minute, I'd almost convinced myself the family had locked a mad relative up there."

"Families tend to keep quiet about things like that. To be honest, that was the conclusion I'd drawn as well." Dad patted her arm. "I wish Mother had lived to see this day," Dad added, his eyes wistful.

"How do you know that she's unaware, Pierce? God works in mysterious ways. I believe He led Anabelle and Eliza to our shop." Erica clicked her tongue.

"I agree," Mother said. "Coincidences like this are rare."

"I like to think so." Erica busied herself, clearing the table when they finished eating.

Anabelle rose to assist her. "I'll do the washing up."

"Nonsense." Erica firmly shook her head. "I can do it in half the time."

Conversation switched to the dogs, and before long, it was time to go.

"Thank you for such a delightful meal, but we'd best be on our way," Mother said.

"Aye. We will speak soon," Dad agreed.

Anabelle fetched Daisy and clipped on her lead.

"You must come back soon and bring Daisy," Erica said. "The dogs enjoyed their play date."

"We will. And be on the lookout for a wedding invitation," Mother said at the door when she hugged Erica goodbye. "The Queen of England will be in attendance."

Anabelle pressed her lips together when she caught the swift glance Erica exchanged with Hank. "We understand if you're busy," Anabelle added to ease any pressure Erica or Hank might feel.

"It is not that. We are entering our second busiest season of the year," Erica explained.

"If you can carve out the time, we'd love to have you," Mother said, taking Dad's arm.

When the front door closed behind them, Anabelle's parents climbed into the back seat while Brodie opened the passenger door, but detained Anabelle from sliding onto the seat. "Erica and Hank might not be able to afford closing their shop."

Though spotlessly clean, Erica and Hank's home lacked modern updates. Anabelle mulled over Brodie's comment on the drive home. If they offered financial remuneration so Erica and Hank could attend, could they do so without offending them?

Anabelle's arm ached as she rounded Soldier's Leap just after dawn the next morning, Daisy dragging her by the lead. On reaching the porch, a large arrangement of purple lupins and yellow flags stood on the stoop by the door. Her heart lurched, and a cold shiver sprinted through her core.

Not again.

Daisy tugged on her leash and propelled Anabelle up the shallow steps to sniff the arrangement. As if sensing Anabelle's horror, she looked up at her, then growled low in her throat at the blooms.

"You're right, my furry friend. Those flowers are trouble." Anabelle rang the local constabulary while her temper bubbled just under the surface.

"Sterling Police," a man answered.

"DI Maxwell, please. It's Anabelle Dewhurst." Her voice trembled, but she pulled herself together.

A click from the other end. "Anabelle," Finn said through the receiver.

"I have another bouquet."

"Is there a note?" he asked.

"It appears so."

"Don't touch anything. I'll send someone over with a fingerprint kit."

"Thank you." She hung up, skirted the massive arrangement, and punched in the house code, dragging Daisy past her latest "gift."

Unease crawled up her spine. She had followed the detective's instructions and ceased wearing her engagement ring, but it hadn't worked.

Temper frothed at the rim of her patience, but a stray thought stopped her from lashing out. Why hadn't movement triggered the alarm and relayed the information to her watch? Had this perverted stalker found dead spots on the cameras and used them to his advantage? If so, it must be someone familiar enough with the site to study their options.

She slammed the front door. Enough was enough. By George, she'd have a camera incorporated inside her porch light. Then she'd catch that stalker red-handed.

"Come on, Daisy. Let's have breakfast." Anabelle unclipped the dog's lead and marched across the ballroom to the corridor beyond, Daisy padding behind her.

When she entered the dining room, complete with its galley kitchen, she found her parents at the table with one of Joanna's carts parked between their chairs. Joanna, bless her, prepared all her parents' meals. That they paid for the service, Anabelle did not doubt, but it ruffled her that Mother and Dad did not fend for themselves.

Daisy whined and pressed against her leg. "Come on, girl. Let's get you something to eat."

Still scowling from her find on the front steps, Anabelle opened a container of dog food and filled Daisy's dish, then washed her hands, the instant hot water almost scalding her skin. She yelped, then shut off the tap, and retrieved a bowl and cutlery from the cabinets, while Daisy gobbled happily at her meal.

Anabelle nudged the cupboard door with her shoulder with a bit too much force. It banged as she poured a bowl of Shreddies, then added milk from the fridge.

"What has you so out of sorts?" Mother asked when Anabelle joined her parents a moment later.

"I'm sorry. That stalker left me another bouquet. I found it just now when I returned with Daisy."

"Oh, dear." Mother closed her eyes.

"Did you call the police?" Dad set down his cutlery and rose to his feet.

"They're on their way."

"I assume there's a note?" Mother's voice wobbled, and she, too, set her breakfast aside, her face pale.

"Yes." Anabelle set her bowl on the table.

"What did it say?" Dad's brows drew together.

"I don't know. I didn't touch it. DI Maxwell intends to have everything fingerprinted."

Her parents digested that in silence and that secret way they had of communicating transferred between them. Anabelle didn't need an interpreter this time to know what they were thinking. They wanted her well away from Soldier's Leap. But that was not going to happen. She had no intention of letting that creeper run her off. The police would find him. The stalker couldn't evade them for long.

Anabelle bowed her head and blessed her food, took two bites, and promptly lost her appetite.

"Anabelle." Mother fiddled with her crockery. "Perhaps it would be best if you—"

"Mother, I'm not quitting my job; Genesis must sack me before I'd leave. I love what I do," Anabelle snapped and was instantly contrite. "I'm sorry."

"Nonsense. It's perfectly understandable considering the circumstances." Dad moved to her side and rested a hand on her shoulder in silent support.

Tears burned her eyes.

"I'll be outside in the back garden until the police arrive." Anabelle stood. She needed to collect herself before the questioning began.

"Of course, darling." Mother still looked somewhat shell-shocked, but at least she had left off insisting that Anabelle leave her job.

Anabelle bent and kissed her mother's cheek. When she started for the door, Daisy lifted her head off her paws and whined. Anabelle halted, mid-step. "I'm sorry, love, but I can't take you to work. Tara's allergic."

"I've got her," Dad said. "She senses that something's wrong."

"Thanks." Anabelle blew him a kiss.

He winked at her, then whistled for Daisy as he stepped into the kitchen and opened a jar on the worktop. Daisy bolted toward him when she heard the sound of her treat jar. She sat at Dad's feet, ears cocked and brown eyes focused on his hand.

Biting back a smile, Anabelle headed down the corridor to the library, a massive space that ran two-thirds of the house's depth. She accessed the exterior door and entered the family's private, walled garden.

The dew-laden sod soaked through her shoes by the time she reached the bridge where Brodie proposed. Resting her elbows on the railing, she stared at her reflection while the trickling fountain soothed her lacerated spirit.

The police would sort this. They'd catch this fellow, and life would return to normal . . .

She exhaled and purposely replayed Brodie's proposal, allowing her most joy-filled moments to supersede the delivery of yet another bouquet. Closing her eyes, she relived the sight of the Japanese lanterns and flower petals glowing under the rising moon. Even her ring arcing through the air and plopping into the pond shoved aside the fear from the frightened corners of her heart. That kiss of all kisses . . . She sighed.

Even Gerald's grumpy yell from the window, warmed and grounded her.

She and Brodie would start their life together when this reno culminated. The long hours that had her tumbling into bed most nights in a chronic state of exhaustion, rousing to an alarm five hours later, all of that would end.

Though she adored Soldier's Leap, the reno provided little time to plan their wedding. Good thing they hadn't set a date, or Grandmama would meddle and make demands.

Neither she nor Brodie cared for society events, and a simple wedding in the small Cotswold village church suited them perfectly. Unfortunately, the Queen's attendance negated that, which meant pomp and circumstance were in her and Brodie's future when they said their I do's. She sighed and pushed away from the railing.

Eloping had never appealed more.

Chapter 28

A loud wailing drew Brodie's attention, and he glanced out his office window just as a yellow and blue police car parked in front of the family entrance. His heart somersaulted, and he rose to his feet as vehicle doors slammed, cutting off the siren. Both detectives disappeared from his line of vision.

Anabelle.

He rushed to the corridor and ran past Hugo, one of Mick's crew members.

"Brodie, hold up."

Halting, he faced the man, impatience simmering. He didn't have time for this. Something had happened to Anabelle.

"We need to handle touch-ups in the music room where the leafing's bubbled." Hugo shifted. "Anabelle said it was all right."

Then what was the fellow talking to him for?

Some of Brodie's frustration must have shown on his face for Hugo added, "We can't get in. The code's been changed."

"Have Mick ring her to let you in." Pivoting, Brodie exited the building and jogged across the drive. He'd not be sharing that the Dewhurst's had added extra security since Anabelle's "secret admirer" had not backed down.

When Brodie reached the family entrance, he found two gloved policemen dusting the doorknob, along with a vase of flowers.

"Did you find prints?" he asked.

One of the coppers paused. "You know I can't tell you anything," he said.

"Brodie," Anabelle called.

Pivoting on his heel, he found her standing beside the path that rounded the house. His breathing settled.

Anabelle was okay.

The tightness in his shoulders eased somewhat, and his gaze drank in her brown hair and pale, but resolute, face framed by darkly lashed blue eyes.

She halted before him and held out her hand. "I want my ring back."

"A little demanding, this morning, aren't we?" he asked in an attempt to lighten the atmosphere.

"I'm serious, Brodie. I've followed everyone's counsel, and it's gotten me nowhere." Anabelle indicated her latest floral arrangement the police were actively dusting.

"Removing my ring to appease that lunatic's demands hasn't made a bit of difference. This person," Anabelle spat the word like she'd eaten something rotten, "hasn't stopped."

"Did the cops say anything to you?" Brodie shifted to watch the officers at work.

"No. They're still busy fingerprinting and have the note to be analyzed."

"I doubt he left clues. This fellow is canny and organized." Brodie folded his arms.

"I agree, but it never pays to give way to bullies. That's why I want my ring back." She stuck out her chin, and her eyes glinted with challenge.

Metal clanked, and they turned in unison as Mick and Hugo approached, each carrying a ladder and a bag of supplies.

Anabelle frowned. Brodie could hardly blame her. The two men couldn't have picked a worse time to appear.

"We're here to touch up the gilding in the music room." Mick leaned his ladder against the house's limestone exterior. "What's all this?" He indicated the policemen.

"Just a bit of bother. Come around the side, and I'll let you in." Anabelle motioned for Mick and Hugo to follow her.

Brodie accompanied them, bringing up the rear. "Is anyone else from your crew on their way?"

"No. Hugo and I can cover this by ourselves," Mick said.

Anabelle unlocked the Archive Room's exterior door and led them into the adjoining music room.

Mick immediately busied himself laying out tarps, while Hugo set up the ladders.

"When you finish, could you exit the way you came?" Anabelle asked.

The doors locked automatically now, and Anabelle needn't worry about hanging around to lock up after them.

"Why are the police here again?" Mick asked as he retrieved his scraper and brushes from his canvas bag.

"A suspicious delivery arrived, and the police are checking it for fingerprints." Anabelle flicked her hand through the air in a nonchalant fashion.

Mick nodded. "You can never be too careful."

Hugo didn't comment. Instead, he climbed his ladder to inspect the bubbled gilding which ran along the bay window's alcove, then stared at Anabelle until she and Brodie departed. Anabelle shuddered when they were out of hearing. "That fellow creeps me out."

Brodie slid his arm around her shoulders and kissed her cheek as they crunched across the gravel drive on their way to the business offices. Clouds scudded overhead and blotted the sun as they stopped outside the external entrance.

"I downloaded an app with a countdown on my mobile," he commented to get her mind off the stalker's most recent gift.

"What for?" Anabelle's mouth ticked up a notch, giving him the notion that she had a good idea as to what he meant. "Why do you need a countdown?" She batted her lashes.

"I'll leave that for you to figure out," He turned the knob, but his gaze dropped to her lips, then slid away. "Just so you know, November eighth sounds good to me. Back to the grind." He held the door for her, then shoved his hands in his trouser pockets as Anabelle moved past him to her and Tara's office.

At the doorway, she paused, her blue eyes glinting at him over her shoulder. "No ring. No wedding planning tomorrow night. Ta." Anabelle wiggled her fingers, then disappeared inside.

Shaking his head, Brodie returned to work, a grin splitting his face. Jings, he loved that sassy mouth of hers. As he booted up his computer, his thoughts snagged on Anabelle's recent delivery, and his mind niggled with disquiet. She might play down this stalker business, but the cad had not relented, even after Anabelle cooperated and removed her engagement ring.

Brodie lifted a mechanical pencil and flipped it between his fingers. Back and forth. Back and forth.

What would that loony demand next?

Chapter 29

Distant banging disturbed Anabelle's sleep. Groggily, she rolled over and checked her bedside clock, then turned on her side and tucked the duvet up to her chin.

More bangs.

Daisy growled, then padded across the room.

Anabelle flipped onto her stomach and burrowed under her pillow. What was Randy doing at this hour? Why couldn't he wait until morning to make repairs? Every time she dozed off, another round of thumps sounded, this time, more muffled than before.

At length, she slept, dreaming of Brodie and a house in the woods, with three pink pigs surrounded by gingerbread walls and a giant wolf huffing and puffing.

Heavy breathing as the wolf drew near—and sniffed. Anabelle stirred. *Daisy?* Anabelle rolled to her opposite side.

A few seconds later, the breathing intensified. Human breathing. She opened her eyes to find a shadowy, hooded figure at her bedside.

Her heart skittered, and the hairs on her neck and arms lifted. Not Daisy. A person.

A weapon. She needed a weapon.

"You told me you loved me," a voice rasped. Then they touched her face.

Anabelle screamed and bolted upright, swinging her pillow like a battering ram and hitting the sniffer in the chest. The hooded figure dashed into the door, grappled with the lock, and sped into the corridor.

"Daisy." Anabelle leaped out of bed and yanked the light off her nightstand, ripping the cord from the wall in her haste and arming herself with the only protection available.

Where was Daisy? Why hadn't she barked? Some guard dog.

Anabelle's teeth chattered as she rounded the bed to the opposite nightstand, almost knocking the lamp over as she fumbled for her mobile and jabbed Brodie's icon.

"Anabelle?"

"B-Brodie," she stuttered, still holding the lamp in her opposite hand, she moved about the suite, switching on all the lights, then bolted the door the stalker had left wide during his escape. Holding the lamp before her like a lance, she inspected the sitting room, then checked behind the sofa, console, and desk—in case the fellow had an accomplice.

"It's one in the morning. Is this about getting your ring back? You're breathing into the mouthpiece like you've run a marathon."

"Someone was just in my room." Her voice trembled, and she forced herself to take a deep breath. To slow her thoughts and exhale. Then she drew in another lungful of air.

"Any chance it was your parents?" Trust Brodie to cover all his bases. Most of the time, she admired his pragmatic mind. But this time, his practical questioning irritated her.

She opened her mouth to snap at him, but his bedclothes rustled, and she heard the zip of his trousers, and bit back the hasty words. Her fellow might be calm on the surface, but he wasn't fooling her. Brodie was coming over to make sure she was okay.

"My parents don't lean over me when I sleep and sniff my face." Anabelle inhaled shakily, then expelled a heavy breath.

"He touched your face?" Brodie growled, his veneer of calm cracking.

"He touched my face," she repeated, her hands now shaking with reaction. Her numbed fingers scrabbled for her mobile. Unable to hold on, she dropped it onto the duvet. Rummaging about, she picked it up again, needing the anchor of his voice to keep her sane.

"Did you update the police?" Brodie asked.

"Not yet." Satisfied that no one was in her sitting room, Anabelle doubled back to the bedroom and repeated the process, poking behind the armoire and the draperies.

"Ring them, then get dressed. I'm on my way."

If Brodie spoke to her like this at any other time, she'd remind him that in their personal relationship, he wasn't her boss. But right now, she needed him.

She nodded, though he couldn't see her. "Be careful, Brodie. He could still be in the house. I should warn my parents as well."

"You might suggest that they bolt their bedroom door." Brodie paused, then said in a rush, "Please wait until I arrive before you snoop around."

"Snoop around?" she repeated, her brows drawing together.

"When you're scared, you go into action mode. Wait for me, okay? I don't want anything to happen to you." He expelled a gruff cough. "I mean it, lass. Be careful."

Attacking a known foe was one thing, but chasing down an unhinged stalker? No thank you. She'd happily wait for Brodie's arrival. "I need to let you in." The idea of leaving her room with that lunatic running free creeped her out.

"Stay put. I know the new security code. Do you want me to talk to you until I arrive?"

"No." *Yes.* Why couldn't she admit how much this incident affected her?

"All right then, I'll be there in two shakes."

The call ended. Anabelle stared at the screen for a second while her sluggish brain processed. Dad. I need to ring Dad. She punched his name on speed dial.

Please, Daddy. Please pick up.

Her father answered on the third ring. "Anabelle? Is something the matter?"

"We've had an intruder. Lock your bedroom suite until the police arrive." She gripped the mobile tightly.

"I'm coming."

"No, Dad. You're at the opposite end of the corridor, and we have no idea if he's still in the house. It's safer if we both lock our doors. Besides, you can't leave Mother. She took one of her pills, didn't she?"

"Yes. It would take an atomic blast to rouse her."

"It's a good thing that she did. At least she'll get some rest." As a joke, it was feeble at best. "Is Daisy with you?" she asked, wondering again where the dog had gone.

"I assume she's not with you, either?" Dad sounded even more alarmed.

"Negative." Anabelle shook her head. Perhaps she'd chased the intruder and bit him. "I need to call the police. Brodie's on his way over. We'll knock on your bedroom door when the coast is clear." She disconnected before her father asked any more questions or changed his mind, then she rang Brodie's cousin.

"Maxwell." The detective's sleepy voice sounded through the line.

"It's Anabelle Dewhurst. Someone just invaded my bedroom. I think it was the stalker."

"Don't touch anything. I'm on my way."

Her screen went dark for the third time. Still holding the lamp and jumping at every shadow, Anabelle drew on a pair of joggers with one hand, then set the lamp on the bed and hastily slid a wool jumper over her head, then grasped the lamp once more. She had just slid into her trainers when someone knocked on her sitting room door.

"Lass, it's me." Brodie's voice reached her from the opposite side of the double doors, the only safe harbor in this night of terror.

She raced across the room, drew back the bolt, and latched onto him like a barnacle to a pilon. He held her tight, his comforting arms banding about her as he carried her to the overstuffed armchair. He sat, keeping her on his lap, then tried to loosen her grip. She was having none of it and clutched him even more fiercely. He couldn't pry her loose if he tried.

"'Tis all right, lass. I've got ye." He smoothed a hand over her hair, then buried his face in her neck, and kissed the skin just below her ear.

"When I woke up, he was breathing over me and muttering. I was so frightened, I couldn't move." She hiccupped, going entirely to pieces as she sobbed out the story. "But when he touched my face, I clobbered him with my pillow."

Brodie kissed her again, his hand rubbing her back, much as her father had comforted her when she had a bad dream.

"Good thinking. You startled him. Do you remember what he said?" Brodie asked.

"Umm. . ." Anabelle shuddered as the stalker's words replayed in her head. "He whispered. Rasped actually. 'You said you loved me.'"

Brodie growled, and his grip tightened to the edge of bruising.

"Do you know how he got inside? The exterior doors were bolted, and the alarm never went off," she asked with her face tucked under his chin. If she could have climbed under his skin to feel safer, she'd have tried.

"That doesn't always stop professional burglars." Brodie rubbed her back some more. "Do you suppose he was referring to the text you sent?"

Anabelle stiffened. "I think you're right." Trust Brodie to keep every detail straight.

"What's Finn's ETA?" He shifted her to his other thigh.

"Another fifteen minutes."

Brodie set her off his lap and pushed out of the chair. Taking her hand, he checked the windows and both doors to the corridor.

"The creeper left through my bedroom door. I bolted it behind him."

"Everything else is locked, and the window alarms don't appear tampered with." Brodie entered the adjoining bedroom and followed the same procedure. "I don't get it." He rubbed his neck, his tone puzzled.

Stepping into the bathroom, Brodie glanced around, then headed into the dressing room beyond. "Well, that answers one of our questions. How did you sleep through this?" He indicated something beyond her field of vision.

She joined him and stared in horror at the human-sized hole in her dressing room wall. "It was real. I heard hammering, but I was so out of it, I thought it was Randy." Her shaking increased, and she rubbed the back of her arms.

"Do you have a torch?" he asked.

"I do." Anabelle retrieved it from the top drawer of her bureau near the bed. Upon returning to the closet, she scanned the broken plaster and sighed in relief when she saw that Granny and her siblings' names remained undisturbed. "Here you go." She passed him the light.

Leading with the torch, Brodie stuck his head inside the opening and flashed the light up the spiral stairwell that connected the dressing room to the attic. "He's not hiding in here at any rate."

Anabelle's mobile rang, and she stared at the unknown number, her heart pounding like hail on tarmac. "Brodie, what if it's the stalker?"

"Let me answer." Brodie took her mobile and hit the speaker. "Who's this?" he demanded.

"DS Ogilvie. Maxwell and I understand there's been a break-in?"

"Aye. Are you here?" Brodie's eyes glinted like obsidian under the overhead fixture.

"Yes."

"Give me a minute, and I'll let you in." Brodie returned her mobile. "We need to change out your phone. When we do, it's probably a good idea not to give anyone your new number until this stalker is caught."

"What about the team? I'll need a way for them to contact me on the job site."

"I'll get you a burner for work, one you can leave at the office. We don't know everyone on the crews. This lunatic could even be a member of Randy's, Mick's, or Mr. Mellencamp's teams."

Brodie had a point. Until the police narrowed the suspects, she couldn't trust any of them.

"Will you be all right if I leave you here?" he asked.

"I'm coming with you. If they find the culprit, I want to be there."

They rode the lift to the ground floor, then cut through the ballroom to reach the entrance, with Anabelle rushing to keep pace with Brodie's long stride. "Did you see Daisy when you came upstairs?"

"No. Shouldn't she be with you?"

"Yes." Though Anabelle hadn't owned Daisy for long, she loved that dog and prayed no harm had come to her.

"Once the police have a look around, I'll find her." Brodie kissed her temple.

"Thank you. It's not like her to disappear." Anabelle peered through the peephole and nodded for Brodie to disengage the alarm before she let the police inside.

The detectives crossed the threshold, looking slightly disheveled after being roused from sleep.

"Thank you for coming so late." Their presence filled her with relief.

"What can you tell us about this perpetrator?" Finn asked.

Standing in the foyer, Anabelle updated the detectives on the evening's event and how the stalker reached her room.

"If you lead the way, we'll start in the dressing room," Finn said.

Anabelle directed them upstairs to her suite, her hand gripped in Brodie's.

Halting before the wall in question, Ogilvie glanced at Anabelle. "Surely, the noise woke you."

Brodie's lips twitched, and Anabelle resisted elbowing him. Instead, she bit out, "This area is two rooms away from where I sleep. The walls are insulated and made of plaster, not simple plasterboard, both of which muffle a great deal of sound."

Ogilvie's lack of social skills surfaced every time he opened his mouth. Why had the police hired him? Was the district short on cops?

"Where does this lead?" Finn indicated the rusty circular stairs inside the wall.

"The attic," Anabelle said.

Finn examined the hole. "We're not crawling through this hole; we'll take the attic stairs at the end of the corridor. It's more comfortable."

Anabelle grinned, grateful for Finn's dry humor. "Perhaps DS Ogilvie would like to meet us there? That way, all the escape routes are covered."

Brodie made a strangling noise that sounded a lot like a laugh.

Straight-faced as ever, Finn nodded. "You make a valid point. Ogilvie, follow the intruder's trail, and we'll meet you upstairs."

Ogilvie sputtered.

"Here's a torch." Brodie tossed the copper a flashlight.

Anabelle led the way, tromping up the attic staircase at the end of the corridor.

When they reached the top of the house, Finn glanced around. "When we were up here before, we were hunting for wires. I didn't walk the entire area. Does this space cover just the family wing?"

"The entire house." Brodie rubbed his forehead. "You're thinking the intruder accessed Anabelle's bedroom from the public side. I don't know why I didn't think of that."

"Is there a way to block the attic's stairwell access from the corridor?" Finn ventured further into the barnlike space.

"Not unless I break fire codes," Brodie said. "We'll install alarms and cameras in both stairwells, with the controls on the family side of the house. That way, anyone who enters the attic must have a code, or a silent alarm will be triggered. Should the security team link the alarm to the police station as well?"

"Aye." Finn moved to the window and glanced out into the night. "I wonder why the perp broke through that wall? Why not access Miss Dewhurst's rooms via the corridor?"

"He probably tried that first, but I keep my bedroom door bolted." Despite her wool jumper, Anabelle rubbed the back of her arms, unable to warm up. Why had the stalker broken into her room? Knocking through a wall spoke of desperation. Had he intended an abduction?

Ogilvie shouted from inside the hidden stairwell. "There's a dog in here. She's in a bad way."

Chapter 30

Brodie frowned at the various printouts Anabelle laid between them on the library's tufted sofa. They'd retreated there after supper to iron out wedding details.

He was still on edge after three days had passed with the police on high alert, but the stalker had not returned to Soldier's Leap. Nor had he left any fingerprints. Brodie fumed at the lack of progress after the creeper's nocturnal visit to Anabelle's room.

He glanced at where Daisy lay on her dog bed near Anabelle's feet on the library floor. Poor thing. She'd gone after the intruder and was repeatedly clobbered with a metal object, likely a prybar. If the cops ever caught that stalker, he'd like nothing better than to use it on the fellow himself for attacking Anabelle's dog.

After a stint at the veterinary hospital, Daisy returned, still off balance from a concussion, severe bruising, and sporting a shaved patch in her beautiful coat where a gash had required stitches.

"I vote that we elope." Brodie pushed the papers aside. "Weddings are supposed to be joyful occasions, but Lady Barbara's list is going to suck out all our happiness."

He lifted the printout and read aloud, "Trumpeters to announce our entrance at the reception? Where does your gran get her ideas?"

"Grandmama Poole has very high standards. When she makes a request, she expects everyone to jump and do her bidding."

"Do you want trumpeters?" Brodie raised both brows.

"Heavens, no."

"Excellent. No trumpeters. Our wedding is not a parade or a royal event." Brodie crossed out the item, then scanned the page even further. "A morning suit," he snorted. "My ancestors would haunt me if I wore one to a wedding."

"Would you settle for a piper rather than trumpeters?"

"I might." He winked. "That would be a lot more entertaining, especially if we surprised your grandmother with one."

"She'd never let you live that down."

"A five-tiered wedding cake? How many guests does she expect?" He slapped the paper onto his lap. "If she keeps this up, I'll insist that we serve haggis at the reception."

Anabelle wrinkled her nose. "That's a hard no for me."

"You're marrying into a Highland family. Trust me, you'll see heaps of Scottish dishes when we visit my parents." He paused, waiting for Anabelle to share her ideas. When none seemed forthcoming, he asked, "What about you, lass? Isn't it customary for the bride to have preferences? My cousin, Sorcha, has an entire mood board for hers, and she's only seventeen."

"I never thought I'd have an option. Grandmama always shanghais our family events."

"I'm beginning to see why your father stays at High Ridge." Brodie's dry tone brought a smile to Anabelle's face.

"Dad refuses to place Mother in an uncomfortable position."

"Smart fellow." Brodie snapped his fingers. "I've got it. Let's request a full-on Scottish wedding and reception at Kirkton Glen."

"Is that where you'd like to be married?" Anabelle's blue eyes rounded with curiosity.

"I don't much care where we say our I do's." He lifted Anabelle's hand and stared at her bare fourth finger. They were engaged, but few people had any clue because of the stalker's demands.

Would the police ever catch that fellow? Usually, stalkers grew more disorganized as things escalated, but this creeper never lowered his guard. He knew every camera's dead spot and never tripped an alarm. That in itself worried him.

Brodie glanced at Anabelle. She sat with her legs tucked under her, poring over her grandmother's lists. The lass had asked for very little. At least he could grant her the one thing she desired tonight, regardless of how far they progressed with this wedding debacle.

Reaching inside his pocket, he tugged out her ring and slid onto his knees. "Anabelle, you were right, lass. You never should have removed your engagement ring. Will you do me the very great honor of accepting it back?"

"Is this a proposal?" Anabelle set aside her paper and uncurled her legs.

"You want another one?" Brodie's brain skidded, and he rubbed his chin, thinking fast. "Should I spout poetry?"

"Brodie Maxwell quoting poetry?" She smirked. "I have to see that with my own eyes."

"Do you doubt my ability? I know a few verses." He rose and struck a theatrical pose.

"O my Luve's like a red, red rose
That's newly sprung in June;
O my Luve is like the melodie
That's sweetly play'd in tune . . ."

"You Scots and your Robert Burns." Anabelle's mouth dented at one corner.

"You dare criticize the best poet this world has ever known?" Brodie placed both hands over his heart as though mortally wounded.

"Robert Burns is a bit difficult to understand these days," she pointed out.

"That poem was apropos. Didn't ye notice the wee bit about the melody played in tune? That reminded me of you at the piano. Pure genius."

"I'll grant you that, but I'm not overly fond of roses."

"Tulips aren't as romantic." He leaned in and whispered, "But I know two lips that strike all sorts of romantic notions in my head."

Anabelle pushed him away. "When you finish clowning around, may I have my ring?"

"Aye." He sobered. "Sorry." He tugged her to her feet, his eyes drinking in this wonderful woman, his elixir of life. *Och*, but he loved her something fierce. Keeping her hand in his, he slid the three-karat stone, surrounded by blue diamonds, onto her finger. "There, lass. It's back where it belongs."

Anabelle extended her hand and gazed at the ring.

The gemstones flashed fire under the light like Anabelle herself. A lump filled his throat, and he kissed her hand, then tucked her against his chest and held her close. Soldier's Leap had grown on him, but strange events stalked Anabelle within its walls. The sooner he got her away from this place, the better he'd feel.

Lifting her chin, she gazed at him through her lashes. "Our engagement isn't complete without one of these." She pulled him down and pecked him chastely on the lips.

"You call that a kiss? Here's one to remember me by." He lowered his head, determined to keep it short, but the softness of her lips drained his brain like the scent of her lemon verbena shampoo—sweet with a bite, like Anabelle herself.

He buried his hands in her silky hair and nipped at her mouth until she wrapped her arms around his shoulders and deepened the kiss. A thousand suns flickered behind his lids and illuminated his soul. Moving his lips from hers, he trailed kisses along her jawline to her collarbone.

Anabelle stiffened in his arms, and he lifted his head to find Lady Huddleton standing in the doorway with Daisy moving toward her for a pet. *Och.* Brodie gave her a sheepish smile and dropped his arms.

"I didn't mean to interrupt." Lady H.'s eyes twinkled with amusement. "Anabelle, your father, and I are off to bed. Do you want Daisy in here, or would you prefer I move her to your room?"

"Leave her with me. She'll just whimper." Anabelle motioned for Daisy, who came and pressed against her. "Won't you, my girl?"

Daisy thumped her tail and nuzzled Anabelle's hand.

Thankfully, the alarm company arrived tomorrow to install additional cameras. With Daisy out of commission, Brodie hoped they would make up the difference and actually capture an image of the perp.

"Night, love." Lady Huddleton blew Anabelle a kiss. "Night, Brodie. Keep her safe."

"I intend to."

"Goodnight." Anabelle kept a straight face until Lady H.'s footsteps faded in the corridor. Then she snorted. "Care to wager that Dad will know all about her catching us?"

"That's a wager I'd most definitely lose."

Anabelle returned to the sofa, and Daisy settled back onto the cushion at her feet. "We still have more of Grandmama's notes to cover."

He set one cushion between them when he retook his seat to withstand the temptation of kissing her again. Lifting the discarded printout, he scanned Lady Barbara's mandates while Anabelle extended her arm and wiggled her ring under the lights.

"Like it?" he couldn't help asking.

"It's gorgeous. You have excellent taste." She gave him a sassy smile.

"Referring to yourself, eh? I agree." He ran his thumb across her cheekbone. "The blue diamonds reminded me of your eyes. Priceless and rare."

"When you talk like that, it makes me all gooey inside." She turned her face into his hand and kissed his palm, a wicked twinkle in her eye. "I do rather miss the green algae on my ring, though."

He chuckled. "Lass, I never know what's going to come out of your mouth."

"I'm serious. The night you proposed was the most romantic night of my life." A dreamy smile flirted with the corners of her lips.

"Wading about in a dark, freezing pond to find your engagement ring was romantic?"

"It was to me." The solemness of her expression bore testimony to her words.

"Me, too. We must be mad." Their eyes locked, and Brodie fought the urge to toss Lady Barbara's list in the bin and kiss her again.

Anabelle's eyes darkened, and she broke eye contact. "Before we change the subject entirely, what kind of wedding band do you prefer?"

"Surprise me." He didn't care what she purchased, as long as the world noted the band on his finger, and the commitment he held for the woman who put it there. He cleared his throat. "I know Lady Barbara runs your family's events, but humor me a moment. If you could have any venue, decor, flowers—anything at all, what would you choose?"

"Hmmm." Anabelle wrinkled her brow in concentration. "I certainly wouldn't have a five-tiered wedding cake or a huge guest list. I do have a thing for lighted punch fountains."

"What about flowers?"

"Tulips, but they're out of season. I wouldn't mind yellow flags. Bluebells or purple hydrangeas. Perhaps stephanotis and lily of the valleys, too."

"Yellow iris, eh?" A sudden inspiration seized him. "The flowers you mentioned are the colors of my clan's ancient tartan."

"Then let's plan our wedding around them. I'm rather excited to see you in your kilt."

"Ladies love a hairy sporran."

"I'm more into hairy legs, myself." Anabelle's eyes danced with the same naughty light as her mother's had a moment ago.

"Is that what you were watching when I stepped out of the pool?" He wiggled his brows.

"You wish." But a tell-tale blush crept up her neck and gave her away.

Holding his grin in check, Brodie marked off two items from Lady Barbara's list. "Flowers and colors. Done."

"You crossed out Grandmama's roses."

"She can get married again if she wants them in a bridal bouquet."

"You two are going to butt heads." Anabelle groaned.

"Has your dear Grandmama Poole never tangled with a Scotsman? We're notoriously stubborn."

"So is she," Anabelle grumbled.

"Lady Barbara has held your family hostage for far too long. I'm surprised you didn't stop her nonsense long ago."

"Grandmama pulls the royal card and steamrolls us all."

"Your grandmother's a good woman, but she's a bully. How did you deal with bullies in school?"

"I ignored them—mostly." Anabelle flushed and glanced away.

"Do I detect a story?" He touched her chin and drew her face toward him once more.

"Not much of one." She shrugged and refused to meet his eyes.

He leaned forward, anticipation mounting. "This should prove entertaining."

"Promise you'll still love me?" Anabelle scrunched her nose.

"Of course, I'll still love you."

"I was called to the headmaster's office when a new girl in our form pestered one of the younger girls."

"What happened?" He'd seen Anabelle in action a time or two and could only imagine what she'd done.

"I was the innocent party, I'll have you know. I *never* started things."

That might be true, but Anabelle had a way of finishing them. "What happened?"

"She pushed me when I stepped in to shield a first-year. Then she slapped me, so . . . I punched her in the face."

"Self-defense. No one can argue with that." Good for Anabelle. She'd never been a pushover.

"I broke her nose." Anabelle winced.

"You broke her nose?"

"Maybe?" Anabelle's voice went up an octave, and she wrapped her arms around one of the sofa pillows and hid her face.

Brodie tossed his head back and laughed. Wiping his eyes, he glanced at her flushed cheeks. "If you stood up to the school bully, why don't you stand up to your grandmother?"

"I can't talk back to her. It isn't proper."

"You can be polite and still get your point across. If you don't buckle, she'll treat you with greater respect." He snatched the pillow out of her hands and draped an arm around her. "After we marry, she will not determine what we do as a family. It's best if we start now on how we intend to proceed."

Her blue eyes rounded.

"I won't be impolite." He reassured her, then picked up the list. "What's next?" He purposely changed the subject. They had accomplished precious little thus far.

"The dress." Anabelle sighed.

"It says you need a gown with a five-meter train for the chapel. Is she expecting a cathedral wedding?"

"She might have mentioned it in passing." Anabelle bit her lip, then said in a rush, "I'd prefer to wear Julia's gown, if Erica can remove the stains."

"Then tell your grandmother, no." Brodie clicked the pen and crossed out the wedding gown with the massive train.

"What if Erica can't salvage it? You saw the dark marks. The gown's riddled with them."

"If anyone can remove stains from that lace, it'll be Erica. She has the greatest motivation possible—pride in her family and her business."

"True." Anabelle agreed.

"I hear a 'but' in there."

"Grandmama made an appointment in London for Mother and me to meet with a wedding gown designer in two weeks."

"Then we had best figure out our preferences before you go." Brodie tapped the paper. "As for your grandmother, a simple no will suffice."

"Easy for you to say," Anabelle grumbled. "She's not part of your family."

"Not yet," Brodie agreed, reaching over to cup her jaw. "But she won't run our family—unless we approve of her ideas."

Anabelle puffed out her cheeks, reminding him of a blowfish. "Grandmama has tentatively booked two cathedrals in Greater London for the ceremony."

"Why don't we get married at the chapel near High Ridge Hall?" he countered.

"Because, according to Grandmama . . ." Anabelle opened a separate page of her grandmother's notes and possible dates from the Queen's itinerary. "High Ridge is not easily accessible, which would make it difficult for Her Majesty to attend. She's at Balmoral until late October, along with several weekends in November, but has an appointment in London on Tuesday, the thirtieth of September. Grandmama strongly suggests that we marry then."

"We don't wrap up here until November. If we marry in September, we'd have to postpone our honeymoon."

Anabelle bit her lip as she flipped through the other available dates on Her Majesty's calendar. "The Queen is booked solid after that until next summer, save for two weekends in November."

"We're not pushing our wedding off an entire year." That would drive them both round the bend. Brodie raked his fingers through his hair. "What about Soldier's Leap as a venue? You love this place."

"I do, but . . . If it's all right with you, I'd prefer a different location, one without a stalker to mar our day."

"Agreed. That was insensitive of me. Sorry, lass." He drummed his fingers on the sofa arm. "Since the Queen is in the Highlands this autumn, why don't we marry at the chapel in Kirkton Glen? She and her security team can easily reach it from Balmoral."

"Brilliant." Anabelle beamed. "Would your mother be opposed to hosting a reception at Kirkton House? The grounds are lovely."

"I'll almost guarantee it will rain, but we can set up tents and outdoor heaters." He leaned back and crossed an ankle over his opposite knee. "Kirkton House is large enough to house our guests, but Dad's an introvert and would struggle with visitors for an extended period of time."

"Are there any hotels nearby?"

A fair question on Anabelle's part, he mused, rubbing his jaw. She had never visited Kirkton House, only his place in London, and was unfamiliar with the mountainous region where he'd been raised.

"Aye. We've one up the lane, but the road's unpaved and heavy going. They'd be better off at the hotel in Mhor or further afield on Loch Earn."

Anabelle added the information to her notebook, then glanced up. "What about food?"

"Mother uses a local caterer. I'm sure they're available."

"Do you have menu requests?" Anabelle poised her pen, ready to jot down his favorites.

"Other than haggis?" Brodie grinned, knowing that would get a good rise out of her.

"We are not serving haggis." She shook her head, her hair swinging around her shoulders.

"That'll be a hard sell." He kept a straight face, but inwardly chuckled at her appalled expression.

"I want pretty food. Haggis looks disgusting."

"All right, lass. I was just having a bit of fun with ye. I do want Cullen Skink, though. Do ye have anything against that?" *Please no.*

"No. It's delicious. Trust me, I won't keep you from your fish chowder. We can garnish it to dress it up." Anabelle added that to her notes.

"Is there anything else you feel strongly about?" he asked.

"The cake. I'd like a chocolate one with chocolate mousse and raspberry sauce filling." Her face lit as she mentioned the dessert they'd shared on their first date.

"Aye," he agreed, touched that she remembered.

"I didn't think you'd fight me on that," Anabelle's sassy smile deepened the dimple in her cheek.

"Ye'll not get any complaints from me." He pecked her lips. "Anything else?" *Please be done.*

"Nothing." Anabelle put her notebook aside.

"Brilliant. We now have parameters for our non-negotiables."

"Grandmama will fight you." Anabelle tilted her head, her voice ominous.

"She'll not be changing this." He'd dealt with demanding clients for ages and refused to allow Lady Barbara to sabotage their wedding.

"No one crosses her. She can be dreadfully unpleasant when she doesn't get her way." Her gaze implored him to reconsider.

"I won't be ugly, lass, but Lady Barbara will not be pushing us about." He slipped his arm around Anabelle and tossed Lady Barbara's list and calendar onto the coffee table. "This is our wedding, not hers. If you don't have strong views about her other suggestions, let her have her way."

"Negotiating?"

"Don't you know it." He chucked her under the chin, his eyes lingering for a moment on her lips.

"You're lucky that you aren't meeting with her in two weeks."

"That's where you're wrong, my lovely bride-to-be." He pulled her close and nestled her against his side. "I've a corporate appointment that coincides with your visit. We'll face Lady Barbara together. I have no intention of having you deal with her alone."

Chapter 31

Anabelle pushed away from the desk. "I'm taking lunch, Tara."

Tara glanced up from the Gantt chart on her screen. The pair of them were similarly dressed in dungarees and T-shirts, with Anabelle's hair pulled up into a messy bun, and Tara's shorter locks pinned back with clips.

"That's right, you have a fitting today."

"I do, and I'd better hurry or I'll exceed my break."

"Good luck. I'd love to see your dress sometime."

Anabelle spun, her eyebrows rising. "Really?"

"I adore fashion, wedding gowns especially. When a bride finds the right dress, it's nothing short of magical. Rather like finding the right pieces for a room."

"I'll remember that." While the two of them would never be more than cordial working professionals, Tara's eye for fashion might prove helpful.

Anabelle jogged down the corridor, pausing in the grand hall, her gaze scanning its transformation. The place stole her breath more than any sprint ever could. Under Brodie's expert management and the team's professional talents, they had turned Soldier's Leap into a showpiece, yet somehow retained its inviting spirit and home-like feel.

Glowing at the success they had achieved, she crossed to the family wing and punched in the code. The smaller foyer, a space no less grand than the one she had just exited, filled her with delight as she ran her hand over the newel post on the original staircase Brodie had incorporated into the family's living space.

Then, crossing her fingers, she stepped into the ballroom where Erica had set up a sewing station on the folding tables Anabelle had supplied for her.

"There you are." Erica bustled forward and kissed her cheek.

"I'd hoped to change before you arrived." Anabelle returned Erica's greeting.

"I left Hank in charge of the shop as I wanted to see the house before your fitting. Your mother accommodated me. I hope you don't mind."

"Of course not. Where is Mother?" Anabelle eyed the growing pile of boxes lining the far wall.

"She went upstairs for more boxes."

Last night, Anabelle and her mother boxed up the things she'd accumulated during her time in Scotland, the amassment of which proved quite shocking. Evidently, Mother had used the morning to bring them downstairs.

Anabelle fidgeted, debating how to broach a subject with her newly found cousin.

"What's bothering you?" Erica asked, accurately reading her body language.

"I wondered if you'd watch Daisy for me while I'm in London. It should only be a few days," Anabelle rushed. "Initially, I'd planned to take her with me, but since her injury—"

"Of course, I will take Daisy," Erica interrupted. "What is family for? I've been hoping she could visit us again. My dogs enjoyed her company. Hank and I will see to her needs."

"Oh, thank you." Anabelle sagged with relief.

Erica chuckled. "Daisy will be fine. We have a brilliant vet who lives nearby—should the need arise."

With the last of her worries put to rest, Anabelle turned her attention to the fitting.

"Should I put on a slip?" she asked.

"Yes. That will give me time to get everything ready." Erica tore off a paper towel from a roll and wiped down the first table.

"I'll be right back." Anabelle bypassed the boxes, then jogged up the stairs, almost knocking her mother over when she reached the top.

"Sorry." Anabelle steadied the load in her mother's arms.

"What's in this one? It's heavy," Mother asked.

"Crystal." Anabelle had gone a bit overboard when she visited a crystal showroom.

"Is this for future design projects?" Mother gave Anabelle a knowing look.

Anabelle bobbed her head. "Partly. I bought a pair of candlesticks for Jecca's wedding present. While I was there, I fell in love with a set of water goblets."

"I assume they were a good deal?" Mother's mouth curved, humor twinkling in her eyes.

"Not really, but they are to die for. I sent Cressida a picture of them, and she asked me to get her a set, too."

"Of course she did. You girls have similar tastes when it comes to art and furnishings. One would almost think you're related." Mother winked, then started down the stairs to add the box to the growing pile they were shipping home.

Smiling, Anabelle entered her suite. No one could miss the family resemblance between her, Wills, and Cressida. With just two and a half years between them, they acted more like triplets than siblings, staying in close touch and planning frequent trips together.

Changing into a tea-length slip, Anabelle snatched up her robe and returned to the ballroom.

"Perfect timing." Erica plugged in her machine.

"Why do I need another fitting?" Anabelle asked, a bit self-conscious wearing a robe in the vast, echoing space. Mother had warned Dad to stay clear for modesty's sake.

"Women often drop weight before they marry. I don't want one of my dresses hanging on you like a sack. This is a Seton gown, and I have a reputation to uphold." Erica held the gown for Anabelle.

She removed her robe and stepped into the dress, turning around so Erica could pin the back.

"I made a new lining with your measurements."

"What was wrong with the old one?"

"The silk shattered." Erica shook her head.

"Shattered? I'm unfamiliar with that terminology."

"The individual fibers in the fabric broke when I cleaned it. It's unusable." Erica's specs winked under the lights.

Anabelle examined the satin in the standing mirror Mother had doubtless removed from one of the bedrooms. "This fabric really flatters the lace."

"Aye." Using the tailor's tape, Erica moved around her, measuring her waist and bustline. "You *have* lost weight." Her comment sounded like an accusation. "You must eat."

"We've been so busy that I sometimes forget."

Erica tacked a few pins around her waist. "Fortunately, your shoulders and torso are similar in size to Julia's. And you are close to the same height. That's grand because the lace has no hem. Those scallops were finished without one. If you were any taller, you could not wear this."

Anabelle winced when a pin poked her through the material. *Breathe. Breathe. Breathe.*

"Don't bleed on the fabric." Erica undid the back and pressed a tissue to Anabelle's side.

Anabelle gripped the standing mirror for support, as the room spun around her. She couldn't pass out, but dark spots speckled her vision.

So focused on preserving the gown, Erica did not notice Anabelle's distress. Nor did she apologize for the jab.

Julia's gown. Anabelle's body went clammy. If she fell, she could tear this beautiful satin. Erica would pitch a fit if she dirtied the new lining. The image of tiny Erica scolding her made the lightheadedness subside.

Anabelle and needles were not besties. They always freaked her out. If needles and blood didn't turn her into such a simpleton, she could admit that Erica had the right of it. Skin healed. The satin might not recover.

"There. That looks better. Not so sloppy around the waist." Erica stepped back. She would not attach the lining until the lace stains were removed.

Anabelle twisted her upper torso, examining the tucks. "It's perfect."

Heels clicked across the marble floor as Mother joined her, both hands pressed to her heart. "The satin is exquisite and almost pretty enough to wear on its own."

"Aye." Erica nodded, a gleam of satisfaction in her bespeckled eyes. "This material has a brighter sheen than the original and will make the lace pop even more. I just hope I can remove the yellowing."

Anabelle bit her bottom lip and forced herself not to place all her hopes on Erica's success. Her cousin was doing her best, but all her preliminary work might be wasted unless those stains gave up their hold on Julia's lace.

"You look at me with those big hopeful eyes. Never fear. I still have a few tricks up my sleeve. Come. I want you to see the dress Louisa made."

The three of them approached where Erica had laid the gown on one of the tables. Save for a slight yellowing in the middle of the skirt, the lace appeared new. Then, with Mother's help, Erica set the gown over Anabelle's head and draped it into place, fanning out the train.

Erica tilted her head. "The cap sleeves on the liner are too long." Like a small bird of prey, Erica attacked the gown and pinned the offending satin into its proper place.

Clucking her tongue, Erica circled, her eyes narrowed. "That peephole in the back has proven most troublesome. It isn't lying right. Hmmm." She studied the lace some more. "If I remove two roses, that bulge will smooth out."

"Won't that unravel the lace?" Mother eyed the material in question, her tone doubtful.

"I'll finish off the ends." A few more tucks, then Erica unfastened the dress and liner.

Anabelle shivered as she undressed, the marble floor cold against her bare feet. Mother handed Anabelle her robe.

"Thank you." She tied the belt around her waist, then started across the room.

"Where are you going, young lady?" Erica called after her.

Anabelle glanced at her mother, then back to Erica. "Upstairs to change into my work clothes?"

"No. No. No. I will take care of this now, while I am here." Erica puffed out her chest like a small bird scolding a wayward chick.

Anabelle exchanged an amused glance with her mother. Tiny Erica would give Grandmama Poole a challenge if the two ever met. When it came to her gowns, Erica was in command.

"I'll fetch a few more boxes." Mother pointed toward the stairs, but she delayed her departure, hovering over the dress as Erica laid the liner on the sewing table.

"You go." Erica pointed to Mother. "Anabelle stays down here."

"While you're sewing, do you mind if I play the piano? It's just across the corridor." Anabelle pointed toward the far end of the ballroom where the music room lay.

"That's grand. I'll get you when I finish."

Anabelle made her escape before Erica called her back on some pretext or other.

"Is it possible to save the lace you remove from the back?" Mother's voice carried across the corridor to the music room.

"Why?" Erica's one-word response sounded somewhat affronted.

"I'd like to add it to Anabelle's veil."

"I will see this veil before we decide." Erica harrumphed.

"Adding the bobbin lace will tie the ensemble together." Mother countered.

"Seed pearls on the hem are a better option." Erica folded her arms.

Anabelle closed her ears. Let Mother and Erica spar over the veil. She didn't give a fig about it, one way or the other, save that it attached to the Poole tiara, a tiara worn by every bride in her family for the last two hundred years.

And Anabelle intended to do the same.

Chapter 32

I TIPTOE UPSTAIRS, intent on crossing the attic to reach Anabelle's room, but a new camera keeps me in the shadows against the wall. Fury ignites and boils over, scorching everything in its path. I try to keep it together. I can't fall apart. Can't let my anger rule my head. I must stay organized.

I move back the way I came, cautious not to step on the squeaky floorboard outside one of the lead's suites. That one has ears like a lynx. More than once, he caught me going down to the basement in the dead of night.

Our magnificent project manager, Mr. Brodie Maxwell, must have installed that camera. I have no way to reach Anabelle now. He's seen to that. Hate fills me, bitter and black like the bark tea Nana forced me to drink as a child when I misbehaved.

Brodie Maxwell—the bane of my existence—the destroyer who tempted Anabelle with that pricey ring. She loves me, but she accepted that diamond anyway—the perfidy of women.

When Anabelle's mine, I'll teach her a lesson for playing me false. But I'll deal with that later. Something else is more pressing, and I intend to address it now.

I reach the ground floor and let myself outside into the chill night air, my hoodie covering the majority of my face as I avoid more strategically placed cameras. A light mist falls, beading on my clothes as I let myself inside the gardener's barn, for once not locked tight.

On a shelf, I find what I seek and toss my head back and laugh. This is child's play.

Reentering the house, I head for the break room kitchen and open the fridge. Brodie dumps our food in the bin if we leave it behind for more than a day or so. But I overheard him admit to eating some when he worked late, which is almost every night.

That's what I'm counting on. I add the pellets to my lo mein, making sure they dissolve, then do the same to Randy's spaghetti and meatballs.

Poison—a fitting end for a pest.

Chapter 33

Anabelle glanced up from her report as Tara stormed into the conference room. "Has anyone seen Brodie?"

"He's around somewhere. I met with him early this morning." Randy paused in his update to the rest of the team. "He asked me to handle this morning's meeting."

Tara's brows squished together. "I specifically asked him to sign off on the artwork delivery as Anabelle had this meeting, and I was on a conference call. Dispatch rang me just now after sending a nastygram to inform me that someone needs to skate down to the Glasgow warehouse and pick up the crate, as no one accepted the shipment when the delivery driver arrived. Do you have any idea how much time that will take to handle?"

Randy glanced across the table at Anabelle.

"I'll go find him." Anabelle rose from the table.

"Do that." Tara gave her a curt nod.

Anabelle slipped from the room and headed to Brodie's office.

His door stood ajar, and the light was switched on, but no Brodie. Spying his mobile on top of his desk, Anabelle experienced the first stirring of worry. Brodie never went anywhere without his mobile.

Perhaps he had chased down the delivery lorry. Anabelle glanced outside, but Brodie's car was still parked on the drive. He never disappeared without leaving word where the team could reach him. Starting back down the corridor, she passed the gents' loo and heard someone inside moan.

She pressed her hands against the door and called, "Brodie? Are you in there?"

Another groan.

Gripping the knob, she turned the handle and found Brodie on the floor, the smell of sickness almost knocking her over.

"Brodie." Her knees hit the floor beside his inert body, and she patted his face, but he didn't respond.

"I'm pure dead brilliant." Brodie shot a sour look across the hospital room. "Leave me be, lass, and quit yer fussin'," he said, his brogue in full force.

"You don't look it." Anabelle folded her arms and scowled. Why were men so difficult?

The doctor suspected poisoning and had pumped Brodie's stomach, then given him a heavy dose of vitamin K and heaven knew what else inside his intravenous bag.

After he'd stabilized, Brodie insisted his parents not be notified. "I'll never hear the end of it. Mother's a ray of sunshine until she worries. I'm not up to handling her just yet."

Anabelle complied, only because he'd pleaded and looked so pale.

But this morning, she was heartily repenting of her decision. The bull-headed Scot had cloaked himself in full-on stubbornness. She rolled her eyes in frustration—it was either that or throttle her fiancé.

"I saw that, lass."

"I don't care if you did." She bent close, right in his face. "You could have died, Brodie!"

"But I didn't."

She pressed her lips together as her fear turned into downright temper, a natural response, she assured herself, especially if one was dealing with an ornery Scot.

"Did they get the lab results?" Brodie had been in and out of consciousness, then slept deeply once the ill effects of whatever he'd reacted to were immobilized.

"Nothing yet. They said they'd know sometime this morning."

Brodie's stomach growled. "I'm starving."

Anabelle shook her head. "I doubt you'd keep anything down."

"Everything's roses. I could eat a horse. Strike that. I'd die for some eggs or a bacon roll. Even a Scottish breakfast sounds marvelous."

"You must have an iron-clad stomach if you can even consider food after what you've gone through. And you aren't going to enjoy the diet the doctor prescribed for the next few days."

"What?" He looked up at her, his face still pale, and the skin under his eyes rather bruised in appearance.

"Broth and clear liquids only."

"A man can't live on that. I'm fallin' apart. And I can't be lying abed, either. We need to get back to Soldier's Leap. We've an inspection today."

Anabelle opened her mouth to soothe him, but the door opened during the last of Brodie's outburst, and a woman in scrubs entered, one not much older than Brodie.

"Mr. Maxwell?" the woman asked.

"That's me."

"Dr. Wilson," she said, turning on her tablet.

Though youngish, the physician did not overflow with bedside manner. She scrolled through the Accident and Emergency doctor's notes.

"You are to remain on clear liquids for several days, until the effects of the rat poison are out of your system."

"No one can live on that diet," Brodie protested.

"Nevertheless, you will, or you'll likely wind up right back in hospital." Dr. Wilson turned off the tablet and appeared ready to leave.

"Did you say rat poison?" Anabelle leaned against Brodie's bed, her legs like an overcooked linguini.

"Aye. There were traces of it in the lo mein and spaghetti you ingested. You weren't in a depressed state when you ate it, were you?" Dr. Wilson asked, her gaze sharp.

Brodie rubbed a hand over his face, his expression dark.

"I didn't try to off myself if that's what you're asking. I'm not even sure how it got there, but from now on, no one touches the leftovers in the fridge." He reached for his mobile on the bedside table, then paused. "When can I be discharged?"

"As soon as we process your paperwork. I need your word that you will stay on clear liquids for the next couple of days."

"I'll see to it that he does." Anabelle patted Brodie's leg through the blanket.

"Excellent." Dr. Wilson departed without a backward glance, and the door swung shut behind her.

"Rat poison?" Anabelle hissed after making sure no one else was within hearing distance outside in the corridor. "How did you manage that?"

Brodie didn't answer. He appeared fixated on his cellular screen.

"What is it?" She moved toward the bed and glanced at his mobile.

> Leave her alone. ANABELLE IS MINE.

Anabelle swallowed. This wasn't a weird coincidence. "We'd better report this to your cousin, Finn. That crazy stalker just tried to kill you."

Chapter 34

The floor vibrated as a London train roared out of the Oxford Circus Station multiple meters beneath her feet. Anabelle stood before the dressing room mirror while Mother laced up yet another wedding gown.

The last few weeks had passed in a blur of activity since her fitting with Erica. And now she and Mother had flown to London to meet with the bridal designer Grandmama Poole had orchestrated.

"Hurry it along, Anabelle. We haven't all day." Grandmama Poole thumped her cane outside in the viewing area.

Anabelle met her mother's eyes in the mirror, neither saying a word, but both in perfect harmony in dealing with Grandmama's impatience.

Doubtless, she should show more interest in reception gown shopping, but she had spent the last two weeks trying to locate where a delayed shipping container of Turkish marble had wound up. Evidently, some inattentive clerk sent it to Singapore. At least that had kept her mind off her stalker.

The unfortunate container prevented the company from meeting its first bonus—not disastrous, but certainly unpleasant for all who had worked to meet those goals.

After she found the container, Brodie had holed up in his office and reworked their schedules yet again to ensure they reached their second deadline in early November, with its compensating kickback. He'd even arranged for local artisans to complete the en-suites as he saw no need for the team to twiddle their thumbs while they waited. The labor for that would break their budget.

Just before she flew to London, a bouquet with a carved alabaster vase appeared on top of her car. Since the alarm company had installed additional cameras around the estate, no further "gifts" or break-ins occurred. But she'd inadvertently parked out of video range and gave the stalker the opening he sought.

Up until then, hope that her creeper troubles were at an end had risen.

But an unknown email arrived in her inbox this afternoon. Though half an hour had passed since she'd read Brodie's text, bile still swirled in her stomach, yet she couldn't cancel the shopping trip that brought Mother and Grandmama so much pleasure.

"This gown is lovely on you." Mother's voice cracked, calling Anabelle back to the present.

She touched the satin folds of the A-line skirt, repressing her lackluster interest as she studied the gown's capped sleeves, Victorian neckline, corseted bodice, and chapel-worthy train. Schiaparelli's timeless gown proved similar in style to Julia's—save for the lace.

Mother held the dressing room door wide, and Anabelle entered the viewing area and stepped onto the dais in front of the three-way mirrors.

Grandmama, enthroned on a velvet chair, nodded to the shop owner. "I think a satin veil would add a nice touch, don't you?"

"No, my lady, it will cover too much of the dress." Peggy James, the owner, waved her hands in protest. "A sheer veil would be a better option."

Harumphing her displeasure, Grandmama's eyes brightened when they returned to Anabelle. She pushed out of her chair, circling the dais to examine the gown's details. "It's nice."

"Nice? She looks like an angel." Mother's brows crashed together.

Anabelle bit her lip, her eyes widening at Mother's response. She so rarely disagreed with Grandmama, that this difference of opinion, though slight, rocked the matriarchal pecking order.

Though she sided with her mother, Anabelle held her breath. If she mentioned the similarities between this gown and Julia's, Grandmama would send it back, then tack more hours onto this shopping expedition.

Anabelle glanced at the dress. If Erica couldn't fix Julia's gown, she'd happily wear this one. None of the other dresses she had tried on that day suited her half so well.

"It'll do." Grandmama sank back into her chair.

"Are we going to select a veil?" Anabelle gazed at the shop wall where the veils hung on display.

"That depends. Are you wearing a heathen tartan across your chest when you marry that Scot?" Grandmama asked.

Anabelle's heart sank. *Here we go again.* "We haven't ironed out all the details."

She and Brodie had discussed several options, one included Brodie draping the Maxwell Clan's tartan sash over her shoulder after saying their vows, symbolizing her joining his clan.

"It will look ridiculous and ruin that beautiful gown. Admit it, Eliza." Grandmama motioned to the dress with the end of her cane.

Anabelle braced herself for Mother's capitulation.

"Mama, you've always been a big proponent of keeping up family traditions. Brodie is a Scot. Adding a family sash to Anabelle's gown is part of Highland culture," Eliza explained, her manner respectful.

Anabelle jolted, her eyes practically bulging from her head. Mother was defending her.

"Harrumph." Clearly ruffled by her daughter's stand, Grandmama zeroed in on Anabelle. "If you intend to wear the Poole tiara, I have stipulations, one being that you do not wear a tartan sash. The two would clash horribly." Grandmama's eyes gleamed with victory.

What? Anabelle opened her mouth, her jaw slack. Grandmama intended to forbid the family tiara just to have her way? The woman played hardball when she intended to win.

Anabelle's chest heaved as she fought for composure. Brodie was right. Grandmama Poole was a bully. And if she didn't stand up for herself, Grandmama would hijack their wedding at every chance.

Squaring her shoulders, Anabelle commanded her quaking stomach to behave. "I'd like more than anything to wear the tiara, but not on your terms. How dare you forbid Brodie's culture from our wedding."

Grandmama fluffed like a disgruntled bird, then bent her a beady stare. Anabelle's tongue thickened, and she longed to beg her pardon, but the injustice of Grandmama's demands kept her from caving. Brodie had a right to include his family's traditions. This was his wedding, too, not Grandmama's.

"Why couldn't you marry someone more practical?" Grandmama complained. "A Scot of all people. He doesn't even hold a title."

"Brodie and I love each other."

"Love." Grandmama crinkled her nose as though she smelled something distasteful. "The Pooles don't marry for love. They marry those whom their parents select, people with class and status—and titles."

Anabelle lifted her chin, but quaked inside like a mass of bramble jelly. "None of the Pooles have struck me as overly happy in their marriages, save for Mother and Dad." Anabelle had it on good authority that her mother's siblings barely tolerated their spouses.

"I know couples who haven't spoken in years. Their arrangements suit them quite well." Grandmama shifted her shoulders like an affronted Edwardian lady.

"Mama, you sound like Violet Crawley," Mother protested, referring to the fictional matriarch of a once popular British television series.

"She sounds exceptionally wise." Grandmama side-eyed Anabelle, leaving her with the distinct impression that she knew exactly to whom Mother referred.

"How long is this train?" Mother asked in an apparent attempt to change the subject. She circled the dais and gently spread the material. "I assume there will be dancing at the reception. Can we put this up into a bustle?" Mother directed her question to Ms. James, who hovered near the doorway, should they need anything.

"The gown makes into a charming French bustle." Ms. James approached, gathering up the train, smoothing and folding as she went, until a streamlined bustle appeared.

Anabelle twisted to view Ms. James's handiwork over her shoulder in the mirrors. "It's so stylish, and I can dance without tripping."

"That particular bustle is quite in vogue." Ms. James stepped back several paces.

"Can this Scot house and dress you in the way you are accustomed?" Grandmama, it seemed, refused to leave off heckling her about Brodie.

Anabelle fisted her hands at her sides, her courage rising. "It wouldn't matter if he couldn't. I have a career of my own."

"You'll rue the day if he cannot keep you in style." Grandmama's dramatic headshake reminded Anabelle of a famous stage actor from London's West End.

"Are you insinuating that Brodie has no prospects?" Anabelle laughed, and the last vestiges of her fear broke free, like unlocked manacles, loosening her of its restrictive hold. "Brodie is a much sought-after project manager, is a talented architect, and receives a handsome salary for his efforts. But even if he didn't, I'd still marry him."

Grandmama's eyes bulged, and she turned to Mother. "How dare she speak to me this way, Eliza."

"Anabelle didn't say anything amiss." Mother rested a hand on Anabelle's shoulder.

The unexpected support warmed Anabelle's heart. Mother rarely stood up for her against Grandmama, choosing silence to keep the peace.

"You have made sly digs about Brodie all day, and Anabelle has borne it admirably. But she's marrying the boy, and if she chooses to wear his clan's sash, that is their decision, not ours. This wedding is a celebration; let's not turn it into a battlefield."

Grandmama gaped as though an inanimate toy had come to life and rebuffed her. No one stood up to Lady Poole, doubtless, due to their misguided notion of respect. But respect must be earned, and Anabelle refused to live in fear any longer. And so, apparently did Mother, if her defiant expression was anything to judge by.

"Don't think I'll loan you the Poole tiara after speaking to me like that," Grandmama sputtered in a last attempt to gain the upper hand.

"You don't mean that." Mother pressed a hand to her heart as though it actually hurt.

"I do," Grandmama snapped, banging her cane against the floor for emphasis.

Tears burned Anabelle's eyes as Grandmama's strike pierced her fragile armor. Every bride in the family wore the Poole tiara. She clasped her mother's hand for added strength but refused to fold. She had fought too hard for her freedom to give way now.

"That is certainly your prerogative, but withholding the family tiara will not change my mind. I'll use something else instead. I love you, Grandmama. You've taught me how to get on in society. I cannot imagine how nervous I'd be without your tutelage, but Brodie and I will determine what is and is not appropriate for our wedding."

Grandmama's features hardened, and she rose from her chair. "I expect an apology before I'll let you touch that tiara."

"I'm sorry you feel that way." Anabelle drew herself up to her full 165 centimeters.

"We are done here." Grandmama stormed out of the shop, the picture of righteous indignation.

"Will she forgive us, do you think?" Anabelle slumped. Victory never felt so miserable.

"I don't know." Mother's voice wavered. "I feel horrid about this, but I couldn't let her ruin your wedding, too."

"What do you mean?" Anabelle asked.

"When your father and I were engaged, every time we planned for our nuptials, Mother switched it. We wanted a simple wedding, one without pomp or circumstance, but that's exactly what we received—all compliments of your grandmother."

"All these years, I thought you and Dad planned that big society wedding. You looked so happy in your pictures." Why hadn't her parents shared this with her?

"We were so in love that we let it slide. It wasn't worth the trouble."

"After what Grandmama said about love, I'm surprised she approved of your marrying Dad at all. He wasn't a prince, a duke, or even an earl." Anabelle forced a laugh, still smarting from Grandmama's edict.

"True. Your father wasn't a duke, but he had a respected title and a lovely estate in a much-coveted area of the country." Mother signaled to the shop owner. "Ms. James, what do you recommend for a veil?"

"Schiaparelli provided several sketches of what she envisioned for that gown. Would you like to see them?" Ms. James asked, the wary expression she had worn around Grandmama a thing of the past.

"Yes." Mother's excitement pulsed in the air. "How thrilling to work with such an amazing design house . . ."

Mother and Ms. James moved out of earshot to admire the sketchbook, then stepped to the wall of veil displays.

Anabelle twisted one last time to admire the French bustle. The dress was stunning from every angle. If she hadn't already set her heart on Julia's gown, this one ticked every box.

"What do you think, Anabelle?" Mother approached, motioning to the veils she and Ms. James carried.

The first veil attached to a tiara, its long, sheer material dotted with pearls. The other, a Juliet cap beaded with minuscule brilliants, hearkened back to the twenties.

"The first one." Anabelle nodded toward her choice. "I think the pearls are a wonderful pairing with Julia's lace and this gown. May I try it on?"

"Of course." Ms. James pushed aside the dress's full skirt, so she didn't step on the fabric, then joined her on the dais. Using a paste tiara, she placed the veil in Anabelle's hair, then, bending low, she fluffed the long chiffon that would partially cover her train.

"Oh. That's lovely." Anabelle beamed at her reflection.

"What will you do about a tiara?" A pucker marred Mother's forehead.

"I'll purchase this paste one or see if Brodie's family has one of their own."

"We could placate your grandmother," Mother said, her voice soft.

"I won't have her insulting Brodie. If she wants me to wear the Poole tiara, I'm delighted to do so, but she will not turn our wedding into a royal extravaganza."

"A compromise might help smooth things over. Both of our families are well-known in society. For that, you'll need your grandmother's talents."

"Having second thoughts?" Anabelle asked.

"No, but whether you like it or not, your grandmother has exceptional taste. She also knows royal protocol better than the royals themselves. It wouldn't hurt to include her with details that you don't care about."

"You sound like Brodie."

"He has a great deal of wisdom. Your father and I have always preferred him to the other fellows you've dated."

Her brows rose at that tidbit of information. "Brodie's lack of a title doesn't bother you?"

"We want your happiness above all things. And Brodie makes you happy." Mother hugged her, veil, dress, and all.

Anabelle mulled over that for a second. "Will Grandmama see it as a weakness if I ask for her assistance?"

"It doesn't matter if she does or doesn't. She's old and set in her ways. Just hold firm to whatever you decide. She campaigned heavily for the Queen to attend your wedding and doubtless intends for everything to be just so."

"I wish she had spoken to me before she invited Her Majesty."

"That's water under the bridge. Let it go. Emotions run high when preparing for weddings. Though we can't change Grandmama, do try to involve her." Mother caressed her cheek, her touch feather-light. "Family matters, Anabelle. I've seen too many estrangements over my lifetime. No one wins."

"I don't have enough emotional stamina to hold out if she attacks again."

"You're stronger than you think. Your grandmother's pride has taken a beating, so expect a few prickles, but I doubt she'll attempt another coup." Mother kissed her forehead, then helped her off the dais.

Mother was right. She needed to stand firm yet yield to things that didn't matter.

Once more inside the dressing room, Mother loosened the lacing, and Anabelle stepped out of the gown and glanced at her watch.

"We have thirty minutes before we meet Brodie for the taste testing. Think we can check something else from our list before then?"

"That depends. Do you want this dress?" Mother placed the gown on the padded hanger.

"Yes . . ." Anabelle's voice trailed away.

Understanding softened Mother's gaze. "You have your heart set on Julia's gown."

"I do, rather, but only if Erica can remove those final spots."

"This Schiaparelli will make a splendid reception gown, and if Erica can't fix Julia's, you can wear this for the chapel and reception."

"I agree." Anabelle tugged on her trousers and buttoned up her blouse.

"It's uncanny how similar this style it is to the other dress." Mother eyed the gown one last time, then lifted it into her arms.

"I thought so too. Let's call Erica and ask how things are progressing."

"Will this veil suit both gowns?" Mother tilted her head, considering.

"I think it's perfect for either of them."

"Excellent."

They left the dressing room with Anabelle carrying the veil and Mother following with the gown. Ms. James, standing near the dais, relieved them of both.

"We'd like to purchase the Schiaparelli and the pearl veil," Mother said.

"Do you need alterations?" Ms. James moved toward the register and packaged the veil in a pastel floral box.

"No, but we'll need it shipped to my address in Scotland." Anabelle intended to pay Erica for any alterations that might be needed.

"Will Erica be insulted that you purchased your reception dress elsewhere?" Mother whispered when Ms. James left to search for a box.

Her question made Anabelle pause. "Are weddings always such a balancing act?"

"I'm afraid so. And not just weddings. Births and funerals are tricky, too."

Anabelle sighed. "Then I'll speak to her."

"Excellent." Mother checked her watch. "Go on ahead. I'll stay while they ring this up. You don't need me for the tasting.

Chapter 35

Twelve faces gazed at the corporate screen as Brodie clicked the final slide of his presentation. "In closing, I've a short video of Soldier's Leap to show the progress we've made."

He'd spent the better part of a year pouring his soul into this project. Hopefully, Genesis's board would appreciate his and the team's efforts.

Images of the former elevation and its update flashed, moving on to the grand salon's conversion into a restaurant, the professional kitchen, the division between the family wing and the main house, which his team had dubbed "the great wall," the wrecked paneling and its refurbishment, the gilding and stencil work, and the former drawing rooms and salons, now converted into a professional business center and conference rooms, their furnishings complimenting the house. Lastly, drone footage featured the newly erected glamping pods down near the loch, hidden from the house by a large hedgerow and swale in the terrain.

Brodie turned off the video. "Any questions?"

"Impressive work. You and your team should be proud of what you've accomplished," Regina Wright, the head of HR, said.

"Thank you. They're brilliant." Brodie beamed.

"You've done some serious juggling over the last few months." Paul

Symonds, the Vice President of the UK Division, looked up from his projections. "Will you meet the deadlines?"

"The team is working long hours to ensure that we do." Brodie glanced around the table at each of corporate's division heads. Hitting those deadlines would provide Genesis with a massive bonus, some of which would be passed to his team.

"How do we sign up for a Soldier's Leap retreat?" Regina asked.

Chuckles rippled around the table.

"The same way as everyone else," Brodie volleyed back.

"We understand you dodged a bullet recently when a designer changed a work order." Larry, the head of Genesis's PR team, folded his arms, his mouth unsmiling.

Brodie clenched his jaw. Why did Larry bring that up? This meeting was to update corporate on the reno's completion schedule.

"An expert has since verified that those orders were forged. I'd say Genesis owes Ms. Dewhurst a massive apology—at the very least." Brodie glanced first at Paul, then Larry, both of whom had originally demanded Anabelle's resignation.

Murmurs circled the room.

"A forgery?" Regina asked.

"Do we know who did it?" Larry asked.

Paul rose to his feet and raised both hands to calm the room. "HR will make it right."

"On it." Regina made a notation on her electronic device.

"Some of you have other meetings, so this concludes ours. Thank you, everyone, especially Brodie, for this presentation." Paul moved toward the exit and opened the door, shaking hands with those filing out.

Brodie shut down the computer, then headed for the door.

Paul cornered him. "Brodie, I've been meaning to speak with you. Genesis won the bid for the multi-story shopping mall in Budapest. Would you be interested in leading the project?"

"If we've already won the project, shouldn't that job be posted on the corporate site?" Though Brodie intended to leave Genesis, he disliked being offered the project without the company following corporate procedure.

"Transki Corps was blown away by your Malaga resort designs and specifically requested you, by name, to act as project manager."

"I'll need time to consider the offer. Anabelle and I are getting married in November."

"I'm sorry about her probation." To his credit, Paul appeared sincere.

"Whoever forged those work orders intended for her to be dismissed. I expect Regina will do something to clear her name. But reputations, once sullied in the design world—"

"Are lost," Paul finished for him. "We'll make it right."

"I hope so. Anabelle is the Dewhurst family representative." Brodie slung his computer bag strap over his shoulder.

"I'll speak with Regina about implementing a whitewashing campaign on her behalf."

"Brilliant."

"Care for some lunch?" Paul accompanied him out of the boardroom and down the corridor.

"Thanks, but I need to pass. I'm meeting Anabelle and her grandmother, Lady Barbara Poole."

Paul stopped mid-stride. "Isn't Lady Barbara one of Her Majesty's attendants?"

Brodie repressed a smile. "I never took you as a Royalist." Most Brits were either for or against the crown.

"My wife follows the royals and keeps me updated." Worry lines creased Paul's eyes. "Anabelle is well connected."

"She is. I hope Regina ropes Larry into that whitewashing campaign."

"We'll pull out all the stops. How does an article in Architectural World, along with a spot on The Morning Show, and an interview on Skye News sound? If we can swing this, it will be sensational dynamite."

"I think you missed your calling. You and Regina should switch jobs. Those ideas rolled off you without a moment's thought."

Paul chuckled. "Not on your life. Tell Anabelle, we'll be in touch." Paul waved absently, then headed down the corridor toward Larry's office.

Brodie remained in the hall, absorbing the environment that had launched his career. He was grateful to Genesis for giving him a chance, but he had other plans, including turning in his resignation once the renovation came to an end and corporate made things right for Anabelle.

Taking the stairs, he stepped outside the glass and steel structure, and texted Anabelle.

Brodie: Are we still on to visit my parents?

Anabelle: YES. Ready and waiting.

Brodie grinned. That was Anabelle speak for, "Please get me out of here."

He dashed to the Underground and took the train to Sloane Square. On disembarking, he made his way to Lady Barbara's leafy Belgravia address. An upstairs curtain twitched in her posh London townhouse, and Anabelle waved, her smile one of relief. He rapped on the bright blue door, and a doorman answered with alacrity.

"I'm here to collect Miss Dewhurst."

"Right this way, Mr. Maxwell."

Brodie stepped into the narrow hall just as Anabelle started down the stairs with her overnight case in one hand and rucksack slung over the opposite shoulder.

He met her on the landing. "What did you put in here, rocks?" he asked, relieving her of the carry-on.

"Shhh. Grandmama is sleeping." Anabelle pressed an index finger to her lips.

"I thought you were having tea?"

"We were, but it ended in a muddle," she whispered.

"Anabelle, is that your young man?" Lady Barbara called from the drawing room.

"Blast," Anabelle said under her breath, then louder, "Yes, Grandmama."

"Bring him in here. I'd like to have a word."

Anabelle groaned. "Be careful," she whispered. "She's still angry with me for standing up to her. I've been walking on eggshells all afternoon. I hope she doesn't make us miss our train."

"We've time before it leaves," Brodie murmured for her ears only.

Setting down her rucksack, Anabelle took his free hand. He let go of her case and accompanied her into a drawing room—a lovely space with high ceilings and tall windows. The room was not the least ostentatious and spoke of old money with its hand-knotted Turkish rug, tufted sofa, and overstuffed chairs. Brodie loosened his tie at the overwarm temperature and longed to remove his suit jacket.

"Hello, Brodie." Lady Barbara inclined her head.

"You're looking well, Lady Barbara." Brodie smiled. He couldn't help it; the woman behaved like a monarch granting him audience.

"I understand you're marrying my granddaughter."

"Aye, that I am." Brodie glanced at Anabelle, and his stomach did a three-sixty. He couldn't wait to call this woman his wife.

"Most couples are engaged for some time before they tie the knot. But with Her Majesty's intention to attend your wedding, we're rather rushed to accommodate her." Lady Barbara raised a sculpted eyebrow.

"Begging your pardon, but waiting a year or two is ridiculous," Brodie said.

His answer surprised a chuckle out of her. "Eager, are you?"

"Yes, ma'am."

"I assume you'll be wearing a kilt?" Lady Barbara's voice chilled on the last word.

"I'm a Highlander. It's customary to do so in my family."

"Mmmm." A world of disapproval came through the sound.

"And where do you plan to hold this wedding and reception?" Lady Barbara asked, both finely arched brows rising.

"At the parish church in my home glen. It's an easy drive for the Queen and her security team to reach from Balmoral, much more so than travelling to High Ridge." Mentioning the Queen ought to grant them points.

Instead, Lady Barbara scowled.

Evidently not.

"You could hold a lovely event here in London next month. I have everything planned."

"Unfortunately, next month doesn't suit mine and Anabelle's schedule. We'll still be in Scotland working." Brodie repressed a silent chuckle. Lady Barbara did not give up easily.

She pursed her lips and stared at him without blinking. If she intended to intimidate him, it wouldn't work. Truth be told, he rather liked her.

"Eliza and Pierce think highly of you," she said after a time.

"I'd count myself lucky if you did as well, Lady Barbara."

"That remains to be seen. Can you provide for Anabelle? I don't want her living in some minuscule flat in the wrong part of London."

"Grandmama." Anabelle dipped her head, a flush coloring her neck and face.

"It's a valid question. The very idea of one of my grandchildren living in a hovel for the sake of love is inexcusable." Lady Barbara swung her piercing gaze back in his direction.

Brodie dropped Anabelle's hand and approached Lady Barbara. "May I?" He indicated the seat beside her.

Another regal inclination of her head.

Brodie bit the inside of his cheek to keep from grinning. "Is it all right if we marry for love and move to Chelsea? I own a townhouse there."

"A townhouse?" Lady Barbara blinked.

"Aye, and a place in Scotland," he added. "Though that might not count, seeing as you're English." He couldn't resist needling her for the fun of it. The woman looked down her nose at any people other than the English.

A speculative gleam came and went in Lady Barbara's eyes. She refrained from commenting, but he received the distinct impression that she rather enjoyed their game of verbal ping-pong.

"Where do you intend to honeymoon?" Lady Barbara asked.

She had him there. Brodie rubbed his jaw, glanced at Anabelle, who stood rooted to the floor just inside the doorway.

"Do you know, that's given me a spot of trouble. Every place I've checked is booked during that time frame."

"Too many tourists visit during the holiday season." Lady Barbara bowed her head in acknowledgment. "I might have another option. A connection of mine on the Balmoral estate hinted that they have a cottage available."

"Is that so?" Balmoral. Doubtless, that connection was Lady Barbara's good mate, Her Majesty, the Queen.

Anabelle's gaze shot to his, her blue eyes alight.

"Tending a fire twenty-four seven to keep a cottage heated is not my idea of a honeymoon." Brodie couldn't resist teasing Lady B.

"Do you think I'd send my granddaughter somewhere primitive? The cottage on offer has all the mod cons one could wish for," Lady Barbara sputtered, giving up her posh act.

"Anabelle, what do you think?" Brodie faced her and winked. "Would you prefer two weeks on the Balmoral Estate or settling into our townhouse for a few months until next spring?"

"Grandmama, can you really secure us a place?" A smile radiated like sunshine from Anabelle's lips.

"Yes. It's very private and only a few miles from the castle. Some of the family will be in residence, but my friend assured me that you have her blessing to stay as long as you'd like."

"That was very kind. Please thank your *friend* for their generosity. You may be assured, we will keep well away from the castle," Brodie said.

Anabelle flew across the room and embraced Lady B. "Thank you so much, Grandmama!"

Lady Barbara, who up until this time had sat rigidly in her chair, crumpled and hugged her back. "There. There, child. Don't make a fuss. If you have other needs for the reception, I might have a few things up my sleeve."

"As it happens, we do need your help, don't we?" Brodie lifted one brow and looked at Anabelle expectantly.

"We do. I haven't the least notion who to use for our announcements." Anabelle moved to the sofa and sat beside him.

"Bingham's are the best. If I put in a good word, they'll expedite your order. May I suggest . . ." And so it went, with Lady Barbara covering items neither he nor Anabelle had considered.

"May I leave the announcements in your care, Grandmama?" Anabelle asked.

"I assume you have an engagement photographer?"

"Brodie's mother is taking pictures of us this weekend. She's won several awards as an amateur photographer."

"Have her email me the file when she's done." Lady Barbara picked up a notepad from the end table beside her and scribbled something, then looked up. "What about the script and paper weight?"

"I trust you to choose something classy. We don't have a preference, do we, Brodie?" Anabelle asked, her question more of a stamp of approval on his part.

"Flowers?" Lady Barbara raised a brow and ducked her chin.

"Covered," Brodie said. The last thing he wanted was to get into an argument about floral arrangements.

"What about your venue? And who's doing the music?" Grandmama referred to her notepad.

Brodie groaned. "I haven't secured a deejay."

"Let me handle it. I know of a fabulous string quartet."

"We'd prefer light rock, Grandmama, not chamber music," Anabelle inserted, checking her mobile, a sudden frown turning down the corners of her mouth.

Lady Barbara snorted, albeit an elegant one, if snorts could be considered as such.

"I can always call in some pipers for Highland dancing," Brodie volunteered.

"Frenzied stomping at a wedding reception? I'll secure a deejay." Lady Barbara jotted that onto her notepad before she glanced up to find both of them watching her. "Don't you two have a train to catch?" She looked pointedly at the clock.

"Yes, Grandmama. And thank you." Anabelle kissed Lady Barbara's cheek.

"Thank you, Lady Barbara." Brodie stood and took Lady Barbara's hand.

"All I ask is that you make Anabelle happy." Lady Barbara did not rise from her chair.

"I intend to." Brodie touched the small of Anabelle's back and led her outside, closing the door softly behind them.

"You're awfully quiet," he said after half a block without Anabelle uttering a peep.

Anabelle wet her lips. "I received an email just now."

"Who from?" He stopped at the zebra crossing and assessed her.

She turned the screen toward him and displayed a seven-word email.

We will be together soon, my love.

Chapter 36

The morning after arriving at the Maxwell's home, Anabelle, sat on a moss-covered log and rested her chin on her knees, soaking in Loch Voil's bronze surface as it shimmered in sunset's golden light. Brodie planted himself beside her while they waited for his mother, Lady Maxwell, to adjust the aperture on her camera.

Birdsong filled the air, and water lapped the shore. The peaceful environs around Kirkton House were a welcome reprieve after London's bustle —and yesterday's shattering email.

Lady Maxwell, a petite brunette with hazel eyes and a sunny disposition, knelt a few meters away. "Lean forward, Anabelle. Brodie is casting a shadow on your face."

Anabelle did as instructed.

"A bit more. That's it. Smile and think lovely thoughts."

Anabelle peeked up at Brodie. His hazel eyes, more green than blue today, were warm and filled with so much love that her heart quivered in response.

The camera's shutter clicked. "Brilliant. Let's get a few shots of you by the rhododendrons."

Anabelle brushed at her clothes, then moved across the lawn holding Brodie's hand.

"How would you like us to pose, Mother?" Brodie asked.

"Just talk to each other while I get the lighting right. Forget I'm here."

A mischievous smile quirked up the corner of his mouth.

"Oh no, you don't." Anabelle read his intent and pivoted, sprinting in her heels. Brodie caught her easily and tossed her over his shoulder, then marched toward the water.

"Don't you dare throw me in that loch." Anabelle squealed and pounded his back. "Brodie Maxwell, you put me down."

"Not on your life. Say, Nessie." Brodie spun her in circles.

Anabelle clung to him for dear life. "There's no such thing."

"Say it, or you're going in the loch. I've got to make a Scotswoman of you. Nessie's part of our culture."

He spun faster, her hair flying out in all directions. She closed her eyes, fighting back dizziness.

"Nessie," she muttered, gritting her teeth.

"What's that? I didn't hear you correctly," Brodie paused.

"Nessie. Nessie. Nessie," she hollered.

He set her down, keeping his hands on her waist. His eyes sparkled with suppressed laughter, then he dipped his head and kissed her. Closing her eyes, she melted into him.

In the last year, she had rarely seen him so carefree. The renovation's demands kept him up most days long into the night. She touched his face, her heart rejoicing that the stress of those responsibilities would soon end.

"Perfect." Lady Maxwell's camera clicked, the flash going off.

Anabelle snapped her head in Lady Maxwell's direction. "I forgot you were there."

"I get my best candid shots that way." Lady Maxwell dimpled, then checked her viewfinder. "I think you'll be pleased."

"May we see?" Brodie let go of her and crossed to his mother, bending his head to gaze at their images on the small monitor. "Anabelle, come look at these." He beckoned with one arm.

She approached, and he pulled her against his side so she could see the screen.

Lady Maxwell clicked from one image to the next.

"Mum, these are brilliant. Could we play them on a rotating screen during the reception?" Brodie asked.

"Aye. It's a lovely way for your guests to share in your joy."

"Which one should we send to Lady Barbara?" Brodie peered at Anabelle. "I vote for the kiss." He wiggled his brows.

"You'd scandalize her." Anabelle twined her fingers with his.

"Can't your granny take a wee bit of teasing?" he asked.

"She's not overly playful." Anabelle bumped Brodie with her hip.

"This one, I think." Lady Maxwell enlarged a picture of them facing each other with Anabelle's hand on Brodie's chest, their heads turned toward Lady Maxwell while golden light bathed them in its magical hue. Lady Maxwell had blurred the background, so the eye remained fixed on them.

"It's a classic pose and quite proper for an announcement," Lady Maxwell said.

Brodie placed his mouth on Anabelle's ear. "Boring."

"I heard that, Brodie." Lady Maxwell shook her head at her son, but her eyes laughed.

"I agree with you, Lady Maxwell." Anabelle couldn't imagine sending a kissing picture to Her Majesty.

"Excellent. I'll enlarge the image on my computer and see if it needs touchups before I send it to Lady Barbara."

"I'll text you her email address." Anabelle retrieved her mobile, and a second later, Lady Maxwell's dinged.

"Very good." Lady Barbara swatted at a midge, those pesky black, biting flies that made even the toughest Scots run for cover.

"Thanks, Mum. The pictures are wonderful."

"I love them, Lady Maxwell," Anabelle added.

"Must we be so formal? Won't you call me Olivia?"

"Thank you, Olivia." Anabelle stumbled over her name. "The pictures are . . . very us."

"I think so, too. I've never seen Brodie so happy." Olivia smiled at her son, her hazel eyes softening. "I'll handle these after supper, but I need to hunt down your father first, or he'll never come in."

"Should we help her find him?" Anabelle asked when Olivia moved out of hearing.

"Dad's in the woodworking shed."

"How do you know that?"

"I heard the lathe running when we came outside." Brodie held out his hand. "Care for a walk?"

Interlacing fingers, they wandered to the shore, swatting the occasional midge until the wind kicked up and blew them away.

"That's something to be grateful for." The breeze cut through her blouse, and Anabelle shivered at the sudden chill. "The wind's a defense against those bothersome bugs."

Brodie removed his jumper and pushed it over her head. When she poked her arms through, her hands were entirely covered by the sleeves.

"Thanks. Aren't you cold?"

"Not in the least. When I was a bairn, Mum put me outside in my pram to toughen me up."

Anabelle's eyes widened. "That seems rather barbaric, especially for an only child."

"Norwegians do it as well. It makes you less impervious to the elements."

"I couldn't do that to our children."

"Our children, eh?" Brodie stopped on the shale, his eyes roving her features.

"Aye," she mimicked his brogue.

He slid his arm around her and ducked his head, his breath warm. "And how many bairns were ye thinking to have, lass?"

"Half a dozen, perhaps more," she said, intending to scare him.

"Six or more?" Brodie's eyes bulged.

She laughed at his alarmed expression. "If you could see your face, Mr. Maxwell."

"We'll certainly have fun trying," he muttered just loud enough for her to hear.

Anabelle's face flooded with fire. Trust Brodie to take it one step further. "Maybe one, then." She walked out of his arms, then glanced over her shoulder and blew him a kiss.

He stood where she'd left him, an unholy smirk on his face. "I think for that, you need to christen our loch, Mistress Dewhurst."

Brodie stepped in her direction, his eyes filled with purpose.

Her heart skittered. "Brodie."

He took another step, his intent clear.

Squealing, Anabelle pivoted and fled.

A brisk gust swept across Loch Earn's blue water and set the anchored boats in the marina bobbing.

"What do you think?" Brodie asked, taking Anabelle's hand and leading her down the hotel's steps and crossing the tarmac to the car park on the water's edge.

"It's not a five-star hotel, but the amenities more than make up the difference."

"Does Her Majesty intend to stay the night before she returns to Balmoral?" he asked.

"Grandmama didn't mention it. I doubt anything in the area is up to her standards. Can you imagine sending the Queen to one of these hotels?" Anabelle indicated the one they had just inspected.

"Definitely not. I'll have Mother prepare the east wing, just in case she does. How many rooms do you think she'll need?"

"Her Majesty, her security detail, and Grandmama in her role as Queen's attendant." Anabelle ticked off the numbers on her fingers. "That's a lot of bother for your mother."

"Don't fash yersel. Mother regularly airs out the east wing to ensure everything remains in working order." Brodie kissed Anabelle's temple, inhaling the scent of her shampoo. "If we produce those half dozen children, she'll likely keep Kirkton House open year-round."

Anabelle groaned. "I created a monster with that comment about children."

"Personally, I'd love half a dozen wee Anabelles running about with your big blue eyes and shiny dark hair." Inwardly, he chuckled. Teasing Anabelle was a favorite pastime.

"With our luck, we'll end up with six stubborn little Brodie's." Anabelle gave him a sassy smile.

"What's the matter with a bunch of wee Brodie's?" He feigned offense.

"One is all I can handle," she muttered, making him laugh.

"Having second thoughts?" He lifted her chin, all but drowning in the crystal pools of her eyes.

"Never. You've my heart, Brodie Maxwell."

Moved beyond words, he drew her into his arms, a sudden lump in his throat making it difficult to swallow. He adored everything about Anabelle, from her sassy mouth to her "take-action" temperament, not to mention her creative "outside-the-box" designs that proved nothing short of brilliant.

If the police identified and arrested her stalker, everything would be perfect. But his worries for her safety remained just under the surface, a constant disquiet at the back of his mind.

He had good reason for his concern. Only that morning, the stalker had hacked into corporate's server—his text on her burner more troubling than yesterday's communication.

You are mine, Anabelle. You belong to me.

Anabelle forwarded both messages to Finn, who promised to catch the nutter. The police traced the cell transmission to the masts in Killicrankie and now monitored all Anabelle's electronic devices. Circumstantial evidence at best, but it verified what they already knew: the creeper must be on the team and living too close to Soldier's Leap for anyone's peace.

Brodie gazed at the rippling loch, its blue water reflecting the sky. "I've missed the Trossachs," he said after a time.

"What's to stop us from living here?" Anabelle asked.

"London's a better location for a startup business."

"You have projects lined up for almost two years. I think it's safe to say you're a sought-after commodity and can live wherever you choose," Anabelle said. "What's brought this on?"

"All our talk about children started me thinking about where they'd be happiest."

"What about your place in Chelsea?" she asked.

"If you don't have an issue with the Highlands, I'll sell my townhouse."

"The Highlands are a wonderful place to raise a family, but you might want to hang on to your townhouse so you can meet with clients from the south."

"Now yer thinking like a canny Scot." He tapped her temple.

"Or an Englishwoman who understands finances and the importance of a London address." A sudden gust tossed her hair into her face. She scooped it up and pushed it out of the way.

"Ye keep me on my toes, lass."

"You'd soon grow bored if I didn't." Her smile made its appearance.

"Diamond cuts diamond?"

"Exactly." Her eyes danced.

He dropped his arms and stepped to the passenger door of his BMW. "Any hesitations about renting a block of rooms in the area?" he asked, returning to the business at hand.

"The hotel is almost thirty minutes from Kirkton House, but I think it's a better option than the one on the carriageway."

"Aye. Those driving up for one night can stay in Mhor. Family and friends who intend to make a holiday of it, will stay here. They'd be much happier at this location in the long run." He rotated his shoulder, and it gave a resounding pop as he worked out the kink.

"Unless they find an Airbnb, those are their closest options," Anabelle pointed out.

"I'll ask one of the gardeners to shuttle guests back and forth between the hotels and Kirkton House."

"This is one of the most beautiful areas in Scotland. Trust me. They won't complain about the distance." Anabelle's gaze swept the blue loch and green hillsides beyond. "If we do move up here, where will we live?"

"The east wing?" He side-eyed her, waiting for a reaction.

"Really?"

She attempted to mask her dismay. Too bad she was such an open book. He smirked. *Och.* She was a fun one to tease.

"No, lass. I love my parents, but we need our own space. The estate has several semi-derelict cottages. We can expand on one of them to fit our needs."

"I love that idea." Anabelle's gaze took on a faraway expression.

"Excellent. So, all we have left on our list is to warn Mother that she might be housing the Queen."

Chapter 37

Anabelle slipped out of Kirkton House well after eleven p.m. and took the path to the loch, pebbles scattering beneath her feet. Here in the Highlands, twilight lingered, leaving her enough light to see by. A bird, startled by the noise, squawked unhappily in a nearby thicket.

Brodie, bless him, had dozed off while watching one of his man shows, all fast cars and death-defying stunts. To rouse him seemed heartless, so she covered him with a quilt and slipped outside, uneasiness crowding her thoughts.

She reached the dock and walked to the end, sitting on the worn, wooden planks and dangling her legs over the dark shallows. A longing rose within her for Jecca, her bestie, and she video-called her without considering the hour.

"Hiya, Anabelle," Jecca answered with a yawn. "What's up? It's been a while."

"How are your wedding plans going?"

Jecca shrugged. "I haven't really thought about it. We've ages before next summer."

Considering that Jecca had planned her wedding in every hue and setting since primary school, Anabelle found the remark rather strange. "I thought you'd have everything nailed down by now."

Jecca sighed. "Geoffrey and I have different tastes. Being so much older, he's a tad set in his ways."

"Oh, dear. I'm sorry."

"Don't be. This is all part of for better or worse, isn't it?" Jecca's over-bright eyes told a different story.

Anabelle's heart bled for her friend, whose romantic tendencies were stifled in this less-than-stellar relationship.

"Did you order that gown you've adored for ages?" Surely chatting about Jecca's wedding dress would lift her friend's spirits.

"Geoff doesn't care for it."

"What?" Anabelle blinked, unable to hide the surprise in her voice.

"He says it's too fussy."

Too fussy? Anabelle bit back the stinging words she longed to say. Geoff deserved a stiff kick in the hiney. He'd love-bombed Jecca and now controlled her completely. The fellow's self-centered lifestyle had not won over any of Jecca's friends.

"What about the venue? You are holding it at the village church, aren't you?" Jecca had always intended to marry there, as her uncle was the vicar.

Jecca glanced away from the camera and swallowed. "Geoffrey doesn't care for the musty smell; it makes him sneeze, so we're going with a more modern venue."

Anabelle's knuckles whitened on her mobile. Jecca adored her uncle, the village church, and its congregation. She longed to throttle the fellow. How dare Geoffrey dash Jecca's dreams. Didn't he care how much that particular wedding dress and venue meant to his fiancé?

"Marriage is a partnership, with give and take on both sides. If you're having doubts . . ." Anabelle let it hang, holding back words that might drive a wedge between them.

"Mum said the same thing." Jecca sniffed as one lone tear slid down her cheek and dripped off her chin.

"Aw, Jecs. I didn't mean to upset you." Anabelle pressed her lips together, her heart filling with sympathy for her friend's pathos.

"I know. It's just that Geoffrey is so much older and wiser than I am." Jecca blew her nose, the trumpeting noise carrying through the connection.

"Is he?" To her way of thinking, Geoffrey thoroughly enjoyed having his way. Anabelle locked her jaw as a few choice words queued for expression–gaslighter being the most complimentary.

A muffled sob.

"Jec's. I'm sorry."

"It's okay. I'm just being a ninny. Tell me one thing, does Brodie boss you about?" Jecca asked with watery eyes.

Anabelle groaned. Brodie, her Type A fiancé, had certainly tried, but after she stood up for herself, he included her in their decision-making loop. That couldn't be easy for a man used to being in charge, but Brodie loved her and made a conscientious effort to change.

"Not so much. Perhaps, if you insist that you have equal say, he'll see reason." At least she hoped so for Jecca's sake.

A hiccup, then an exhale from Jecca's end. "Thanks for listening, Anabelle. I didn't want to say any more to Mum; she's not exactly team Geoffrey."

That made two of them.

"What's been happening with you?" Jecca asked, sounding more like herself.

Anabelle lifted her eyes to the hillside silhouetted by the moon's radiant beams. She glanced back at the screen and shuddered.

"I have a stalker." And out spilled the story, with Anabelle doing her level best to keep the fear from her voice.

"The police are involved, and your father's now hired a minder?" Jecca asked.

Anabelle could see the worry in her eyes. "I'll be fine."

Jecca didn't need another worry, not with Geoffrey's issues, issues that could ruin Jecca's life if she married the fellow.

"You will be careful, won't you?" Jecca asked.

"I will. I am. It's all good. Stop worrying. I was just updating you on what's been going on. I miss you, Jec's. We need a girl's weekend with Cressida—a getaway where we stay in our jammies, watch movies, and eat unhealthy food."

"I agree. We're definitely overdue." Jecca yawned. "I hate to break this up, but I gotta go. I've an early morning. Ta, luv."

"Cheers." Anabelle blew her a kiss and disconnected. So focused on her conversation with Jecca, she hadn't registered the soft tread of trainers on the wooden dock behind her until hands came down on both of her shoulders.

She gasped, twisted at the waist, and peered up in the dark. "Brodie! You gave me such a fright."

"Sorry about that. I thought you heard me." He reached down and helped her to her feet.

"Couldn't sleep?" She snuggled into his arms, partly for warmth and partly to gain closer access to him.

"I woke up when you left the house. I started worrying when you didn't return, so I came outside to see if everything was all right. I hope I didn't intrude on a private conversation."

"Jecca and I were catching up. Brodie, she's not the least bit happy. That fiancé of hers is all about himself and completely wrong for her."

"It's probably best if she figures that out for herself, or she'll likely resent any interference."

A cold breeze blew off the loch and ruffled her hair. Brodie pushed the stray strands out of her face.

"You're right." He had such a level head, even in times of high emotion. "But what if she goes through with it?"

"Then you'll be there to mop her up and help her back on her feet, like the good friend you are." He kissed the tip of her nose, then brushed her lips with a featherlight touch that erupted tingles all over her body. She lifted her arms around his neck and pressed her mouth to his.

The inky night around her seemed to vanish, replaced by a limitless dark expanse—an emptiness that matched her sense of awe. His warm lips moved over hers—first gentle, then with increasing urgency. She answered him eagerly, kiss for kiss. Above them, stars spun wildly, as if the universe itself revolved around the heat they generated from their own personal sun.

Abruptly, Brodie stepped back, letting her go. The swirling stars slowed and steadied, shining once more as distinct points of light scattered across black velvet. A strong gust tossed her hair into her face and brushed her arms. Anabelle shivered, reality sinking in once more. "Come lass, time to return to yer room before I forget myself and behave badly."

Sighing, Anabelle slipped her hand into his and glanced up at his profile.

The muscle in his jaw bunched, the way it did when Brodie fought for control.

"Quit looking at me like that, lass," Brodie ground out, keeping his eyes forward.

"Like what?" Her mouth curved.

"Like ye want to take a bite out of me. I'm doing my best to be the gentleman here," he growled.

"But what if I want to take a bite out of you?" She ran a finger along his wrist.

"I'd love nothing more than to toss ye over my shoulder and have my way with ye."

"What's stopping you?" Curiosity welled within her, rising above the desire that had consumed her only moments earlier.

"Respect for ye, and a promise I made to God."

"What promise?" This was news to her.

"That if *He* ever let us cross paths again, and I could persuade ye to accept me, I'd protect yer virtue until things were legal between us."

Admiration coursed through her. "Brodie Maxwell, you are a legend." This fellow of hers wasn't anything like Jecca's fiancé. Brodie never lost sight of the big picture and intended to save their intimacy for their wedding night.

Old-fashioned. Yes.

But Brodie held to his standards, and she loved him all the more for it.

Her heart melted into a puddle, and she blinked her stinging eyes. This fellow was her knight, one of those ancient protectors who swore an oath of fealty to their liege lords—only hers had covenanted his allegiance to God.

A hot tear trickled down her cheek, and she wiped it away as the well of joy inside her overflowed.

He brushed it away. "You all right, lass?"

"Happy tears. I'm grateful you're such a good man." *Thank you, Heavenly Father, for Brodie.*

The clouds of doubt had obscured her confidence in Brodie's love when the reno demanded his time, but his feelings for her remained unchanged, constant as the sunrise over his granite-clad Munros.

Steady, determined, and stubborn. That was Brodie down to the ground.

Smiling, she twined her spare arm around his waist and pressed her head against his shoulder as they made their way back to the house.

Brodie was right. Jecca would figure things out. If not, Anabelle intended to help her glue the pieces back together.

Chapter 38

A WOMAN COULD GET USED to this, Anabelle thought as she reclined on the sitting room sofa, her gaze drifting to where Brodie lay on the yoga mat, sweat glistening on his bare arms as he counted out another set of reps. They'd returned to Soldier's Leap several days ago. While Brodie didn't hover, exactly, he came up with every possible excuse to be nearby since that last text arrived from her stalker. Today, he'd shown up after work, towing a cart loaded with a gym bag and weights.

She picked up the controller and changed stations on the telly, while absently rubbing Daisy's silky ears with her free hand. Her gaze boomeranged back to Brodie and his bulging muscles, and she tried not to stare at the sight. Stalker or no, she was thoroughly enjoying the view before her.

"Getting anything out of that?" Brodie jerked his chin toward the telly when he paused between a set of reps.

"Not really."

If she had a choice, she'd rather turn on a movie and cuddle with him on the sofa, but the prospect across the salon might be her next favorite option. He caught her ogling and winked, a sparkle in his eyes.

Daisy nudged Anabelle's hand and whimpered.

"I'm warning you, Daisy. Once I shower, you are moving," Brodie said.

"When will that be?" Anabelle batted her eyelashes at him.

"Soon, lass. This is my last set." Brodie wiggled his brows at her.

Anabelle snuggled into the pillows, no longer bothering with the remote as she eyeballed her fellow. The renovation wrapped soon, and though deeply attached to the estate, the idea of leaving didn't trouble her the way it once had—doubtless, because she could return any time she pleased.

"Done." Brodie ran a small towel over his shoulders, neck, and arms, then jumped to his feet. Even with his demanding workload, he never skipped a workout.

And oh, how she admired its effects.

A wicked grin quirked his mouth. "Ye keep staring like that, Miss Dewhurst, and I'm liable to join ye as I am." Grabbing two sets of free weights, he deposited them on the cart, then rolled up his mat and laid it across the weights.

"Where can I shower?" Brodie asked, picking up his gym bag.

"The laundry room has a shower. That one is closest, but you're welcome to any of the others."

Brodie saluted before he disappeared, whistling down the corridor.

"Don't get too sleepy, Daisy." The dog lifted her head and placed her muzzle on Anabelle's chest. "Brodie meant every word." Anabelle ran her hand down the dog's spine. Moaning with pleasure, Daisy rolled, belly-up to give her greater access.

Her mobile vibrated, and she checked the ID before swiping to video chat.

"Hiya, Grandmama."

"Anabelle. You're looking peaked." Grandmama frowned. "Brides should take every precaution to look their best for their wedding day."

"I've been working overtime. That's what happens when you have a career." Her grandmother had never worked a day in her life, though she kept busy serving the Queen.

"Don't be cheeky, young lady. Show some respect. I've been handling your wedding affairs."

"I'm sorry, Grandmama." Anabelle plucked at the pillow beside her, shame setting fire to her cheeks. Lack of sleep was no excuse for unkindness. She cleared her throat. "Is there something I can do for you?"

"I thought you and Brodie would appreciate an update. Your announcements are mailed, and the wedding cake is ordered. I even located the fountain you selected for nonalcoholic beverages."

"Wow. That's brilliant." A burst of excitement rushed through her. The cascading tower, with its muted lights, added a magical element to events she had attended.

"I also rang the florist with your peculiar request. You must know that roses are best for weddings."

Anabelle clenched her jaw and fought a childish urge to roll her eyes. They'd been through this a half a dozen times already. "The yellow iris, myrtle, stephanotis, and lily of the valley match the Maxwell tartan."

"Such garish colors." Grandmama tossed her head.

"Brodie's clan chief, the Duke of Strathclyde, is coming and will appreciate our choice."

"That's quite a coup." Grandmama's tone shifted, and she beamed. "The Queen of the United Kingdom and the Duke of Strathclyde will be your guests. This wedding will be the event of the season." Grandmama shuffled several papers. "Has the Duke of Devon accepted his invitation?"

"He's in the south of France," Anabelle informed her.

"A shame that your mother never uses that connection from her father's family." Grandmama clucked her tongue against her teeth.

"Devon is Mother's third cousin. They've only met a half dozen times and are hardly more than passing acquaintances." With a twenty-year age gap between them, Mother and Devon had little in common.

Grandmama sighed, doubtless finding her daughter, Eliza, a lost cause when it came to social hierarchy. "Did you secure a venue for the reception?"

"We intend to use the gardens at Kirkton House. They're lovely and have a view of the loch." She'd updated Grandmama with this information in her last email.

"That's rather risky, isn't it? Scottish weather is notorious. And November? Is that wise?"

"We've reserved heaters and tents, one of which has a dance floor. And if the weather is too inclement, we'll move the venue indoors."

"It storms dreadfully in the Highlands," Grandmama continued.

"As I recall, the Queen's last Garden Party proved quite dismal," Anabelle countered. What was keeping Brodie? She needed an excuse to ring off.

"Is Kirkton House large enough to accommodate your guests if the party is moved indoors?"

"It's similar in size to High Ridge Hall," Anabelle said. "And the public rooms flow from one to the next."

Grandmama lifted her brows at the camera lens. "I had no idea Brodie's family lives so lavishly." She cleared her throat, a sign that had Anabelle metaphorically girding her loins.

"Have the Maxwells reconsidered their choice of attire? Kilts are tacky."

Anabelle closed her eyes and bit the inside of her cheek to hold back a disrespectful response. Grandmama might be in her early seventies, but age had not mellowed her tactics. She manipulated, or steamrolled, anyone who kept her from having her way.

"All the men, including the Duke of Strathclyde, will be in kilts." Anabelle's jaw ached from clenching it so tightly. "Including Father."

"Barbaric. All those men in that incessant wind with their skirts flapping. You know what they say—"

Brodie entered the room at that exact moment, his hair still wet from the shower. Sighing with relief, Anabelle turned her mobile so Grandmama could see him. His entrance saved her from further disparagement of kilts, Highlanders, and Scots in general.

"Say hello to Grandmama. She's mailed the announcements and ordered our cake. Isn't that lovely?" Anabelle made a face out of camera range.

"That's grand of you, Lady Barbara. Thank you."

Grandmama inclined her neck in that regal way, as though granting royal favors—a mannerism that generally drove Anabelle to the edge of sanity.

"I don't know why young people are in such a rush these days to get married. In my time, engagements lasted for years."

"Things are much less proper than they used to be." Brodie's sympathetic tone went a long way to soothing Grandmama's prickly attitude.

Anabelle repositioned the mobile. "Grandmama, we need to go. We'll talk soon." Without waiting for a response, she disconnected the chat and leaned against the pillows.

"That was rather abrupt. Was your conversation that bad?" Brodie joined her on the sofa, dislodging Daisy, who jumped onto the floor with an indignant air.

"Not in so many words, but I know Grandmama. She was gearing up for another flower and kilt skirmish."

"She doesn't care for the flowers?" Brodie questioned in an innocent tone.

Anabelle did roll her eyes then. Grandmama's relentless push for roses and the exclusion of kilts made her temples throb. "Why can't she be more like Granny Dewhurst?"

"Because, my bonnie bride-to-be, she isn't. Lady Barbara is one of a kind. Would your Granny Dewhurst have the connections to get those announcements printed and mailed so quickly?"

That made Anabelle pause. "You're right. Granny Dewhurst excelled at cuddles, stories, music, and listening." She had no right to compare her grandmothers—they were as different as tart apples and sticky toffee pudding.

"Grandmama found a fountain." A smile broke through Anabelle's frustration.

"Nice." Brodie gave her a high five.

"What do I do the next time she mentions roses?" Anabelle rested her head against the sofa cushion and stared at the ceiling.

"Encourage her to remarry and show us what we are missing. Speaking of missing. . ." Brodie snaked an arm around her shoulders and dipped his head for a kiss. "Better?" he asked at length.

She cocked her head. "I'm not sure. I think I need more convincing."

Chapter 39

Morning sunlight streamed through the ballroom's clerestory windows as Anabelle hammered the final tack into place on the business center's topper. *Finished at last.* Those window treatments had taken longer than anticipated, but they were finally mounted and ready for installation. She stretched, working out the burn in her upper back from bending over for so long.

Daisy whined from her doggy bed beside Anabelle's feet. "There, there, love." She stroked the dog's silky ears.

Four days ago, she and Brodie returned from Kirkton House. Upon her return to Soldier's Leap, she met the security detail Dad had hired for her protection, a burly fellow by the name of Stanley, who hung about in doorways and rarely spoke. After several forays at conversation, with muted, one-syllable answers, Anabelle had given up polite conversation and even forgot his presence for long stretches.

Rising, Anabelle returned the straight pins to the cushion just as the doorbell sounded. She paused, her heart banging against her ribs. *Please don't let it be another bouquet.*

The bell rang once more, followed by a knock.

"Stanley, could you answer that?" she called over her shoulder to the security detail.

"Right." Stanley left his post and stepped into the foyer, his shoulders almost as wide as he was tall.

She put away the hammer and upholstery tacks, then stretched to relieve her burning back one last time. Male voices carried from the foyer before Paul Symonds, Genesis's Vice President over the UK division, entered the ballroom.

"Nice digs." Paul lifted his eyes to the gilded moldings. "This is stunning."

"Thank you. How are you, Mr. Symonds?" Anabelle stepped forward to greet him, questions churning inside. What was he doing here? Inspecting the job site? Or did he have a meeting with Brodie?

"It looks like I've interrupted something." Paul eyed the toppers.

"I just finished the business center's window treatments. We're hanging them this afternoon. That's why I'm working over here today instead of at my desk." Anabelle indicated the organized mess.

Paul shifted his weight from one foot to the other.

"Mr. Symonds, may I offer you a cup of tea?"

"No. No."

When he didn't say anything further, but continued to look uncomfortable, she asked, "Is there something that you need?" Was he looking for Brodie?

"I'm here to formally apologize on behalf of Genesis for placing you on probation. Nothing I say can undo what you must have suffered, but we'd like you to accept this as a token of how badly we feel about the situation." Paul pressed an envelope into her hand.

Not knowing what else to do, Anabelle opened the flap and glanced inside. A check for £20,000.00! Utterly gobsmacked, she reread the number. "That's incredibly generous."

"We're dreadfully sorry."

"In all fairness, the evidence seemed conclusive. I'm just grateful the forensic specialist proved my innocence, or I'd be returning to university for a degree in another field."

"About that," Paul hesitated, then cleared his throat. "Sky News is cooling their heels in your foyer. It was the best idea we had to clear your name in the industry."

Anabelle blinked at him. Sky News? This situation smelled of Brodie. In fact, she was almost certain of it.

"Where will this interview take place?" Truth be told, she'd rather not do the interview.

"Our publicist thought to open with a shot of you playing the piano, then introduce you as the granddaughter of the renowned composer, Belle Lindsay Dewhurst."

Anabelle fisted her hands as self-consciousness overwhelmed her. At least she could partially hide behind the piano. Perhaps this interview wouldn't be so terrible.

"What do you think?" Paul asked.

"I like the angle." Anabelle nodded slowly. "It's gimmicky but has heart." Playing the instrument where Granny took her first lessons was a brilliant way to segue into the interview.

She motioned for Stanley to join her. "Could you escort everyone to the music room while I change into something more appropriate?" Anabelle indicated her jeans and paint-spattered T-shirt.

Starting for the doorway, she paused. "Paul, do you have a copy of the interview questions? I assume there's a script?"

"Brodie forwarded them to you," Paul said.

"It would help if I checked my emails, wouldn't it?" she smiled brightly, holding back a tremor. Ever since her stalker's last communication, she struggled with opening her electronic messages.

"Right this way." Stanley motioned toward the open doorway, and Paul, along with men carrying cameras and equipment followed him to the music room–a well-known British presenter trailing in their wake.

Anabelle took the lift upstairs to her room, playing the interview questions via text-to-speech while she changed into a blue dress that hugged her waist. She sat at her dressing table and slipped on a pair of Gianvito Rossi pumps, then ran a brush through her hair, and touched up her makeup.

Lastly, she added a pair of medium-sized gold earrings to complement the ensemble–simple, classic, no-fuss chic. She didn't have time for anything elaborate. After a glance in the full-length mirror to check for lint, she dashed to the music room.

Five men, including Paul and Stanley, turned as one when she entered.

Stanley once more planted himself in the doorway with a clear view of the corridor and the adjoining library.

"Anabelle, come meet Michael Evans. He's conducting your interview." Paul motioned her over.

"Welcome to Soldier's Leap." Anabelle crossed the room and extended her hand to the television presenter.

"A pleasure." Michael nodded respectfully. "This is quite a place."

"Thank you. Genesis has done wonders with Soldier's Leap on this renovation." Anabelle reclaimed her hand, then faced the cameraman.

"I'm Jimmy." A tall man with a protruding Adam's apple clipped a mic to her collar and asked her to speak several times. Satisfied with the sound reading, he gave her a thumbs-up.

"I'm Howard, the director, but I'm wearing two hats today. He moved, tinkering with the camera lights for a moment, then set up the shade screens.

Nerves danced, doubtless a close relative of stage fright, and made her limbs weak. Michael Evans was in her music room. This was real. What if she froze up on national television?

Michael read over his notes, then set them aside when Brodie sauntered in. Paul made one last round of introductions.

"Sky News?" Brodie stood alongside Paul and folded his arms. "You outdid yourself, Paul."

"Miss Dewhurst, I'd like to start the segment with you seated at the piano," Michael said. "I understand you play."

"Yes. Did you have something particular in mind? Or should I play one of my grandmother's favorites from Mozart's *The Marriage of Figaro*?"

"That should do marvelously," Michael said.

"I'll need a moment to warm up." Anabelle moved to the piano to limber up her fingers.

"Go ahead. I need to tweak one more thing." The cameraman adjusted a shade, then checked her for shadows, while Jimmy programmed an electronic device.

Taking a seat, Anabelle ran her fingers over the ivories in a series of short scales. All nervousness eased as a feeling of peace distilled upon her soul. Looking up, she nodded. "I'm ready."

"Brilliant. In three," Howard said. "Three. Two. One," Howard, the director, called out the seconds.

Anabelle pressed her fingers to the keyboard and played the last few stanzas of Granny's favorite Mozart piece *The Marriage of Figaro*. The music pulsed with emotion as the melody filled the room, taking full advantage of the acoustics. On the last chord, Howard motioned for the cameraman to shift to Michael.

"This is Michael Evans with Sky News. Today brings me to the former home of celebrated composer Dame Belle Lindsay Dewhurst, the dowager Lady Huddleton. Mozart's piece was a particular favorite of Belle Dewhurst's, and was performed by her granddaughter, Anabelle . . ."

With the house now emptied of television crew, Anabelle changed back into grubbies and spent the next half hour carting window treatments to the business center. Stanley even offered his services, or it would have taken ages to lug them all to the far side of the house.

"That should do it." Anabelle pushed hair off her sticky forehead. "Thank you, Stanley."

The security detail grunted his acknowledgement.

One of these days, she intended to see if the fellow could rub two sentences together. He took his job seriously, though, which gave her a sense of peace, the first since her stalker had amped up his game.

"Back to the office we go." She forced a smile, then headed to the conference room with the loquacious Stanley on her heels. He took up his vigil in the doorway where he had a view of the corridor and the conference room.

Mr. Mellencamp bustled past, acknowledging her with a curt nod, his arms loaded with linens. His wife must have snagged him for gopher duty. But why was he in this sector of the house?

"Welcome to our organized chaos." Randy glanced at her from his position in front of the enormous white board.

"I passed Mr. Mellencamp just now. He looked like a man on a mission," Anabelle commented, her gaze taking in the updates on the board.

"The Mrs. lassoed him to help move the bedding to the linen closet."

Randy snorted, clearly enjoying Mellencamp's discomfort. "I meant to tell you, those backordered headboards arrived."

"Finally." Anabelle placed a hand on her hip. "I almost cancelled that order. It's amazing how they magically appeared after that nastygram Tara sent them."

Randy chuckled, then returned to the board and updated the list of his completed projects. Even though everyone shared an electronic chart, the whiteboard proved easier to read than the multitude of colored entries on the calendar.

"The toppers are in the business center and are ready for installation." Anabelle joined him, eyeing what he'd checked off.

"Nice. I'll have my guys hang them after lunch." Randy texted his team the information.

"Thanks." Anabelle headed into her shared office.

Tara looked up from her computer desk, where a pair of work gloves lay beside her keyboard. "There you are. How was the interview?"

"Nerve-racking. But it's done." Taking a seat at her workstation, Anabelle booted up her computer.

"Your sister rang," Tara said.

"Cressida?" Anabelle raised both brows. "Did she say why?"

"No. She asked that you to ring her at your earliest convenience. Keep it brief. When you return from Stirling, you'll need to handle any loose ends that popped up during your absence. This trip of yours couldn't have come at a more critical phase in the reno."

"This isn't a pleasure trip, Tara. We're finalizing the menu for our wedding." Anabelle tapped the keyboard with more force than necessary. Sometimes, Tara's myopic focus made her long to tug the woman's hair.

"I do understand, but you're leaving us in the lurch, and it's too late for me to hire a replacement." Tara flipped her hair and returned to her screen.

Replacement? Anabelle's lips stretched, her smile fake as saccharine. "I'm no longer on probation, *remember?* A forgery expert ruled in my favor, and Genesis extended a formal apology."

"Do they have any idea who did it?" Tara didn't apologize, but her attitude softened a tad.

"I couldn't say."

Chapter 40

I ENTER the restaurant where the tasting is taking place for Anabelle's reception and scout around until I locate a storage cupboard with uniforms and hair nets and caps. I find the right size, then slip into the men's room to cover my clothes, and put on the mask to disguise my features, a rubber one I paid one-hundred and fifty quid for.

Cameras aren't a problem now.

Grinning behind my mask, I head for the kitchen. It's best if I memorize the floor plan before they arrive. Being prepared for every eventuality is my motto.

I offered to pick up a shipment for Tara in Perth. No one knows my real errand. The idea of being so far from Anabelle is intolerable, even for just a day. I need to see her skin—that creamy, flawless complexion that is so essentially her. Beautiful flesh I yearn to touch.

A server, carrying rolled napkins around cutlery, passes me in the corridor. I hold my breath. Is she going to stop me and ask who I am? Silencing her would ruin everything.

She doesn't so much as give me a nod. I exhale and continue to my destination, a plan forming in my mind.

It's so daring. It just might work.

Chapter 41

The corner booth tucked in the back of the restaurant seated eight, an overindulgence for a party a little over half that size. The ever silent Stanley sat at the adjoining table, alert and uncommunicative. Anabelle shifted, the cool vinyl banquette making a disgusting noise as her bare legs stuck to the material. Cressy, seated beside her, laughed, and Jecca's lips twitched from across the table.

Anabelle gloried in both responses, Cressy's because of the year she'd had battling cancer, and Jecca, because she rarely smiled these days. Her bestie had flown up with Cressy to meet them for the tasting, and Anabelle sincerely hoped it would help her clear her head and see Geoff for the gaslighting beast that he was.

Brodie intended to join them later after they'd narrowed the options. Right now, he was handling several errands for Randy, who had run short on basic construction supplies.

Everything for the wedding had been set until yesterday, when the caterer fell and broke her femur. Mother had gone into full fix-it mode, forcing her and Cressida spend the entire day ringing every known restaurant in Stirling to find someone who could cover the reception.

The restaurant manager, Alina, a slender woman with extra-short hair and a Polish accent, whose name tag and title, manager, were listed on her crisp white shirt, approached the table. Behind her came a server with a large circular tray loaded with small-sized samples.

"We have a variety of appetizers for you." Alina circulated cards and short pencils to everyone. "Please fill out these forms as you go along, rating each between one to ten. It will help in your selection."

The server set an array of small crockery on the table with everything from stuffed mushrooms all the way to muscles.

"This looks so good." Cressida selected a small fork, speared a mushroom, and popped it into her mouth. "Mmm."

Warmth permeated Anabelle's heart to see her sister, who'd been so ill from the treatments, actually enjoying food again. Mother's eyes teared, and Jecca's shadows lifted as they all watched Cressy eat.

"What?" Cressy paused with her fork hovering over the shrimp. "Do I have something on my face?"

"No, dear." Mother sniffed, then eyed the smorgasbord before them with interest.

"It's just nice to see you eating," Jecca said.

"Trust me, it's heavenly." Cressy wrinkled her nose at the sea urchin eggs. "But I think I'll pass on those."

Anabelle made a face, selecting one of the smoked muscles on a separate platter. "This smells delicious."

The tasting progressed, with Alina bringing in a selection of soups, including Cullen Skink, a smoked fish chowder. "Brodie's going to miss out if he doesn't hurry up."

"Alina, is there a way to garnish the Cullen Skink to dress it up a mite?" Mother asked.

"Yes, we can do that. Paprika, or fresh herbs, would add a dash of color. We've done that for other occasions."

Anabelle's stomach cramped. She kept a smile firmly pasted on her face until Alina and her team left their table.

"Is something wrong?" Mother set down her cutlery.

"Did you have a bad oyster?" Jecca asked.

"I didn't try any, but I did have one of those smoked muscles that I love." Nausea clawed its way up her esophagus. "I'm going to be sick."

She climbed over Cressy and dashed into the ladies' room around the corner from their table. By the time she reached the toilet, a rushing filled her ears.

"No," she moaned and pressed her hands to her face, her skin ice-cold, her heartbeat erratic and so loud it drowned out all sound. The room spun, faster and faster, darkness invading the edges of her vision.

What was happening? She tried to push up off the cold tiles, but her body didn't respond. She couldn't move. She groaned, her breathing shallow, her body frozen, bereft of warmth, and the black closing in, blotting out the space.

The stall door beside her opened. Footsteps. Then hands tugged her backward, out of the stall, and lifted her onto the open window ledge before she lost consciousness.

"Sorry, ladies. I tried to get here before the tasting began, but traffic was a beast on the M9," Brodie said, a frown forming between his brows. "Where's Anabelle?"

"She ate something that didn't agree with her," Lady Huddleton said. "I need to check on her. She's been gone a while." She hurried toward the ladies.

"It wasn't a muscle, was it?" Brodie asked the table's two remaining occupants.

"Yes."

"Did either of you have any?"

"No. Anabelle was the only one. They had an orange substance on top that didn't appeal to me. But you know Anabelle and smoked muscles."

"Aye." Brodie tapped the tabletop, debating whether to enter a women's toilet and check on her himself. Stanley appeared of the same mind, shifting from foot to foot.

Lady Huddleton returned to the table but did not take her seat. "No one's in the ladies, and the kitchen staff haven't seen Anabelle," she informed Stanley "She's gone."

"I'll check the alley." Stanley rushed out the entrance.

"Gone." Brodie's hands transformed into cold blocks of ice at Lady Huddleton's words. He jumped to his feet. "She didn't leave by the entrance?"

"No. Nor by the kitchen."

"Is there a storage room she could have holed up in?"

"I'll ask." Lady H. spun and all but crashed into the restaurant manager. "My daughter's ill. Do you know of any place she might have gone for a lie down?"

After a brief explanation, Alina shook her head. "We only have shallow closets for our table linens. I will check the freezer. Sometimes new workers accidentally get locked inside."

Taking matters into his own hands, Brodie barged into the ladies. The room with its three stalls proved empty of people, just as Lady H. had said. His scan of the room ended on the low-hung sash window, and an entirely new scenario took shape.

He bolted across the tiled, checkerboard floor and gripped the window. It slid up in silence as his worst suspicions accelerated at warp speed. No one else had eaten a muscle. If they had, they would be sick too. Did the stalker know enough about Anabelle to realize her love of muscles? If so, had he followed her to Stirling and deliberately poisoned her food? After all, the guy had poisoned him before. In a normal situation, he wouldn't jump to such conclusions, but with a stalker after Anabelle, he couldn't sit around and wait for the police to figure this out.

Brodie climbed out the window. A blurred shoeprint, much too large for Anabelle's foot, made a slight depression in the soil. He rushed to the road and scanned the pedestrian traffic in both directions on the pavement in time to spy a man carrying a woman with long brown hair.

Brodie sprinted in pursuit. "Stop that man," he hollered up the block. "Stop him. He's kidnapping my fiancé."

A few people turned to stare as he pushed past. "Call the police. Stop that fellow." Brodie rasped, his feet never slowing as he closed in. The fellow glanced over his shoulder, exposing a weathered face full of wrinkles.

Brodie faltered. Huh. From the back, he could have sworn the man was much younger.

"Stop. That. Kidnapper," Brodie bellowed now only fifty meters from his target.

This time, two university students approached the man. "Hey. Put her down," one of the male students stepped closer.

The man dropped Anabelle, then slashed out with a knife. The student jumped back, narrowly escaping the weapon and tumbling backward onto the curb.

A woman screamed. "Call the cops."

Panting heavily, Brodie arrived and drew the fellow's attention, keeping the man's knife a healthy distance from both Brodie and the male student. The young man jumped to his feet and shifted to the opposite side of the blade-yielding man, helping split his focus.

Anabelle lay on the concrete, her eyes closed, skin a waxy color.

He yelled, deep from his gut, the roar of a wounded bear. The fellow, now surrounded by pedestrians filming his attack, turned tail and darted into traffic. Horns honked. Brakes shrieked.

Brodie followed, his focus solely on Anabelle's kidnapper. Kicking out with his leg, he caught the fellow in the back of the thigh, sending Anabelle's stalker down on one knee. Snarling, the fellow bolted to his feet and darted into the crowd across the street.

Torn, Brodie, halted, glancing back toward Anabelle, her injuries unknown. Did he chase her attacker or check her for wounds? Concern for her welfare won the day, and he raced to her side, kneeling to check her pulse. It was much too rapid.

"Someone call an ambulance," he yelled.

"Already did, sir." The university student, who had almost taken a gut swipe from that butcher's blade, rejoined him. "How is she?"

"I don't know." Brodie searched the youth's face. "Thanks, man. Glad you're safe."

The kid shrugged. "Just doing what anyone else would."

Brodie stroked Anabelle's cheek. "Anabelle, love. Can ye hear me?"

Her eyelashes fluttered, but she didn't regain consciousness, not even when the ambulance arrived and loaded her onto a gurney. Brodie climbed inside the back with her, not giving the medics time to object.

Loaded with questions and brimming with fury, he rode to the hospital, ringing Lady H. on the way.

Then he rang Finn, blistering his cousin's ears with Gaelic obscenities.

"Haven't heard you speak like that since we were fifteen. I'm proud you remembered the words," Finn said when Brodie paused for breath.

"If you weren't a copper, I'd pop you for that."

"I'd like to see ye try," Finn countered right back.

"That lunatic almost got away with kidnapping Anabelle–in broad daylight." And where was that blasted bodyguard Lord Huddleton hired? Why hadn't he returned? Her father paid him an exorbitant salary to protect his daughter.

Finn let him rant until he'd exhausted his repertoire of words. "I'll meet you at the hospital, Brodie. I'm glad you got her in time."

Brodie lifted Anabelle's hand, clasping her cold fingers, and found that his were shaking.

Chapter 42

THAT DOCTOR IS NOT GOING to cut Anabelle's flawless skin. That is my privilege alone, and only if she misbehaves.

I push the surgical theater's double doors wide and enter a sterile environment. Not one person has questioned me. Confidence and quick thinking work like a charm.

Up ahead, I spot a curtained partition and step behind it, just as two nurses hurry past. A patient lies asleep on the bed behind me, tubes and driplines attached, and beeps fill the space from a monitor. This must be a recovery room. Grabbing a tablet off the desk, I peek into the corridor between the fabric, my heart beating fast.

Medical personnel confer with one another in subdued voices, not two meters from where I hide.

"Anabelle Dewhurst is in partition 2D," a nurse says, her voice high-pitched and nasal sounding. "Check for allergies before we stitch up that arm."

Pushing aside the curtain, I determine which way the prep and recovery partitions are numbered and head toward Anabelle. I reach her compartment, but a voice stops me cold.

"It's all right, lass."

Brodie Maxwell is here!

"Take this, Miss Dewhurst. It will help settle your nerves," a nurse said.

"What is it?" Anabelle's voice is higher than normal, like she's scared.

I frown. Anabelle isn't easily frightened. Her response makes me long to soothe her worries. But I'll do one better. The idea of someone piercing her perfect flesh, even for stitches . . . It's an abomination.

"I'll be back in a few minutes after that valium takes effect." The privacy curtain opens, and I jump out of the way as the nurse exits Anabelle's cubicle.

"Sorry," I mutter, ducking my head so she can't see my eyes.

The nurse hurries off, reading her chart, doubtless for the next patient's treatment plan.

"Are you all right if I use the men's? I'll be back before the nurse returns," Brodie said.

"I'm not surprised after you drank an entire sixteen-ounce Irn Bru," Anabelle said, her voice teasing.

I ease into the privacy cubicle next to Anabelle's just as Brodie enters the corridor. I tap my fingers on my leg as I watch him through the curtain's gap until he disappears from view, that long confident stride of his eating up the distance. I detest the man and everything about him. Especially his relationship with Anabelle.

She's mine.

I check my watch, making sure to wait until the valium kicks in. The minutes stretch, and I grow impatient. But I keep it together and wait out the time, then, keeping my face averted, I slip into Anabelle's bay. Only my eyes show above the medical mask. I won't give away my identity just yet. Not until we're alone.

What good luck that I followed the ambulance. No more wasted time apart. No more Brodie Maxwell calling the shots.

I move behind Anabelle's bed and release the brakes, then unhook her from the intravenous bag. "Off we go now," I say, rasping to disguise my voice.

"You aren't going to sew me up right now, are you?" Anabelle wobbles upright, her eyes big but not scared. Her speech is already thick from the sedative I laced in her food and the valium the nurse gave her.

I grin behind my mask and file that away. Anabelle's disarming in a drugged state. "Not until later," I say in that same fake tone.

"Oh." She lies back and closes her eyes. "I'm dizzy."

I wheel her down the corridor to the lifts, my breath shallow and fast. I must get her out of here before Brodie returns.

Chapter 43

BRODIE TUGGED open the curtain to Anabelle's bay and blinked at the empty space. He'd been gone less than two minutes. The nurse couldn't have whisked her away. The valium had barely had time to take affect.

He spun around and bumped into the nurse in question. "Sorry. Did they take Anabelle for scans?"

"No. I'm here to prep her for sutures." The nurse craned her neck and took in the empty Accident and Emergency bay. "There must be a mistake." She hurried to the nurse's station, with Brodie hard on her heels, his worries mounting.

"Did someone move Anabelle Dewhurst?"

A nurse seated behind the desk clicked on her screen and typed Anabelle's name on her keyboard. "No."

"She's not in her bay."

A tingling started in Brodie's limbs, raising the hairs on his neck and arms. Anabelle's stalker wouldn't have followed her in here, not after they'd almost caught him. Would he?

But the feeling persisted.

Without Stanley to guard her while in the loo, Anabelle had been there for the taking. Gah. He could kick himself for that blunder, and now Anabelle was to pay the price for it.

Brodie scanned the area, but no one pushed a gurney down the main corridor. Following his gut, he sprinted down the hall, gripped the end cubicle of the nurse's station, pivoted around the corner, and bolted to the lifts.

Sliding to a halt, he glanced at the lights above the metal doors. Two elevators were in use. One going up. The other down.

Gah.

He charged to the stairwell, jumping over the handrail down a half flight of steps to save time. Reaching the next floor, he burst into the corridor, only to find the elevator car open and empty.

His chest heaved as he entered the car, punched the next floor, the metal sliding shut with a ding and starting its climb. "Come on. Come on," he panted.

When the doors pinged, he stuck his head out, checking the corridor. Private patient rooms. Blast! He swept his gaze over the lift buttons. All were going down.

Hitting the button, he waited for the lift to respond, precious seconds ticking. He almost bolted back into the stairwell, but the doors closed and started their descent.

His heart thundered like a summer storm, loud and harsh. Two floors later, he again peeked into the corridor outside the lifts. Two patients in push chairs moved toward the exit, each maneuvered by medical staff in scrubs. But one of the patient's heads lolled to the side, exposing long dark hair.

Brodie erupted from the lift, a Highland battle cry erupting from his lips. The fellow pushing Anabelle's chair partially turned and scanned the area. His eyes widened when they landed on Brodie bearing down on him in full Scottish fury.

The creeper let go of the pushchair and sprinted out the hospital exit into the car park.

"Aaargh," Brodie bellowed, the sound erupting from his diaphragm. He didn't follow, only gripped Anabelle's chair and swung to face her. She smiled up at him, her eyelids at half-mast, the irises dilated.

"Bro –" Anabelle's head flopped forward, her chin resting on her chest.

He scooped her up into his arms, his heart still racing like a druggie on a meth high. Ten seconds more, and he would have lost her. So close. Much too close.

Brodie kissed her, his body shaking from reaction.

Ninety seconds. He'd only been gone ninety seconds, and that lunatic had pounced. Two times in one day.

They couldn't leave Anabelle alone for a second.

"Hiya, sis."

Anabelle moved her head, her vision swimming as she roused from the oddest dream about a pushchair and someone petting her face, telling her no one was going to mar her pretty skin.

She blinked twice, and her vision cleared. "Wills. What are you doing in Scotland?"

"I flew up this morning. You gave everyone a scare when you disappeared."

"I disappeared?" Her memory remained a massive fog.

"Your stalker paid you a visit." Wills's jaw clenched, the skin tight. "It's a good thing Brodie found you before that monster wheeled you out of the hospital."

That strange dream with the pushchair had been real. Bits of the experience floated through her misty mind. A man had stroked her neck. Crooning. His voice familiar. She told him to stop. Had he?

"When can I go home?" she asked.

"Tomorrow."

She made a face. She hated hospitals.

Shifting on the mattress, she attempted to move her arm, but it felt weighted. "Why is there a towel over my arm?"

"Brodie put it there, so you won't peek at your IV. We know how much you love needles."

Her stomach twisted. "There's a needle in me?" her voice rose, high-pitched as a child's.

"Just for a bit longer," Wills assured her. "You had so many drugs in your system, the doctor needed to flush them and monitor your condition."

Brodie rapped on the doorframe, then entered, sending Wills a meaningful look.

Wills bent over her bed and kissed her cheek. "See you soon. Only one of us can be in here with you at a time. Mother, Dad, and Cressy are in the lobby." He slapped Brodie on the shoulder as he left.

Things must have been much more desperate than Wills let on if the entire family had arrived.

"Lass, it's good to see you awake." Brodie took the single chair in the small, private room and squeezed her arm, the one not connected to a needle. Dark circles under his eyes belied his confident manner.

Anabelle closed her eyes, exhaustion weighing on her lids as everything returned in a rush. Brodie picked up her hand and pressed a kiss to her cheek.

"What's the date?" The drugs in her system made her lose all sense of time.

"October fifteenth."

"You should be at the airport," she said without opening her eyes.

"Change of itinerary." Brodie leaned in and whispered for her ears alone. "I can't fly to London for corporate meetings with my only girl in hospital."

"They release me tomorrow, and I'll be back at work very soon."

"Anabelle, those drugs affected your kidneys," he reminded her. "The doctor wants you to lie low for a few weeks. There could be a genetic weakness, and they intend to use every precaution."

"I'll be fine. We can't afford for me to miss work, not with that deadline."

"Sorry, lass. You've medical restrictions." Brodie tapped the end of her nose, then followed it up with a kiss. "And I won't allow you on the jobsite."

"Killjoy."

Chapter 44

THREE WEEKS LATER

My heart pumps fast, making me pant, as I park in front of the Soldier's Leap offices. Workers scurry across the graveled drive like a colony of ants, each intent on their job. Each focused, with their eyes on the goal.

My contract is done, and I shouldn't be here, but Anabelle is due back this morning after that leave of absence —her perfect skin marred by those sutures.

My mouth is dry, and I bite my tongue, filling the cavern with saliva as Anabelle climbs out of her car with that rotten dog of hers on a lead. I clench my hand. Why did she bring her dog? I should have finished off that mutt when I had the chance.

As for Stanley . . . I grip the knife inside my jacket pocket and hold my stencil kit in my other hand, my excuse for being on the property.

My heart ratchets up, and my breathing intensifies.

One way or another, Anabelle leaves with me today. I'm done waiting.

Chapter 45

Brodie grabbed a file from his credenza that contained all the employee signatures and drove to the forensic specialist's office. He needed to return to Soldier's Leap before the team meeting at 9:30 am. He had unfinished business with Mr. Crouch. If the fellow had an opening, perhaps they might get lucky and find the name of Anabelle's forger. Then he could surprise her with the result tonight after work.

On entering the building, the receptionist greeted him warmly. "Mr. Maxwell, your timing is impeccable. Mr. Crouch had a cancellation and is available to see you."

"Excellent." Brodie followed her to Crouch's lab.

His mobile vibrated inside his trouser pocket. He ignored it. The team could wait. Anabelle's safety came first.

George Crouch straightened from the half-bent position over his microscope, wearing a scowl at the interruption.

Brodie stepped forward and shook his hand. "I brought signatures of the two individuals I think bear looking into. The first is Hugo Jenson. The fellow puts off weird vibes. Though that's not a crime, I'm going with my gut on this to see if he's responsible for forging Ms. Dewhurst's name." Brodie cleared his throat before he continued.

"The other person is one of our team leads, a fellow called Mick Aiken. Miss Dewhurst was recently kidnapped. Even though her abductor wore a mask, he couldn't hide his build. Mick's height and weight are similar to the perp's, much more so than the other employees. Since the forger accessed documents, that narrows the field considerably, as only our team leads can access the on-site business offices." Brodie slapped the file against his thigh.

"After Anabelle's kidnapping, I started wondering if the two crimes might be connected, especially after I was poisoned. It's all too coincidental."

For all Brodie knew, the stalker was trying to get Anabelle fired so he could steal her away from him.

"Forgery is the lesser of the two crimes, but I'd appreciate it if you'd check these signatures first before we tackle the others."

"Ah. I wondered if you might know the culprit." Crouch's face underwent an immediate change.

"Why is that?" Brodie passed Crouch the folder.

"Because I generally recognize the work of clever forgers. But this one is new to me." Crouch placed the folder beside the microscope, then stepped to a filing cabinet, retrieved a binder, and returned to his workstation.

"Have a seat." Crouch pointed to one of the rolling stools near his workstation.

"It might be a shot in the dark, but I'd like to close the loophole on this forgery in case these signatures don't match. As it stands, we only assume one of my team members was the forger, but we need verification. If it's someone else, we need to know."

"I understand." Crouch took the file containing Mick and Hugo's contracts with their subsequent signatures, then opened an odd-looking scanner.

"What's that?" Brodie moved to the stainless-steel worktop.

"It's an infra-red scanner that separates ink shades and ultraviolet light to examine modifications to paper via erasure or chemicals." Crouch switched on the device with a click.

"Can't a computer do that?" Brodie asked.

"It would certainly make my job easier if they did. Unfortunately, we can't program computers to detect fraudulent handwriting at this time." Crouch fed both samples, one after the other, into the machine.

The scanner beeped, spit out the original work order, then scanned the second document. Crouch then moved to the microscope across the room. Brodie trailed after him, fascinated at the process, despite his pressing need for answers.

"What are you looking for now?"

"Give me time to read the printout first," Crouch snapped.

Brodie fought the urge to check his watch. Though an expert in his field, it didn't make Crouch any less of a crank.

The fellow compared the printout three times, then entered his findings in the binder. "This looks promising." Crouch bobbed his head as he set Mick's contract with its accompanying signature under the microscope.

"I'm checking for the pen weight and pressure." Crouch focused the lens and stared at the image.

Brodie fought the urge to squirm. Couldn't Crouch speed this along?

"I can tell you one thing. This individual is detail-oriented and exceptionally precise." Crouch lifted his head, his admiration apparent. "In fact, they're one of the best mimics I've encountered in quite some time." Crouch then compared Mick's signature to his findings on the work orders.

Long minutes passed, the sound in the lab came from the ticking clock and the hum of electronic devices.

"The pen weight is identical. Come look at this." Crouch motioned for Brodie to join him at the microscope.

"See here?" Crouch exclaimed, fairly bursting with energy.

"What am I looking for exactly?" Brodie pressed his eye to the lens.

"The weight adjustment. He lifts his pen on the *h,* just like in the forgery," Crouch exclaimed, excitement permeating his declaration.

Brodie squinted at Anabelle's signature, then exchanged it with the forged work order. For the life of him, he couldn't see any difference between Anabelle's signature and the forged document.

"The pressure Ms. Dewhurst uses on her name is lighter. And her forger lifts his pen instead of continuing through as she does."

"I'm not seeing it," Brodie apologized.

"Trust me, this is incredible luck."

"Why did it take so long to tell the difference between signatures?" If it was that easy, why had Crouch dragged his feet?

"I was backlogged. I also needed to document every stroke of the pen.

Since this signature was previously recorded, I was able to jump straight into the comparisons today." Crouch tugged his left earlobe. "If this fellow chooses, he could make a fortune in white-collar crime."

"You're positive that Mick Aiken is Ms. Dewhurst's forger?" Brodie needed absolute confirmation.

"Yes, Mr. Aiken is most definitely your forger, Mr. Maxwell. I'll forward this information to London."

Anabelle filled her lungs with moist air as she unclipped Daisy's lead and hung it on the hall tree, closing the outside door with her heel. Stanley stood nearby, saying little. She'd almost grown used to his quiet presence.

"You be a good girl." She rubbed Daisy's ears, and the dog leaned into her, groaning in doggie ecstasy. "I'll see you at lunch."

Aside from the doctor's order to avoid heavy lifting, she had a green light to return to normal activities, and that included work. In a nutshell, life was good.

And if the police caught her pesky stalker, life would be perfect. But until then, Anabelle side-eyed the silently lurking Stanley, who shadowed her every move, something Anabelle appreciated more and more as each day passed. In a nutshell, Stanley helped her feel safe..

Still dressed in raingear, Anabelle exited the family wing, followed by Stanley, and proceeded to the business office's conference room. Inside, she found Randy at the whiteboard, a printout in one hand and a marker in the other.

"Morning, Randy."

"Anabelle! It's good to see you back." Randy looked up from the printout and gave her a welcoming smile.

"Thanks. It's fabulous to be here."

"Looks like we're going to hit that deadline." Randy acknowledged the schedule, then snapped a picture of the whiteboard a second before his mobile buzzed. He glanced at it. "Duty calls." He bustled off, pressing the device to his ear. "Hiya. What do you have . . ."

Anabelle checked the daily schedule and all but rubbed her hands, a smile stretching her lips, and her heart thrumming with anticipation. The first six suites were ready for setup. She adored this phase of a project, the pinnacle, where everything came together.

Pivoting, she entered her office, hung up her outerwear, then sat at her workstation.

Tara glanced over from her computer. "Anabelle, I'm glad you're back. Can you take the lorry into Stirling and pick up the rugs for the second-floor suites?"

"Didn't we pay a delivery fee on those?" Anabelle scrunched her brows, positive she'd placed that order and covered the accompanying charge.

"We did. Unfortunately, we're setting up the first suites today, and the rug shop can't deliver until Friday."

"On it." Anabelle snatched the lorry keys, then grabbed her jacket.

Accompanied by Stanley, Anabelle slipped outside onto the drive via the office exit and ran into Mick and Gerald.

"Anabelle, it's nice to have you back," Gerald greeted her with a brief smile, an unusual occurrence for the taciturn fellow.

She jingled the keys in her hand.

"Where are you off to? Mick's expression sharpened on the keys.

Anabelle frowned. Why did Mick sound so odd? As if he were almost disappointed that she had returned.

"Stirling. I've a pickup."

Gerald's mobile buzzed. He read the text and groaned. "Someone's scratched the floor moving furniture. Gotta run." He headed for the office entrance, leaving Anabelle, Stanley, and Mick on the drive.

"I've an errand in Stirling as well. Care to give me a lift?" Mick asked, his eyes on Stanley.

Mick's coming would delay her return, but would save her from a long, quiet ride with the silent Stanley.

"Sounds good." She reached the lorry and climbed into the driver's seat with Stanley taking the passenger side. "What do you need in Stirling?" Anabelle asked, starting the engine when Mick plopped onto the bench directly behind her bodyguard.

"Bits and bobs at the paint supply shop."

Odd that. According to the whiteboard, Mick's team had completed their touchups and signed off yesterday. Someone must have damaged the gilding, a common enough occurrence during installs.

She released the parking brake and backed up, her eyes sweeping the front elevation of Soldier's Leap, before she put the lorry in gear and headed for the gate.

Chapter 46

Still seated inside Crouch's lab, Brodie rang Finn. He needed to update him about Crouch's verification, and toss his wild idea out there for Finn to shoot down. The call went straight to voicemail.

Expelling a frustrated breath, he disconnected.

A second later, Brodie's mobile vibrated. With Crouch, still on the line, expediting the evidence on Mick Aiken to his London counterpart, it gave Brodie time to answer.

"Maxwell."

"Brodie, it's Finn. I'm trying to reach Anabelle, but she isn't picking up. Is she with you by any chance?"

"No." He checked his watch. "She should be at work by now. What's going on?" His heartrate ticked up. "Have you identified our stalker?"

"I've narrowed it considerably."

Brodie straightened on his stool. He'd share Crouch's findings later. If the two crimes were not connected, forgery seemed the lesser of two evils when it came to Anabelle's crazed stalker.

"All your employees came through with flying colors, save for two. Retrieving this information took extra time as one isn't a British citizen," Finn said, his words clipped. "I've sent a patrol car to collect Hugo Jenson from his flat."

"May I ask why?"

Finn had obviously figured out Brodie's color-coded work schedule and used the team's temporary addresses to go after Hugo after realizing that Hugo no longer worked on site.

"Hugo Jenson spent seven years in a Latvian prison for kidnapping and abusing a tourist."

Brodie tugged at his tie, the material a lariat around his throat. Genesis had run background checks on all the team leads and staff, including Gerald, Tara, Mick, Randy, and Lance Billings, who handled the grounds crew. How had anyone with a record slid past them?

"Hugo completed his contract yesterday and cleared out last night."

"Mr. Jenson is a person of interest. If you see him hanging about the estate, ring me."

"We would also like to question Mr. Aikin." Finn's comment regained his attention.

"He cleared out yesterday, too. But, I agree both men should be apprehended. Crouch just identified Mick as Anabelle's forger."

Silence.

"You there?" Brodie asked.

"Aye."

The hair on Brodie's neck rose, a premonition stilling his thudding heart. "What else do you have on Mick?"

"I received a report fifteen minutes ago. Granted, Mr. Aiken was never convicted, but two of his former girlfriends disappeared without a trace."

Finn's words burst through Brodie like an atomic blast.

"And you can't reach Anabelle?"

"No. I was hoping she was with you. I rang you earlier to see if she was."

"She's not. Stay on the line. I'm calling my team. Maybe one of them has seen her." Brodie punched through to the team video chat, refusing to give way to panic. A likely reason existed for Anabelle's unanswered calls.

Randy picked up, with Tara and Gerald behind him. "What's up, boss?"

"Have any of you seen Anabelle?" he asked.

"I sent her to Stirling in the lorry to collect the rug shipment." Tara looked at him oddly.

"Yeah, and Mick went with her," Gerald said, "which I found strange. Didn't his team sign off yesterday?"

Brodie forced himself to breathe. "Do either of you know if Stanley accompanied them?"

"Yeah, he's with her," Gerald said.

"How long ago did they leave?" Breathe. Anabelle was okay. Her protection officer was with her.

"They left a few minutes ago." Gerald's gaze sharpened. "Is something wrong?"

Brodie assimilated that bit in silence as prickles danced across his flesh. "I sincerely hope not." He hung up without another word.

When he switched to Finn's line, Brodie fumbled the call and disconnected. He punched the number, but Finn didn't pick up right away.

"Come on. Come on. Don't go to voicemail."

Just when it seemed likely to do so, Finn answered. "DI Maxwell."

"Mick showed up this morning." Brodie's nostrils flared. "He and Anabelle are on their way to Stirling in the company lorry to collect a rug shipment."

"I'll put out a BOLO. Is her protection officer with her?" Finn fired off.

"Yeah."

"We'll pick them up, Brodie. Anabelle will be okay if her bodyguard's with her."

Chapter 47

Anabelle downshifted, handling the lorry with care as they descended the steep slope to the main road. The small truck, with its manual transmission, was not her favorite to drive.

"Do you always take the private entrance?" Mick asked.

He had a point. The main entrance was much easier to navigate than the hairpin turns on the private drive.

"It's just habit. I've been using it since I arrived, long before they cut the new entrance," she said, glancing at Mick in the review mirror.

"So, you and Brodie, huh?" Mick stared pointedly at her engagement ring.

"Yes." She tapped the brakes and eased into the first turn, rotating the wheel as she approached the curve.

"That was fast," Mick groused.

Anabelle glanced at him again, then back at the road. "Not really. We've been seeing each other for almost a year." Why did she feel the need to defend herself? Her personal life was none of Mick's business.

"No one here said anything about you two until that ring showed up on your finger." Mick stabbed the air, motioning toward the diamond.

His tone made her engagement sound like a crime. Stanley must have thought so too, because he looked over his shoulder at Mick when she slowed for the second bend. The pinched expression she caught in the rearview mirror set off a niggle of worry.

"Brodie and I keep things professional during work hours." If Mick had any sense of decency, he'd drop the subject.

"How could you act the way you do around me, then get engaged to that . . . robot."

Robot? Alarm bells pealed like mad and made the hair on her arms rise. Mick sounded like a jealous teenager. *Or a stalker . . . ?*

Could it be?

She took the curve faster than she should, the tires squealing for purchase, then grabbing hold. Stanley shifted in his seat, his dark eyes narrowed on the stenciler as he reached into one of his pockets—pockets that held TASERs.

So, it wasn't just her catching the weird vibes rolling off Mick. "You and I enjoy a pleasant professional working relationship, just as Randy, Gerald, and I do. But you're overstepping personal boundaries."

Mick's face went white. "You never cut loose with them the way you do with me. You love me. You're only marrying Brodie to further your career," Mick growled, fury biting through his words.

Anabelle slammed her foot on the brake. "Get out. You can find your own way to the city. I'll not listen to this all the way to Stirling and back."

"You'll do as I say," Mick roared, losing all semblance of control.

Stanley whipped a TASER from his pocket but fumbled with the seat belt release.

Mick pounced, yanking a wire from his jacket and wrapping it around Stanley's neck.

With one hand on his neck to keep the wire from cutting off his oxygen, Stanley pressed the TASER's trigger, the barbs shooting half a meter from his intended target. Mick's fingers, so skilled at stenciling and gilding, tightened on the line, making Stanley's eyes bulge.

"Stop it. You're hurting him," Anabelle shrieked, stamping on the brake.

Stanley kicked out in an effort to shift his position and remove the pressure off his windpipe.

Mick laughed and cinched the wire tighter. "Not a chance."

"Let him go," Anabelle cried.

"I call the shots, dearest Anabelle. It's time you learn that."

She laid on the horn, hoping to draw someone's attention.

Mick dropped one arm and clipped her upside the head with a hard chop. "Stop."

Her ears rang, and she shook herself. Mick's shift in attack gave Stanley time to gasp for air before Mick yanked with both hands on the cord. He was going to kill Stanley.

Anabelle slammed the accelerator to the floor, aiming for a boulder. If she hit it hard enough, the impact might throw Mick forward and free Stanley, and maybe hurt Mick, who wasn't wearing a seatbelt. Metal crunched. She jerked against her seatbelt, but Mick must have braced himself as he crouched over Stanley, still pulling the wire. Whipping the drive stick into reverse, she backed toward the pines and rammed the lorry into the hillside. If she could render the vehicle undriveable, Mick couldn't force her to leave . . .

She missed the trees and smacked into the mossy bank instead.

"You daft cow." Mick yanked ferociously on the cord, and Stanley went limp.

"You killed him." She gulped at Stanley's inert form and fumbled with the door handle to escape.

With glittering eyes, Mick pulled a knife from his jacket's inner pocket and pointed it at her.

Her breath whooshed, deflating her lungs as she fixated on the sharp metal tip.

Mick slipped between the driver's and passenger's seat, unlocked Stanley's door, and shoved him outside, onto the hill.

"What a fine bodyguard he turned out to be. Your dog did a better job." Mick planted himself in Stanley's seat. "Drive."

Anabelle bit her lip.

"Do as I say." Mick flashed the knife in her face, coming within centimeters of her nose.

She panted, and her hands trembled on the wheel as she lifted her foot off the brake. *Do not pass out. Do not pass out.* It's not a needle . . . just something much sharper and deadlier.

Her mind scrambled, thoughts whirling. If she jumped from the lorry, could she escape? Doubtful. Mick was taller. The odds of outdistancing him were less than optimistic.

Brodie's face flashed behind her eyes. She had to act. She refused to give in—not without a fight. She had too much to live for.

Lifting her chin, Anabelle floored the accelerator. The engine revved, and the lorry shot down the lane. *Lord, help me.*

"Slow down."

The tip of the knife touched her flesh—the sharp, pointy end. Her lungs froze, and her vision tunneled, like it did before she blacked out.

Not this time!

She hit the brake, then cranked the wheel, sending the lorry into a spin. Mick grabbed the hand strap above the passenger door. The box truck hit the berm and stopped, horizontal to the lane, its bonnet centimeters from the steep drop to the loch.

"You did that on purpose," Mick hollered.

"Why would I wreck a company vehicle?" Of course, she did it on purpose. Too bad her plan hadn't worked.

"Get us back on the road, and no more funny business." Mick pressed the knife tip into her throat.

Anabelle sucked in through her nose as blood trickled, warm and sticky, down her neck. The black dots enlarged, clouding her vision. *No fainting.* Fight.

"You're scaring me," she gasped. "I can't drive with that pressed in my skin."

"I don't want to cut you, Anabelle. I love you," Mick crooned. "You're not like Stella and Elizabeth. They never listened to me. You do."

"Who are Stella and Elizabeth?" Her gaze darted over the hillside, looking for a way out.

"I loved them both so much." Mick sighed. "They tried to get away. Said they hated me. I couldn't have that, could I?" He smiled as though speaking about the weather, but his eyes were mad—devoid of the merest hint of humanity.

Anabelle dropped her eyes on the knife; it proved less scary than the madman holding it. "Who were Stella and Elizabeth?" she asked again, unable to keep her voice from shaking.

"They told me they loved me. Just like you did, remember? But they lied. They didn't love me. I was respectful and gave them a funeral, even though they didn't deserve it." Mick stroked her arm with his free hand while the knife remained at her throat.

Terror clawed at her mind. He'd killed those women. Did he plan to kill her, too?

The words looped through her mind, repeating over and over. She gripped the steering wheel and filled her lungs. Exhaled. Then filled them again, forcing her mind to function and not freeze up.

For months, she and Mick worked together, and never once had she suspected that behind his face lurked the stalker—a delusional madman who functioned like everyone else. Sometimes.

When Finn removed the camera, Mick had broken into her room, attacked Daisy, and crept to her bedside. Had he intended to kidnap her that night, just like he had in the hospital? Was this always his plan?

Anabelle shuddered. She must escape, but how? If he kept that knife against her throat, she'd pass out.

But she couldn't do that. He'd steal her away, and she'd end up like those other two women. Could she reason with him? Was he capable of that? Clenching her teeth to keep them from chattering, she put the lorry in reverse, gears grinding.

"You need to remove that knife." Her voice quavered. With her pulse at a low roar, she put the gear stick into drive but kept her foot on the brake and waited.

Mick's eyes softened. "All right." He lowered the blade to his lap. "I won't hurt you if you do what I ask."

She pressed the accelerator and edged around the last bend, then rolled to a stop at the gate. The engine ticked over as they waited to enter the carriageway along Loch Tummel, and she prayed for the alarm company's security camera to swing in their direction. Surely someone would notice the feed. But with everyone scurrying about to complete their tasks, the chance of them noticing her absence might take too long.

Her shoulders slumped, her hope snuffing out, like a candle flame in a stiff wind.

She was on her own.

Chapter 48

While the lorry idled at the Soldier's Leap gate, Anabelle's mobile rang, sending her lost hopes surging back from the ashes. Only Brodie, her parents, and the police had this number. Her heart raced, galloping like an unfettered colt. Help was in reach!

She dropped one hand from the steering wheel and stretched for her purse.

"I don't think so. Hand me your bag." Mick squeezed her wrist, his fingers crushing.

"Ouch!" Seething, she surrendered her only contact with the outside world.

Mick fished inside her handbag, drew out her mobile, then flung it out the window and into the stone pillar. The black plastic shattered. "You won't be needing that where we're going."

A smile lit his face, flickering eerily in the lorry's cab. "Now they can't track you. No more interruptions. No dog. No bodyguard. No parents. And no more Brodie Maxwell. You're mine."

He motioned toward the carriageway looping the loch. "Turn left."

"Where are we going?" Anabelle's gaze lingered on the knife as an ember of temper inside ignited into a full blaze.

"You'll see." Cars continued to buzz past, making the turn impossible.

"We're still on the estate, Mick. You haven't kidnapped me yet. If you let me go, it will be easier for you." Killing Stanley, along with assault with a deadly weapon—any of which would land him in prison—she bypassed entirely.

"I can't do that. Not until you love me. All I need is a chance," he whined. "Then we'll marry, and you and Soldier's Leap will be mine, like it was always meant to be. Your family stole it from ours, but I'm a generous man. I'll share it with you."

"What do you mean? No one took Soldier's Leap from you. It's belonged to my family for ages." Had he lost all sense?

"Soldier's Leap belonged to my great-grandfather and should have gone to Gran after *The Titanic* hit that iceberg and sent him to the bottom of the sea."

Thanks to Erica, she knew the family's history enough to follow Mick's claim. But she cringed at the distant relationship.

"Your great-grandfather never married." Anabelle kept her voice soft, to hinder his agitation from flaring further out of control.

"That wouldn't matter in today's world," Mick insisted.

Anabelle begged to differ, but wisely kept her lips sealed. Her great-grandfather had reinstated Grandpa Simon as his son and heir upon Mick's relative's death. She did not know about there being an illegitimate child. But the stories about Grandpa Simon's wild cousin's behavior came as no surprise.

Was Soldier's Leap the reason behind Mick's fixation and kidnapping?

"My family will miss me at some point," she said.

"You won't need your family. You'll have me." Mick tapped his mobile screen and turned on a playlist. "Remember this? Remember how much fun we had?"

Beatles' music filled the lorry, and Mick joined in.

Anabelle tightened her hold on the steering wheel as tremors took hold, spreading, until they shook her entire body. She could not, she absolutely could not allow this fellow to drag her off to heaven knew where. He was mad, like the hatters of old.

"Sing, Anabelle." Mick shifted in the passenger seat to face her.

"I can't." Her voice cracked.

"You must learn to do what I ask." Mick pressed the knife to her throat again. "Sing."

She opened her mouth, her voice off-pitch and cracking, the sound anything but musical. Mick didn't seem to mind, though, and set the knife on the console between them.

"Turn left." He said when a break in traffic gave her the opportunity to follow the direction he wanted her to take.

Anabelle's hands clutched the wheel so tightly, they lost all feeling. Left took them through sparsely inhabited countryside, with nothing but Munros and an occasional farm. If they turned right, they passed hamlets and villages, and her hope of escape.

"Where are we going?" She hit the blinker and followed his instructions.

"I have a place just for us. I was going to take you there earlier, but you woke up and screamed the house down. I've forgiven you. You didn't know it was me." He ran a finger up her bare arm.

Her flesh quivered, and bile burned her throat.

"You have the smoothest skin, Anabelle. I was angry they were going to put sutures in your arm."

She swallowed convulsively. "Where is this place you're taking us? Will I like it?" The hillside rose steeply above the loch as she drove, and the trees gave way to occasional patches of granite and gorse.

"I don't know." Mick's brow wrinkled in concentration. "I should have asked you first. That's the gentlemanly thing to do, of course. It's no Soldier's Leap, that's certain. But when we're married, you can move back into the Lindsay wing with me."

He smiled, and for two beats, he was once more the affable fellow she knew, then in a flash, the Mick she knew was gone.

"Until then, we have a cow you can milk, and you can make butter like my Gran."

"I don't know how to milk a cow or make butter."

"You're smart. You'll figure it out." He lifted a shoulder and faced the road. "There's a stream for washing."

"Is this shelter in the country?" She kept at him, anxious for information that could help her escape.

"It's miles from the closest village. No one will bother us."

Anabelle's knuckles whitened on the wheel, the skin stretching taut. If

Mick's hideaway was that deep in the country, her best chance of escape was before they arrived.

Help me, Lord. Help me escape from this madman.

To the right of the lorry, Loch Tummel stretched for miles, charcoal gray under the gloaming sky, its slopes of pine and larch, growing more barren on the steep hillside. She side-eyed the drop to the water below. No one could survive that fall.

She shivered, and her gaze moved to the knife on the console between them. She'd rather die at her own hands than suffer the same fate as those two other women. Once they reached Mick's destination, he'd kill her, because she had no intention of cooperating with his delusional plans.

Steeling herself, she spun the wheel and left the road, bouncing down the uneven hillside, and knocking the blade to the floor. Mick dove for it, but its tip nicked his hand. He howled, and blood dripped from his fingers. She swerved to avoid a granite outcropping, and the knife slid further and wedged between the door and the step beside his seat, blade up.

Anabelle fumbled with the power buttons to unlatch the doorhandle but instead lowered her window partway. Correcting her mistake, the lock clicked, and she opened the door, ready to jump.

"No." Mick lunged past her and yanked it shut.

She narrowed her eyes, pressed down on the accelerator one last time, and aimed for the drop. Saplings snapped as the lorry jounced over the rough terrain and hit a boulder, shifting the van sideways. They hung there, suspended, teetering halfway over the verge.

"Are you daft?" Mick yelled, bracing his hands against the passenger window and dashboard.

Anabelle hit the automatic door lock. Click. Click. Click. No power. Her heart dropped. She must have severed the electrical line. Letting go of the wheel, she unbuckled as the box van listed to the side.

"We're tipping," Mick screamed.

In slow motion, the lorry lurched forward and plunged nose first, somersaulting through the air, flinging Anabelle into the roof, and knocking the wind from her lungs. The second rotation tossed her body like a ragdoll into the steering column. She clung to the wheel and gasped for air.

Mick wrestled with his safety harness as the box truck dove the last ten meters—free-falling in slow-mo.

They hit the loch, the impact like concrete.

Icy water rushed through Anabelle's partially open window and stole what was left of her breath. She tugged at her door handle, but it refused to budge. Trapped, she pushed up to the ceiling and gulped in the last bit of oxygen as it funneled out.

Then the lorry tilted and sank. Murky water engulfed the vehicle, and darkness claimed them in its frigid grasp.

Anabelle squeezed her head and shoulders out the partial opening as they plunged, but her hips stuck. Scraping and heaving, she twisted to be free. The window dug into her, and pain radiated through her torso. She gritted her teeth and crammed herself out the small gap.

Just when she had all but pulled loose, something latched onto her leg and hindered her escape. She lashed out with her feet, connecting with something hard. The hold gave way, and she followed her air bubbles in the dark water.

Breaking through the surface, Anabelle gasped. But the frigid loch numbed her, and her clothes weighed her down. She thrashed, fighting to stay afloat. But her movements slowed, and she floundered.

A car stopped on the single-track road above the loch, not far from the lorry's descent.

"Help," Anabelle croaked and inhaled water. She gasped and swallowed more.

Heavy. So heavy. And cold. Sinking, she returned to the inky blackness.

There, in the distance—a feeble light glowed through the gloom. She floated toward its warm glow, the brightness increasing the closer she drew. At the light's center, music played, an unknown melody, the notes pure and sweet, filling her soul with joy.

At the center of the light, Granny sat at a piano playing a song from her handwritten notes. But this Granny was young and vibrant, not the old woman Anabelle had known. Granny Dewhurst lifted her head and smiled at the man leaning against the instrument's side.

Anabelle had only seen Grandpa Dewhurst in pictures, but she knew him immediately. He and Granny seemed so happy together, the music a projection of their love.

The melody pulsed all around Anabelle, and she longed to join them.

But an arm snaked around her waist and pulled her away from the music. From the light. From their all-consuming love.

It jerked her to a place of pain. Anabelle fought to return—to Granny and Grandpa. To the music. To the light.

Time dragged, agony wracking her body.

The light, so bright at first, faded, along with the music, leaving her adrift.

"Granny," she called. "Where are you?"

Utter blackness fell, and crushing pain consumed her. Then, something shifted.

Out of the darkness, she heard it again, faintly at first—the melody Granny had played, its notes pulsing with love. This time, though, words accompanied the tune.

"Please save her. Please, Lord. Please save Anabelle," a man's broken voice pleaded.

Chapter 49

Anabelle floated in a sea of black nothingness. Then she surfaced. To beeps. To agony. And to Darth Vader sounds.

Where was she? Where was Granny? Where did the music go?

Panic filled her. Light stung her eyelids, and her lungs moved without her aid. She hurt everywhere and longed for the dark void.

But she heard the music again. It was here–in this place of pain.

Someone pressed against her stomach. Their shoulders heaved, and deep, masculine sobs shook the bed. Someone was crying. Why were they crying? *Don't cry. Please don't cry.*

Anabelle flexed her hand to comfort them, and her fingers touched short hair. A man?

She fought to open her eyes, but the light hurt, and the beeping noises sped up. Her lungs inflated and made her chest ache.

"Anabelle?" A warm hand touched her face, the thumb stroking her cheek. Granny's song filled his voice, a voice full of tenderness and love.

"Lass, can ye hear me? Blink if ye can," a man said, his voice hoarse and broken.

Brodie. Brodie was here. Then understanding flooded through her. Brodie had called her back. Brodie needed her. Brodie loved her.

Anabelle squished her eyes, the effort exhausting.

He kissed her cheek, and water dripped onto her face. Brodie was crying. Brodie never cried. His stoic nature was like the granite beneath his Scottish soil. Nothing upset him. He was her rock.

A buzzer sounded, and she winced. So tired. Darkness, with its siren song, tempted, and she longed to sleep.

"Stay with me, Anabelle." Brodie held her hand and kissed it. "Don't leave me, lass." His voice broke.

Footsteps.

"Is something the matter, sir?" a woman asked.

"Anabelle's awake."

"Mr. Maxwell, people in comas often blink and even open their eyes," the female said.

"But she can hear me. I know she can." The mattress compressed slightly near Anabelle's waist. "Anabelle. Can ye blink to let the nurse know that ye can hear me?"

Blink? That was so hard.

"Please, Anabelle. Show them you're awake. They don't believe me." Brodie stroked her cheek, his fingers trembling.

Why didn't they believe Brodie? He never lied.

Using every ounce of energy she possessed, Anabelle squeezed her eyes.

"There. See?" Brodie said, his voice triumphant.

"Well, I'll be. Let me get the doctor," the nurse said.

Retreating footsteps.

"Ye did it. I'm so proud of ye." Brodie kissed her cheek, then ran his fingers through her hair. "They don't know what a fighter ye are. If they take this tube out, I know ye can breathe on yer own."

A tube. So, that was the weird noise.

"Does the light bother ye? Is that why ye won't open your eyes?"

With her last ounce of energy, she squeezed her eyelids.

Brodie let go of her hand, and a moment later, the massive pain brought on by the light eased. He picked up her hand again. "I've prayed like I've never prayed before. I begged Heavenly Father to keep ye here. Our future children need ye, all six of them."

She moved her lips, but the tube didn't allow her to smile. Slowly, she pried her eyes open—it felt like someone had superglued them shut. *Brodie.*

"Anabelle." Brodie ran his finger across her cheekbone, the lashes above his blue-green eyes wet, his eyes shining with joy. "I love ye, lass."

A doctor and two staff members entered. Anabelle winced at their loud voices.

Brodie moved to the foot of her bed to allow them access.

"You've had a nice sleep, Miss Dewhurst. I'm Dr. Verdun. I'm here to check your vitals. If all looks well, we'll remove your tube. How does that sound?"

Anabelle slid her gaze to Brodie, then back to the doctor.

And blinked.

Brodie stood in the doorway of Anabelle's office, his eyes bulging from their sockets. He fisted his hands and longed to punch a wall. That stubborn lass. He should have known she wouldn't follow the doctor's instructions.

Anabelle lay on a blue chaise lounge, a computer on her lap and a Gantt chart on the cushion beside her. Balloons—not bouquets—tied to colorful weights littered the entire space, compliments of Jecca, Wills, Cressida, and Stanley, who had miraculously survived Mick's attack. Brodie had carted the entire lot of balloons home from the hospital at Anabelle's request.

He shoved his hands inside his trouser pockets. Had she conned Randy into moving that chaise in here? Or had Gerald or Mr. Mellencamp caved to her wishes? Doubtless, all three men had fallen over themselves to do her bidding. Whoever had disobeyed his orders, Brodie intended to find the culprit and give them a piece of his mind—right after he put Anabelle on probation.

Again.

He marched into her office and halted at the foot of the chaise lounge, half a meter from where she lay. "May I remind ye that the hospital sent ye home with the stipulation to rest for one week? It's been exactly twenty-four hours."

"I love it when you go Scots on me." Anabelle beamed up at him, her voice still raspy from the ventilator. "Don't be cross. I can't rest. I'm worried about our deadline–it's making my heart race. I can lie here just as well as in bed, but here, I can ensure that my part of the installation goes to plan."

"You're not popping upstairs to make adjustments." Why couldn't she see reason? Anabelle had drowned—quite literally—just as Mick had done, only he had not survived.

If that farmer hadn't happened along as the lorry sank, Anabelle would not have pulled through. The fellow rang emergency services, then dove into that frigid water and fished her out, unknowing of Mick's existence.

Unresponsive when Anabelle arrived at the hospital, she spent the better part of a day attached to a ventilator. Every time Brodie thought about it, he broke into a cold sweat.

"Two design students from the university are going to be my legs."

Her saucy smile undid him.

"What am I to do with ye, lass?" he asked, kneeling beside her.

"Marry me in a few weeks?" She stroked his jaw, her touch tender.

He shook his head. *Och.* But he loved her. "Two more on payroll will bust our labor." He used their narrow profit margin to keep his wits together, instead of burying his face in her neck and clutching her tight. Her experience still gave him nightmares.

"*Oh, ye of little faith.* I'm not a ninny, Brodie. It's free labor. Both students need internship hours," she rasped.

"Way to think outside the box. You're amazing, do you know that?" He kissed her cheek, unable to maintain a professional distance, not with her drowning so fresh on his heart.

Anabelle took his hand in both of hers. "I know how tight our deadlines are. Trust me. The students are working wonders, plus they're posting content on social media. Mrs. Mellencamp's already noticed a bump in reservations. I can only attribute that to their posts."

She looked so pleased with herself, lying there in her comfy clothes that he couldn't restrain himself.

"Hang the rules." He wrapped his arms around her and covered her mouth in a satisfying kiss.

"Keep that up, and I'll never get anything done." Anabelle pushed him away, blushing.

"Brodie," Randy called from the doorway. "Might I have a word?"

"Duty calls, but I'll be back." Brodie wiggled his brows at her. "There's more where that came from."

"Promise?" Anabelle taunted, her blue eyes sparkling.

Och. The tease. "Count on it. Ye know I always keep my word."

Anabelle stroked the piano keys, unconsciously picking out the melody she'd heard that day in the loch. Pressing D, she winced. That wasn't right. She switched to D flat and smiled. There it was. Closing her eyes, the melody swirled through her mind, and her fingers stretched for the notes.

Footsteps rang out in the corridor, the firm heel strikes of a man.

"I thought I might find you here." Brodie poked his head inside the music room doorway.

"Brodie." Anabelle grasped the front of her robe. "You can't come in here."

"Why?"

"I'm not dressed."

"You're covered. Besides, that thing's more modest than regular clothes." Brodie motioned to her thick robe.

He did have a point. Her dressing gown reached her chin, and its material hung from her shoulders all the way to her calves.

"How did you get in?" She remained seated at the grand piano.

"I know the code. Your mother asked if I could ship some boxes home to High Ridge for you, so I've borrowed Randy's lorry. It's loaded now. What did you pack in some of those containers? Weight sets?" he asked, stepping through the doorway.

"Nothing so boring." Anabelle made a face. "Try Wemyss Ware."

"I should have known. You make straight for that pottery whenever you find it in a shop."

"Those hand-painted pieces are highly collectible, I'll have you know. I picked up a few for our warehouse."

"Thinking ahead?"

"Yes. Can you blame me?"

"No. I hope you got them for a bargain."

"My thrifty Scot." She laughed at him.

"Waste not. Want not," he quoted, rounding the piano and sitting beside her, facing the opposite direction. "What were you playing just now? It's beautiful. I've never heard it before."

Anabelle bit her bottom lip. Brodie's pragmatic, no-nonsense way of thinking did not bend toward the metaphysical, so she had held off sharing her experience in the loch with him.

"I heard it a few weeks ago. Do you like it?" Anabelle played the melody once more.

"It's hauntingly beautiful. I'm not familiar with the composer."

"Promise you won't laugh?" She touched the back of his hand.

"Why would I laugh?" He wrapped his fingers around hers.

Anabelle steeled herself. "Something happened the day I went into the lake."

"Besides drowning?"

"Yes."

"I promise I won't laugh." He took both of her hands in his.

"When I squeezed out the lorry's window, the water was horribly cold. I tried to make it to shore but kept swallowing water. Then I saw a light. Granny was there, sitting at a piano composing a song, and my grandfather, Simon, who died before I was born, was there, too. I tried to reach them, but they disappeared."

She squeezed his hand. "Then the same melody called to me again, but I heard your voice pleading for me to return."

Brodie slid both arms around her, clutching her tight, and buried his face in her neck, "This was the song you heard? I love it even more."

She nodded, her head bumping his chin. "I've been picking it out." Anabelle wriggled from his grasp and played the tune for him.

"Anabelle." Erica entered the music room. "I haven't heard that since I was a little girl."

"You know this song?" Anabelle's hands froze on the keys.

"My grandmother often hummed it when she made lace," Erica said.

"The composer is unfamiliar. Do you know who it is?" Anabelle asked, holding her breath.

"Louise Morrison made it up." Erica hummed the refrain, a smile curving her lips. "She was quite musical and played several instruments."

Chills coursed through Anabelle, and she stared wide-eyed at Brodie.

This melody was part of her heritage. Had Julia hummed it to her children before her passing? But if she did, Granny never once played that tune. Anabelle would surely have remembered. Perhaps Granny had hugged it close to her heart, like a precious gift filled with memories and love.

Erica bent a scathing glance on Brodie, only just noticing his presence. "You cannot be here."

"Why not?" Brodie's brow furrowed in confusion.

"Anabelle is about to try on her wedding gown for the last time, and it's bad luck for the groom to see it." Erica waved him away with both hands.

"Just one wee peek?" Brodie winked at Anabelle, a teasing light in his eyes.

"No. No. No. You must leave." Erica frowned at him like a small gnome and pointed to the doorway.

"All right. I'll go if I must." Brodie leaned over Anabelle and kissed her, his mouth lingering too long for a simple peck. He was doubtless enjoying himself at Erica's expense. "Cheers, lass." Brodie's eyes clung to hers before he left through the open doorway.

"That man is so in love, he won't be able to say his vows when he sees you in Julia's dress." Erica chuckled as they reentered the ballroom.

Erica halted, motioning toward the dress lying on the table.

Anabelle squealed, examining the skirt for the stains that had proved so difficult to remove.

"There were times I almost gave up." Erica clucked, shaking her head, and making her specs blink under the chandeliers.

The only thing lacking now was the Poole tiara.

A frown tugged the corners of Anabelle's mouth. It didn't matter. Not really. Other things in life were much more important. But a shadow of sadness shrouded her as she stepped into the gown and faced the mirror while Erica did up the back.

Wearing the Poole tiara would have linked both sides of her family, something she longed to do. But she couldn't change Grandmama Poole or soften her heart. Nor did she intend to allow bitterness over what might have been to ruin her day.

Best to look forward and focus on the good. Had Julia done the same when she married her beloved William?

For a moment, she imagined the four women linked to this wonderful gown, Julia, for whom it was created, Louise, whose clever fingers had fashioned the exquisite lace, Granny, who lost her mother so young, and Erica, of whom divine providence had reunited to their family circle and restored this precious heirloom for generations to come. Each added a portion of a bloodline that once was lost, and now was found.

Chapter 50

Nerves pulsed through Anabelle's veins, and a wild desire to flee consumed her. The discordant chant, "*Run. Run. Run,*" filling her head. Brodie had the right of things. They should have eloped.

The kirk's antechamber, a small room with a flagstone floor bathed in the refracted light of the stained glass windows, did not soothe her in the least. Dad stood in the doorway, eyeing the guests, while Erica ensured that the small bridesmaids and pageboy did not step on Julia's gown. In the far corner, the wedding planner, florist, and photographer conferred one last time over Grandmama's to-do list.

Grandmama Poole had put the fear of the Almighty in them to get this right.

Anabelle's mobile dinged repeatedly inside Dad's pocket. He checked the messages and passed it to her with a smirk.

Wills had started a group text.

Wills: How many weapons do you suppose the security team has in here?

Jecca: Too many for my liking.

Cressida: I hope one of them has a sniper rifle. That would be exciting.

Wills: How much do you think the cumulative value of jewelry inside this chapel is worth?

Cressida: Millions.

Jecca: The Queen's is worth that much alone. Did you see her brooch? The center diamond must be over twenty karats.

Cressida: Do you think Anabelle will remember to curtsy to Her Majesty?

Will: NO.

Jecca: Yes!

Wills: Do you think the Duke of Devon will doze off before the service begins? I vote yes.

Jecca and Cressida responded with resounding noes.

Anabelle rolled her eyes and handed the mobile back to her father. "They're being ridiculous."

"You aren't shaking anymore. I'd say their silliness did the trick," Dad pointed out.

Mother squeezed through the door, a familiar case in her hand, and a smile like a searchlight on her lips.

"Is that—" Anabelle covered her mouth with a trembling hand.

"Yes." Mother set the case on a wooden bench and unfastened the clasp. Diamonds sparkled, their red and blue fire reflecting the vibrant colors of the stained glass windows above. Carefully, she removed the veil from Anabelle's hair, detaching the paste tiara in exchange for the baroque pear-shaped pearls set in filigreed platinum and diamond clusters.

"I know Grandmama's not warm and engaging like Granny Dewhurst, but she's immensely proud of the woman you've become. And she loves you, Anabelle." Mother secured the tiara to the veil, then attached it to her hair with deft fingers. "I don't think she ever intended for you not to wear the Poole tiara."

"Grandmama's love language needs serious tweaking," Anabelle whispered, emotion stinging her eyes.

But as Brodie had pointed out earlier, Grandmama might be prickly, with a propensity to have her own way, but her actions told another story.

Mother stood back to admire the effect, and a tear tracked down her face. "You look beautiful."

"Stop, or we're both going to ruin our makeup."

"I can't help it." Mother kissed both of her cheeks. "Next time we speak, you'll be Anabelle Maxwell."

"I love you, Mummy." Oh, bother. Anabelle fanned her face. Now she *was* crying, and she hadn't even made it down the aisle yet.

Mother blew Dad a kiss, then slipped into the chapel. Anabelle caught sight of Brodie's cousin, Sorcha, sitting in the back pew before Mother shut one side of the double doors behind her.

Erica appeared at Anabelle's elbow and mopped her up.

"Thank you." Anabelle exhaled, then chanted to herself as nerves took command of her mental acuity. "Curtsy to the Queen. Curtsy to the Queen. Curtsy to the Queen."

"The Duke of Devon just arrived," Dad said, his tone one of surprise.

Anabelle squinted through the small opening, unable to accept what she was seeing. The Duke of Devon, leaning heavily on his cane, moved toward the kirk. *Two dukes?* Her stomach roiled. Grandmama would never stop crowing after this.

Erica took one look at her face and held her by the shoulders. "These people are here because you and your family matter to them."

Anabelle gulped. She couldn't breathe. *Is this what a panic attack feels like?*

Understanding softened Erica's features. "Julia was very nervous when she married William. She didn't want a society wedding, either."

"How do you know that?" Anabelle asked as Erica adjusted her gown one last time.

"My grandmother served as one of her bridesmaids."

"But I thought Great Grandpa William was disowned?"

"He was for a few years. But Julia's family, though merchants, had piles of money and covered the expenses. William's friends and relatives showed up in force to attend their nuptials, despite his parents' actions.

The connection Anabelle had experienced when she removed Julia's dress from the trunk intensified.

"Better now?" Erica asked.

"Yes. Thank you."

Though a distant cousin, her and Erica's relationship felt closer. And no one could convince her that they met by accident. God had placed Erica in her path, guiding her to the one person with the answers she sought who could reconnect their families.

"Do you have Brodie's ring?" she asked, turning to her father.

"I do." Dad patted his pocket as the organist started the introductory notes of the processional.

"That's my signal." Erica slipped into the chapel.

"Ready, children?" the wedding planner asked the oldest bridesmaid, one of her Poole cousins' daughters, a precocious six-year-old.

"Yes," the bridesmaid replied, her brown eyes solemn.

A moment later, the doors opened, and the children started up the aisle—the girls' soft yellow dresses and the pageboy's mini kilt garnering a series of oohs and aahs.

Dad held out his arm.

The photographer snapped a few candid shots of her and Dad, then the chapel doors swung wide, and the congregation rose, the Queen right along with them on the front row beside the aisle.

Gulp. Right now, she'd rather face a needle than that royal stare.

"Focus on Brodie," Dad murmured as they crossed the threshold and started up the aisle. "This is about you and him."

She squeezed his arm in acknowledgement. Dad was right.

The music changed keys, and the first bars of the song that had haunted her since the day of her drowning swelled to the rafters.

Brodie stood in his kilt before the altar, his stance wide and strong with Finn, his best man, standing at his side. Breaking protocol at the change in music, he twisted at the waist and gazed at her over his shoulder, his eyes shining with love.

This remarkable man had called her back to him that day in the hospital—his voice echoing the melody of the loch—the music of love.

A sense of peace engulfed Anabelle.

She brushed the lace of Julia's gown. This beautiful dress linked her to past generations, and her thoughts sped to those yet unborn. Perhaps one day, one of her descendants would wear Julia's gown, linking them to their Scottish heritage, and visit the place that made it all possible.

Soldier's Leap.

Have you ever closed a book and wished you could stay with the characters just a little longer? I felt that way about Anabelle and Brodie. That's why I'm sharing something special—a deleted scene from *A Royal Request,* written just for readers who want one more heartbeat of this story (and perhaps a hint of what's to come later in the series).

Don't miss out—sign up for my newsletter and be the first to read Anabelle and Brodie's special deleted scene and get exclusive updates about the series!

https://www.authorpaigeedwards.com

Stalk Me

Paige Edwards is an award-winning and best-selling author. Due to her deep British roots, Paige's books are often set in the UK, and she hops the pond whenever she gets the chance. For over a decade, she served on her region's Interfaith Community Council, sponsoring humanitarian projects alongside those of numerous faiths. When she isn't writing, she and the hubs take off on occasional adventures in their newly converted Sprinter van. Paige loves connecting with readers. You can reach her by visiting her website

https://www.authorpaigeedwards.com

DEADLY DEPTHS

ROXBURGH SCIONS

Inspirational Romantic Suspense

FALL 2026

PAIGE EDWARDS

Deadly Depths

Chapter 1

Air bubbles drifted in a steady stream to the ocean's surface as Rod Henderson exhaled. Floating above his dive group, he tapped his oxygen tank, the metallic sound carrying underwater, and pointed to the surface with his thumb—time to go topside.

The neoprene-clad scuba divers flutter-kicked their fins, halting at the rest stop to equalize their lungs after such depths. Rod counted their number. One person short.

Lowering his head, he swept his gaze over the coral head below, a massive formation with its own microclimates. Not finding his missing diver, he moved through the water, searching for the lone delinquent. A moment later, Rod chuckled, bubbles rushing past his mask, when he spied the lad lifting a starfish from the ocean floor.

The Caymanian government had strong regulations against disturbing the ocean's natural habitat. Rod thunked his tank with force. Tap. Tap. Tap.

The lad looked up and dropped the starfish.

Caught you, dude. He could hardly blame the lad for touching the forbidden. That was one granddaddy of a starfish he'd found. Doubtless, at that age, Rod would have done the same.

Rod motioned for the teen to move toward the boat, then followed.

If only his childhood and youth had condoned such a carefree lifestyle. But it hadn't. Since birth, his parents had drummed duty and responsibility into him, every bit as much as the Scottish countryside had drummed cold rain on his skin. With an eye on his delinquent diver, Rod rose through the warm sea. After more than two decades of Scottish rain and gale-force winds, he couldn't get enough of Grand Cayman's perennial sea and sunshine.

It certainly beat working in chill temps back home and marrying a lass with the right pedigree. He eyed one of the attractive twenty-something-year-old women who chattered with her friends in the bow of his dive boat, then glanced away.

His parents' expectations. He shook his head.

Proper protocol was not for him.

When it came time for choosing a bride, he wouldn't pick a stuffy one who understood which piece of cutlery was used for what. Or how to address the toffs in his parents' circle. He wanted a companion, not a flashy, posh lass who spoke like she had marbles in her mouth.

Treading water beside the ladder, he removed his fins and draped them over his forearm, then climbed aboard. He scanned the horizon, where dark clouds hovered, moving toward them. They'd likely have rain tonight.

He unzipped his wetsuit and let it hang from his waist, the August sunshine baking into his torso. Smiling, he faced the group of novice divers. "There are sliced oranges in the cooler that will help cut the salt taste in your mouth."

Moving forward, he raised the anchor.

After everyone resumed their seats, he revved the engine, eased through the reef's opening, and started for Georgetown to drop this lot on the cruise ship's quay. Their happy chatter assured him that they'd enjoyed their time in the water.

For him, diving was like exploring another dimension, one where gravity held little sway, and the vivid blues, yellows, greens, oranges, golds, and pinks were worlds away from the stormy skies and freezing lochs of home.

Clearing the reef, he opened the throttle, the salt air buffeting his face as they bounced across the turquoise swells. A boat bobbed in the shallows.

Odd that. Rod squinted, noting the name on the ship's hull.

Neptune.

He didn't recognize the yacht. Doubtless, they were visitors, as he knew every dive operator on the island. What were they doing? Didn't they know the danger to their yacht? He should probably check it out. All the maps were well marked with depths. Just in case they didn't know, he should warn them.

He lowered the throttle, but one glance at his dive watch had him increasing speed. This group needed to reach the cruise terminal in time for their tender. He'd stop by later and hope they suffered no ill effects for their folly.

People avoided that stretch of ocean on the East End because of the risk of running aground. The place was a veritable graveyard of shipwrecks. It didn't keep him from glancing over his shoulder one last time, questions swirling.

Everly Patterson faced the bank manager, her heart racing as he reviewed her falsified documents. "I'm here to review your offshore accounts and ensure that all clients are paying their taxes." She managed, her flat tone belying the onslaught of nerves wreaking havoc on her nervous system.

The Caymanian bank manager, Jasper Twining, a tall fellow dressed in a top London brand, frowned. "I have no idea why you are here, Miss Patterson. I assure you that our bank follows all protocols. Before I let you loose on our records, I intend to verify your authorization before we proceed." He folded his arms, as two lines beside his mouth deepened. "You do realize that what you ask will take several weeks, if not months, to oversee."

"I'm aware of that." Everly dipped her chin.

"While I make that call, I'd appreciate it if you would join Susan, our new accounts manager." Jasper Twining's Caymanian accent purred through the request, the smile on his lips not reaching his eyes.

Everly stiffened. The man suspected her and insisted she have a minder? How had she tipped him off?

"I'd be happy to join Susan." The only way forward was to bluff her way through this standoff.

Mr. Twining motioned for Susan to join them. "I'd like Miss Patterson to join you at new accounts until I return."

"Yes, sir. Right this way, Miss Patterson." Susan motioned toward her desk, positioned in the carpeted section where two mahogany desks stood near the roped-off teller queue.

Jasper Twining moved off, leaving her with Susan in a vacuum of silence. Everly exhaled. Safe—at least for the moment.

When she'd been briefed for this mission, nothing about an unbelieving bank manager had been discussed. She'd need every bit of her wits to pass this wicket. But why had Mr. Twining given her such a hard time? She'd presented him with authentic credentials. Had her nerves betrayed her?

Or did he have something to hide?

Until this assignment, she had assumed, like many others, that an offshore account protected clients from taxation in their home country. However, Cayman Island banking was not equivalent to unmarked Swiss accounts. Strict regulations were adhered to in this region, but recent random monitoring of this particular bank suggested otherwise.

"Please make yourself comfortable, Miss Patterson." Susan motioned for her to take a seat in one of the two unoccupied chairs across the desk from her. "I'll be back soon. I'm due for a break."

Everly crossed her legs and scanned the teller line. Island time ran much slower than London's big smoke. No one seemed in a rush, and those in the queue chatted to one another in a friendly manner.

Movement in the doorway drew her attention to a tall, tanned fellow with bright blue eyes, wearing a pair of ripped jeans, flip flops, and a T-shirt that said, "I don't have to outswim the SHARK. Just my dive buddy." His overlong brown hair, bleached by the sun into burnished gold, and stubbled cheeks failed to camouflage his indecent good looks.

"Hiya, Maisie," he greeted one of the tellers, his deep voice carrying.

"Hi, Rod. Good to see you," Maisie, the teller, waved, a bright smile stretching her cheeks.

Two other tellers smiled at him from their stations. He must be a local, Everly mused, clocking his movements as he joined the queue and slapped the Caymanian gentleman in front of him on the shoulder. The man turned, and the two immediately struck up a conversation.

The shaggy-headed individual, by far the scruffiest person in the bank, made her shudder. His untidy appearance rattled her need for order, and she pressed her fingertips, one by one, into her thumb pad, counting.

Unable to focus. She removed her spectacles and cleaned the lenses on her pencil skirt, then crossed her ankles, ensuring her feet, clad in low-heeled loafers, rested under her chair. She laced her fingers together in her lap and eyed the clock.

Surely, Mr. Twining's call did not take this long . . . How could he identify her as anything other than her credentials stated? MI6 did not make errors. And Sir Roger, head of British Intelligence, had assigned her to this case, her first in the field, after her audit of his office had unearthed a few discrepancies. Everly shifted uncomfortably, the thin material of her blouse tugging at her flesh before it separated after the dried sweat from her walk had adhered it to her body.

A large, warm hand landed on her shoulder. "I'd like to open a new account," a low voice said.

Everly squeaked, then craned her neck to meet Mr. Scraggle Hair's sparkling blue eyes.

"Sorry. I didn't mean to startle you," Scraggle Hair said, a boyish grin belying his words.

Cheeky lad.

She cleared her throat. "Susan stepped away for a moment and will be right with you," she responded, prim as a schoolmarm.

"That's all right." Scraggle Hair pulled the chair out beside her and plopped onto it, his gaze taking her in with a full-on sweep that sent the color flooding into her cheeks.

"You must be new to the island," he said.

"What gave it away?" She frowned. First, Mr. Twining, now this ragtag fellow suspected her–of what, she had no idea. The acrid taste of failure burned in her mouth. How had she betrayed herself?

He jerked his chin toward her clothes. "Because you look like you just got off a flight from Iceland."

Iceland? She glanced at her wool skirt and low-heeled loafers, then touched her tight bun on the back of her head to see if any hair had escaped its confines. "For your information, I'm an auditor," she huffed, sitting more upright in her chair–if possible. "And these are professional clothes." She gave his attire a disdainful sniff.

"That makes sense." He stretched his legs in front of him as his mouth curved higher, and an impish sparkle lit his eyes.

"Why?" She prickled at his insinuation.

"Because people who holiday in the islands are a lot more relaxed."

She narrowed her eyes and opened her mouth to respond, just as Susan and Mr. Twining returned.

"Miss Patterson, sorry that took so long." Mr. Twining halted several meters from her chair. "Come this way, and we'll get you situated."

Everly stood and tucked the chair legs into the carpet's former indentations to ensure she'd returned it to its proper place. Mr. Scraggle Hair rose as well, dipping his head to her in a courtly manner at odds with his appearance.

"A pleasure to meet you, Miss Patterson. I hope to see you around." He winked and flashed his straight white teeth.

Everly nodded, tightened her grip on her handbag handle, and stomped after Mr. Twining, serenaded by Mr. Scraggle Hair's rumbling chuckle. *Ugh.*

Iceland indeed. If she ran into that repugnant fellow again, it would be too soon for the likes of her.